MW01016529

The Truth About the Night

The Truth About the Night

a novel by

MARTYN BURKE

HarperCollins*PublishersLtd*

Published by HarperCollins Publishers Ltd

First Edition

HarperCollins books may be purchased for educational, business, or sales promotional use through our Special Markets Department.

HarperCollins Publishers Ltd
2 Bloor Street East, 20th Floor
Toronto, Ontario, Canada
M4W 1A8

www.harpercollins.ca

Library and Archives Canada Cataloguing in Publication

Burke, Martyn
The truth about the night : a novel / Martyn Burke.

ISBN-13: 978-0-00-200601-9
ISBN-10: 0-00-200601-4

I. Title.

PS8553.U638T78 2006   C813 .54   C2005-905471-9

HC 9 8 7 6 5 4 3 2 1

Printed and bound in the United States
Set in Monotype Baskerville

For Doug Morton,
who left the race trailing
kindness in his wake

Palomar

We're up on the mountain waiting for the sun to go down so we can look into the skies for an apocalypse that would wipe out life as we know it. Or at least life as we know it for a light-year or so around us. With whatever images of cosmic hellfire can be coaxed into the telescope. But all Charger wants to talk about is Marilyn Monroe.

He's leaning on the pile of logs staring down at the valley, the way he's been since I noticed him there as I was driving up to the Palomar dome.

It looks like it came out of a postcard. All green and lush below us, surrounded by forests and nestled into the side of the mountain. Like you should hear yodeling. Or see happy milkmaids cavorting in dirndls. Except that Charger's got that rifle hanging down at his side, the kind that the street gangs use up in L.A., the ones with a big fat metal banana curving down under the barrel. It makes a pretty scary image, especially with Charger being about the size of a doorway. But that's all it is—an image—and Charger and I both know the problem.

Which is that he's a big pussycat.

With that overgrown boy's face and that haystack of hair stuck on top of this man-mountain body, he has trouble being scary when it's time for one of life's close-ups. But from the other end of the valley Charger must look pretty intimidating. Which is why the Colonel hires him to come up here and be the last line of defense against the invading hordes of ravished humanity pouring into America, laying silent siege to everything that lets the Colonel sleep at night. Namely, the long thin lines of illegal aliens coming across the mountains from Mexico or sometimes farther, some of them led by coyotes—guides—who butcher the Colonel's cattle for food.

But it's not just the cattle the Colonel cares about. He looks around and sees the fall of Rome happening all over again but this time with Vandals in running shoes, T-shirts and a few other historical and geographic anomalies thrown in for the hell of it.

So he hires Charger to plant himself below the white dome of the Palomar observatory like some warning sign to the Vandals. More out of instinct than planning, Charger always manages to find a place that makes it look as if the huge dome and he are growing out of the mountain together like they're connected by the same root system.

With the telescope inside it, the Palomar dome looms above everything else like some inverse beacon, sucking in light and any collateral metaphysics from the heavens. The Indians thought Palomar was some kind of mystical place. Malava, they called the valley in front of us—Magic Place. And I have come to believe it. Just staring at the dome rising up from the mountain and the forests is like watching the sun come up over Stonehenge. You know there's voodoo and science going on all at once.

In the daytime when the dome is closed, the observatory sits there hibernating in silence, blasting its eerie pure whiteness out in all directions, the creation of Druids in tweed who built it before any of us were born. One of the last great analog wonders of the world. But now at twilight the dome has stopped blazing whiteness as it awakens and settles back to soak in the ambers of the fading sun. The long curved shutters on the dome leave their due north hibernating position and blink open like vertical eyelids as the telescope the size of a locomotive slews and rumbles inside, waiting for darkness and the photons that have traveled the trillions upon trillions of miles just to reach earth on this very night. Digitized images of past violence with stars bursting, shredding, incinerating, a billion or so years ago in places beyond our power to imagine in anything but the crudest of worldly terms.

But Charger's concerns are more basic. "Marilyn coulda had any man she wanted," he says. "JFK even. She was having a thing with the president of the United States. And who does she end up with? Freddie!"

Ever since Charger came back from meeting another lawyer in Los Angeles he's been all wired up over Marilyn Monroe's plight. The lawyer's office was on Wilshire Boulevard just east of the San Diego Freeway. Charger found himself looking down at this dinky little graveyard wedged in among office towers. The one where Marilyn Monroe is buried. "Who does this guy Freddie think he is anyway?" he asks again. Watching Charger work his way up through the various stages of indignation on Marilyn's behalf is like watching a bubble build to a geyser.

"I'm still waiting for you to tell me," I say again. But Charger has perception valves that clog up sometimes and things don't always get through the way they do with other people. He sits down and stares out across the valley. Then he takes out a piece of paper with some writing on it.

"Richard F. Poncher is this dead guy's full name," he says, reading from the piece of paper. "But they called him Freddie. The guy is buried right above Marilyn Monroe. In a wall! They put Marilyn in this big marble wall. Like in a marble box or something. And right above her is Richard F. Poncher. 1905–1986. *You're one in a million, Freddie,* it says carved into his marble slab. I mean, can you believe it?"

"No I can't," I say.

"One in a million? Christ, this Freddie gets to lie there stacked up on top of Marilyn Monroe forever. We're talking eternity here, you know."

Eternity's a fairly relative concept up here at Palomar. Some of those photons racing toward their destiny with the big telescope in an hour or two have been blasting through nothingness for untold megaparsecs. Which is to say so many billion years ago that the earth was just soup when they began their journey.

"They're dead," I tell him. "Marilyn and this Freddie character are both dead. So why worry about it?" But Charger isn't interested in nuances of existence. He's pretty much the same conversationally as he is physically. When he sets a course it's almost impossible to recalibrate. Which maybe is why he kept running into his own quarterback in the three games he played for San Diego last year.

"Did Marilyn have anything to say about it?" he asks. "I mean, she's only the most desirable woman in the history of the world and all of a sudden this Freddie shows up dead and lies on top of her forever. Does that seem fair?"

Time to recalibrate, even a degree or so. Or at least try. "Charger? You're not going to get carried away and shoot someone, are you?" Or put another way: Under no earthly circumstances let the Colonel use you as cannon fodder for the cause. His cause.

"Marilyn's only got one dinky little rose. Freddie, that pervert lying on top of her, has got zilch. Not a flower in sight. Figures. But right in the center of the graveyard there's a bunch of new dead people with a damn Rose Bowl parade's worth of flowers."

"If you see anyone coming up through the valley, don't hurt them," I say. This gets his attention. You never know what's going to sink in. His face clouds over. Sometimes I think that Charger's mind is like the telescope inside the dome. You can almost hear it rumbling.

"I wouldn't hurt anyone," he says, looking a little hurt himself. "Scare them maybe. Nothin' wrong with that, is there?"

Some of these people don't scare. "Depends," I say after thinking about it.

I've forgotten Charger's real name, if I ever really knew it. He just showed up here doing odd jobs after one of the times when he got cut from the San Diego football team—the Chargers. When the name stuck to him up here on the mountain he never objected, almost as if it kept him closer to a dream that kept slipping away into some fog of his own. Charger really couldn't figure out why he wasn't wanted by the team. I'd seen him once in one of the televised games, a human plinth rumbling down the field. Opposing players bounced off him as if he was armored.

And yet he lacked some requisite instinct of raw destruction. Some killer instinct that could leave an opposing linebacker in geometric rubble. That, and some synaptic linkages that were not working properly—the sensimilla buzz, he called it—had too often left him still figuring out which opposing players to mow down long after the play had ended.

So now on bad knees Charger stands guard for the Colonel, a one-man Praetorian guard stopping the Roman Empire from collapsing all over again, defending against the Huns and the Vandals and the Franks and the Goths. And Mexicans. And whatever OTMs—or Other Than Mexicans as the Immigration cops call them—are joining the endless hurried processions led by the coyotes through Mendenhall Valley at twilight.

When he's not standing guard Charger goes back to the brick shack he's rented across the border in Mexico and writes letters to lawyers who might take on his case against his old football team. And buys cartons of cheap Xantac and Prozac in the Tijuana *farmacias* that he resells out of the back of his car to Americans who can't afford the prices on this side of the border.

"What are you guys looking for tonight?" he asks as he always does.

"Neutron stars," I tell him, and he thinks about it, nodding in apportioned approval.

"Neutron stars," he says. "That's good. Really good." He thinks about it some more, a picture of perfect stillness and roiling motion all at once. "You know probably the best thing about being smart?"

"What?" I know the answer. He's told me this before.

"You get to forget better stuff than the rest of us." Which is when he grins. A boy's grin full of teeth and secret mischief like he's pleased with what he's said.

"Don't shoot anybody." Or better yet, don't get shot.

"I'll remember that."

When I'm going back up the hill Charger calls out, "Marilyn Monroe really needed someone to look after her." Then the pause and the silence of thinking you can almost hear. "I'd look after her. I'd be better for her than Freddie."

"You would." And I mean it. But forget that candle-in-the-wind business, her blowtorch of fame would leave someone like him a smoldering cinder of gentleness.

"Hey!" yells Charger. Then again, louder. "Hey! C'mere."

Back at the top of the valley Charger's staring out at a black mark merging into storm clouds that looked like a fat bruise in the sky. "A helicopter."

"So?"

"So something's going on. Over there in Barker Valley."

"It's probably the rich oil guy who owns the big house down here in Mendenhall." But it's not. You know it.

"Listen to it," he says. The distant *thwap thwap thwap* of the rotors ricochets off the untreed folds of the mountain. "Military. Civilian choppers don't sound like that."

"Maybe marines." The whole area between Palomar Mountain and the ocean is fragmented with marine bases. The coast highway north of San Diego sometimes turns into a mobile amphitheater as the Sea Stallion helicopters blast low through the air above the traffic to the nearby ocean, ratcheting troops into the water. Preparing the forces of the Free World for storming beaches straight into the teeth of a defending force of television cameramen.

"They're never over this far," he says. "I'm telling you, something's going on." I realize that whatever is going on out there I don't want to get involved in it. At least not with Charger. Not now when I've got neutron stars out there just waiting for their screen test in an hour or so. The helicopter descends into the part of the distant sky that has turned obsidian. "What the hell they doin' over there if a storm's coming?" The silence returns, this time seeded with a wind that comes in from the southeast.

The sun is making long shadows as I walk toward the Palomar dome, up through the woods where incense cedars get to dress up and fool the unsuspecting into thinking they're redwoods, towering in silent groves that release you suddenly into meadows billowing with deer grass where the Colonel's cattle are grazing. And then along a path leading to the South Road that winds, dips and finally rises to the top of Palomar Mountain.

It's as if those roadbuilders back in the 1930s designed the South Road for visual impact, the kind that makes people gasp and shriek on amusement park rides when something leaps out at them. The first time I drove up the South Road and turned that final curve I almost lost control of the car, contorting into the windshield, magnetically pulled toward the dome as it suddenly levitated out of the trees, its whiteness as unexpected as its size. At that moment I pretty much figured out the genius of those medieval cathedral-builders in Europe, the ones who decreed that visual power was the way to catapult dull minds into an awestruck appreciation of the Kingdom of Heaven.

There is something about the silence of the Palomar dome that creates sounds in your mind. Booming voices and choruses rising above the intense clatter of science and reason that is practiced within.

Inside, the telescope reposes in silent obedience, a gray gargantua awaiting the orders of its puny masters. Next to it, the data room hums with digital readiness as we prepare for the evidence to be gathered. In these hours until dawn I will be one of those who are looking for what is not there, at least not now. Detectives, never allowed at the scene of a cosmic crime that happened a billion years ago and whose light is only now reaching us. Sherlocks with a massive magnifying glass in search of clues to a case of violence committed by stars or galaxies that may no longer exist. Our task is to assemble evidence and photograph the ghastly remains as they fester largely outside our jurisdiction of human understanding. Piecing together the evidence in varying nanometers and parsecs that tell of the sheer immensity of the assaults that occurred as stars blew themselves to pieces, battered each other, fused, cannibalized or otherwise stretched the laws of physics and God so long ago that the earth was not yet even forming out of its primordial ooze.

How long ago? If the length of your arm represents from the present back to Julius Caesar, these cosmic crimes happened somewhere past Tokyo, past Beijing, past the moon and Saturn. And finally past Pluto. In some place where time and space are part of the same alloy of incomprehension.

"Not looking too photometric," says Carl, one of the astronomers, staring into the storm clouds churning in the south. Carl's the lead astronomer for the next four nights, and he's in his uniform—the short-sleeve blue shirt bulging with pens in the pocket and slowly shredding from age. He usually just ambles around with the imprint of a grin somehow finding itself onto his face no matter what's being talked about. Just sort of radiating some secret celebration of the absurd on that face of indeterminate age (I'd bet on fifty) no matter how many lines etch into it.

He must have academic fangs though. He's one of the few astronomers to wring more than a few nights a year on the telescope from the Caltech worthies who dole out the Palomar treats up there at the Pasadena campus, a hundred and fifty miles north of here.

Carl's in my own little pantheon of good guys. Which is not the case with all the astronomers who come through here. Pull a personality spectrograph on any given cluster of them and you'll run the gamut from dweeb to High Priest with all the attendant gradations of ego and rampant self-importance. But Carl doesn't bother to take himself all that seriously.

Carl's idea of beauty is an equation. The longer the better.

"Since when do storms come up from Mexico at this time of year?" says Yannic, a grad student who works with Carl. Super-serious, jet-black hair in tight little curls, maybe twenty-five, and just possibly possessing the soul of an anarchist, but red-shifted just enough toward the dweeb end of the spectrograph to make him academically domesticated. Carl doesn't reel in what he has to throw back.

We are waiting for the clouds to part. Like disarmed members of the IRA, Carl says. *The Infra Red Army*. Some astronomers are strictly optical, others X-ray, but Carl has always been loyal to the infrared part of the spectrum.

I sit at the control console; the numbers start dancing in red on the digital gauges and I stop what I'm doing like I'm expecting a revelation. This always gets the astronomers' attention. In a flash Carl's beside me squinting into the gauges as the numbers keep bouncing. "We got other problems," I tell them, looking at the dewpoint depression readout, which is getting up close to 3 degrees.

I don't have to tell him what it means—that the cool outside air is hitting the warmth of that big photon-trapping mirror in the telescope. All of which will produce a nice little corrosive fog boiling off the delicate surface of the mirror.

That is, unless I close the shutters and wrap up the whole operation for the night.

Which is basically a major part of what I, as night assistant, do for a living—rein in scientific wet dreams. The ones erupting full blown from the fevered math-filled desperation of astronomers unlocking eternity *and definitely on the way to the Nobel Prize,* thwarted only by their measly allotment of a mere three or four nights per year on the big telescope.

I've had High Priests throwing world-class shitfits in the data room when I broke the news that I was buttoning the place up for the night. To them it's kind of like some deckhand telling the captain to drop anchor. But they know there's nothing they can do about it.

Astronomers can come in trailing attitude, doctorates and published rectitude, but I'm the one who has to operate it, nurture it, slewing and aiming it into the night, roiling through declinations and coaxing ascensions from my control panel, and if I say close then baby we close, this tent folds.

Nobody's messing with the work the Druids in tweed did a half century and more ago. Not on my watch. Those guys built Palomar to exactly the same dimensions as the Pantheon in Rome and with the precision of a Swiss watch on a grand scale. Turning science into art and religion all at once. The 200-inch mirror alone took them fifteen years to get right, all 20 tons of it. For eleven years they polished it, then carted it across America and installed it here on the mountain. They cared. It shows. And I revere them for it.

Astronomers come and astronomers go. But this place is amazing, especially when you look at the prefab junk they're dropping onto mountaintops around the world nowadays in the name of science.

"Hey," says Yannic, peering into the stereo system. "Someone took out the Rolling Stones CD."

"Editorial statements come in many forms," says Carl, who believes culture more or less stopped with Bach.

"Dewpoint's acting up again," I say, squinting at the changing red numbers. "We're back up to 2.8. We're probably out of business anyway."

"Shit," says Yannic, shifting toward the weenie end of the spectrum. He gets a sulky quality whenever we talk about dewpoint depression. "We've got to 3.0, right?"

"That may be the least of our problems. The windspeed's up to 41. And climbing."

High above the floor of the dome I heave the heavy, creaking door aside and step out onto the catwalk high above the ground where the vertical walls meet the curved upper part. The mountaintop view is as close to infinite as earthly restrictions permit. Catalina Island rises up out of the Pacific about sixty miles to the west. And then tracing the coastline upward, the lights of Los Angeles are coming on almost a hundred miles away, a gauzy glow filtered through the haze and smog. A veil on an old whore, the people on the mountain call it. Most of them up here loathe L.A. It's practically a moral issue with them.

I'm looking south and there's lightning somewhere down around the Indian reservation off the mountain. I've never seen lightning at this time of year. Usually it rolls up on thunderous chariots of Mexican hot air in the waning days of summer.

The more we walk around the catwalk, the more the twilight air snaps at us in sharp, cold little bites. Yannic's in front of us and calls out, his words pulled away from us by the wind. He's pointing to something.

Another helicopter. Barely visible hovering in the angry turmoil of clouds in the distance.

"Something's weird."

"Yeah. No Grimes light," says Carl. "The flashing red light on top of the helicopter." Neither Yannic nor I even think to ask him how he knows about such things as Grimes lights. Carl's a kind of technical archaeologist dwelling among electronic rubble he finds in junk stores and by some alchemy fashions into infrared gizmos in his cluttered, windowless Caltech office in Pasadena. Gizmos that actually work when he hooks them up to the big telescope.

He squints into the wind. "No lights, period. He doesn't want anyone to see he's there."

"Yeah but a storm's coming up," Yannic says. "What the hell's a helicopter doing out there in this weather?"

The far darkness is suddenly bisected by a powerful funnel of light that shoots down from the helicopter. For a moment the helicopter seems suspended, jostling in the wind on top of some lambent cone of phosphorus.

Carl disappears inside the dome and returns with binoculars.

"Someone's in trouble," he says after looking for a moment. He passes the binoculars to me. The quivering compressed image is blurred by the enveloping storm, but in that magnified blast of white light the silhouette of a man can be seen lowering into it on a rope. And then, instant blackness. The light, the helicopter vanish, and the clouds and the night take hold.

"Jesus Christ. What the hell is this?" Yannic pulls his jacket around him and leans into the jolts of cold air outside the dome.

Yannic's moving around the catwalk with a lithe sureness I don't have. Unlike me he never looks down through the metal grating to the concrete far below. We all have our own dweeb factor. Mine is heights. Looking down makes my thoughts go cubist and my legs buckle. I'm trying to fake it by acting cool and sort of caressing the railing but looking down at the facsimile of the ground far below as rendered by the flashlight beam *True identity of Palomar observer discovered* that jerks all over. *Missing grate cause of tragic fatal fall.* Truth be told if it was just me alone up here I'd be positively palsied. But Yannic, bless him, doesn't seem to notice my fear.

We get to the huge shutters and the flashlight beam catches a stream of moisture running off one of them. Major Druid alert. "We're closing up," I tell Yannic.

Before he can react, a flash of light like a strobe but not so white comes from somewhere around the curve. It lasts only an instant and ricochets off the moist white smoothness of the dome.

"What the hell was that?" I ask. Yannic's already running around the curve. Me, I walk more or less.

"Something going supernova at five air masses?" It's what passes for grad student witticisms. Yannic stops, his face squinting above the futile beam of the flashlight beam that vanishes in the wind. "Listen."

I hear it. Gunfire. It comes in stutter bursts from the area where we saw the helicopter.

"Who'd be using an automatic weapon out there?" Yannic asks.

"Charger" is all I say. Then, except for the wind, there is silence again. Until the next burst of gunfire, this one framed by distant yells that send a different kind of chill through me.

But Yannic doesn't hear them. He's vanished back into the dome.

Inside, my priorities overwhelm other thoughts for the moment. I race to the console, checking gauges and typing instructions on the computer. The rumbling reverberates through the walls of the data room as the shutters close and the dome lumbers in its relentless circle, spinning just fast enough to shed any gathering ice from its surface like some shattered and discarded chrysalis.

My thoughts have flown. I am out there. Out on the mountain, in the forests, in the storm, out where the gunfire came from. "It's got to be hunters" is all Carl says when I tell him. But he's not convinced, you can tell because he says it twice. And then: "Maybe we should take a look."

"Take a look?"

"Yeah. In case..."

"Yeah." Yannic sounds even less sure than I do. Then, almost as an afterthought: "Look for what?"

I am definitely not supposed to leave the telescope. I am the sentry. The lookout tied to the mast of enlightenment peering out in search of beacons in our turbulent nights. Leaving my post is somewhere between AWOL and desertion. If scientists had a firing squad I'd be in front of it, cut down in my prime in a volley of e-mail. But Charger's out there somewhere. I beg forgiveness from the Druids in tweed and hurry out of the data room, trailing Carl and Yannic.

In sharp shadows the ancient elevator creaks and groans down to the ground level. From the elevator and the corridor it could be 1948, the aura of old steel and dark wood dimly lit preserving a different kind of time travel.

The imprint of the puzzled grin is back on Carl's face, now that irony and absurdity are again openly rampant in a world that has carelessly ignored the mathematics of life itself. We hurry through the heavy entrance door, leaving the faint interior amber light and stepping into the blast of cold rain. In the jarring absence of any discernible light in the parking area next to the observatory the vertigo of blackness almost takes the legs out from under me until I grope to the outline of Carl's battered truck, the IRA limousine he calls it.

Yannic's busy explaining why all that gunfire has to be from hunters.

Carl drives down to the South Road below the dome, and suddenly the IRA limousine spins on a patch of black ice invisible through the impressionist's swirl created by the ragged remains of the windshield wipers. Yannic's in the middle yelling while I hold on to the door handle and Carl steers with one hand and defrosts the window with the other. Electrical junk, coffee mugs and old newspapers are rolling around in the cab of the truck. And that damn grin is still there like a gash in the night.

"This isn't funny," Yannic yells.

"Statistically it is," Carl yells back, grappling with the steering wheel as the big cedars on either side of the road form a momentary merry-go-round. Carl loves it. The crazier things get, the more he fires up that grin.

We get up to the crossroads where the forest retreats behind the parking lot around Mother's Kitchen, the restaurant that serves as the only meeting place on the mountain. One light burns low inside it.

"Closed," says Yannic.

I see a movement back on the fringe of the light. I get out of the truck, into the freezing rain with Yannic stumbling after me, skidding across the parking lot muttering about it being just like Seattle where he grew up. The rain's the kind that stings your face like there was something in it. And in the flashlight beam it's coming at us as if it was fired from ground level. I motion for Yannic to shut up, which does no good until I grab his arm. The flashlight beam catches something. A pair of gemstones blazing back at us. And two huge ears almost like a rabbit's sticking up from a small brown head surrounding those ruby eyes.

"Jesus Christ, we got Bambi on our hands," Yannic says, holding the light on the deer. "It's got to be hunters. That's where the gunfire came from."

We're very close, closer than I've been to an animal in the wilderness before. Our motions are slow, non-threatening, and I can hear my breathing echo in my ears. Yannic's gently turning the light around when it catches something else. A blur, a muted flash that jams some overload system where fears are stored in my head.

That's when Yannic screams. Or maybe it's the deer in some otherworldly shriek, I can't tell in that one terrifying instant when a grenade of fur and blood explodes.

Yannic's light careens all over. There's no cover. The darkness and the violence within it become even more horrifying because of the shrieks and the groans and the sounds of bones being snapped like twigs and flesh making a ripping sound. I can't tell if it's blood on me or maybe just the rain that suddenly got hotter, but whatever it is there's a viscosity factor to this terror.

I'm dragging Yannic, whose feet have turned into anchors, tugging at him until I can jumpstart his brain to link up with the rest of him. Then he's practically a cartoon, his legs like pinwheels and yelling all the way to the truck. I race after him, screaming at Carl to get back inside, and I'm almost there ready to dive—I mean literally dive in after Yannic in a flurry of arms and legs—when my brain suddenly turns into one massive strobe light of the purest fear. Because I realize something:

It is coming after us.

Whatever the hell *it* is, whatever that strobe of fear lets through into my nearly extinguished conscious thoughts. It is coming, roaring, slashing. I slam the door and behind me an instant later comes a crash when it hits the truck. Not once but again and again in a desperate fury.

I'm extricating myself from whatever loose ends of Carl and Yannic are entwined around me, sitting up into the rheumy, stale air of the truck. Staring into the contorted and wildly snarling face of a mountain lion.

I've never seen any creature like this one. Thrashing and turning wildly with furies that have made it mad, crazy, insane. The thing's spinning on some axis of its own rage, twisting and flailing at something only it can see. And with a howl that comes from some other world, the mountain lion leaps onto the hood and slams its head into the windshield, drooling deer's blood and slobber that are quickly painted across the glass by the wipers.

The thing spins on the hood and then lunges back into the drool, ripping a windshield wiper off like it was a flower pulled up by the roots. Yannic's yelling something about getting the hell out of here but Carl's frozen, strangling the steering wheel like rigor mortis has set in. No grin this time, just a little gurgling noise that comes from his throat. Whatever possesses me, I don't know, but I instantly realize something fundamental to the situation: we're in here. And it's out there.

"Nice kitty," I say.

It breaks the trance. Carl looks over.

"Hey. Don't worry about it. He can't open doors, you know," I say sweetly, almost lyrically like my happy-go-lucky self had finally after all these years chosen this moment to make its debut. "Simple. Just put the car in gear and we go." And as I'm saying this the mountain lion spins into the air like it had been snapped off the hood by an unseen chain. It lands on the ground, lunging and pawing at unseen demons.

"Jesus, what's with that thing?" says Carl. "It's like it's drunk or something,"

"Go go go go go!" Yannic yells.

The headlights lurch in a circle, Carl peering around the gore on the windshield trying to steer us back onto the road. From out of the side window we can see the steaming husk of what moments ago was the deer. The mountain lion's landed in it in a frenzy, ripping, slashing and spewing blood all around. This isn't about nature or even killing like in some National Geographic hyena film. This is about destroying.

The lion is trying to find the soul of that deer and devour it.

For a long time we sit in the enforced silence of the big front room of the old, vaguely Tudor building they call the monastery. It's where the astronomers stay when they're working up here on the mountain. Yannic brings down some brandy and we whisper questions at each other as if we're trying to make sure it really did happen. And in case we try to tell ourselves it was just a hallucination there's always the IRA limousine parked outside with the viscous goo congealing all over the windshield.

Carl goes upstairs to bed first. Then Yannic. I sit there in the darkness with the last of the brandy, and some sudden gravitational field comes out of that ugly old overstuffed armchair, pinning me to it with a force of exhaustion that makes my arms and legs feel like lead. The thought of driving back to my cabin over at Bailey Meadow is bad enough. But walking through that storm to the 200-inch dome where my car is parked is worse. I can't stop the visions of that deer. And the bloody steaming rubble that it became.

Hanging on the wall in the dining room is the white eraser board diagram with a square for each of the rooms in the monastery. In each square is written in Magic Marker the name of whatever astronomer is occupying the room while working at Palomar. I stand there staring into the eraser board, still seeing the deer. Room 11 is blank. So I write my name on that square, take the room key off the hook and walk up the carpeted stairs. In the spartan room looking out over the front of the monastery I fall across the bed, not bothering to pull down the black metal shutters that lock out all light in the daytime while the astronomers are sleeping. Pinned to the bed I drift, held suspended somewhere between dreams and death in some hammock of consciousness, some porous state of being through which rush all the seething images and terrors that we have locked away in the cages of our own traveling emotional circus. And suddenly...

...*the beasts are loosed. Racing into the center ring!* Into this cage of unconsciousness as the spotlight whips around and the audience roars while I desperately crack the whip keeping the beasts on their stools pawing the air and snarling—anything to keep them from devouring me because these are my beasts and I am the lion tamer I am the—

Lion?

I sit up as if I was spring-loaded, hurtled out of my circus and into the starkness of the room. I remember something. Or do I? I look out the window at the silhouette of Carl's old truck. It's too dark to see the windshield. But something is not right. There's a lion somewhere—not the one Yannic and Carl and I saw—a different lion in the cage of my own fears coming at me and no matter how much I crack the whip ...

I run out of the room, down the stairs, through the kitchen to that white eraser board. In the space for Room 11 I had written in marker pen *Michel Berard.* And right then I know why the other lion, the one that had been lying quietly, the one that I had thought was now tame, toothless even, had returned.

I quickly obliterate the name with the eraser.

Then I write my name as it is now: *Michael Braden.* Then exhaustion folds around me like a cloak of infinite weight.

I am aware of someone standing over me in the darkness.

Before I can even pull myself out of sleep, I hear Charger say, "Shhh." And then: "I went into your house. I had to."

"What do you mean you had to?"

"The woman."

"What woman?"

"The one who had blood all over her," he says. "I had to have some place to hide her."

The storm has passed. Out on the South Road, cutting through the forest, the silence seethes with activity. For now it can only be felt, not seen, not heard. The kind you just know is out there. The blackness of the trees forms a canyon wall down the mountain as the full moon comes through the breaking clouds, aiming at the rainsheened road like a spotlight.

It's Bright Time on the mountain when the moon is so full that only the infrared guys can use the telescope. On nights like this, the moonlight wipes out the visible-light guys, the ones who work in Dark Time delving way out there into the extragalactic edges of the universe. "Thank God for the moon," says Charger.

The seats in his old Cadillac are still damp from where the rain came through the holes in the convertible top. It groans up the incline past where the deer was killed. "Right there." I point. "Over past Mother's." The carcass—if you can call it that—is still there, a festering stew of body parts and blood. Charger stops the Cadillac, gets out and stares at it like he's thinking of something that's partly secret.

"I seen kills before," he says. "My daddy and me used to hunt. You'd see 'em all the time. What the wolves'd do to sheep or the like. But you know something?"

"What?"

"This ain't no kill. At least no ordinary kill. Bet the lion didn't eat a mouthful of that deer. Just tore it to shreds. Which makes sense."

"Yeah? Well I was there. And nothing made sense."

"Does too. That lion was stoned, man," he says. "You're never hungry when you're doped up."

"What dope?"

"Stoned. Coked out of its head. You know."

"Know what?"

"That helicopter we saw. Something happened over in Barker Valley. I don't know what exactly. Someone ran into a bunch of Mexican illegals in the dark. Someone started shooting and one of the Mexicans got shot."

"What's that got to do with the lion?"

"The guy was dead or dying when the lion got to him. Bleeding a lot. A meal waiting to happen. The guy had stuffed himself full of condoms of cocaine. He got shot up in the stomach and after whoever was with him dragged him a mile or two away they had to leave to go look for a road. The lion must have smelled the blood. So when they came back it was eating the guy. It ate the coke too. I'm tellin' you, the lion got stoned."

"How do you know this?"

"The other guy told me."

"What other guy?"

"The other guy with the woman. Dressed like he was going out to play golf or something. But he had a lot of blood on him too."

Bailey Meadow is over on the west side of the mountain, a few miles from the dome. It's like something you used to imagine when you were being read fairy tales as a kid. One of those gorgeous woodsy places with cabins nestled in among the big evergreens where sunlight only comes through in patches and shafts. You almost expect to see gnomes or elves happily working away. But that's not why I rented a place there. It was because there's no meth labs anywhere nearby.

Not like on the other side of the mountain, where the collection of shacks and houses set back off the road dead-ends at the old lodge. On that side of the mountain meth labs are a growth industry. There's just enough walking hair triggers standing guard and peering through acetone vapors to make a random neighborly visit not too advisable.

One of those local wild-eyes, a stringy apparition everybody calls Vern, actually spent part of a Sunday afternoon trying to shoot down a dentist flying his homemade ultralite plane over the mountain. Vern was convinced it was the Feds.

But Vern's no worse than any of the others over there, just some burned-out guy who's been living in the fumes of his own meth lab for too long. Long, mangy hair, a shirt that smells of two Mondays ago and an automatic rifle always by the window. If there's a scent to paranoia it's there. Or maybe it's just all those chemicals wafting through the woods on the east side of the mountain.

And that's not the worst of it. Those places are like bombs waiting to go off. A year ago a meth lab blew up just off the mountain near Lake Henshaw. It leveled the place and the fire scorched the grass for a field or two around. Bits and pieces of a couple of Mexicans were found later. At least the deputies presumed they were Mexicans from Tijuana.

Fire is an obsession here on the mountain. It's a living being around here, a marauder that's never gone, only hibernating. And ever since I've been here I have felt a sense of fire, like something deep in the woods waiting to lunge.

Some nights I've even dreamt of fire. Being swallowed up by it.

Which is why it's weird that Charger and I don't even pick up a whiff of smoke when he pulls up to my cabin, this old frame cottage nearly buried in the woods at the end of a lane.

"I knew they'd be safe here," Charger says. "No one would ever want to break into your place." Charger has a way of making compliments that sound like insults.

The headlights sweep the cabin and already there's something not quite right. Whatever it is—the scattered pattern of the old deck chairs, the clumps of leaves by the door or the birdbath being knocked over—it doesn't really register in mental alarm bells. It's just a sense. An uneasiness. Something in your mind that creaks.

When I try to open the door, it's locked. In the three years I've rented the cabin I don't think I locked the door more than twice. One of the true joys of living in a place with nothing worth stealing. After the key finds the lock, I push the door open and there's a noise that comes from the darkness inside. Like breath being expelled. Then we hear it again. Sharp and jagged in a way that makes the darkness stand on edge until the frayed halo of Charger's keychain light pushes it away.

I'm moving in front of the light. Forming shadows that come to rest on the crumpled form of a woman pressed against the wall with tangled dark hair and trembling hands held out in front of her like she's warding off what only she can see.

It's her eyes I see first, wild and dark and blazing terror from the corner of the big room. Her dress, *a dress in the mountains? With sequins on one sleeve?* is soaked and torn and has a dark bloody stain running from somewhere beneath her breasts tapering down almost to her knees. Like some pointer forcing you to look to her feet, which are, bare and scratched. It's her shoes she's holding on to, or what's left of them. Flimsy silken things that were never meant for the mountain.

Terror etches its patterns into the mask of her face, beautiful and contorting all at the same time. With all those waves of fear coming off her it's even hard to tell how old she is. The penlight flashes to me and then Charger in darting halos.

"It's me again," Charger says to her soothingly. "And my friend who lives in this place." The light flashes back to me for an instant. "No one's going to hurt you."

I turn on the lamp on the wall, the 15-watt wonder that the old couple who own the cabin had insisted was for atmosphere. It barely pushes the darkness away. But it's enough to break the fever. She looks from Charger to me and then her hands sink down, pulling her into the floor as she slides down against the wall.

Charger says in a low voice, "I'm not so sure she's okay."

She's trembling and staring into the floor like it's a thousand miles away. When I reach out to give her the old plaid blanket from the couch her eyes flash over to me. It's like gunsights being trained on you.

"Here," I say softly. Those eyes never leave me—I can't approach her with the blanket. I have to leave it on the old couch, slowly back away and then let her reach out for it. She picks it up like something that may have to be hurled aside. And finally when it's wrapped around her something lets go. As if she's struggling to cling to the last vines of consciousness. Then she sinks onto the couch and all of a sudden she's asleep.

"She's really pretty, you know that?" Charger says.

And she is. The madness and fear flee from her face as she sleeps. The mask slips away. You can see that she's probably even younger than I thought, somewhere in her twenties. Her matted hair dries out and falls loosely around her face in dark cascades.

I motion Charger outside. The strands of light coming from the orange bulb over the front door cast a sheen across the boughs hanging lower because of the rain that has now stopped. The silence of the cedars is complete.

"You said there was a guy with her."

"There was. Nervous jumpy guy who looked like he should have been handing out menus at one of those restaurants that's not as fancy as it thinks it is. I don't know what someone like her was doing with a guy like that." Already Charger's got scenarios going for her.

We walk aimlessly to the end of the lane where the orange light runs out. I'm ready to go back into the cabin. Which is when that first whiff hits me.

"Hey," says Charger. He smells it too.

Smoke. Not just chimney stuff. This is real smoke. The scary kind that sets off alarms almost genetically embedded within anyone who's spent more than a long, dry summer on the mountain. And the light. The orangeness now isn't just from that one little bulb way back at the door. It's coming from the opposite direction.

Over where the old hotel is.

They've called the old barnlike structure the hotel for longer than anyone remembers even though no one has actually stayed there for decades. It's been used more for parties and weddings, the kind where people want to pretend they're from pioneer times surrounded by oil lamps and deer heads sticking out of the walls.

A ball of orange light blossoms through the trees. We run toward it, stumbling through underbrush now illuminated by the walls of the hotel that are now exploding in flames. We're the first ones there but voices are rising into the night behind us. Charger gets to the door and I can hear him yelling over the snapping noise the fire's making. Even through the dirty side window I can see what he's pointing to.

But I just don't believe it. I can't. It's like when something has to register but your mind keeps rejecting what your eyes insist on. Because how else can you explain this?

Flames rising around a man nailed up on the wooden beams?

Like he was nailed to a cross?

The fire rips through everything as if it too is a creature seeking prey.

I am awed by the will, the consciousness of the fire. It wants to destroy. Or maybe avenge. At its most awful it practically sucks the whole building into it with smaller explosions maybe from the oil lamps, flinging flaming debris out at the cedars. It's the moisture from the rain that saves these trees, except for the ones closest to the fire that now stand steaming and charred, looking somehow humiliated, like people stripped naked in a public place.

They give off a sizzling sound that rises into the roar all around me. Then there's a kind of cry, more like a confused howl of fear and fury. It's Charger. Lurching into the inferno, pointing as the old building explodes around him. I bellow his name, loud enough that he hears and turns, pointing again. Pointing at this thing, these remnants of a being, distorted in the flame-whipped heat, this form of a man.

Or what used to be a man. Nailed to the massive, blazing crossbeams, high above the disintegrating floor of the hotel.

Charger's words are sucked into the inferno. As are my screams, warning him, ordering him. He hears but does not hear. All he can do is stand there, somehow unable to move, and point as the creature devours everything around him.

There's a star that Carl and Yannic talk about, one you can only see from the southern hemisphere at a declination of -60 degrees. It's about 150 times as massive as our sun, and the death throes it's going through are creating some serious labor pains, hurling the kind of fire into the galaxy that has definitely got the attention of the Druids' descendants. Because the inferno from this star when it explodes, even from a few thousand light-years away (read: trillions and trillions of miles) might just rewire our dinky little solar system in ways we don't even want to think about.

But out of that kind of awesome destroying fire comes something else: life. Literally. Us. We're all made up from bits and pieces of dead stars that have annihilated themselves, blasting their elements through the universe and finally lodging within us as iron in our blood, the calcium in our bones and the oxygen flowing within us. We are all the product of all that destruction of stars out there in the eons.

And there have been moments watching the Colonel when I am reminded of all this.

Like now, severe and serene all at once, he's walking through the edges of this fire as if he was inspecting his forces. Enjoining the elements for the next great battle with an enemy that the rest of us cannot see.

It was sometime after the hotel walls fell in that I first noticed the Colonel. Even as I'm pulling Charger out of the flames I am aware of that white Jeep driving up and the Colonel getting out, seeming to trail some spectral fire of his own behind him. The Colonel could almost be my grandfather but no one thinks of him as being old. Even with everything crashing down and exploding all around, he gives off a certainty, a kind of command from some emotional alloy that has so often reduced others in his presence.

It is not just some certainty encrusted with age, the way some older people get fixed in their ways as the mental steering mechanisms seize tight as they're plowing through the petunia beds. His is a certainty you're born with.

And with it, in his fashion, he rules the mountain. As has his family for turbulent generations, going all the way back to when some of the men on the mountain looked in books to find out where France was before they rode horses down the mountain on their way to fight a war.

The Colonel approaches as I pull Charger from the flames, the hues of the fire playing off his hair that has grown longer since it went almost pure white a few years ago. It flows back now, long and straight and completely unmilitary in a way that's daring you to ask if he ever was a real colonel.

I'd always assumed he was. Most people here do, presuming that Vietnam or maybe the Gulf War is probably somewhere in a past that he never talks about. And few people get far enough past the barriers of those clear, pale blue eyes to ask him questions about his life. His presence alone, that fierceness that comes from within and emerges as a controlled, often silent sense of command, has a way of fending off inquiry.

But the true mountain people, the ones who have a way of saying a lot by saying almost nothing, will sometimes talk about how the Colonel was always in trouble as a kid, that he used to herd cattle for his father, and that his family has owned most of the land on Palomar Mountain for over a century.

And right now he's probably the only element of serenity in this maelstrom. It's as if he somehow simply belongs in all the flames and smoke-veiled chaos. Which is maybe why he fascinates me.

I deal in fire. I look for it out there in the cosmos and I have come to worship it at the altar of creation itself.

Maybe it's hard to comprehend—until you've sat in the solitude of the dome as the telescope serves up images of enormous stars cremating themselves, shedding their own mass and spewing it out in million-mile-an-hour firestorms. Devouring their own helium and carbon and oxygen, fusing into neon at hundreds of millions of Celsius degrees—a cosmic hellfire that in a pitiless millisecond would turn our puny little planet into a cinder.

But that's just in the throes. The actual death of these stars is beyond what we can imagine. Somewhere out there, one of them is exploding every single second, an entire sun going off like a bomb, and its explosion is to what we can comprehend as the fire of the sun is to a glowing match. Some of them die with the power of a billion suns exploding in that one atomized second right after they've collapsed back in on themselves.

Or when they've cannibalized another star that has been pulled too close, literally ripping the surface off their prey in a colliding pirouette of death.

It was only later that I wondered if the Colonel had seen the incineration of the man nailed up into the inferno. By the time the six members of the volunteer fire department arrive in their old fire truck it looks like the sky is inhaling the flames. Charger and I are stumbling through the smoke in that moment when the ceiling starts crashing down.

The fire has devoured the man nailed up on the beams.

The Palomar Volunteer Fire Department doesn't have the kind of equipment to fight a fire like this so at first we're all flailing away unloading hoses that don't really do anything. Charger and I are running around helping, not really knowing what to do. It's more out of mental numbness than anything else. My mind is still yelling *Liar!* at my eyes. Or maybe it's the other way round.

As we're dragging hoses through the woods, Charger's yelling into the commotion. "It was him—the same guy!" he keeps saying.

"What same guy?"

"The nervous jumpy guy with the girl at your place. The guy I told you about. The guy in the country-club clothes."

"You saw his face?"

"No—there was nothing to see."

"You got close to him, didn't you?"

"Listen to me," Charger's yelling through the noise of the fire. "There was no face to see. The guy in there didn't have a face any more. It was gone. All except for where the duct tape was covering his mouth."

"How can a face be gone?"

"It just was. Like someone just scalped his face. Pulled it right off him."

Scott, the volunteer fire chief, is shouting at us to grab the hose connections that keep spraying water all over the place. Which is sort of like holding on to a big hungry snake that got into one of the meth labs and ate the product. But by the time we get it all fixed we're drenched and my hands are aching. It's simply no contest. That fire has made up its mind.

It's as if it's going to obliterate whatever evil has just happened there. And when the hotel walls fall away I swear I'm not imagining the outline of the crucified guy still nailed up there in the moment before the flames change direction and blast downward like something was hurling bolts of fire at him.

Part of the huge top beam comes crashing down like a bomb as Charger and I are looking all over to see if anyone has seen the crucified guy. But fire fever's got them all running around and in the commotion and yelling and noise you'd never notice him through the flames unless you knew exactly what you were looking at. Even then your brain would be feuding with your eyes like mine still is.

In the middle of it all Charger stops, looking like a thought is being pulled out of him with difficulty. "They didn't even do that to Jesus, you know," he says. "I mean, they hung him up on the cross and all. But they didn't do what this guy had done to him. What the hell is that all about? Ripping a guy's face off?"

But now, as the hotel is collapsing in on itself, the Colonel heads through the smoke toward Charger and me. He always makes Charger nervous, shuffling from one foot to another and looking around like some new puppetmaster of his hasn't quite figured out how to pull his strings properly. Eye contact is the toughest thing because once the Colonel gets Charger with that blue-eyed stare, he's locked for the duration. The Colonel's eyes are pretty much hunting weapons when he wants them to be.

But it's me the Colonel is looking at. Actually it's not so much looking as sending out a flare with his eyes. "You saw it too?" he asks, coming out of the smoke. "The helicopter?"

"Twice," I tell him. "Or maybe it was two helicopters. Over at Barker Valley."

"It's coming. I tell you it's coming." He's already walking away as he speaks. He turns and speaks directly at me. "You're new here, aren't you?"

"Been on the mountain for about eight years."

"That's new," he says turning away. "Good work with the fire here."

It's as close to a compliment as I've ever heard from him.

The Indians from the La Jolla reservation down in the valley have come roaring up with their foamer, the shiny new truck they've been aching to show off in front of the white guys who are still cranking out mere water from all their creaky volunteer fire department equipment. Even the fire figures this out. Before their white foam starts billowing all over, it loses its fury. In the jagged array of fallen and steaming timbers vanishing under the foam, only the remains of an antique piano protrude, looking like a black spire in a sea of whipped cream.

Charger and I are both staring at it picking thoughts out of each other's head. "That guy's in there somewhere," he says. "The dead guy."

"His bones are. Or maybe just his ashes."

"Ashes?" says Charger, looking upset. "Where's the justice in all that? The guy didn't have a face left and now there's nothing even left for us to bury?"

You can always sense one of those subterranean shifts in Charger's emotional plates. Which is sometimes a tricky balancing act when you're the one up on the surface. For all his gentleness, Charger's tectonic qualities can never be taken for granted.

"Nothing's gonna get buried. Don't even talk about it. Okay?"

"We gotta tell the others. That poor guy. He's probably got people who love him. Maybe a mother or something." The thought of a mother always gets Charger worked up.

"We're not telling anyone anything."

"Why not?" Said through game-face lips that don't move very much. He's hearing audibles above the roar of some crowd in his head.

"What if she's illegal?"

"Oh yeah." This stops him in mid-rush. "They'd deport her. That poor woman," he says, looking concerned, as if he's forgotten something.

"And what if the same people who crucified this guy are looking for her?"

And the revelation seeps through. "You think they're gonna want to do something to her too?"

"They killed the guy she was with, didn't they?"

"Oh yeah, for sure," he says. "And the mountain has no secrets. Not once you tell someone."

This silent woman has the stillness of marble in the darkness yielding to the first faint veils of dawn.

The fear that had cinched her expression has fallen away as she sleeps on the couch, and only the faintest pursing of her lips yields clues to life. While she breathes, pale sheets of light sculpt changing complexions across wide cheekbones, flaring below her eyes, which begin to flicker in a jagged rhythm of whatever reveries struggle toward the surface of consciousness. She makes a sound, a kind of whispered little cry, and then falls still again.

Silently I move past her, betrayed occasionally by the creaking of the eighty-year-old pine floor, long since worn down to bare wood on the path between the front door and the kitchen. My home, more accurately the cabin I rent, is what they describe in real estate brochures as rustic. In other words almost nothing has been updated in it for years. There is a natural state of darkness, occasionally yielding to this, the oblique and earliest sunlight of the day. The room where she sleeps is the living room, dining room and kitchen all at once, with hewn log walls interrupted only by the stone fireplace and an enamel-deficient sink next to the ramshackle stove. The one bedroom and bathroom and the sunporch that Charger often appropriates as his room are similarly rustic, exuding the permanent fragrance of a well-cultivated dampness that resides in the log walls. And for an added decorating touch, my landlords located the refrigerator on the sunporch, where it has resided for all the decades of its existence amid the impromptu garlands of dead pine needles and the spread acne of rust.

The light fights its way through the trees, stronger now in shafts that have their own weight. I have become attuned to light. After emerging from so many nights in the dome, I've come to respect the light of dawn. Unlike the twilight that nurtures dreams, the pale stain of dawn strips away our protective layer of lightly held truths.

Illusions are impossible at dawn

But now in this gathering of faint light I look at her and she seems almost Mediterranean, dark and with large eyes. I have no idea what, or who, is there, clinging to sleep in the next room. She is a different kind of illusion as I fill in histories for her. Fleeing a husband. A rich heiress. An impoverished woman who—*Hey hey Mikey, you can come up with better than that, man! How about a Vegas showgirl on the run from some rich industrialist with eight wives on his belt! A Mata Hari type spy who—*

Tommy. Not now.

An hour ago I returned from the dome, where, in all that echoing silence I heard the Druids' intonations, like the Inquisitors' chorus, convicting me of leaving my post. My penitence is to check and recheck. The instruments are properly shut down. The dome is securely closed. Silent. Safe. Awaiting the photons of another night.

Charger's note sits on the bed. Apologies scrawled in pencil for leaving before I got back. Charger left just before dawn. He had deliveries to make, cheap pills and insulin for the senior citizens of San Diego County bought from one of the Tijuana *farmacias* he has a deal with. So now it is my watch as she sleeps in the gray light settling across her.

I sit on the bed. I will not sleep. I cannot. Not yet.

I awaken, hurled from sleep into the sifting heat of afternoon, expecting the enfilade from those eyes again. But she's gone.

At the back door I can see out into the woods, where the sunlight is bleaching the clearings amid the darkness of the trees. Stillness. Then something moves. In the layers of forest she turns, the movement giving her away, lithe and almost floating, this time without all that wild and blazing fear. For a moment she's invisible as if some natural camouflage has embroidered her into the trees and the ferns.

I get closer. A twig snaps underfoot. Her response is instantly feral, a stillness that sears.

She is kneeling in the water completely naked, washing the blood from her dress. I stop, walking into that stare of the hunted, in equal parts indignation and fear. She raises the dress in front of her, the sequins on the sleeve glinting in dull flashes.

It is a gesture more protective than modest.

Her eyes do all the moving, wide and dark, filled with uncertainty and firing off looks that lacerate.

"I won't hurt you," I say, backing up behind the huge, horizontal trunk of a fallen tree. Only her face and shoulders are visible.

"What's your name?"

Her defenses falter. She looks confused. And says nothing.

"Your name," I ask again. She forms some sound that never makes it past her lips.

"My name is Michael." Then, silence. "Do you speak English?"

She makes a shrugging motion that says Yes. No. Maybe.

"What happened to you last night?"

She starts to say something and again no sound comes out.

"Can you talk?"

It's as if she nods yes and then tries to take it back.

"You understand what I'm saying?"

This time another nod. A simple yes.

"Then... why don't you say something to me?"

At first I think she hasn't heard. For a moment she looks around and then walks into the clearing holding the dress in front of her. In front of a patch of damp, bare earth she kneels, reaches out beside the little stream and runs a finger through the mud.

And writes *No lo se.*

The phone is ringing. In volleys that quicken in my head.

Back at the cabin. It's Charger on his cell phone.

"*No lo se,*" I tell him. The words rise from the mud.

I don't know.

"Why would she say that?" he asks.

"She didn't say it. She wrote it. You're sure it means 'I don't know'?"

"You think I don't know Spanish?" he says indignantly. Two years of living across the border in Rosarito Beach and now all of a sudden it's *Señor Charger, por favor.* He's almost yelling. But it's not really Charger being cantankerous, it's the Vicodin. He's hooked on the stuff. Has been since he mangled his leg throwing a block against some Seattle linebacker and then kept playing with shredded ligaments.

"Charger."

"What?"

"You're getting ornery again. Just take a dump, willya."

"Aw, Michael, I been taking laxatives all week." A long deflating sound. We're back to a normal decibel level now. "All week I tried. I can't."

Long ago I stopped bitching at him over the Vicodin. I said my piece and now that's a demon he'll have to make his business if he ever gets around to it. What's my business is the effect the Vikes have on those around him. Namely me. I have had to sit through some tantrums that suspiciously resemble the terrible twos. But then that's what Vicodin does. It dehydrates you so much that you're walking around with a week's worth of cement hardening in your innards.

"Where are you calling from?"

"The doctor's place."

"Which doctor?"

"The shrink."

Dr. Herrera, the South American psychiatrist in San Diego. Charger's friend whom he met through some of his crazier Mexican pill customers. Dr. Herrera's been sort of talking Charger through his own problems in the last year or so.

"Just ask him if you can use his washroom."

"It's no use. It doesn't work. Besides, I can't. Not after what happened last time."

"What happened last time?"

"He thinks I blew up his toilet bowl."

"Get real."

"It had a crack in it before. It had to have." Immediately the story gets assigned a reality factor of fifty-fifty. On the yeah-it-could-have-happened side of the ledger, you definitely don't want to be anywhere in the neighborhood when Charger starts shipping that cement. The Vicodin express, when it finally comes rolling through town without benefit of mufflers and catalytic converters.

Again I hear Charger talking to someone in the background. He comes back on the phone and says, "Ask her if she could speak before last night."

"Who were you talking to?"

"Just ask her."

"Charger, who were you talking to?"

Silence. "Dr. Herrera."

"I thought we agreed we wouldn't tell anyone about her."

Confusion sifts through the phone, the kind that always comes when Charger thinks he's done something wrong. "Aw c'mon, you know Dr. Herrera."

Another voice comes on the line. "Hello, Michael?" Heavy and melodic all at the same time. With an accent of indeterminate origin. "Forgive my curiosity," Dr. Herrera says when we get past the preliminaries.

"Doctor, no offense, but I didn't want Charger talking to anyone about her."

"Why?"

"Because we don't know who it is who wants to hurt her. And up here on the mountain it's impossible to keep anything a secret."

"Well don't go to the police. Not yet at least. I think it is maybe advisable to take her somewhere. Far away. Immediately."

"Why?"

"I have a feeling, that's all."

A feeling? "I think she's okay here. For the moment at least."

"Michael, I commend your concern but time may be of the

essence. But no matter what, I think from what Arthur"—*Arthur*? I can never think of Charger as Arthur—"has told me, I should see her. Soon."

There is an insistence, an imperative at work in the doctor's tone blocking out what follows with questions strewn behind my thoughts. "Michael? She may need medical attention."

"You're a psychiatrist."

"All the more reason."

And then nothing but the sound of my breathing making a loop through the mouthpiece and back into the ear. "Take the phone to her," he says. "Michael, this is important." The loop grows louder. "Are you there?"

"Yes. I'm here." I'm on a cordless phone. Its signal could reach the little stream.

"A professional habit, so please, Michael, take the phone to her and ask questions."

"What questions?"

"I will tell you." Almost urgently now. "It's important."

But there is something else—*Oh for christsakes No, a jillions time No! don't listen to a shrink! NoNoNo! they are the worst, man, they'll glue your eyeballs inside out and have you staring into your own goddamn brainpan as they fricassee your gray matter for their own jollies I know, man, I was there you know that Mikey, Mikey look at me for—*

Tommy. No.

Holding the phone, I walk back from the cabin, through the trees, following the silky red tendrils of blood sifting through the stream that runs across the mountain.

There in the middle of the woods holding a phone, talking to a psychiatrist and standing in front of a naked woman washing blood out of an evening dress, I make a quick assessment of the absurdity factor.

"Are you still there? Michael?"

"You talk to her," I say into the phone and then hold it out toward her. She has covered herself again, her eyes darting back and forth between the phone and me as if it's going to burn her ear.

She leans into the phone and listens. And then nods. She listens again and then pushes the phone back toward me.

"How did she respond?" Dr. Herrera's voice is urgent.

"She nodded."

"Nodded meaning yes?"

"Yes."

There's a pause you can almost hear coming through the phone like the rush of all that I tried to forget. "Her condition could be..."

"Could be what?"

"I think it might be important that I see her. Very soon," he says again. "Please ask her if this would be acceptable."

I want to throw the phone and run from the voice in my head that has become a chorus of fears. *MikeyMikeyMikey*. The chorus does not want these intruders—these police, these psychiatrists and all the rest of the social ornamentation snooping around up here on the mountain. This is my fortress, my refuge where I have fled both in body and in soul.

It is my escape from all that happened back in Canada.

From all that I did.

To the last psychiatrist.

I had lain in wait for him.

Watching Dr. Baymer get out of his car in front of his magnificent log house in the clearing on the granite of the Canadian Shield overlooking Georgian Bay, an expanse of water so vast it could have been the ocean. I lay there telling myself I intended to aim carefully. But not really knowing what I intended.

Except that I wanted to make it right for my brother. So that what happened to Tommy would not have gone unpunished.

I had rehearsed it all—walking over to Dr. Baymer as he lay pleading for a life that was no longer his. I had seen that moment in my mind, letting him see my face and fill his last moments with the realization that this was for what he had done to Tommy.

But through the scope of the rifle that image of coiled intellectual arrogance and devastation melted away into a sad and nasty little clerk. Furiously I conjured up Eichmann and Himmler and all the feckless little inquisitors whose savagery must have been stoked daily by their own chinless image in the mirror. Looking through that scope and praying for rage, a rage that would carry me through into the bloodlust of vengeance and killing that would make a Sicilian jealous. But my prayers were unanswered by God or whatever god got the call that day.

I wanted a tyrant. What I got through that scope was a sad little man. I lost my fury. I could not go through with it. Instead I aimed into the cedar boards behind him, settling for what I thought would be some revelation of sniveling fear in him and a moment of crippled redemption within me.

But in that instant of communion between my finger, the trigger and the bullet Dr. Baymer turned quickly back toward his car.

And walked into the bullet that was meant to miss him.

There was a splattering of human tissue on the cedar exterior of that magnificent house. But it was not his brains. It was his nose.

It was not the way I planned. Not with him lurching all over without a nose. I never wanted to shoot off his nose. That's just humiliation. That was his game. The game he played as he destroyed Tommy.

The revelation when it came to him was not what I expected. A gaping mouth working noiselessly at the sight of me. As blood spouted around it and the stare of a terror that gradually transferred itself to me. At that instant there was an unexpected death. A form of suicide. Michel Berard died.

And Michael Braden was born.

I turned and ran. From Penetang. From Canada. From myself.

And then the flight into America: nurturing, forgiving, forgetting America where old lives vanish and new lives are born.

Just as new stars are born every moment somewhere out there in the cosmos. Maybe that's why I found Palomar. To watch other kinds of violence through the massive telescope as worlds explode and devour and die in cosmic agonies that make what I have done trivial in the eyes of God, or a god who enforces the cycle of creation.

Out there in the unimaginable light-years of the cosmos, violence is what gives new life. It is necessary.

It is our paradox, our terrible truth. And there's no way we can accept it.

Penetang

As much as they all had suffered in Oak Ridge, it would have gotten worse after what I did.

Because for a while the tin-nosed Torquemada returned to that grim place to burn more already messed-up minds at the stake of renewed psychiatric rectitude, the kind that burst forth in those days of fashionable enlightenment after *One Flew Over the Cuckoo's Nest.* Nurse Ratched came in more socially acceptable forms, but the effect was the same. And probably still is. Insanity breeds piety from those who know what's best. And Dr. Baymer always knew what was best.

Tommy was not insane. The opposite. My brother was born with a grin that could not be pried off his face. And that was probably most of his problem because the people who did him in couldn't stand having someone like him around. They were people who got to be important and powerful, and could never shed the nagging fear that maybe all their lives they really were trailing toilet paper from their shoe and Tommy was the only one who knew it.

But it was just the way Tommy was. Something about the world just didn't add up and I think he figured that probably God wanted it that way. So go with it and laugh. He gave off this invisible light, the kind that shines into the dark places inside other people. Or at least those who wanted to let the light shine in.

He was my hero.

Even saying that now after all these years gives me a thrill just like it did when I was five years old and he was ten and he invited me to play Knock Knock. *Knock, knock. Who's there?* I even got to say the punch line, which was about as big an honor as I've had in my life. *Thumping.*

Thumping who?

Thumping's crawling up your leg.

And for hours at a time we'd be rolling around on the grass in front of our house and laughing so hard I'd pee my pants, which always ended the game with our mother yelling at Tommy.

Even then I should have known that getting yelled at was to be part of Tommy's destiny. By the time he was a teenager everyone around Penetang had a favorite Tommy story. Mine was Father Nunzio chasing him down the aisle of the big shrine yelling at him that he was going to go to damnation for what he had done. Tommy had got bored with being an altar boy, always waiting for Father Nunzio to finish polishing off a bottle of sacramental wine in the rectory. So one day he poured something called Neutral Red, a kind of dye, into the wine. And later from the bathroom when Father Nunzio was yelling panicked prayers to the Holy Mother as he was pissing bright red it was Tommy's giggling out near the altar that gave the game away. Even when Father Nunzio chased him all the way past the statues of the martyred Jesuits, swatting him with a rolled-up newspaper, Tommy was still grinning. At least until Father Nunzio caught up with him.

No one ever wanted to be on the receiving end of Father Nunzio's wrath. He terrified us all. He was a big heavy man with a scowl that almost never left him and an Italian accent that got thicker as he got angrier. The only time that accent almost vanished was when he talked about California and the Indian mission the Jesuits had sent him to run near San Diego. You could tell he regarded our little town of Penetang as some lower form of Purgatory, especially in the winter when he muttered a lot. Getting transferred there from San Diego was almost like his life was over. Every February when the rest of us were rejoicing on the ski slopes and outdoor rinks, California became some Eden from which Father Nunzio had been banished.

We grew up in Penetang, a place that American tourists of a certain age always thought sounded like it should be in Vietnam. Actually it was properly called Penetanguishene from back in the 1600s when the Huron Indians used to carve up, roast and generally martyr the French missionaries in droves. But a few hundred years later the Chamber of Commerce–type wisdom of the day was that tourists wouldn't visit a place they couldn't pronounce, so the name got shortened to Penetang. As an added bonus the name change pissed off the French Canadians in the area, who took their martyrs seriously.

Penetang is more or less straight north of Toronto, up on a hill overlooking the kind of bays and inlets you see on postcards. It's where the land changes and with it, the people. The loamy softness of the south abruptly surrenders to the craggy rockface of the north, and Penetang, like most border towns, avoids declaring loyalty to either side. Once the tourists and summer-cottage types clear out in September the place settles into the grim task of consuming large amounts of beer and recruiting a hockey team that will fulfill its civic duty and beat the shit out of Midland, the town a few miles down the bay road.

We lived in a house off Champlain Road on the other side of the harbor, and from our bedroom window Tommy and I could look out to the bay just beyond the three rusting cars and one washing machine that our neighbors, the Robillards, had abandoned on their front lawn. One day Tommy set off firecrackers in one of their abandoned cars and the blaze it started in the upholstery brought the fire department screeching in with hoses blasting away.

The flames pretty much caused the car to blow up. I loved being around Tommy when he laughed like he did then, as we were peeking out of our screened-in porch. He got so crazy that I tried to put my hand over his mouth. He just couldn't stop giggling as Mr. Robillard yelled at the fire department that his brand-new car was ruined and the insurance would have to pay for it.

Tommy had this weird kind of music around him when he laughed. It was what I remember the most.

Miss the most.

Beyond the rooflines of the small houses on the other side of the road was the harbor and then the town on the other side of the little bay. On some days we'd watch through binoculars as our father—we called him our old man—supervised the launchings at Grew Boats.

He haunted us, Tommy especially. When we were really small Tommy kept asking why our old man was called Lightning. That's what everyone called him back when he was truly the golden boy, the one who made the town forget what it was. Didn't Lightning come down from the sky and go ka-boom! And then make a big fire? Something like that, Lightning would answer. And then Tommy would run all over like a wind-up doll yelling *ka-boom!*

But the haunting feeling Lightning cast over us like a shadow grew with the silent revelations of him not being the hero we needed him to be. It all happened in slow motion, as if plates of shining armor had silently fallen off our father piece by piece until there was nothing left but a startled man who had somehow shrunk to be smaller than we were.

When we were little kids there was still enough mythology trailing around behind him. And us—we were the proud sons of the great Lightning LaRue. He got the name Lightning because of his speed when he was carrying a football or racing down the ice playing hockey. And the LaRue part came because when he was a kid he always wanted to be like that cowboy movie star Lash LaRue.

When Tommy was old enough to know who Lash LaRue was he wanted to be him too. It was his way of making sure he turned out to be just like our old man. For a year after his ninth birthday Tommy dressed all in black just like Lash did in *Lash of the West* or *Phantom King of the Bullwhip*, which he made me see eight times at the Pen Theatre. It was this bullwhip part that created the most problems for Tommy. No one around Penetang even knew how to make a bullwhip, so Tommy figured he'd be the first.

You just knew he'd get yelled at a lot over that one.

Pretty soon everything from the elastic in the Tummy Tucker—the name was written on the label of Mother's steel-belted underwear—to the fan belt in Mr. Robillard's only working car was being disassembled in an effort to make a proper bullwhip. When Tommy finally got something close to what Lash LaRue would call a bullwhip he tried it out on mother's juniper bushes.

That night Tommy and I both hid under the bed. It was about that time we started figuring out that it was always Mother who did the yelling. Never our old man.

He was drifting off—the great Lightning LaRue was getting quieter and quieter. It took us years to realize what was happening, that it was Mother who began making more of the family decisions. We never noticed the moment where something in her voice became permanently different when she talked to him. Or about him. Something had slipped in both of them. And neither could talk about it.

They would not have even known how to get back to where they began.

Their old photographs have a kind of magic to them. Mother looks like she gave off the same light he did. In those pictures she was beautiful in a way that she never seemed to be later on when we were growing up and something in her face tightened around her mouth. There's one photo taken after a football game where she's staring up at Lightning LaRue looking just like Vivien Leigh with Clark Gable in the poster for *Gone With the Wind.* A lot of people in Penetang thought Mother was better looking than Vivien Leigh and after the movie played for one night in a revival showing at the Pen Theatre she bought the poster from the projectionist. It hung in our front hallway where anyone entering our little house would have to see it. Once in a while you'd catch Mother standing near the poster pretending not to look at it.

Our little house with its aluminum windows and screen doors quietly became a war zone, with skirmishes fought between Mother and Lightning over things that didn't matter but were meant to represent things that did. The less they touched each other the more the fights flared over things like insulating the attic. When he quit another job selling insurance, the lawn suddenly needed resodding. And when the garage and all its tools became a refuge for him, the more we absolutely needed shutters on all the windows. So our place would look like the villa in that Italian decorating book.

I was about ten years old when I first remember Mother on her own in the bedroom crying in the middle of the day.

For a while she cried a lot but she always tried to keep it from us. She'd do her best to protect us from whatever she was going through and always came up with some reason for why she was upset. *Thinking about your grandfather. A bad headache. Allergies.* But neither Tommy nor I believed her. We knew better.

Even at that age we knew she was crying because of a future that never happened.

One afternoon when I was secretly listening to her cry I started to choke. I fell across my bed because I couldn't breathe. It was all my fault—it had to be, all of it. I mean, it was so simple, wasn't it? There had to be an answer to her problems, Lightning's problems, and I wasn't seeing it.

I was letting them down.

When she heard me and came running into the bedroom and calmed me down, I didn't want her to touch me. Some vaguely formed impulse was gasping to escape from it all.

I wanted to cling and flee all at the same time.

Everything became worse after the mahogany-boat argument. If there was one thing that our old man was good at other than being Lightning LaRue, it was making wooden boats. He had learned the craft from one of his Berard uncles, the French Canadians who had migrated to Penetang and brought with them the skills that were passed down in the Saguenay River towns of northern Quebec. At first it was a canoe slowly appearing like magic in our garage, the strips of wood that he planed, molded, glued, doweled and shellacked until Tommy and I had this sleek vessel that we paddled triumphantly all over Penetang harbor borne by winds of lightness and hope we had never known.

It was one of the last times I remember seeing our old man smiling a real smile, not one of those bleary, dialed-up versions that he came to rely on later.

He was waving to us from the shore. And then he was actually laughing. We could see him laughing, but not hear him. We were too far out in the water and the wind was coming from behind us.

But now I can hear him. In those times when I wake up in the silence of Palomar hearing that laughter. Remembering Mother standing behind him, up near the house. But she is not smiling, she cannot feel those winds of lightness even though in my waking dreams I yell back through time pleading for her to see what we see—that the great Lightning LaRue is laughing again.

But she can't see it.

Because those were days when no one in Penetang talked about the great Lightning LaRue any more unless they were asked to remember. The last training-camp tryout with the Toronto Argonauts had been way back when Tommy was in kindergarten. And in hockey, the Canadian Olympic team had stopped calling a couple of years after that. And then the jobs dwindled through a succession of shorter durations.

It was only the talk of making those mahogany boats, first the canoes and then the real beauties, the mahogany inboard cruisers, that seemed to resuscitate the spark in our old man's eyes.

It was his belief that mahogany boats had never been made properly in our part of the world. Not like the great wooden boats of Italy that were works of art, each made from one tree so that the grain on the starboard gunnel was the same as that on the port gunnel. With single planks of mahogany that ran from bow to stern, not the cheaper butt-plank method that created joins of smaller pieces of wood. Or the even more inferior way of using overlapping mahogany plywood planks.

No, none of that would be for the great boats Lightning would build. His boats would rival the work done by the Italians who built the gorgeous Riva, the most beautiful boat in the world. Especially the Riva Acquarama Special that Tommy and I lusted over. We lusted—that was the only word—because it was what got Lightning excited. He came alive. And as he did, so did we. He even started using the word *art* when talking about the boats he would build. The art of boat building. He believed it. And even better, so did we, listening to him talk about ordering entire Honduran mahogany trees from which these works of art would emerge. For connoisseurs. Who truly loved classic boats. People of taste.

People who were not remotely seduced by vulgar fiberglass.

Pretty soon our kitchen table became the wooden boat research center. There were photographs and specifications of all the great wooden cruisers that were no longer being made. Tommy and I would argue the merits of a Hacker-Craft versus a Gar Wood, and when we found out that the Van Dam Wood Craft, a company in Michigan, an *American* company, had just started building wooden boats again, that settled it. There was no time to waste. The great Canadian wooden boat was waiting to be built. A genetic maelstrom had been silently unleashed with unknown generations of Quebec canoe builders ringing the noiseless DNA chimes within Tommy and me.

Plans were hastily made for converting the garage, making it larger, and the financing schemes were drawn up for investors—mostly local car dealers, farmers and lawyers. All of whom were certain to remember the mystique of Lightning LaRue as they stood on the shore and watched us paddle the canoe in a demonstration of the kind of nautical quality that they, as investors, could expect once the mahogany cruisers started rolling out.

It was when we were paddling in the demonstration for the dentist that I first saw the changes in Tommy. He was almost seventeen and I was eleven, but even then I knew there was some difference that mattered in Tommy. On the surface it was in the way he talked to me, as if his words were fired from close range in ways that stung. I don't think he even knew he was doing it.

The dentist, a small, bald-headed man from Alliston, had been the football team's trainer in their senior year when Lightning made the final thirty-two-yard run to glory on a fractured left foot. Even when we were paddling out in the harbor I could see the dentist on the shore catching himself looking up at our old man the way he probably did years ago.

"You're wrecking everything," Tommy hissed at me from the back of the canoe.

"What are you talking about? I'm not wrecking anything."

"You are too! You're just gawking at them."

"Eat your nose, I am not."

"Dammit, paddle! Faster!"

"I can't."

"You can!"

I was straining so much I thought my lungs were going to catch fire. The sound of Tommy's paddle slicing the water behind me was like someone pounding a hammer. "The dentist is gonna... cough up the money... if we show how... fast this thing is." Tommy rasped out the words in bursts like he was firing them from a slingshot. "Go! Go! Go!" I couldn't believe it. The world was winning and Tommy was losing. I didn't have to turn around to know that the grin he was born with wasn't there any more.

"It's no use."

"It is!"

"It's not. Lookit."

On the shore the dentist was retreating with the same *have to think about its* and *talk to my accountants* that the others had left with. You could always tell. Just by the way they moved with the awkward looks and the darting smiles as they staged a tactical retreat to their cars.

But even more depressing for Tommy and me out in that canoe was the way you could see it all playing out in Lightning, a kind of cinching-up of that old bravado with all those grins we never saw around the house any more. And then after the inevitable *I'll get back to you* there was the exhalation of hope. The terrible shrinking. As if the great Lightning LaRue had suddenly come unhooked from some hose that kept him inflated to the manufacturer's recommended pressure.

With every disappearing set of taillights it took him longer to turn back toward the house and face the empty space in the doorway where Mother had been standing only moments earlier.

This time, as the dentist drove away, Tommy slashed at the water in a frenzy that almost tipped the canoe. It was the first time I saw the different Tommy, the one who couldn't laugh at the world because now it was laughing at him.

The world was laughing because it didn't want classic mahogany boats any more.

It wanted fiberglass. And only fiberglass.

I didn't know it. Tommy didn't know it. The great Lightning LaRue, deflating on the shore amid the wreckage of a future, didn't know it. Or maybe didn't want to know.

But Mother knew, at least now she did—that her whole life from the age of about seventeen had been heading toward fiberglass.

The life Mother was now living had been invisibly hanging out there in front of her, waiting to emerge from the vanishing mists of hope.

It had been that way ever since she was the one that so many of the other girls had wanted to imitate. The one who never tried to be liked but simply was. It was an attraction borne aloft by some effortless energy that went into everything she did and was. The old photographs are all the same, with that smile that even now sends waves of hope and heartache crashing down on the distant, uncharted shores of what might have been.

Lightning was the one she fell in love with. Maybe even the only one she ever loved. And it was unconditional. The evidence is there. The photos. And the letters from the summer jobs at the Muskoka Sands resort hotel. Shoeboxes full of letters almost radioactive with longing.

Even from those letters, Mother's restless need for activity, for simply making things happen, burns through the intervening years in a way that was never apparent to us, her sons, until it was all over.

And if you read those letters as I did before I fled, another name emerges like something flashing across some darkened sky of past lives and then fading forever. Or so you think.

Steven Atwater.

The name careens through her letters, at first congealed among *the gang*, the other teenagers working there for the summer like Mother, the ones who went into Gravenhurst for milkshakes, and then more or less the same group—Gayle, Karen, Nick, Warren, Lorraine, Steven and me—who went waterskiing on their days off. Or over to Gull Island on one of the little sailboats. Or to the Saturday-night dance in Bala.

In one of the photos Steven Atwater is standing on the dock behind the rest of them looking straight at Mother while everyone else is waving into the camera. I always thought that because of what he became, the power he accumulated, he'd look different like maybe handsome or tall and blond, the kind of imposing-looking guy who'd draw your eye to him. Actually he does draw your eye but not for the reasons I thought; he is shorter than the other males and not much of a physical specimen—except for his eyes.

Those eyes go all the way back to China. Like two dark pits of furious will, they burn through the rest of the group to get to Mother.

Steven Atwater wanted Mother more than all the other trophies he would ever buy, acquire or plunder.

For the longest time he was never any real threat to the legend of Lightning LaRue. Not even two months after the photo on the dock was taken, when he made the mistake of driving up from Toronto under the pretense of bringing a few of the group together for an autumn reunion weekend. He had to pretend to smile through the aftermath of the victory over Midland, the game where Lightning got photographed for *The Free Press*.

Even in the glory days that lay ahead of him, Steven Atwater would have known a contract of the heart had been forged so irrevocably that not even his legal battalions could rend it asunder. Not the way they did with corporations he routinely ripped open in the name of underlying value.

In those days this unacknowledged contract between a quietly complicated man and a loving woman, made on the shores of Penetang, had as its consideration, the one element Steven Atwater's own life lacked, the missing piece of his existence that could not be willed into being: sheer joy.

And on that "reunion" weekend Steven Atwater's very presence, his lacerating will, would have been obliterated by the light that Mother and Lightning gave off from somewhere inside them. And being what he was, Steven Atwater would not, could not, ever have forgotten that defeat.

For Mother more than any of her friends, the future was the source of all light.

Because from somewhere behind her in that dreaded terrain of the past, all that was bad and frightening resided.

Her own mother was still making collect calls to her sisters on Church Street in Penetang. The calls came from payphones outside a motel in Niagara Falls where the latest husband or whatever man she was with may or may not have been lying across the bed. Mother had been in those motels too, a child bouncing obliviously through a steady progression of her mother's onrushing addiction, across the Ontario landscape, hurtling toward the tawdriness of the Falls, that degraded postcard where small-time hoodlums ginned their scams under the noses of proper Protestant somnolence.

Yes, Mother had been there. Until her own mother's sisters had taken action, a flotilla of aunts swooping in while their own sister was dripping from collapsed veins and spewing some incoherent syntax of rage at the official documents, the ones invoking the Holy Wrath and Writ of the Catholic Children's Aid Society that took the child away from her. And landed Mother in the custody of her aunts on the quiet, shady streets of Penetang. A little girl playing hopscotch and dressing her dolls and raised by aunties. And who charmed the neighbors by being the most cheerful of all the children in the area, the one who never cried.

Who never seemed sad.

Or talked of her past.

Only the future was bright. Pure. Joyous.

And then one day the future became Lightning.

Palomar

Since I left Penetang there has been a kind of dream that sometimes overtakes me, a cortical fusillade of reinvented memories I do not want to remember. It usually comes at times when I am telling myself everything is normal. And in my attempts to place the dream in some rational world, I am unable to find an immediate catalyst that would have pushed it up from whatever depths have been nurturing it. Only later, usually much later, can I even vaguely discern the fears that gave it life.

The dream almost always starts as benign, almost playful. But over succeeding nights it is repeated, playing itself out endlessly, revealing its true nature, Medusa tangles of consciousness descending into unslayable nightmares that transform themselves, each more virulent and terrifying than the one before.

But the one today is different; it has no gentle antecedents that change virulently with each visitation. This one starts where the others have ended.

It is less than half a day since I looked into the inferno of the hotel and saw the man nailed up in the flames. But there is nothing about those flames that intrudes into the tangle of fear from which I cannot awake as the exhaustion of that night and day clings to me like a narcotic.

Instead I see that mountain lion, a maelstrom of fangs and claws on the hood of a car crashing toward me in a kind of slow motion that I cannot escape by rolling away from beneath it.

But it is mostly the glass from the windshield I see descending on me slowly in beautiful slivers, a lacerating cascade that sparkles and shimmers in its lethal descent. The slivers of glass descend forever, hurtling toward me as if all my responses are glued together in helplessness.

But then in one instant a chill shoots through me, flinging aside the shroud of unconsciousness. It is a chill that comes from somewhere on my arm.

From where the woman has touched me. Waking me. She is standing over me looking both concerned and startled.

She is holding a knife.

Then she quickly backs away, toward the window as if returning to a post she had left. Through the fog of exhaustion, I watch her staring out the window, gripping the long-bladed knife with the serrated edge. The one used for cutting bread.

The back door of my cabin acts as a kind of sundial, the shafts of light coming through it telling me that I have slept until early afternoon.

For a moment nothing registers and then even as sleep falls away at the sight of the knife I do nothing, just lie on the couch watching her. Her concentration is total. Whatever it is she sees outside is all that has any claim to her attention. Even when I get up she does not look over.

There are voices from outside. Her hand tightens and loosens on the knife handle as if searching for the best grip. The muscles on the side of her face faintly contract. For an instant as I approach, her eyes dart toward me, flicking tendrils of fear.

"What is it?"

It's as if she doesn't hear me at all. The voices subside as I get to the window. A furniture delivery truck is driving away from a house in the woods across the road. I reach down and gently take the knife out of her hand. "It's okay," I tell her. Her expression subsides and she leans against the wall and closes her eyes, shaking her head slowly as if there is some kind of pain at work.

I am only partly aware of how much I want to make this pain go away. It seems almost natural to reach out to comfort her, my hand brushing her shoulder. She recoils as if she's been jolted, that spring-loaded stare snapping open for the instant it takes to register that no harm is present.

Then, breathlessly, she takes my hand and gently places it back on her shoulder. As a gesture, almost an apology for her reaction. She nods the faintest of smiles as her breathing subsides.

"Police," I say. "Maybe we should go to the police."

She just stares at me. Through me.

Again. "*Policia.*"

She shakes her head, at first slowly. Then, as if seized by something, her hands splay open in front of her in sharp little waving motions. Her mouth makes words but no sounds come out.

Outside she sits in a deep wooden chair at the back of the cabin, her knees raised up protectively in front her. With her eyes closed and her face turned toward the sun she is like a plant finding the light. It is one long moment of serenity that ends only when the sun goes behind the clouds and she shivers under my old football sweater that she wears.

Her dress hangs across the railing, torn and flimsy in silken folds that catch the gathering breeze, and when I say we need to buy some clothes for her she looks at me as if I'm speaking a foreign language.

"Can you understand me?"

A blank stare until she nods as if with difficulty.

"Can you say something to me?"

She replies, her mouth moving. And still no words come out. She tries with the same result, over and over again until she slumps back in the chair, closing her eyes and shaking her head.

Charger returns. "There was a message for you. Right after you left for the dome last night. On your answering machine. I heard it. I couldn't help hear it," he says, looking somehow guilty. "Could I?"

The voice on the answering machine is gruff, uneasy at being ordered around by a machine. "Phone me," it says. "Tonight. Not tomorrow." And then the *click* comes like a blade.

"The Colonel," says Charger, filled with wonderment. "Wow."

"Why wow?"

"He never calls anyone." He looks around to see if she's watching. It unnerves him to find out that she is. "Did you talk to the Colonel at the fire?" he whispers.

"No more than you did."

"Do you think he knows about her?"

"No."

"Dr. Herrera says we have to do something about her."

"What does Dr. Herrera know about anything?"

"He says she needs help. Right away. He wants to see her." He's whispering and I can see her eyes raking us with flickers of suspicion.

"No."

"No?" Charger's waiting for me to say I don't mean it.

"Why's he so insistent on seeing her?"

"He's good."

"I don't care. I don't want him up here. Not right now. Not till we know what we're doing."

Charger suddenly won't even look at me. Always a sign of impending news that makes him uneasy. "Michael?"

"What?" He won't look at me. He's looking all around. "What?"

"It's too late."

"What's too late?"

"I told him it would probably be okay if he came here. So he's going to show up here."

"Are you serious?"

"I'm sorry, okay? It was a really weird time at Dr. Herrera's."

"Weird how?"

"Like I didn't even get to have a session with him. Like he was upset about something. He wasn't like he usually is." Charger gets that guilty look that comes when he thinks he might have offended someone. "But he really wants to see her," he says, not whispering this time.

I turn toward her. "We're talking about the doctor, the one on the telephone," I say. "Do you understand? The doctor? The one you talked to."

She shows no comprehension. Her eyes are on Charger.

"I wasn't whispering to hide anything, honest," Charger says to her. "I thought maybe it might upset you."

"The doctor," I say again. "In San Diego. He wants to see you."

Still nothing.

"See, he's not really a doctor," says Charger, still sounding apologetic. "He's a psychiatrist." He points to his head. "But that's okay, you know. Nothing to be ashamed of. I go to him, you know. See, I'm sort of having personal-type problems ever since..." He stops.

She looks from Charger to me as if she understands nothing.

When I return with sweaters, jeans, socks and moccasins—whatever can be bought for her at the General Store—there is a man standing near my cabin. He is better dressed than people from the mountain. No one from here wears a blazer and flannel pants in the middle of the week. The man is standing by a large black car, maybe a Lincoln.

Even before I open the car door I catch a glimpse of the woman in the shadows of the doorway. She challenges me with a look of confusion, maybe fear.

The man, with gray hair and vaguely olive-toned features that yield nothing, is scanning the forests like someone trained to see what others miss. From where his old Cadillac is parked Charger calls out, "You remember Dr. Herrera."

I do. From the days of driving Charger when the shattered ligaments in his knees could not be trusted to work the brakes well enough to go to the therapy sessions that were keeping him marginally stable. And sometimes sitting in the waiting room talking to Señora Herrera, his wife—Sonia as she insisted on being called—on the days she acted as his receptionist. There were two therapy sessions going on then. One on either side of the closed office door as this dark-eyed woman with hair pulled fiercely back like a ballerina's told tales of longing for a life they once had. A life before they had money. Before success took its silent, corrosive toll.

In those hours, waiting outside the closed door of her husband's office, she would talk until she reached some inner circle of indiscretion. Then she would pull back, realizing the glare that for a moment she had shone into their lives like a ringmaster introducing some new act in a flash of the spotlight that is instantly extinguished. She would become flustered. Then silent.

After several weeks of driving Charger, all I really knew for sure about her was that her husband cast more of a spell over her now than he had when they married. And that somehow I felt sorry for her.

After driving Charger to those sessions for a few weeks, I made an excuse and told them that I was needed in the dome for the installation of a new optical device. I never went back.

"Hello, Michael," Dr. Herrera says in that faintly undulating accent, radiating the same formal reserve that makes him almost unapproachable.

But he is not looking at me. He is looking at the woman. An appraiser evaluating a purchase.

Dr. Herrera Jimenez, or Jorge as Charger calls him when he feels his therapy sessions are going well, is Peruvian with all the coarse elegance that the Castilian *oligarchía* of Lima had passed down over its centuries of rule. Decades ago, first as a student radical and then as a young doctor, Jorge Herrera had been teargassed in the name of this Reforma Agrária that so enraged his father's friends. And then had fled into the vastness of the Peruvian Amazon, barely eluding the Interior Ministry people who were hunting him. Settling near the jungle town of Iquitos and treating *campesinos*, he waited to join the revolution that would happen when the great Che arrived. To hear it told by Sonia, these were days of minor triumphs and for her, at least, quiet rapture.

The rumors were all over—that Che Guevara had left Cuba to start the revolution in Colombia. And from there, Peru. Or Bolivia.

But Che never came.

At least not to Iquitos. But several American military men did show up, the ones advising the Peruvian army on counterinsurgency. One of them, a captain, spoke perfect Spanish and sought out the most passionate of the local intelligentsia, no matter what their political views. In fact the greater the political challenge, the more the captain sought them out. And Jorge Herrera Jimenez was the biggest challenge. So one day the captain appeared at Dr. Herrera's clinic with a surplus X-ray machine, supervised its unloading and installation under the Marxist banners and then left without a word.

That night Jorge marched into the captain's compound with a bottle of rum that he slammed down on the table between them. "Let me tell you where you and all those like you are wrong," he said defiantly, pouring the first drink.

Into whatever mists of rebellion the chimera of Che faded, there emerged out the other side Dr. Jorge Herrera: psychiatrist.

Whose psychiatric studies at Provincetown had been paid for by the U.S. government, an arrangement facilitated by the captain and his contacts at the embassy. And now with a practice in the Hillcrest area of San Diego and a large home on the coast near La Jolla, he has become a man of parts. There is the Lincoln. Which replaced the Jaguar. And the conferences in New York and Madrid.

And the revolutionary past that bubbles silently beneath the floor of this new life.

"Arthur." Dr. Herrera is setting up some equipment on the table next to my bookcase. There are a vials of liquid and wrapped syringes. Only his pale green eyes move, flickering between us. "Please. Explain to her. As I asked you."

"No," I say.

"No?" His eyebrow arches, an expression all its own as he sees me staring at the syringes. The vials… *Chemicals, Mikey, they jam you full of chemicals and then—*

"Outside," I say, nodding toward the door.

On the porch Dr. Herrera is impatient, almost aggressive. "It's sodium amytal," he says. "Known in lay circles as truth serum. If she is indeed a mute it will do nothing to her. But if she cannot talk because of a conversion reaction—where trauma renders them unable to speak—the sodium amytal will lessen whatever unconscious factors are preventing her from speaking."

"And that's all that's in the syringe?"

"You don't trust me, do you?" he says with a contained exasperation that I have never seen in him before.

—no no no no—

Inside, the woman stands utterly still, backed up against the far wall of the cabin, her eyes not blinking.

"Dr. Herrera's treating me in San Diego," Charger is telling her. He's winding up for something, I can see the inner gears slipping. "See, I got this problem, I got to have an operation on my knee for a torn ACL. From football and all. And what they do is replace your tendon from a dead guy, you understand? The doctors put a dead guy's tendon in your knee for godsakes and—"

"Arthur, maybe we can explain to her in a different way?" says Dr. Herrera.

Charger's unruly thatch of vaguely blond hair jerks forward, the way it does when he furrows his brow. Instead of talking to the woman, he suddenly turns to me, as if I'd be an easier audience. "I'm trying to tell her that Jorge—Dr. Herrera has been helping me to get over having part of a dead guy in my body."

"Maybe just try a different approach?" says Dr. Herrera.

"Yeah," says Charger. "Yeah." He turns to face her. "Not any shrink could get your mind into a place where you can handle having part of a dead guy being inside you, you know. Jorge's good."

She's looking from me to Charger and back again. Confusion flickers in her eyes. I'm looking for a verbal exit when Dr. Herrera says, "Perhaps I can help you." Nothing. And then: "*A lo mejor le puedo ayudar.*"

At the sound of Spanish something within her cinches.

"*Solamente quiero hablarle.*" Nothing. "*Soy psiquiatra*... psychiatrist... You understand? *He visto casos donde de repente alguien no puede hablar.*"

She nods slowly but yields nothing more.

"*Me quedaré aqui. No me acerco al menos que usted me de permiso.*"

She nods again.

They sit. Dr. Herrera talks slowly, gently. It is a flow of soft Spanish that eventually elicits another nod. "*Digame algo loque, sea,*" he says.

"I've asked her to talk to us," he translates.

Her mouth moves. But no sound comes out. She stops as if gulping for air and then tries again, with fragility engulfing the clenched protectiveness. Only a jagged rush of breath.

And then: shaking her head slowly back and forth, slumping into the wall, she pounds her fists into her legs. Her hand flashes past her face as if angrily trying to hide the need to wipe away tears.

"Do you have a pad of paper?" Dr. Herrera asks me. When he passes it to her he asks, "*Que le pasó a usted?* What happened? *Por favor. Escríbalo.*"

At first it's as if she did not hear him. She is sitting on the floor, the light catching the curvature of her face, beautiful in its unadorned state emerging in and out of the curtain of luminescent dark hair that falls around her face. She is looking somewhere into what already has passed, into some place that none of us can see. Then she takes the paper and writes quickly.

In perfect English are two words:

Plastic surgery.

I sometimes wonder about infinity. Because if it is true that all mathematics, all physics, break down at infinity, that not one single equation or theorem survives when the concept of infinity is introduced into their mix, what does that tell us?

That there is no infinity?

Philosophy, religion, science—all need infinity, the infinite, in one way or another.

Where are we then?

Twilight comes quickly.

I have to leave Dr. Herrera and Charger with her.

And three hours later I am in the dome overwhelmed by a death.

A cosmic death so colossal that even among the High Priests there is a general worldwide groping through a confused fog of equations none of which can grasp the immensity, the terrifying violence of a blast that, were it near our part of the Milky Way, would make us and our sun look like billiard balls in play. Our puny planet would be flung into eternal blackness, a carom shot into some side pocket of the universe.

This night begins as most nights in the data room begin, with the routines of opening the dome and setting up for whatever kind of observing is to be done. In this case it's Yannic chasing brown dwarfs, which are sort of wannabe stars, objects hanging out there in space without enough mass to achieve nuclear fusion at their core.

So they end up being a hundred thousand times dimmer than the sun, which until the last few years made them invisible to the equipment we were using on the telescope.

We're working in the constellation Lepus again, which is a favorite celestial fishing hole for Yannic and Carl. They like to troll somewhere around 8 parsecs, which for the rest of us is still trillions and trillions of miles away but for astronomers is the shallow part.

While I'm checking dewpoint depression and weather forecasts on the Internet, Carl's looking at the infrared spectrograph on an object that showed a high methane reading, usually the signature of a brown dwarf.

"Do you know that Charles Babbage, the guy who invented the first primitive computer in the nineteenth century, calculated that the chances of a man rising from the dead were one in 10^{12}?" he says.

"Hey, do we have to listen to Bach again?" asks Yannic. No answer from Carl. "I might need you to do an R.E.T."

"But why 10^{12}?" asks Carl. "I mean, Christ rising from the dead was probably no more than 10^4 odds when you look back on it."

Yannic thinks about this for a moment. "I'm going to want to go to Gliese 566B," he says more to himself than to me, but I put it up on the stack anyway. "If you're an atheist it would definitely be 10^{12}," Yannic says. "Religious belief decreases the order of magnitude."

"Get real," says Carl with that permanent grin taking on a more quizzical quality. "Atheists deal in infinity."

"Infinity is where all equations fail," says Yannic.

"Precisely," says Carl, still fine-tuning.

I turn the Intercom Selector dial, which activates microphones all over the dome. Through the little speaker comes the creaking, rumbling and groaning noises of a hundred tons of moving glass and steel. I listen like a doctor through a stethoscope and then go out through the doors into the eerie silence of the dome. Brief moments like these are when it's so easy to find religion with the telescope, barely visible in the pitch blackness, a massive scientific fuselage aimed through the slit into the heavens far above.

I'm flicking the toggle switches that control the oil pumps when the dome echoes. "Michael! Get in here!" It's Yannic, almost leaving the floor with excitement.

We have a gamma ray burst.

Nothing matches this. It is the holy grail of astronomy.

Of course there's a different holy grail every other year. But this one hurls us into observational waters for which we have no charts. Gamma ray bursts are one of the few pre-emptive clear-the-runway events that instantly wipe out any long-nourished plans the astronomers working that night may have had. Forget about brown dwarfs. Or anything else.

When I get back into the data room Carl is pacing and yelling into the phone to some guy in Italy who's talking about what their X-ray satellite just picked up and Yannic has got the Caltech guys up in Pasadena on the other line. He's also pacing at the end of another long phone cord like a dog on a leash. "I'm getting the coordinates. We're gonna be about five and a half hours over," he yells.

"Impossible. The telescope'll be lying on its side," I yell back, pounding away at the console, shutting the dome and putting the telescope into temporary hibernation while we change the instrumentation. Everything's done at panic speed because the gamma ray burst itself lasts only for a few seconds or sometimes minutes. What we're going to try to get is the optical aftermath, which can last hours or days if we're lucky. I sprint into the dome and start lowering the new CCD camera into the tertiary focus.

Why all the panic? We're delving into cosmic death on a scale that cannot really be understood. A kind of death that could affect us, whoever the *us* happens to be at some terrifying moment in the next thousand or maybe million or maybe billion years.

Before I came to Palomar, astronomers working here on the 200-inch found a faint star called Geminga, the remnants of something that exploded a few hundred thousand years ago and basically blew a hole in space. For one cosmic moment it would have been a searchlight in our night sky, maybe twenty times brighter than the full moon. And then the million-degree battering ram of interstellar gas and gamma rays started racing through the cosmos at 60,000 kilometers a second. Earth was spared. But the thinking is that the outer planets, Uranus, Neptune and Pluto, got hammered.

And that's the good news. The bad news is that Geminga may not have even been a real gamma ray burst like the one we're chasing after tonight.

It was probably too small.

Right now the High Priests are thinking that maybe gamma ray bursts are caused when the most massive stars in the universe explode—hypernovas as opposed to mere unimaginably enormous supernovas. Or maybe it's the moment of a black hole's birth, also a contender for causing a gamma ray burst. Who knows? They're churning through theories on this one—like black holes colliding. Or neutron stars colliding. Or a neutron star getting sucked into a black hole—neutron stars are the dinky remnants of huge stars that blew up. They're only about the size of a mountain but these things are so dense that one teaspoonful of neutron star material would weigh billions of tons.

But whatever these things are, you just have to throw off the fetters of rational thought in order even to remotely grasp a gamma ray burst. For that one cataclysmic moment when it explodes it is simply the most powerful force in the entire universe, pumping out more energy in those few seconds than all the billion billion billion galaxies—each with its billion billion blazing stars—combined.

Take all the nuclear weapons ever made and explode them all at once—in other words, incinerate the planet. The entire amount of energy released by all those nukes would only equal the sun's energy output for 1/100,000th of one second. Now take all the energy ever produced by the sun in its entire ten-billion-year shelf life.

And?

And all that ten billion years' worth of energy from the sun would only amount to one—*one!*—puny percent of the energy released in those few seconds by a gamma ray burst.

Which is why I'm scrambling and sweating to lower the CCD onto the tertiary and finish the coupling as Yannic is yelling from the data room.

I race back in there, phone lines and Internet crackling with coordinates, and begin hunting for the optical transients, the residue of that gamma ray burst as it fades into celestial embers. The Druids must be shrieking from their tombs as I start typing in the Dec and the RA and then start working the black buttons on the aluminum pad that send the huge telescope groaning into action. It's the RA—the right ascension—that is shorting all my personal circuits. At an RA of 5 hours and 30 minutes I can almost feel the shrieking as the telescope turns over, way over.

Which is another way of saying that the telescope, all hundred tons of it, is practically lying on its side. Pointing west almost into the treetops. But there's nothing I can do about it. That's where the gamma ray burst is coming from.

Carl is on another phone to the Keck telescope in Hawaii, talking to them about the spectroscopics they're doing on the same gamma ray burst.

But right now all I care about is capturing that optical transient on our cameras without pushing the telescope so far over that it hits the limit and just shuts down. I'm afraid to look outside into the dome and see that huge steel yoke lying on its side. I'm grabbing exposures but Yannic is yelling at me to move another hundred arc seconds.

Yannic's got the munchies, the way he always does when he gets nervous. He's delving into the brown paper bag with his midnight lunch, the one prepared by the ladies at the monastery. Every astronomer shows up with a little paper lunch bag with his name written on it. It's kind of like having a stand-in mom up on the mountain. "Man, we're dealing with 10^{54} ergs."

"More," says Carl

"Hey!" Yannic says, looking into the bag. "I asked for tuna salad."

"Are we still at plus 73?" Carl asks.

"On whole wheat," says Yannic. "I wanted rye."

We follow the burst, tracking it with exposure after exposure. And what we end up with are images on a screen—basically smudges and dots—and one of them, the gamma ray burst, having blown everything to bits, will be fainter by at least one magnitude when we do the same thing tomorrow night.

Smudges and dots are what pass for high drama in my profession. The apocalypse as seen by pointillists.

Carl is busy contemplating God's little joke in all this. "Do you know that we're all going to die laughing?" he says. "If a gamma ray burst happens within a few thousand light-years of us, it will cause a reaction between nitrogen and oxygen, which don't normally react. So the whole planet will be smothering in nitrous oxide—laughing gas."

"Mayonnaise," says Yannic, examining his sandwich again.

The phone rings on the private data room line. It's Charger. "You should see this," he whispers. "Some pretty weird stuff has been coming out of her."

He's whispering.

4 a.m.

We have wrapped it up for the night. The earth, on its axis, has tilted our latitude away from the gamma ray burst, leaving only the exhausted mechanics of a telescope never intended for such celestial gymnastics.

Tomorrow at twilight, and for several nights after that, we'll be chasing the fading traces of the gamma ray burst until there is nothing left. It is watching a form of history unfold—the only kind of history that will eventually matter. None of us talk about it but we're all pretty much awed by this moment we have been entrusted with. Entire careers, lives even, flash past without witnessing such an event.

Carl and Yannic depart for the monastery an hour before I step into the pre-dawn blackness of the parking lot beside the dome. If bodies have memories then mine knows every one of the eighteen steps it takes me to walk from the heavy door of the dome to the place where I always park.

On step fourteen I am blinded by headlights that snap on, scales falling from the night in an instant.

"You didn't phone," says the voice from behind the piercing beams.

The Colonel's white Jeep pushes through the glare of its own headlights, sifting through the darkness toward me. "That helicopter last night? The one that people say was somewhere on the mountain? You saw it, right?"

Before I can even finish nodding his reply comes. "Get in," he says. Half request, half order. "Show me where it was."

There's a kind of large spigot sunk into the side of the mountain on the Colonel's property over near the South Road. It is where the mountain bleeds its water. The Colonel's shiny tanker trucks hook up hoses at the spigot and pull water from artesian depths, destined for the plastic bottles in the supermarkets and convenience stores of America. Fueling the joggers, the homes, the offices with what had coursed ceaselessly for millennia through the undisturbed darkness. His tankers labor up and down the mountain's roads, shined to mirrored perfection, reflecting all they pass in images that never stay the same from one instant to the next.

Day and night the mountain yields its water. It is the source of the Colonel's fortune. His authority.

Water is power on the mountain.

I've never spent more than a few minutes in the presence of the Colonel. But even before his Jeep turns off the paved road onto the dirt tracks I know I have this fear of telling him—or anyone else on the mountain—about the woman. Like Charger, there's some protective instinct at work.

"It always starts with one immutable truth," the Colonel is saying. "Most of these people coming here don't belong on the mountain." Then he turns for a moment in a way that engulfs me in thoughts of ulterior motive. "You seen anything strange up here lately? Apart from the helicopter?"

"No." Then again, redundant and involuntary: "No."

Then there's a silence and I'm waiting for the next declaration, some explanation of who these people are. But it never comes. Some people can exist easily in silence. Others live to fill it. With talk. I am one of the latter. Silence is a weapon in the hands of others.

The silence settles around us like something I'm desperate to swat. Say something. Anything. *A guy was crucified and*—Except for the sizzle of the tires, silence—*had his face sheared off before they burned up every trace of him.* The road vanishes evenly beneath the Jeep as it turns east and then south. *And there's a woman*—The image of her eyes hangs in front of me in the darkness and I forget the silence.

We round a curve and the night is peeled away by a whipping motion of red and blue lights that flick out from where a sheriff's cruiser is one of two vehicles idling on the side of the road.

A deputy sheriff and the local California forest ranger stand around what looks like a huge dark smear on the side of the road. They're wearing their official looks but you pretty much know they're talking about sports or women, the way they always do when they're having coffee at Mother's Kitchen. When they realize the vehicle pulling over is the Colonel's Jeep they start doing the poker-faced investigator number.

The Colonel looks out at them through the windshield. "Damn fool Lone Ranger without the mask," he mutters, staring at the forest ranger, who recently started wearing a gun to make himself look more cop-like. "Probably shot himself a tree. And is trying to figure out how to arrest it."

As we approach, the ranger points to a trail of blood that comes from the bushes and ends on the side of the road. "Had a report some guy was dead or dying," he says in a voice that sounds like a tenor trying to be a baritone. You get the impression the ranger's one of those guys who'd be lost without starch, the kind that's laid on so thick his shirt looks like a slab.

"Don't see anyone dead or dying," says the Colonel, ignoring him and looking around.

"Neither do we."

"Appears someone stole the body," says the deputy.

"Why the hell does someone steal a body?" says the ranger.

"It's tied in to all the other foolishness going on around here," the Colonel says.

"We had a report that some guy had crawled out of the brush here," says the deputy, ignoring him. "Dead or dying by the time he reached the road. Wasn't clear which. A couple of ladies from Valley Center were up here visiting. Came across him. A big ragged hole in his belly, real mess. Went to make a phone call and when they came back there were some Latinos loading the body into a Porsche. And this is all that's left," he says, shining the flashlight down toward a smeared white tube-like object on the ground. "Condom. They must have wanted what was inside him. Guy must have been crammed full of dope."

"Said they were real scary-looking," says the ranger. "Shaved heads an' all. Tattoos. Woman remembered one of 'em having a big number 30 tattooed on his fist."

"Thirtieth Street. *Calle Treinta*," says the deputy. "Mexicans from San Diego. Logan Heights area." He's talking about the area from where the Tijuana gangs weave their power into Southern California, recruiting kids born in America but still Mexican inside their heads. "Never seen those guys up here."

"A Porsche? Damn," says the Ranger. "All that blood? You'd mess up the leather seats big time."

Six miles later the Jeep is relentless in its 4-wheel assault on the dirt road that is vanishing beneath us. I'm only hearing part of what the Colonel is saying. "Never seen Logan Heights types up here. Smooth-looking thugs. Not like the damn cholos, the peasants who cross over from Mexicali. Ever seen 'em? Dressed all in black because their coyotes told them they won't stand out at night. The ones who mostly end up as a pile of bones in the desert. Poor dumb sonsofbitches practically boil in their own clothes when the sun's straight overhead."

And the woman back at my place? In that flimsy dress with sequins? And shoes meant more for a cocktail party?

"Are you okay, boy?" asks the Colonel, prying open what must have been my blank stare.

"Fine," I say, which holds the silence intact for several hundred yards of rutted tracks before we plunge through onrushing tree branches that flash past and close in on the Jeep, lashing at its sides.

"Nothing changes," he says. "Just business as usual."

"This is usual?" I say. "I've never seen nights like this before."

"In the grand scheme of things this is just nuisance stuff. Keeps the locals up late and gets the dogs worked up. I'm talking about Zeno. Seneca. Marcus Aurelius. The Stoics knew what it was all about, son."

On the mountain people figure that the highest compliment the Colonel could pay was to talk about something other than his water business. It meant he thought you were worth it. And if you didn't live up to his assessment, you were instantly enveloped in an impatient silence before a sudden departure.

"The Stoics knew there ain't no such thing as progress," he says. "Not really. Maybe indoor toilets, central heating and anesthetics. All the frills. But when you get down to the basics—good, evil with maybe misery and joy thrown in on a grand scale—the Stoics got it right. It's all a constant. In any given era some categories are up. Others down. It's a zero-sum game. Up till some charismatic psychopath like Hitler comes along and throws a match into a pool of genetic gasoline. And then the slaughters start. You want to be born way before or way after all that crap starts."

In the headlights the path in front of us widens into a dirt road, maybe a dried-out riverbed. "'Cause if you're not, you gotta wait out a hell of a lot of killing till the next era starts."

He stops the Jeep and quickly turns off the engine and the lights. We sit in fragments of moonlight. I am about to fill the silence when he whispers, "Tell me about the helicopter you saw."

I tell him what I saw. Or didn't see. The darkness. The Grimes light. Hoisting men up. Gunfire.

"Well now, this is where we get a choice. We can either get scared of the night or we can light a damn candle. So let's just go find out what we're up against," he says quietly.

Then the door handle clicks and an interior light goes on in the Jeep for an instant. His hand passes through the darkness in a beckoning motion.

Outside in the forest I can hear my heart beating a hole in my chest. The Colonel is crouched not far away holding on to something that I can't make out in the darkness. But my mind tells me it's a pistol. Something on the dirt path ahead makes a crunching sound. And again. The Colonel holds his hand out a little farther in front of him.

There is someone approaching. Again my mind tries to fill it all in.

In an instant the night lights up. The headlights on the Jeep.

Blinking and blinded, two young marines in full camouflage wave their rifles into the headlights and yell things I can't understand.

"Stand down, soldier!" snaps the Colonel. You can tell he's said this kind of thing before.

There is a confused pause and then one of the marines barks, "Sir! Request permission to approach! Sir!" Every word is spit out.

"Permission granted," says the Colonel quietly, edging into the light. I see that what he has in his hand is not a pistol but the remote control for the Jeep. It was what lit up the night.

"Sir! Request permission to speak!"

"Lighten up, boys. You're with your own. What's going on?"

"Not at liberty to say. Sir!"

"Are you lost?"

It is obvious they're lost but don't want to admit it to mere civilians. They look at each other, trying to figure out how to answer. One of them is taller and looks young enough to be denied entry into any bar. He's skinny, with the residue of pimples and an Adam's apple that bobs up and down.

"Could be. Sir!"

"C'mon. I'll drive you to wherever you gotta be," says the Colonel. "Get in."

"Sir! We cannot! Sir!"

"Why not?"

"Sir! We are not clean. We are dirty."

The Colonel comes as close to a chuckle as I've ever heard. "I'm giving you an order. Get in." This seems to confuse them for a moment. Then the shorter marine mutters something and walks over to the Jeep. As he's about to get in he turns and says in a hill-country twang, "You wouldn't happen to have a beer, would you, sir?"

Inside the Jeep they sit silently in the back seat, their rifles occasionally clicking against one another as we jostle across the rutted trail.

"You've been up here for four days," says the Colonel into the rearview mirror.

"Not allowed to talk about it, sir," says the taller one softly.

"You guys been all over the valley here, knee deep in camouflage telling yourselves no one can see you. Some kind of behind-the-lines war game."

"Maybe, sir. Then again, maybe not."

The Colonel checks the rearview. "I started out in recon, son."

"Copy that, sir."

"Been watching you guys. Obviously an expeditionary unit. Like we sent into Afghanistan or Iraq or whatever hellhole we decide to save for a while."

Silence from the two marines.

"If I had to guess I'd bet you're stationed out of Twenty-Nine Palms—probably originally from Camp Lejeune in North Carolina. Not from Pendleton or these parts. But something went drastically wrong."

"Could be, sir." And then the Jeep fills up with a tense silence as it jolts along the path. The Colonel's eyes keep flickering to the rearview mirror.

"And you," he says to the shorter marine, "where are you from?"

"Not at liberty to say, sir," says the marine softly and with the hint of a Hispanic accent.

"I don't mean stationed, son. I'm talking hometown. Sounds like you're from somewhere."

"I am from somewhere, sir. Born near Acapulco. But raised in America. Outside of Dallas. Sir."

"You know that by the second century, Rome didn't have any of its own citizens in the military?" says the Colonel.

"No, sir. Didn't know that, sir."

"Anyone they got to join the military automatically became a citizen."

"Worked for both sides, I guess, huh? Sir."

"They're still debating that, son."

"Yes sir."

We keep bouncing through the darkness for a while and then the Colonel says, “Appreciate what you’re doing. Both of you.”

“Yes sir,” says the shorter marine.

The Colonel’s eyes keep shooting to the rearview mirror and a tiny grin flickers. “You boys like cartoons?” he says. In the moment of silence you can feel their confusion radiate from the back seat.

“You mean like Dragon Quest?” says the taller marine.

“Cartoons,” says the Colonel as if he enjoys catching them off guard.

A pause, muttering and then: “Like Grand Theft Auto?”

“Uh-uh. Cartoons. The old Warner Brothers stuff.”

“Is that like Bugs and Daffy?” says the taller one, his voice instantly shedding its protective wariness.

“Exactly!” beams the Colonel.

“Oh man, check out ‘The Rabbit of Seville.’ It is so cool!” says the taller one. “The one where Bugs is a barber.”

“Work of art!” says the Colonel. “But you gotta see ‘Long-Haired Hare.’ Really underrated. Hilarious. A comment on our society.”

“Sir! Sir!” the shorter marine is yelling, trying to get into the conversation. “Sylvester and Tweety.”

“‘Bad ole puddy tat!’” yells the taller marine.

“‘I’ll raith thuch a thtorm over ththat dog’s houseth,’” the Colonel sputters like Sylvester the cat to the shouts of laughter from the back seat. And suddenly I understand that control is an instrument the Colonel plays with perfect pitch and in whatever key he deems necessary.

Imitations of Wile E. Coyote, Yosemite Sam and Daffy Duck fly around the Jeep and the two marines are shouting over each other in gales of laughter as they tweet and sputter and beep-beep with the Colonel.

And then in an instant it changes.

In the depths of Barker Valley an officer and several marines step out of the void, standing in front of the Jeep as it shudders to a halt.

It’s like some deluge has opened up above us. We are blasted and jolted into a roar that buffets our yells.

It is a helicopter. It descends above us, hovering like some vast bird of prey. Orders are yelled into the rotor-whipped vortex that feels as if it sucks the two marines out of the Jeep. In a moment they are gone. As if they'd never existed. The slapping of the rotors echoes briefly and then is swallowed by the night.

Utter silence. Complete blackness.

And then a tiny clinking sound from out there in the darkness. The Colonel hits the remote and the headlights flash on again. "Shell casings," he says from the blackness. "Something went way wrong. They never do live-fire operations around here."

Something on the ground near the edge of the light draws me over. It's as if a small fire had been started and then covered over. A few sticks, carved to a sharpened point, are lying around. One of them skewers some kind of processed meat that looks like it came out of a can.

"That's what happened," says the Colonel, picking up the sticks. He looks around, searching for something. Behind us are the smooth-barked manzanilla, their branches shiny and scarlet even in the darkness. The Colonel walks farther, past cactus, stunted bougainvillea and then to taller flowering plants, blooming in organized riots of red flowers. Several of them have been hacked off about waist high, their flowers stripped off and lying on the ground.

"Oleander poisoning," says the Colonel. "Damn fools cut down oleanders and used the stalks to roast something. Sap from these bushes is worse 'n snake venom. Whatever else happened, they had a bunch of poisoned marines on their hands. That explains the helicopters you saw. Medevac."

"And the rest of it? The shooting?"

"Or that guy who got his innards chewed on by the mountain lion?" he says. "God knows."

"Are you really a fan of cartoons?" I say. We're driving back toward the dome, the first faint wedge of dawn prying at the eastern night behind us. "Or was that just some kind of show?"

"Both," he says. "Those boys were a touch on the tense side, don't you think? Had to do something. Matter of personal principle. Three elements you never mix in your own vehicle: tension, strangers and loaded weapons."

As we cruise toward the intersection near Mother's Kitchen, other lights appear from the side and grow stronger, flooding the wall of trees beside the road. They are headlights, coming from the road leading to Bailey Meadow. A big black Lincoln slows to a half stop and then rolls through the intersection and speeds away on the road toward San Diego.

"Psychiatrist," says the Colonel.

"How do you know that?"

"He's on the mountain, isn't he?" says the Colonel as if there was really no reason for me to ask. "Coming from the direction of your place," he says almost as a challenge.

"Yeah?"

"Yeah." Then after a while: "You ever see a psychiatrist?"

"No. Never."

Penetang

Tommy was born during what should have been Mother's second year at the University of Toronto. Her exams the Christmas before were the last she ever wrote, and on the second weekend in February when she was cleaning out her room in the women's residence, her biology professor, an old Irishman from Donegal, came by to inquire if perhaps there was some way she could return the following year. When the baby was born, of course. Perhaps when things were more settled.

If she really did want to be a doctor it would be a shame for someone with her obvious abilities to…

In his confusion the old Irish professor directed his encouragement to Steven Atwater as well as Mother, thinking that he was the husband-to-be. Instead of just someone who had offered to help pack her books.

The real husband-to-be was playing his final year with the Kitchener Rangers. And that weekend in the game against Belleville he would be scouted by two National Hockey League teams, the Philadelphia Flyers and the Montreal Canadiens.

The next season when Lightning played for the Hershey hockey team, Tommy was born in a rented farmhouse in Pennsylvania. When he was old enough to talk, the facts of his birthplace endlessly fascinated him.

"'Melica," he would say again and again when asked where he was born.

At first Mother corrected him, "A*mer*ica, Tommy. You were born in A*mer*ica."

"'Melica," Tommy would reply, grinning through his baby teeth "'Melica, 'Melica, 'Melica," and then running all over the house yelling,"I'm 'Melican but you aren't."

For the first three years of his life Tommy was shuttled, chortling, between Penetang in the summers and Pennsylvania in the winters, where Lighting played for Hershey until he was cut from the team when three Swedes headed for the National Hockey League were brought in. But even after he and Mother returned to Penetang, the reality of their lives had not yet set, as if the perception of what was still possible had only just been poured and was waiting to harden.

Although neither of them would have thought this way, there was still the legal tender of their unacknowledged contract: there was a future. A glorious, success-filled wonderful future. It was this way with most of the women of Mother's age who remained in Penetang or the other towns in the area. In an era when they endured moments of confusion about their roles, and then surrendered their own future in exchange for their husbands providing one that was better. Or at very worst, equal.

That was the unspoken deal, made a thousand times over by most of those women who had been girls together.

This unspoken deal seldom bubbled up into conscious thought until the Reckoning drew closer. It had all started as hope and joy and then as the years passed and the rowing grew faster, more panicked, illusions were heaved overboard to lighten the payload. It became a terrified, tearful, sometimes sulfurous confusion as the finish lines first appeared over some inner horizon.

As the couples headed into their thirties, there were all around them the scoreboards of these unspoken contractual obligations blinking with triumph or bitterness, both of which were unsuccessfully hidden by the women forced to wear the results like either a tiara or a secondhand dress. Susan Vivash with the awkward walk and bad pageboy hairstyle, who nobody even looked at in school, proved a far better dealmaker than Alice Sanders, who was easily the most popular girl in Tay Township but married the charismatic fool Calvin Barker, whose bulldozer business had dwindled to a junkpile out past the cases of empty beer bottles behind their unfinished house on the sixth concession road.

And where Alice now foraged through the Goodwill store in Barrie—it was far enough away that no one she knew would see her trying on secondhand clothes—Susan Alter *née* Vivash and her husband, who owned the Toyota franchise now, regularly shopped at Holt Renfrew in Toronto.

Somewhere around the age of forty was always the Reckoning. The age when the finish line was still off on the horizon but now—barring a lottery win—the positioning of the rowers was becoming locked in. With all its desperation and fury pounding at the sides of such delicate crafts, the re-examining of the contracts was everywhere.

Acid silently ate holes in the vessels themselves, or they were capsized in the rapids of envy, betrayal or depression that now surrounded the women of our town as they looked at one another.

And judged themselves. And their choices.

And then the rumors about Steven Atwater began.

It was said that he wanted to return to Penetang. Not permanently. Maybe just for the summers. And in the style to which he was now accustomed, a criterion that sent local real estate agents into muted frenzies of hope. As the water rises all boats go up, they told themselves and each other for months.

A legend would be returning, the man who had enraptured Bay Street from the highest suite in the burnished gold tower of the Royal Trust building in Toronto. The Venezuelan oil penny stock was the most prescient of his moves, but the Bay Street analysts all had their own favorites. They often embellished the Atwater legend on the CBC or CTV. The regulars at the corner table closest to the wall-mounted television could hear them over the din in the tavern at the Brûle Hotel.

Lightning had become one of those regulars.

When Lightning returned home from the Brûle he would usually want to talk in that way that drunks flood you with sozzled wisdom once the valves of reticence and coherence have seized open. Most times it was me he'd want to talk to, I think because Tommy scared him a little. It was as if he couldn't stand the reflections of his own image. For a long time he'd seen that reflection in Mother's eyes. And now it was showing in Tommy's eyes, framed by the roiling frustration and fury that got boiled away into a residue of fear for himself. As if this bleary vestige of former greatness swaying sadly before Tommy was somehow his own future arriving early.

On the nights when Lightning didn't make it home for dinner I knew that long after dark I'd be hearing his faltering steps on the stairs leading to the basement where I did my homework. He'd usually show up acting like he was looking for something.

"Oh, are you still here?" he would say.

"I'm always here, Dad."

"Oh. Yeah? Huh." Then he'd lumber through some transition until he came to: "You know, I been thinking…"

It's strange how I now sometimes miss what I used to dread, all the rambling introspection that followed. And grew more intense with the news that Steven Atwater was returning. The name was never mentioned but it hung like a mirror in front of Lightning, who took to looking at photographs of himself from when he first met Mother.

"You know, some guys stop playing to win," he said. It was always *some guys*. "They never know it but one day they silently slip over the line and start playing not to lose. It's always the end."

So I'd promise him I'd never just play not to lose. And then he'd smile that beery smile, feeling that he'd done his paternal duty in inoculating his son against his own disease. And then begin the cycle all over again a few nights later when *some guys* were back at the Brûle.

It went on like this until that night, the one when Tommy barged into the Brûle and dragged him out of the place.

I never knew the whole story but the local legend is that Tommy punched Lightning, sending him sprawling over the hood of his own car in a volcano of vomit and fury. Lightning stood up swinging at phantoms and crying until he sunk to his knees surrounded by the darkness of a town that had forgotten and a son who was sobbing more than he was.

It was the last time Lightning ever touched alcohol.

Steven Atwater returned that summer when Lightning was into his third year at Grew Boats, having worked his way up to foreman. Part of his duties were to send the sleek fiberglass cruisers down the ramps and into the waters of discontented prosperity that rose around us all. The first time I even heard Steven Atwater's name was when I came home from school to find Mother sitting in front of the television staring into a CKVR newscast about the Liberal candidate in the Simcoe riding for the next federal election: Steven Atwater.

Not just a candidate—a resident!

Or at least in the sense that he and his second wife were also residents of New York, Frankfurt and Toronto. The legend of Bay Street was building a mansion overlooking the eastern part of Penetang harbor, a vast faux Lloyd Wright edifice, officially announced as blending in with nature but in reality subjugating it with blasted, sculpted and manicured hillsides contoured to conform to the design of the house and the will of its owner.

You could see it through our front window rising out of the distant hills.

But not only from our little home. Even from where Tommy and I rode the old horses we rented by the hour, galloping across the fields, pretending to be Lash LaRue, Jr., the iron girders began looming like a skeleton awaiting its skin of stone and wood. One afternoon I reined in my horse and yelled for Tommy.

Silently we watched the silhouette of a distant crane lowering another girder into place.

"I don't think I like horseback riding any more," Tommy said.

It was the last time he and I went riding.

But the most overpowering view of the mansion was from the

water, where we still paddled our old canoe. Which was also where Lightning took the fiberglass cruisers out for test drives before Grew Boats turned them over to its customers.

There was no way he could miss that mansion as it grew into the statement it was always meant to be. Steven Atwater had bought the one piece of property that could be seen from anywhere on the whole bay.

Mother never used to watch television in the early evening. But soon we noticed that the CKVR news was on every night before Lightning came home. We didn't know about the phone call she had received. It had been made not by the candidate but by his staff. A Liberal Party election office for the riding of Simcoe was being opened next month in Midland. Her name had been suggested. And would she be interested in ...?

Mother's announcement that she was going to join the campaign staff of *Steven Atwater—A Candidate for Our Times* was buried in an argument about Tommy. "Tommy's becoming unmanageable now" was always the code for letting Lightning know she was the only one holding the household together. Which in the complicated semantics of our family meant that she was fed up, something had to change, so she had the *right* to do whatever it was she'd spent days trying to figure out how to tell him she wanted to do. And the best way to do that was bury it in a fight over Tommy.

Unmanageable had become whatever Tommy was doing in school that made him reckless, outrageous, irreverent or otherwise exactly like Lightning had been when she met him.

"Father Nunzio can only put up with so much, you know."

"Father Nunzio's never put up with anything in his life. The man's a bad-tempered tyrant."

"You better cross yourself for what you said."

Then a silence. Until: "He stole the clicker."

"What are you talking about?"

"Tommy stole Father Nunzio's clicker. The TV remote control.

He didn't steal it exactly. He just hid it. But the poor man had to get up out of his Barcalounger chair and change the channel by hand for three nights in a row."

Lightning thought about it for a moment and then grinned as if she wasn't watching. Lately it was one of the things he did that really bugged her.

"You think this is funny. It's not. Tommy's always in trouble now."

"Aw c'mon, it's not trouble."

"Father Nunzio has hemorrhoids. He doesn't want it known, but he does. And getting up out of his Barcalounger—"

"So light a candle and say three Hail Marys for Father Nunzio's ass."

"That's not funny."

"You're right. Anyone who lit a candle around Father Nunzio would risk dying in a gas explosion." Father Nunzio was well known for what was called in polite company "his emissions." Which to us kids were just rotten, sneaky, silent farts that could practically level a mule.

"You don't show disrespect to a man like Father Nunzio. That's exactly what Tommy does. And I bet you're both going to pay for it in the afterlife."

"Forget the afterlife. I'm already paying for it."

"That psychology class thing alone was the limit." Mother always said this knowing the response she'd get. Just say *psychology class thing* and Lightning would start to chuckle. Which would make her predictably indignant—exactly the state she wanted to be in. *It's not funny!*

And of course just as predictably Lightning would laugh. This always provided Mother with the added benefit of feeling that no guilt could be attached to her indignation

Like most families we knew, guilt was the one indispensable ingredient in the daily stew of domestic jostling. Without it the routine of everyday life would soon settle into the tranquility that was so publicly longed for and so fervently undermined. It was pretty much understood that nothing worked as marvelously as guilt as a means of seizing the real prize: The Moral High Ground.

And I'm the one who has to live with the consequences!

With most of the other families we knew, once the Moral High Ground had been seized, the real fighting began.

It was a battle Lightning learned how to fight. Like some guerrilla group who never held territory when their opponents opened up with the big guns, but instead just retreated into the foliage.

Especially when she talked about *the psychology class thing* he seldom gave her a good target to aim at from this Moral High Ground. "You know, you're probably right about all that," he'd say with a little laugh. Which drove Mother crazy. The fact that I laughed too didn't help, of course. But what else could you do?

The psychology class thing was probably the closest Tommy came to being a true genius.

He'd spent the first part of the previous school year being berated by Brother Eugene, his psychology teacher. Brother Eugene taught the course that had lab rats pushing levers to get fed. Conditioned response he called it. But Tommy's problem—if you can call it a problem—is that he started feeling sorry for the lab rats.

So around Christmas he decided to conduct his own experiment. Using Brother Eugene as the lab rat.

Brother Eugene was a pacer. Spewing nervous energy and darting stares he would stalk back and forth in front of the class, never able to sit behind the desk. His long legs would scissor back and forth in front of the rows of desks and his bony finger would skewer toward whichever poor unfortunate caught his wrath that day. Brother Eugene possessed the tyrant's genius for sensing terror in the hearts of the wretches he taught and using that terror like a whip.

In early January Tommy organized the thirty-four other kids in his class in the experiment. There were seven rows of desks. Tommy rigged it so that whenever Brother Eugene went past the sixth row they would all react more slowly to his questions. Their answers would be less precise. Some would act drowsy. Others would mumble or stammer out garbled answers. *Galvanic response? I…um…I…you mean like galvanic, right, sir?…Responses that are galvanic? It's um … Sir? Could you repeat the question?*

But when Brother Eugene was in front of rows one to five, the answers were instant, precise, *Sir, it's the electrical response of the skin, usually measured by a device that records changes in the resistance of the skin, to the passage of a weak current produced by the body of the subject,* the respondents alert and eager to ingest the knowledge that he so generously bestowed upon them.

For the first couple of weeks nothing happened. But then one Friday, they noticed that Brother Eugene never went past row five for the entire class. The following Tuesday he ventured into that forbidden territory only once and the dozy answers sent him scurrying back to the safety of the other rows, where he stayed for the rest of the class.

Brother Eugene was a definite lab rat.

After the breakthrough, Tommy laid out the lab rat experiment schedule: next week they'd expand Brother Eugene's no-go area to anything past row four.

Brother Eugene didn't have a clue what was happening to him. And a few weeks later, after he was reduced to an invisible cage in front of the first three rows of students, he chicken-walked around his tiny area, his long, thin face looking like someone was giving him electrical shocks. His voice had gotten screechier. Beads of sweat appeared soon after he entered the room, and that high-strung quality of his was soon exquisitely torqued into some low-grade hysteria that rendered almost comical his attempts to induce fear in his students.

I know for a fact that Tommy was seriously wondering about the possibilities of a Nobel Prize for science—shared with the rest of the class if necessary.

On the night before the end, I had my head under the pillow listening to the Leafs playing the Canadiens on the little plastic radio. Tommy was lying on his bed in the darkness asking me things like whether or not you had to go to Stockholm to get the Nobel Prize, and if I thought you'd get a parade down Main Street if you won. Or free tickets to the matinees at the Pen.

The only parade Tommy got was us watching him run for his life as the wrath of God as interpreted by Father Nunzio descended upon him. Father Nunzio chased Tommy all the way up to the seminary.

We should have known the experiment was doomed when we saw

Oinky Lalonde's mother in the office talking to Father Nunzio. Oinky was this poor fat kid who wet his pants if he got nervous. His mother was shaped like a barrel, scowled all the time and had two long hairs growing out of a mole on the side of her chin. We figured that if she'd been our mother, we'd wet our pants too. We called her the Pope's secret weapon because she was always in the Martyrs' Shrine fiercely praying for forgiveness along with the Ukranian, Polish and Filipino Catholics who came up from Toronto to be photographed at the exact place where the Indians massacred the Jesuits.

When we asked Oinky what his mother was doing in the office he wet his pants instantly. We should have figured out Oinky's mother wasn't visiting Father Nunzio just to get blessed.

But how were we to know that Oinky had ratted?

A few days later Tommy and the others discovered some new decor in Brother Eugene's classroom. There were big posters of the saints, Paul, Joseph, Mark and a couple of others no one recognized, hung at the front of the class. And unless you looked for it, you'd never see the little hole cut in the dark part of one of the saint's robes, about waist high.

It started off as Tommy's finest hour. The lab rat experiment was at its most Pavlovian, with Brother Eugene trapped in his corner and flinging tics in all directions.

It was only the loud fart from the other side of the chalkboard that ended this potential Nobel Prize–winning experiment.

It instantly puckered the minds of an entire class. Mental and observational powers were suddenly compressed as fear and revelation came down upon them like an avalanche. *Wednesday!?* Was it? Yes, it was Wednesday!—the day the cafeteria always served fried food. And no one ever went near Father Nunzio after he ate fried food, for gastrointestinal reasons that now ricocheted through panicked young brains. The janitor's closet? On the other side of the wall? Even Brother Eugene turned and scanned the front of the room, his pale, watery gaze finally fixing on the single spying eye reappearing in the hole cut in the middle of the saint's robe.

"Father?" he said.

"I'm the one who has to put up with it, not you." Mother's code was getting less encrypted now, heading toward the plain text handed down from her Moral High Ground like stone tablets. "I can't stand being the one who's trapped in here having to deal with him all the time."

Lightning squinted into some unseen light the way he did since he quit drinking. "So what do you want to do?"

"He's unmanageable."

"Tommy's a sixteen-year-old boy."

"Honestly. Sometimes I wish you could listen to the way you argue."

"I'm not arguing."

"I'm going into politics." There. It was out. All the trappings of guilt and indignation fell away like a chrysalis, once vital, now unneeded. Finally.

There was a silence, with Lightning not quite absorbing the heft of the instruction manual to their new life that he'd just been handed. "Excuse me?"

"Politics." She waited for a response from Lightning. None came. "Why are you looking at me like that?"

"I didn't know you were interested in politics."

"The Liberals called me." Nothing from Lightning. "They want me."

"The Liberals want *you?*" Lightning had just stepped on a marital land mine and he knew it. It was the surprise in his voice that was the detonator. Nothing else mattered—all the rational explanation about being surprised she even knew any Liberals. Or that she might just have been phoned at random. None of it could save him now.

"Perfect, just perfect! You act surprised that anyone would want me"—a coded message that it was all obviously just a declaration of survival, a lonely soul saving itself as the waters of an indifferent world rose all around.

"That's not what I meant and you know—"

"You never think I have any real worth."

"Aw come on, I do too and you know it."

"*They* think I'm worth something. *They* obviously know what I can do."

"Who's *they*?"

"The people over at the Simcoe riding office in Midland." It had all been leading to this, her wanting him to have to piece it all together, to have to say *his* name himself.

After a long time checking one of his fishing reels, Lightning said, "Isn't that Steven Atwater?"

In the end it was Lightning who made the decision for her, the way most decisions had been made because it was just the way things happened, the pattern they had fallen into.

Even the following day, when Mother was overcome by second thoughts, it was Lightning who simply said, "Do it. If you don't we'll both pay for it."

Who ever has a sense of your parents' age when you're a kid? We didn't. Tommy and I always thought of them as being like the rest of the parents in the area. *Older*. Which was some amorphous demographic. Mother was *Older*. And a mother besides. Ours. And mothers looked a certain way. Acted a certain way. Were that certain way.

Older. Mother was thirty-five years old. But suddenly she stopped being that certain way.

She came home with her hair done like the model on the front of *Vogue*, the magazine that suddenly replaced *Better Homes and Gardens* on the kitchen table. And her clothes were different than what she had ever worn, going from earth-tone sweaters and corduroys to dresses in cool white, grays and blacks. With maybe a red silk scarf or rhinestones thrown in just to accessorize—a word we heard a lot in the beginning when she was worrying about what to wear. But mostly we heard about the great Liberal Party battle for Simcoe against the dreaded Conservatives and the shifty New Democrats. Our kitchen started filling up with advertising flyers until *Steven Atwater—A Candidate for Our Times* overflowed into the dining room.

During the fifty-four days of the campaign, Mother was often gone before we left for school and sometimes she would not return until after dark. Most nights she'd phone from the Midland office and say that we should order in food because she'd be late. In Penetang "ordering in" really meant getting food from the Greeks or from the fish-and-chips place on Main Street. But Lightning usually cooked dinner for us and acted like everything was normal.

It wasn't. We were amazed at Mother and how she seemed so different. Everything about her was quicker. She talked faster, moved faster and paced back and forth while she was talking on the phone, her new high-heeled shoes tapping out a rhythm of impatience that we could hear from our bedroom even when we put pillows over our heads. Talk of polling stations, door-to-doors, canvassing and advance teams kept stitching its way into my hockey broadcasts from the little plastic radio. It really started to bug me. The Leafs would be on a power play and I'd all of a sudden start tuning in to Mother and some crisis in elections posters not being delivered.

It was in the playoff game against the Chicago Black Hawks that Tommy started pounding on my pillow when I wouldn't listen to him. When I pulled the pillow tighter around my head he sat on it until I almost suffocated and the radio got imprinted into my face and my nose pushed the dial around to some country-and-western station. "Listen!" he hissed at me as I was gasping for air.

"To what?"

"*That,*" he said, pointing through the walls toward the kitchen.

"What?" All I heard was Mother's heels clacking on the linoleum floor.

"Are you thick or what? *Listen!*" Even in the near darkness you could almost feel the sparks off him. I still didn't get it. "You can't hear her voice. She's *whispering!*"

"So?"

"So she does that every time when she's talking to that moron Atwater."

"Huh?"

"She doesn't want the old man to hear her talking to him. She's hiding stuff."

She *was* talking differently, in this low voice except for when she laughed. Actually it wasn't so much laughing as it was giggling. She was never like that with Lightning. At least not that we could remember. "What's she hiding?"

"Do you know that Oinky's mother is saying prayers for us over at the shrine?"

"Oinky's mother would say prayers for roadkill."

"Yeah? You know how Mother never gets home till late?"

"She's working."

"Not according to Oinky's old lady. She says that Mother and that Atwater moron were over in Midland Park. Just the two of them."

"Big deal. They got a rally there. Remember? They shoulda been there."

"At ten o'clock at night?"

"Will you go fuck yourself!"

"I'm telling ya." Through clenched teeth, spitting the words out. "Oinky's mother knows everything!"

Which was true. She did. And the problem was that Oinky's mother always told everything she knew, spreading it around like her own brand of manure, nourishing the fields of hurt all over town. Waddling from beauty parlor to drug store, working the street with malicious piety. It was as if she'd bugged Father Nunzio's confession box and then broadcast the results.

Pretty soon Tommy and I were getting strange looks from people on the street. And when he pounded out Fat Abbott for saying our mother was getting laid by the *Candidate for Our Times*, Father Nunzio threatened to have him expelled if he ever fought any other students. So Tommy nodded contritely, went straight to the cafeteria to get a sugar container, and poured its contents into the gas tank of Fat Abbott's Honda.

It was as if all of a sudden neither of us had anything in our lives that was fixed. Everything seemed turned upside down. We'd lie in bed at night and wonder why Lightning just didn't get up and do something—anything. Rip the phone out of the wall. Punch Steven Atwater. Yell. Get mad.

Something.

He was, after all, the great Lightning LaRue.

Lightning spent the long spring evenings clearing the back parcel of land on the little plateau above our house. He seemed utterly solitary, working with a rake, shovel and a hoe as if that chunk of ground had some invisible wall around it. It was the fortress he retreated to whenever there were questions with no answers—like when his mahogany-boat plans fell apart and he spent days up there clearing the land like a homesteader with a lot on his mind.

There was something about the very earth itself on this piece of land, no bigger than a tennis court, that held his attention, that transported him into some place where no one else could go. Asphalt patches of an old road led up to the plateau, which in the early 1900s had been the site of an open-air market that sold preserves. But in tales told in French and English on both sides of Penetang harbor, the land was abandoned after all the violence done to it. The Gignacs, the family who owned the market, began a feud among themselves that ended when the disinherited son returned at night and burned all the storage sheds before being shot through the head by his brother. What was left was a charred and festering piece of earth, lacerated by all the glass that had been stored there, the bottles and jars smashed and dumped onto the abandoned ground.

For decades the shards of glass had been silently absorbed deeper into the earth. The lacerations healed, leaving only a smooth, grassy softness on which our family would sometimes spend warm summer evenings, Tommy and I running barefoot through the sprinkler or playing catch. And usually at dark Tommy would want to make a fire up there, a kind of bonfire that would worry Mother as she worked on her flowerbeds, and she would call to Lightning, who was tying whatever fishing lure he'd just created. Lightning would tell Tommy to make only a small fire and then go back to tying his lure.

And Tommy would make his little campfires that always seemed to get too big until Lightning had to come and bank them, snuffing out the last embers as Tommy laughed and protested, lunging at the sparks trying to catch them like fireflies in a net. It was a part of the ritual of our family. And it somehow carried with it the false sense of permanence, as if we would all be found there in that same place, years and years into the future.

It must have been like that for generations, serene and unblemished as if the earth had pulled everything under, wanting to forget whatever furies had disfigured it all those years ago.

And then the glass began to cut through and rise up.

One spring when I was very small it suddenly thrust glinting, jagged and pretty up into the light, like something out of nature lying in wait in slashing packs. All across the ground were the jagged fragments, bottle brown and light and dark green with occasional cobalt blues, pushed into the light, extruded from the silent depths after all those years.

The same way that battlefields, scenes of horror and slaughter, will at first swallow the spent shells, the barbed wire and bayonets and all the other awful trinkets of war, and then decades and centuries later release them back into the open air, pushing the horror out of itself as a signal, a reminder of the truth beneath all that quiet serenity.

We spent the first few weeks of every spring picking the long hidden fangs of glass that were waiting to do unto others. "The frost," Mother would always say. "The frost is what pushes the glass up." But Lightning never said anything about it. He always had a mystical side that Mother blamed on his days as a drinker. It made him less social, she said. Drinkers get like that. Off in their own thoughts. Or some drinkers, at least.

But it was not his drinking.

Lightning started finding something the rest of us missed, wandering alone on that little piece of land looking for jagged shards of glass.

Or sitting out there in the canoe or walking for hours on the edge of the water near the end of the harbor where it leads into open waters and the vastness of Georgian Bay. Occasionally he'd mention the flight patterns of the wild geese. Or the deer tracks. Or whatever else that Mother and Tommy and I weren't all that much interested in.

But there were other times when this inner sanctuary of his came from simply tending to the wounds of that piece of land up behind our house. When all the stories about Mother and the *Candidate for Our Times* began ricocheting around Penetang, Lightning spent hours up there with the glass that kept coming out of the ground. Every evening after work he'd clear the shards away, nursing the ground until by twilight it was again smooth and silky. And then the next night he'd return to find the new glass that had been pushed up by the damp coolness of the night before.

Tommy watched him through a firstborn's eyes.

"He's planning his moves," he said on the first night. "I'm tellin' you, Lightning's gonna clean that guy." But by the end of the week Tommy was in mouth-breathing intensity as he waited. And waited. "What's he doin'?" he asked from the kitchen window, looking up at Lightning working on the plateau in the fading light. "Jesus Christ, what the hell is he waiting for?"

And when Mother came home that night it was Tommy who said, "Why are you home so late?"

I just wanted it to be over, all of it that was driving me so crazy, the seethingly polite silences that wafted through our little house like some invisible poison gas. But who knew how? I didn't know what to say, who to get mad at. My problem was I loved them all, Tommy as my big brother hero. And Lightning too. And Mother. With all her sharp, cornered answers, which had barbs on them now.

Mother announced one night that she'd be staying overnight in Orillia. With several other members of the campaign. To set up the big rally on Saturday.

Tommy went outside in the darkness and beat a tree until the baseball bat broke in his hands. And then sat in the darkness like he couldn't think what to do next.

A few days later, on Saturday, Tommy took action. Or at least whatever action he *could* take. "C'mon," he broadcast from the loudspeaker screwed into the top of the battered old station wagon with the Perkinsfield Drive-In sign on the side. "We're going to do some campaigning of our own."

One of Tommy's weekend jobs in the warm weather was driving

along all the beach roads blaring out the details of whatever movie was playing at the drive-in that weekend. He'd cruise up and down from Balm Beach to Wasaga holding the microphone in one hand and droning out the details through the loudspeaker. "*Rocky IV*—how many *Rocky*s can they make, for godsakes? Come and see for yourself." When he got bored he'd do things like play the theme from *Jaws* just as he got to the public beaches. Or give his own movie reviews. "The most tasteful family drama since *Texas Chainsaw Massacre*."

Then when he was finished he'd take the station wagon back to Mr. Brunton, the Pentecostal Bible-thumper who owned the drive-in, arriving with hymns blasting from the loudspeaker. Once in a while, just to vary the program, Tommy would arrive blaring quotes from Romans because Mr. Brunton was big on Romans 3, 5 and 6 *As it is written, There is none righteous, no not one* and it always resulted in a three-dollar tip, as he told Tommy he was doing the Lord's work.

On this one Saturday, when he was supposed to be advertising some dopey teen comedy, Tommy headed for Orillia, where the big Liberal rally was going on in Couchiching Park. Usually it took about an hour but Tommy drove the whole way with a cassette recording of a police siren playing through the loudspeaker. Cars in front of us were pulling over all over the place.

We got there in about twenty minutes. I was on the floor in the back seat yelling at him to slow down when he yelled "Hold on!" and all of a sudden I felt like I was in the middle of a blender. With my jaws clattering I grappled my way up from the floor to see trees and shrubs flashing past the side windows.

"Wh-wh-what are you doing, you moron?" I yelled, bouncing all over the car.

"We're late!" he shouted over the explosion of branches that flew all around us. "Put the other tape in!"

"What other tape?"

"The one marked *X-rated*," he screamed over the din, before swerving onto a paved road in the park festooned with red and white *Candidate for Our Times* banners. People on the edge of the crowd were looking at us.

I put the audiotape in the machine. "Push Play," Tommy said, sweetly smiling and waving to the crowd. I couldn't see Mother anywhere but I could see Steven Atwater up on a stage over near the lake, waving to people through a blur of flailing posters and banners. He was in the middle of his speech as I pushed Play. And then I heard it. But I didn't believe it.

"Tommy, what the hell is *that*?"

He smiled innocently at the sea of confused faces turning in the direction of the slowly moving station wagon. "The sound track from a porno movie," he said waving.

The entire park echoed with *Yes! Yes! Uh uh uh uh! Do it!* coming out of the loudspeaker on top of the station wagon as Steven Atwater was making his speech—something about it being time for responsible government—*Yes! Fuck me harder!* and all those flailing election posters looked like they weighed a thousand pounds in the hands of confused supporters as the anger on Steven Atwater's face flashed into a rictus smile that only partly masked the kind of death-stare look—*Oh Baby! Baby yesss!*—that must have been used to fire a lot of people down there in Toronto.

Later that night, when Tommy and I were lying in the darkness of our bedroom listening to Mother's car come up the driveway, Tommy whispered, "Know what I'm gonna do to really nail that Atwater bastard?"

"You already nailed him. You just wrecked his campaign speech."

"No way. That was just tactical. I'm talking strategic." Tommy had been reading military books about World War II.

"What's that mean?"

"His wife."

I whipped the pillow off my head and sat up like I was spring-loaded. "His wife?" I was twelve, and the thoughts of grown men's wives were not even on the charts of hormonal magnetism. My old catcher's mitt was of more interest.

"She's hot." You could hear the pained squeal of the side-door hinges being opened with futile stealth as Mother tiptoed into the darkened house. "You saw what his wife looks like."

I vaguely remembered the photograph in *The Free Press*. The candidate's wife standing beside him, tall and sort of blond with some Swedish-type name that I couldn't remember. It wasn't like she was a starlet type, she was a little too old for that, but you could see that maybe once she was. Probably when they met. "What about his wife?"

"I'm the pool man," said Tommy triumphantly, like that was supposed to explain it all.

"The what?" Nobody I knew had a pool, never mind a pool man. Who needed a pool in Penetang when you practically had an ocean right outside your door?

"The pool man—the guy who shows up to clean the swimming pool. Half the porn movies in Mr. Brunton's locked cabinet have a pool man who screws the bored rich housewives whose husbands are too busy making money to pay any attention to them."

"Are you crazy?" From the bedroom down the hall we could hear voices getting louder. Actually only one voice got louder. Mother's. It was like that now. Ever since Lightning stopped drinking. He mostly listened.

"Lightning should do it. To get back at that bastard. But he's too good a guy. So I gotta do it for him."

Tommy didn't look like the pool man. But then I didn't really know what a pool man was supposed to look like. He'd just turned seventeen and he was tall with a mop of dark curly hair that sort of worked with that big grin he usually had. But the rest of him was what was different now. With tight jeans cut off so high that from behind you could see where his legs stopped and his rear end started.

"Pool men are weird," I said the next day, as he left in the back of the pickup truck that was taking the carpenters over to finish work on the Atwater mansion. Tommy just gave me the kind of smile you see in movies when guys are going off to war and they want to look brave for the sake of those they're leaving behind.

It didn't work the way it was supposed to. You could tell because that night Tommy didn't want to talk about it. "She's hot, I'm tellin' ya," was all he would say. And then once when we were almost asleep he said, "I'm close. Very close."

"You don't sound close," I told him.

"You're too young to understand women," he said.

The next day after school Tommy got into his pool-man outfit like he was dressing for a bullfight. But this time he cut one finger off an old baseball glove and stuffed it down the front of his pants to make a bulge. But the bulge made him walk funny like his feet were going off in different directions. He got on his bicycle and peddled over to get hot with the candidate's wife. But even before he got down to Champlain Road you could tell he was having trouble keeping that baseball glove finger in the right place.

That evening he pedaled back home just before dark, looking irritable and jumpy. "She's not a normal woman," he said. "I mean, any normal woman would go for the pool man, right?"

I said probably. But what did I know?

"She's definitely not normal."

"Why? What she'd do? What'd you do?"

"None of your business."

I found out later from the carpenters that Steven Atwater's wife had yelled at Tommy for leaving footprints around the pool and then made him look for the problem with the septic tank that kept overflowing, which made Tommy throw up on the lawn furniture. And then later, his baseball glove finger fell out of his pants and got caught in the pool filtration motor causing the whole system to seize up. Which is when she told him not to come back.

"Not a normal woman," Tommy kept saying.

Havana

Dawn.

Dr. Herrera has gone. Charger waits, protecting her.

"Dr. Herrera left around four in the morning," he says. "There's something wrong with his wife."

"Was that why he was so antsy tonight?"

"You don't ask Dr. Herrera things like that."

"He's different."

"He's nice, Michael." Said almost pleadingly. "You know he's nice."

"What's wrong with his wife?"

"Sonia's been sick. I think."

"Sick how?"

But Charger's staring at the sleeping woman. "He injected her. You know that?"

"With what?"

"Something that made her talk," says Charger. "It was like a miracle. You know what else he said?"

What else? "No. What?"

"He said he wants us to get her out of here."

"He said that yesterday."

"Yeah, but now he's real serious about it."

"Then you'll have to take her somewhere."

"No, Michael. Not without you. I'm not good at stuff like that."

"I can't leave here. For at least a week."

"We may have to."

"I'm stuck here. We have a gamma ray burst."

"What's that?"

"Something no one else can handle. The telescope was almost horizontal tonight. I can't leave."

"Jeeze," says Charger.

She sleeps in my bed, turning and making gentle whimpers that sound like words or maybe names. She is wearing one of my denim shirts instead of the cotton nightgown I bought for her. The illusion of familiarity pleases me in some way I can't quite identify.

She stirs again. And I find a different kind of gravity at work. I go over to the bed and pull the covers over her shoulders. She murmurs.

"You like her, don't you?" Charger fills the doorframe, almost blocking the rays of the sun.

"I don't even know her."

But yes, I do. Know her, that is. In the way that we know people by filling in what we want to know. The wonderment, the fear and exuberance and from the way she shook her head and smiled when she looked at the clothes I had bought for her. And I know that there is some force of attraction that has come from me filling in the vast blanks of her life.

"I know nothing about her," I repeat. For my benefit. And somehow those blanks have become the qualities that have filled the vacuums in my own existence. I have conjured up her life—Mexican, probably she's Mexican. Maybe Salvadoran. Maybe—

"She's Cuban," says Charger, interrupting my thoughts. "It's on the tape."

"What tape?"

"Of her. Talking. It's on the table. Dr. Herrera wants you to hear it. Michael?"

"What?"

"I told you. He wants us to get her out of here."

"Where to?"

"Anywhere."

An hour later: Charger has left to make his pill runs. The gullets and psyches of San Diego county await their Xantac and their Prozac. And in front of me, the tape deck sits in silence, waiting to tell its tale:

You know that I am taping this?
Ah.

That is a yes?
Yes.

How do you feel?
Different.

Different?
Yes. Like in dreams. Sort of like floating. You gave me a needle?

Yes.
What was in it?

Something to help you… What is your name?
Elena Garcia Molina. Why are we speaking in English?

Other people may have to hear it.
What other people?

Where are you from?
From Cuba. From Havana.

Havana?
Centro Habana. Avenida 47. Entre Calle Catorce y Dieciocho. *In a house on the side of a hill overlooking the Almendares River. I grew up there. I miss it.*

How is it that you speak English?

My mother taught English at the University of Havana.

What happened to you?

You mean back then?

Then. Now. What happened to bring you here?... Are you all right?

I don't know how to answer.

You wrote the words "plastic surgery."

Yes.

What does "plastic surgery" mean?

That is why I am here. That is how it all started.

Tell me about it.

I was kidnapped. From Cuba. And taken to a place in Mexico where we operated and put a new face on a man. A whole new face. And now his family wants to kill everyone who gave him this new face.

Why?

He died.

Who kidnapped you?

The man. His family. And the doctor who was running away with me. Where is he?

Who?

The doctor who I was with when I came here to the mountain.

He was a doctor?

Yes.

I don't know what happened to him.

Does your friend here know?

No, ma'am, I don't, I really don't. Know anything, that is.
Apparently no one knows what happened to this doctor.
If he comes back keep him away from me. Please.

This man, this doctor, took you out of Cuba?
He was a—how do you say? son of a bitch? I had no intention of being here. Actually that is not true. Everyone I knew dreamed of leaving Cuba. But not like this. Not this way.

What way?
What did you give me? The injection?

Sodium amytal.
Ah yes. Of course.

Of course?
I am a doctor.

... You are also a doctor?
Yes. It—the sodium amytal, it makes you talk. Under certain conditions. Yes?

Under certain conditions.
You mean when the causes are not of the body, yes? Not ... physiologia, is that it? They are all in the mind. Yes?

Fear can do terrible things to the body. I have seen people go blind for a while. It is called a conversion reaction.
I could not talk.

Yes. That is another kind of conversion reaction. People turn mute. After some terrible trauma. What happened to you?
I can't ... I can't ...

It's okay. You're safe …

I don't believe you. People have been telling me I am safe for months. And they lie. Nothing is safe.

What would you like to do?

Find someone who does not lie.

We are here to help you.

I will find out, won't I?

Yes. You will. Tell me… tell me about your life.

This is not a trick?

No.

My life?… My life?… Okay… Before the revolution my grandfather was a doctor who went to the mountains in Oriente, where he met Che Guevara, who was fighting with Fidel against the government.

Your grandfather knew Che?

Yes. Is something wrong?

No. No, not at all.

You seem …

Please continue.

Well … I went to medical school. The Hospital Docente Calixto Garcia across from the University of Havana. For six years I worked hard and got the third-best marks in my class. That made me a general physician. And that was when it started to go crazy.

What made it go crazy?

He showed up.

He?

Dr. Reyes.

Who is he?

The son of a bitch. Dr. Francisco Reyes. The man I don't want to see. Ever. As a visitor he came to the ESP class I was teaching.

ESP?

English for a Special Purpose. I was helping Francisco, the instructor. The classes are divided into brigades of between five and ten students. Each brigade would come in—it was in the ORL, the Oto Rino Laringologia classroom—and we would give them white cards with a topic—like malaria—on it. And they would talk about it in English. When one of the students came up to speak about the topic in English I was aware of talking behind me. I turned and saw two men and the woman from the CDR—the Committee for the Defense of the Revolution. The shorter man looked ugly. He was rude and he didn't care if he interrupted us. But the taller one—Dr. Reyes—was different.

How?

He was not rude like the ugly one. You could tell he had manners. And you could tell immediately he was Mexican.

How?

You should know. He spoke in sharp little spikes. Mexicans talk that way. Not like Cubans. You are Colombian, no?

Peruvian.

Really. I would have said Colombian.

Why was this Dr. Reyes there?

I only found out later. The CDR woman told me that they wanted me to go to dinner with them that night. They were staying at a private villa they had rented in Siboney. I didn't want to. But I did. It was a mistake. In every way. The villa was big with guards around it. Inside there was Dr. Reyes, the shorter ugly man and three jinateras*—you know? Girls who sell themselves?*

Prostitutes?

Sort of. It was supposed to be a dinner party but it didn't really turn out that way. The ugly one—I finally was told his name, Ramon Cabrera—was already drunk when I got there …

Yes?

I'm just remembering. I almost don't want to. The three jinateras*—they were just girls. One was from Cerro, a poor area of Havana, and the other two were from small towns. In Pinar del Rio, I think. They were very pretty. Ramon Cabrera was getting them drunk and making them undress each other. When they were naked he told them to do things to each other. You know, like sex things. He did not understand these girls at all. The* jinateras *will go to bed with men, no problem. But the other things, like what he wanted them to do, they would be too ashamed. But in one way maybe he did understand them.*

In what way?

He brought out money. More money than I have ever seen. A big plastic bag stuffed with American money. Hundred-dollar bills. He pulled out a fistful of this money and said to the jinateras*, "Now maybe we understand each other?" And these girls, they looked at all this money he was holding and it was more than they would make in their lifetime. I was disgusted. I said I had to leave. Ramon ran over to the table and put a pile of money in front of me. I just looked at it and left. He laughed and yelled to Dr. Reyes, "I like her. I like this one." Dr. Reyes caught up with me outside and persuaded me to talk to him on the patio. He had something important to tell me, he said …*

What was so important?

Freedom.

Freedom?

That's what it seemed like … At the time.

And what does it seem like now?

It is why I am here … At first he began by apologizing for Ramon Cabrera. He said he was not usually like this. That it was just that Ramon's wife had become a very strict Catholic back in Mexico. And that the only power she had between them was the power of sex. And she would only let him touch her on religious saints' days. It was her form of having some control. So Ramon Cabrera went wild with women when he was not around his wife.

What did you say to that?
I laughed at him.

How did he react?
He just smiled. He knew what he was saying. Like I said he was more refined. He told me that Ramon was a businessman. That's the word he used. That he had planned to invest millions of dollars in Cuba because he wanted to come here for an operation. That's why they were at the hospital. But after looking at the conditions at the hospitals and clinics they had changed their mind. Dr. Reyes was recommending that the operation be performed in his own clinic in Mexico.

What kind of operation was he going to have?
I asked that. But Dr. Reyes said it was secret. Actually the word he used was "personal." Inside the villa, I could see two of the girls through the window. One of them was upside down lying on top of the other while Ramon Cabrera was pulling his pants down behind her. I told Dr. Reyes I knew what kind of operation I would do on Ramon if I was holding the scalpel at that moment. And he laughed. He said that Ramon liked my spirit. Good, I said. I like my spirit too. And then I started walking toward the gate. That was when he made me the offer. The offer of freedom. He told me he could get me out of Cuba if I wanted.

Why couldn't you get out of Cuba yourself?
You know. The government. People were dying by the hundreds trying to escape. Just trying to get to Florida. The bolseros*—the people on the rafts and the inner tubes—were dying at sea, being eaten by sharks. Some mornings on the Malecon they'd find body parts washing up. Arms. Legs.*

But your grandfather—
My grandfather was why I could not leave. He was very powerful. And he would make sure I was not given a visa to go. And he also knew that I wanted to get out because of Juan Carlos.

Who is Juan Carlos?

Juan Carlos Tieles Curbelo. He was the son of the man who was in my grandfather's orchestra in the psychiatric hospital.

An orchestra? In a psychiatric hospital?

It's complicated.

How?

It just is.

What about this Juan Carlos?

I knew him as a boy and then I met him again while he was playing trumpet—like his father, but he was playing Latin music in a band at Café Cantante. I wanted to leave Cuba with him. And go to America. And start over... Do you know what that means? Starting over?

Yes. I do.

The first time I saw Juan Carlos he was on the bandstand. I had that feeling—you know the one where it's like you've known someone all your life? I didn't think he was Cuban at first. He had hair that was light, almost blond, and he was tall with those amazing laughing eyes and when I laughed back from the dance floor he played some funny notes imitating me. Laughter...

What about laughter?

Maybe some people need it more than others.

And you?

I am one of those who need it.

And you found it with him?

For a while.

For a while?

I don't know that I was truly in love with him. But he was a good person.

And I think maybe I felt so bad about what my grandfather had done to his family that I would to do anything he wanted. Just to make it up to him.

What had your grandfather done to his family?
Terrible things. I don't want to talk about it.

What did Juan Carlos want?
He wanted to leave and all he talked about was getting to play in New York or Miami. A lot of his friends had done that and returned. Some musicians were being allowed to leave and return, unlike ordinary people. But there was some problem—the government would not give him a visa to leave. Maybe because of who his father was. So that night when Dr. Reyes made the offer, I turned around and went back to him and said, "Does that include Juan Carlos too?"

And he agreed?
Yes. Lies. All of it.

How?
They had a boat, one of the very fast ones that rich Americans own and use to sneak over to Cuba. They go to Marina Hemingway outside of Havana and tie their boats up and then go back to America. Not a lot of people knew about this. I would be hidden under the front of the boat in a special compartment where the Cuban Coast Guard would never find me when they searched the boat. There was only space there for one person so we had a plan that Juan Carlos would leave after dark from a village west of Marina Hemingway and swim out to a little light about a hundred yards out in the water—the kind that tells ships to be careful. The boat would pick him up and make the trip to Florida.

But you are here without him.
Yes . . . yes. I am here without Juan Carlos.

What happened?
They lied. And I was a fool to trust them. That is what happened.

How did they lie?

When the boat left it was hours after dark. After several minutes I crawled from the hiding place and looked out. Right away I knew something was wrong. I yelled to the two men who drove the boat. There was a big storm coming and one of them pushed me under the deck. I yelled and I screamed at him to go back for Juan Carlos. "Your man is dead," he yelled back at me, pointing to the waves pounding the boat. "Dead!"

...Are you all right?

I don't know how to answer that...

What are you thinking?

They had never intended to stop for Juan Carlos. They knew he would die out there.

How do you know that?

The boat went straight out. To the west. Right from the moment they left the Marina Hemingway. Instead of going along the shore about a hundred yards out. To get Juan Carlos.

If you want to stop for a while...

One day later, the boat got to a place where there was nothing but sand. Just like a desert. But there was a big black truck-car with dark windows. It was waiting on the shore. I was taken to it by a man with the dead eyes. And then he and the driver took me a few miles to a flat place where a plane was waiting. It was an old-looking plane with propellers, the kind where the nose sits higher than the tail. Inside the plane there was nothing, it was all bare with the metal beams showing. The plane took off immediately. It was so noisy my head was throbbing and I had trouble breathing. I was all alone and the door to the cockpit was locked. I kept crying and yelling that I wanted to talk to someone, but it was almost like no one was flying the plane. It landed somewhere in the dark and by this time I was so exhausted that I no longer cared what they did with me. Another big black car was waiting and when it finally stopped after about an hour, I was there.

There?

In this compound. Owned by Ramon. The short, ugly one. And his brother Antonio. With high white walls all around a large house. Dr. Reyes was waiting. Even from his first words I could see that he was different now.

How?

It was like there was no need for the charm any more. The good manners. All that was gone. He got tense and irritated when I became emotional. Like I had no business being upset. There were other men with dead eyes around, three, maybe four of them carrying guns. He just turned and nodded to one of them who grabbed my arm and led me inside the house. But inside it was not a house at all. It was like a hospital. All white. With an operating room where the living room should be. I was led down a hallway to a little room with a bed and a bathroom. They locked me in there.

Did you know where you were?

*I was somewhere near Tijuana. In a room that locked from the outside. There was a television, which I turned on. The stations were all Mexican. And a few American stations from San Diego. I fell asleep. Crying. When I woke up the next day the door to my room was still locked from the outside. I got dressed in the clothes they had there for me. All the right size. Amazing. Dr. Reyes was a man of details. But no taste. The clothes were shiny. With things that glittered on them. How do you call them—*lentejuelas*?*

Sequins?

Yes. Sequins. They were all over those dresses. Like someone who wanted people to look at her all the time would wear... They let me out of the room and nobody seemed to pay any attention to me. There were the same three or four men with guns who didn't speak to me. I might as well have been invisible. The entrance to the compound had two big metal gates that swung open when one of their cars came or went. It was like a—how do you say, castillo*?*

Castle.

Castle? No. Maybe more like... a fort. Yes? For two days I stayed there and no one talked to me. It was like I didn't exist. Then Dr. Reyes came back. I could tell he was there even before I saw him. That cologne he wore. You could smell him before you saw him. He cared about such things. And the way he dressed. He always wore clothes that were somehow not quite right. Too good. But somehow wrong. Too shiny. I was angry at him, I yelled, but he slapped me and pushed me back into the room. He was shaking. And then he told me… He told me why I was there. I was to be a nurse.

A nurse?
Yes.

But you said you are a doctor.
Dr. Reyes didn't care. He just needed someone to act as a nurse. After he convinced Ramon not to have the operation in Cuba, Dr. Reyes needed someone to help him when he gave him a new face.

A new face?
Dr. Reyes was a plastic surgeon.

She does not awaken even when the sound of gunfire comes from somewhere nearby and I quickly switch off the tape recorder.

A single echoing shot swallowed up by the forest and then nothing but the silence of the mountain. I turn off the tape machine and go outside.

Silence. As only a forest can be silent, swarming with noises from inside your head.

Then there is a crunching sound of a car rolling slowly across gravel. A sheriff's car is on the road at the end of the lane and in its idling growl it takes on a sense of something predatory. The jagged sounds of its two-way radio scrape against the dawn.

Turning back to the open door I can see her eyes, open now and locked on me like talons. She doesn't move and her expression has not changed from when she slept. But her gaze is unyielding as I go toward the door and close it.

It is another sheriff's deputy. I recognize him—the one who lives on the east side of the mountain. Tall, older and deeply tanned with silver hair. Sort of a former leading man type now working character parts.

"Strange nights," he says from the car.

"Yeah. Really strange." The marines? The woman? Or the man without a face hung up on the beams? "Especially that hotel fire." I move past him a little, wanting to shift his attention from my cabin.

"Naw," he says. "The old place was a disaster just waiting to happen. You ever look at the wiring in it?"

"Never did."

"Half chewed by rats and god knows what. Forty amps total in that whole nailed-together pile of wood. And cedar-shake roofing. Musta told them a hundred times the place'd go up in smoke one day." He reaches for the shotgun clipped vertically beside him against the dashboard. "Damn strange."

"Yeah."

"Have any problems inside your place?"

"Nothing." *He knows.*

He's out of the cruiser and staring straight at my front window. "Yeah," he says and then turns and walks across the road. "You're lucky." He laughs a little. "Baileys were luckier. Damn lion."

"What about the lion?"

"Tried to eat Bailey's house."

The Baileys are my neighbors across the road and back into the woods a little. An older couple, with his family being mountain royalty for a century or more. The deputy cradles that shotgun like it's all no big deal. But his finger never leaves the trigger all the way over there.

Old Mr. Bailey is sitting on his porch holding up a gun of his own, a big hunting rifle that makes him look about three sizes smaller than he really is. "Dammit, Don," he yells to the deputy, "you gotta do something about these break-ins."

"Yeah sure," says the deputy. "Serves you right. Told you about leaving cat food out around the house."

They go back and forth for a while, sort of half-kidding each other about whose fault it was for what happened. Mr. Bailey's sitting beside what used to be his big front window that's now just shards of glass scattered all over the porch. And beyond that, lying in the middle of the living room in a pool of its own blood, is the dead mountain lion.

"Damnedest thing," says Mr. Bailey. "It woke us up with all the screechin' it was doing. Right out in front here. Staring into the window like it was gonna attack it. Turning in circles, twitchin' and jumpin' all over like someone shoved a firehose up its ass."

The deputy's walking back and forth doing a Sherlock. He stops in front of another, smaller window. "Know what it was? He saw his own damn reflection. Thought it was another mountain lion. He attacked himself."

"He was slobberin' and droolin' all over the place."

"Strange night," says the deputy.

"Shootin' a mountain lion in your own living room?" says Mr. Bailey. "What's so strange about that?"

The audio tape yields its secrets again. This time she is awake. But she does not want me to know it, lying there in the bed facing the wall. It is her breathing that gives her away, a different rhythm than when she sleeps.

Why was Ramon getting a face-lift?

Not just a face-lift. A whole new face. He and his brother, Antonio. They were two of the biggest cocaine people in Mexico. You must have heard of them.

Yes.

His brother, Antonio, was the first one to get a new face. Using his own doctors. Whatever Antonio did, Ramon copied. He was a fool. Antonio was really the one who ran it all. He was supposed to be a genius. In his way. But evil. Truly evil.

Yes.

Ramon was stupid. And brutal. But Antonio was the one everybody there really feared.

Yes.
They had both decided to have new faces. So that the American police would not recognize them.

Yes.
Antonio had already got his new face when I arrived. His own doctors had done the operation a couple of weeks earlier. None of us knew what he looked like now. He was a mystery man. Once at night I saw a man in the courtyard with his head all in bandages. It was Antonio, I was told. You could tell because the gunmen there were all nervous. Antonio was terrifying. Even to them.

And you were scared?
Of course. After I told Dr. Reyes that I refused to have anything to do with it, he said, "Fine, they will kill you like they are killing a bug. The way they kill people all the time."

Why did he not get a nurse from Mexico?
Dr. Reyes said that Ramon did not want a Mexican woman for a nurse. She might tell her relatives, he said. And besides, Ramon had heard that Che Guevara had a face-lift done by Cuban doctors over in Africa. So that he could not be recognized by the people who were hunting him. And so to Ramon that was a sign that he needed a Cuban woman as a nurse. He thought he could be made handsome like Che. He was that much of a fool.

Che was caught. And killed.
Ramon didn't think about that. He was stupid. An evil little tree stump of a man.

Was?
He's dead. He died on the operating table.

How do you know this?
I am very tired.

There's only a few more questions.

But I have a question for you.

Yes?

You said you are a psiquiatra—psychiatrist, right?

Yes.

No psychiatrist would give a patient sodium amytal the first time they met. Maybe the second or third time. But never the first.

You gave permission.

That is not the question.

No. But I thought that in your case there was some urgency.

And then the tape runs out. Or maybe the recorder was shut off. The whirring stops. The click signals the end. On the other side of the tape there is nothing.

Why? Doctor, what was the urgency?

Watching her lying there, I am part of the stillness in the cabin, with the only motion being the slowly rising rays of the sun. And replaying the tape over and over in my thoughts. But it is her words, not his, that tumble through my thoughts and somehow unleash a fear.

She stirs.

And then as her eyes open, I wait until she is looking at me, lying perfectly still. "I need to ask you more questions," I say. "About why you came here. Why this place? The mountain?"

She is perfectly still. At first I think she hasn't heard me. But then she shakes her head slowly. And her mouth forms the word *No.* But no sound emerges. Nothing.

Only the fierceness of her stare that will not release me.

Penetang

The twilights in late May were always my favorite time in Penetang. They seemed to go on forever and yet they vanished so quickly. There was the newness, of life being created all around as the carapace of late-winter grayness cracked under the bursting green of the maples and the birches and the walnut trees budding. It taught me the eternal equation of value from scarcity, prizing those endless warm twilights because they were so few.

But this year I feared them.

Seething silences rose from the ground like fumes. Lightning would come home from work and make dinner, which was when the voices, the din began. It hung over the dinner table. It seeped and swirled through my controlled terror, my just wanting everything to be fine.

But it was Tommy to whom the din, the voices, really spoke to. And through.

"When's Mom coming home?" he'd half ask, half announce.

When Lightning came out with his usual answer—"When she's finished work"—Tommy's face would become a mask that had pressure building behind it like some inflating inner tube with a weak spot.

On this night, Tommy threw down his fork and left the table. Lightning said nothing. After dinner he retreated to the ground up behind the house, where he tended to it, raking and prying the latest glass to appear from the earth. It all seemed so peaceful, but it terrified me. I knew it was coming.

Even from the dock where I was tying up the canoe I could hear the shouting. It was Tommy. With all kinds of *what kind of man are you?* stuff. And all the yelling about Mother that should have got him slapped by Lightning, his own father. That part was bad enough. But not nearly as bad as what suddenly struck me, standing there on that dock, the distant sight of this man, my father whom I realized I didn't know at all.

I knew only the shell. The legend or what was left of it, but not this shrunken, distant reality waiting out the storm of his oldest son's humiliation.

And then Lightning went off on his own, walking into the darkness of the harbor's edge, not to return until long after everyone else was in bed. I lay there listening. Waiting for voices from down the hall. There was none. In the silence of that night I felt like acid was eating me away from the inside out.

Something in Tommy's grin had changed. I saw it the next day when he left. It had lost its innocence. "Tommy," I said as he tried on the construction hard hat.

"What?"

"You're my brother, okay?"

"Yeah." He was tightening the plastic sizing strap on the helmet. Totally engrossed.

"You don't get it, do you? Stupid!" I don't know why but I started crying and punching him, kicking the hard hat out of his hands. It caught him by surprise and in the fury of his reaction he cuffed me on the head, making my ears ring as I sprawled onto the floor of our garage.

"You idiot," he said, retrieving the hard hat. "You still believe in your fairy tales. Well, it's not going to turn out like that. And if Lightning had any guts he'd leave her."

"Leave Mother?" I was horrified. It was more than I could comprehend. It was the only world I'd ever known. However bad things got, him leaving her—us!—was beyond the limits of my imagination.

"Tell me why he's stayed. Huh?"

"Because …"

"See, you can't."

And then he turned and walked out the door as an old Pontiac with rusted-out fenders approached on the road below. Tommy got in.

And I knew more than I have ever known anything in my life that nothing would ever be the same again.

I tried to make it all go away by asking myself why Lightning didn't leave. Pretty soon I was silently asking the question every day.

And every day the answer seemed to drift farther away.

Tommy had a favorite trick. It was the road crew thing. His theory was that most people are so conditioned to obey anyone who looks like they're in charge that they will behave like sheep. All you have to do is make yourself the shepherd. Or maybe the wolf.

He tried out his sheep theory after the Penetang Kings lost to the team from Collingwood on a cheap penalty. The referee was the uncle of one of the guys from the Collingwood team and when Tommy started arguing he got thrown out of the game.

One morning a few days later he organized the Kings' goalie and two defensemen to go over to Collingwood with him wearing those orange fluorescent construction vests and hard hats. Tommy had sort of borrowed—that was his word—a backhoe owned by the goalie's father. When they got to the other team's arena they offloaded the backhoe and set up traffic cones and, with the two defensemen acting stern and waving traffic around a detour, Tommy dug a massive hole right in the road in front of the entrance to the arena.

A police car drove up, stopped and a window rolled down.

"Gas main," said Tommy from the backhoe and returned the policeman's *Yup-okiedoke* salute.

When they had dug a hole that two houses could fit into, he loaded the backhoe onto the trailer and they drove away.

The hole remained for the rest of the hockey season while confused arena officials tried to fix blame on various civic departments as well as Ontario Hydro and Consumers Gas. Eyewitness descriptions of the road construction crew varied widely, but the one thought to be the most accurate described the backhoe operator as being mid-forties, possibly with a mustache and overweight.

When Tommy left the garage that morning I knew the road crew thing was going to get used on *Steven Atwater—A Candidate for Our Times*. And of course a big hole got dug in the road leading into the park in Midland, the route that the campaign procession was going to be using.

But it didn't make much difference because the storm canceled everything anyway. It started in mid-morning, coming from the west straight over Thunder Bay, and by noon there were marine warnings all over the place. The water in the harbor got that slate-gray churning coldness as the miniature waves slammed into each other in confusion when no single direction could be found. But farther out past the channel, toward Beausoleil Island, the waves marshaled in angry unison, gathering power and size, driven on by the rain that overtook them in stinging volleys.

It was into these volleys that Lightning blasted through the waves.

A test run, he yelled over the wind-whipped protests of the men he worked with. The new 23-foot fiberglass Grew cruiser. A chance to see what it could do, he called out. What it could withstand. The Scotsman who managed the factory came stumbling down to the dock, yelling at Lightning, ordering him to return immediately. But the roar of the storm flung the Scotsman's words back at him. It was only the look that passed from Lightning through the horizontal rain to those on the dock that constituted a transmission of any kind. And what it said sent the Scotsman running for a phone. But no call to the provincial police could have helped. Lightning was already full throttle, heading for the open channel and the 30,000 Islands, where the storm was at its most punishing.

The cruiser cut through the waves, hitting them like an explosive charge that detonated the spray in all directions. The *Georgian Queen*, the tarted-up old scow that wheezed through the summers as a tourist boat, had just turned back, seeking shelter behind the north shore, when Lightning cut across its bow heading in the opposite direction. The crew ran to starboard, yelling through bullhorns at the rain-lashed figure receding into the swallowing gloom.

Lightning never looked back.

The boat was found the next day, capsized near Methodist Point. On Friday, Lightning washed up on the southern tip of Giants Tomb Island.

In the fog of pain that never really lifted, one image got strobed into what I remember to this day. It was Tommy. Not so much the screaming and swinging baseball bats at lampposts. Or spewing torrents of fury at Mother as I tried to push him away, crying and falling all over him, a thirteen-year-old pleading with his older brother, his hero, to stop please stop.

It was the sight of him running toward the road at night that got etched forever. Screaming at me not to follow him. Threatening. And then vanishing.

After midnight, when I pulled the pillow off my head and watched the bedroom wall turn from invisible blackness to a flickering orange, I knew why Tommy was not in the other bed.

Through our window I could see the flames mirrored in the harbor, leaping with every new explosion as shock waves rolled in, out of synch with whatever my eyes had seen blown up moments earlier, rattling the panes of glass in front of my nose.

Grew Boats was an inferno.

The chemicals used to make fiberglass were what trapped Tommy. When they exploded in 50-gallon geysers his escape route was cut off until the fire department had put out the flames.

There was no bail.

Oinky's mother trod her well-worn path. The Tories swept the Liberals. Steven Atwater lost. Mother sat for hours staring out across the harbor. No one phoned.

Mother and I existed in the silence of a house that was slowly shrinkwrapping around me until I couldn't breathe in there. And the term *psychiatric evaluation* drifted unspoken through the terror of a bedroom that was now mine alone.

And sometimes I'd walk as far as I could go along the north shore to where it met the open waters of Georgian Bay and I'd yell at Lightning, telling him how angry I was. On most days the wind stole my shouts and flung them away like so much chaff. It never made me feel better anyway.

Tommy was taken in handcuffs to Toronto, where he was locked up in some psychiatric institute for three days, and then he was brought up to Barrie, where they were going to try him. I was sitting in the visitors' place with him when some big old policeman limped past with another prisoner and abruptly stopped. He looked at Tommy and that *Yup-okiedoke* salute went into instant replay. All of a sudden that guy on the backhoe wasn't middle-aged, didn't have a mustache and wasn't overweight.

This got Tommy sent down to the psychiatric institute in Toronto again.

Extreme antisocial behavior was the latest word-lashed whisper that flashed through the town. Causing massive damage to public property. Holes—*giant* holes, dug callously at peril to life, limb and probably public order.

And Life, Liberty and the Pursuit of Happiness.

And Peace, Order and Good Government. Or so it was alleged.

In my seething, my punching at smoke and air, I tried what Tommy did. I took a baseball bat to the nearest telephone pole, blazing away at it, trying to pull the pain out with every blast against the pole, yelling and cursing into the night. It didn't work. Not like it did for Tommy. All I was left with was sore hands. And the same terrible ache that wouldn't go away.

And then Tommy was brought back up to Barrie, where he laughed about the answers he gave the guys at the institute. "I told them I dug the hole in Collingwood because I thought there was a worldwide conspiracy and Steven Atwater was at the center of it."

"Tommy, I don't think that's such a good idea. Don't joke about this stuff. There's already been some provincial police guys asking questions about you all over town."

"Yeah? If they're doing their job they'll find out it's true." He said it with a jittery stare like they'd hooked up his toe to an electrode.

"Tommy?" That stare scared me.

And then he laughed. It was the same old Tommy. Go with it. Goofin' around. It'll all be over soon.

But it was not. Could not.

The terror in that bedroom exploded in those long nights when I called out for Tommy. Who wasn't there. And would never be. Not with the gale force of accusations that Oinky's mother was dutifully reporting, trundling on her appointed rounds within sight of the ashes of Grew Boats. In school I punched Oinky in the leg for what his mother was doing. I didn't punch him hard, just hard enough so

I would feel better. But I didn't. I just ended up apologizing to him when he cried.

But the more I apologized the more Oinky wailed. I figured out that he was sniveling so loudly because he wanted Brother Eugene to notice. I heard Tommy's voice saying *Fuck it* and I buried a knuckle in Oinky's big blubbery arm. Which of course was like jumping on a car with an alarm system. You could've heard Oinky way over in Midland.

I got thrown out of the class and sent through the empty halls to meet my fate at the hands of Father Nunzio. Transgressors usually had to wait on a bench outside his office until he deigned to open the door and loom in towering wrath over the assembled wretch. But this time his door was open just enough so I could hear the two provincial policemen who were asking about Tommy. Asking Father Nunzio about the things he'd done. Hostile acts. Antisocial behavior. Endangering others. The court-appointed psychiatrist had requested more information.

Because the Crown Attorney was recommending Oak Ridge.

The Ridge! Every schoolkid in Penetang knew the litany—*nuthouse looney bin rubber room.* We made fun of what we were afraid of. But we also knew other words: *Psychotic. Psychopath. Paranoid schizophrenic.* The worst wackos of all were shipped to our little town from all over the province and crammed into one synaptically festering wedge of inhuman madness and criminality. Right here in that big old Gothic building overlooking our quiet harbor.

And Tommy!—funny, grinning Tommy—was not part of that wedge.

But Father Nunzio—that traitor who would not know a joke unless the Pope told it—that gaseous inquisitor, was telling tales about the frightening hostility, the sheer menace of this boy Tommy.

"The boy is seriously disturbed," I heard Father Nunzio say.

And even before he'd finished talking I suddenly figured it out: Father Nunzio was the worst thing that ever happened to us. Because if it wasn't for him, none of this would be happening to Tommy. Or us.

Which is when I kicked in his door and yelled, "*Disturbed?* You wanna know disturbed?" And some other things about Father Nunzio being a big fat liar.

As I stood there in my full thirteen-year-old fearsomeness.

That August, when Tommy's pretrial hearing was just weeks away, something, *anything* had to be done. Or so the lawyer told Mother, who was still crying most nights after she went to bed. So one evening I rode my bicycle to the Kiwanis Cub banquet, where you'd always find Father Nunzio if there wasn't a Knights of Columbus dinner on the same night. I waited for hours in the parking lot for him to come out. He was one of the first to leave, lumbering toward the old Ford he drove.

I'd rehearsed it all over and over, the part about being sorry for kicking in his office door when the policemen were there and calling him a big fat idiot and that I really did want to touch God and that Tommy was sorry for everything he'd ever said about him too—but please, please just tell the court that Tommy was not like the experts, whoever they were, were saying he was.

I wove through the parked cars and rounded the back of his Ford just as he was opening the door. But suddenly I saw that bulk of his cinch up and then slowly let go in a practiced peristaltic wave of his digestive tract that almost sent me crashing into the fender trying to stop. I knew what was coming. But it was too late, I had committed myself, and the wave crested just as he turned around. The worst part was that he panicked when he saw me and tried to stop the wave. But it was too late for him too. The wheezy fart he'd been uncorking announced itself to the world as a damp little explosion.

It might as well have been a bell the way it clanged in my head. I stood frozen with my mouth open.

Father Nunzio looked momentarily suspended between embarrassment and fury and then recovered with his characteristic whip-flicking stare, looking at me like I'd crawled out from under a rock. He quickly got into his car. I ran to the side window and started telling him everything, *everything!* He was backing out when he stopped and rolled down the window. "I pray for you," he said. "And your mother."

"We pray for you too" was all I could think to say. He kept backing out and I kept running beside his car yelling about Tommy. He stopped before he got out of the parking lot and opened the window. This time that scariness was gone, the bulging eyes and florid lips thinning into a slit—none of it was there. He almost seemed to want to hear what I had to say.

"My brother's not crazy and you know it," I blurted out.

"Your brother is the author of his own misfortune," he said quietly. "And he continues to be."

"That Houdini thing was just a joke and you know it," I blubbered. Tommy had invited a friend of his, a kid from Victoria harbor who was practicing to be the next Houdini, to visit him in jail. The next Houdini was demonstrating lock-picking techniques to Tommy in the visitors' area when the guards figured out what was going on.

And then Tommy laughed at me when I got angry at him for this. "No big deal," he said as I yelled at him and told him it *was* all a big deal stupid, that he was in jail and they wanted to throw away the key.

"I can only pray for your brother," said Father Nunzio.

"Don't pray. Help! You were the one who told those cops Tommy was a nutcase."

"Your brother is a troubled soul. He needs help."

"Not the kind you're talking about!" I was yelling now and slobbering all over but I didn't care any more.

Father Nunzio looked at me for a moment and then rolled the window up and drove away. It was last time I saw him for almost two decades.

I had ridden my bicycle home, seeing nothing and shouting at the night. When I got back I was afraid to go inside, into the house from which Lightning and Tommy had been ripped forever and where the muffled sound of crying would hang in the darkness.

The sky was alive. Something was happening in the darkness. It lit up above me in a towering luminescence. It was the northern lights, scary in the bizarre wafting curtains of light like some deity—like God—had taken the entire enormity of the sky from one horizon to the other and draped it with an undulating faintly green veil of light.

I groped my way up to the land that Lightning used to clear and lay down on it.

Glass cut into my shirt but I didn't care. I stared up into the exhilarating fearfulness of the aurora whipping slowly back and forth above me. I could feel blood soaking into my clothes as I lay there under the lights yelling for Lightning and Tommy to come and watch.

I yelled at them until the northern lights faded and an obsidian blackness settled around me.

’Melica

I am here because of Father Nunzio.

Pulled into this place by some gravitational imperative that wove through the lower depths of memories replaying themselves, unseen, unheard, in all those years I was fleeing.

Am fleeing.

Memories of Penetang when he was our very own Grand Inquisitor. When the only heaven he described that seemed remotely accessible to wretches like us was California. He rhapsodized about the place. Spinning reveries about the mountains of San Diego County. And all the old Spanish missions where lucky Jesuits from freezing climes could bask in Mediterranean warmth.

In the depths of the Penetang winters you could see that for him hell was not molten, it was frozen.

It was when the blizzards tore into Penetang like amphibious assaults off Georgian Bay that we would hear most fervently of this one mystical California mountain with orange groves and palm trees below it and the gleaming dome of the observatory on its crest. The snow would be whipping at the windows around us but the visions that were painted in our minds were of quaint missions, beaches, and Palomar!

A place where you touched God through the massive telescope on the mountain that saw all the way back to creation.

Staring out at the snow, I decided that I too wanted to touch God.

It was the one religious impulse that Father Nunzio seared into me. There was once a moment when I wanted to tell him this. For Tommy's sake.

After that single shot blew Dr. Baymer's nose off his face, my lost decade began.

First, Toronto. But then, imagining *Wanted* posters of a twenty-year-old College Street bartender tacked up in the downtown police stations, I bolted for Niagara Falls and the border crossing. I just walked into America. In those years false identities and documents were mere psychic misdemeanors in the grand scheme of things. Especially when you were being swept into the roiling, exuberant currents of American life. And telling yourself you were on your way to touch God.

But God waited. As I tumbled across America. Or 'Melica as I could almost hear Tommy saying on those long nights alone, thinking about what I had left behind.

First there were odd jobs in Chicago, and then Omaha for a month, and then other places whose names blurred under the gathering fugitive's mentality that I could not make go away, always expecting to be rammed by the fears filling up the rearview mirror. For a year, maybe more, I never stopped speeding even when I was alone in some dingy rented room waiting for sleep to smother those fears in exhaustion. But every morning it would begin again, the feeling of being sprayed with tension through a fine nozzle. Any sense of tranquility dissolved in the puddles of acid that collected in my memories whenever I stayed in one place too long. Always expecting to be found out. Arrested. Deported.

And then there was Colorado. And something in the isolation of the mountains and the forests around the ski resorts gave me the illusion of safety. After four years I was almost forgetting to look in that rearview mirror.

Those years ended one cold night when Susan Alter—the one who had been Susan Vivash when she was in Mother's class—and her husband walked through the lobby of the expensive ski lodge where I was working. She was dressed up in her latest Holt Renfrew *après-ski* clothes and stopped like she'd seen a ghost when she saw me. When she gripped my arm I almost lost the tray of daiquiris, and she wouldn't let go until she made sure I knew how much she felt sorry for my mother.

And that if anyone turned me in it wouldn't be her. Definitely.

I knew she was telling the truth. She wouldn't have to turn me in. Her husband would do it for her. He was glaring at me through a cluster of auto dealers like he was mentally dialing 911. I served the daiquiris, went back into the kitchen, got my parka and walked out through the back door. Into my future.

A week later the Greyhound bus from Phoenix stopped in Temecula. I hitchhiked the twenty-minute drive to the base of Palomar Mountain and walked uphill for six hours until I could see the observatory dome. And then I unpacked my parka, lying down in the long grass, waiting for night and for the stars to appear.

Waiting for glass to cut through the parka.

I could now give a marginally scientific explanation of what causes the northern lights, one wrapped in talk of magnetic disturbances, negatively charged electrons and cathode rays that blast off the face of the sun and bombard the earth.

But none of that could ever reach the mysticism of that night as a boy in Penetang staring into the vastness of those supernatural curtains of light, bleeding into the earth that was cutting me. If there was a moment of foreordination in my life it was then, when Palomar became the only inevitability I possessed.

I was destined to be here.

In this place, this shrine with its enormous mirror at the heart of the telescope, one enormous piece of glass, lovingly ground and hand polished into an infinite smoothness all those years ago.

And playing out the mysteries of existence and creation as they are incrementally revealed from the fires out there in the universe, those infernos that from here twinkle lovingly in the serenity of the night.

But there is a truth about the night, a truth behind all that serenity, all that beauty. It is a truth we may always crave to ignore.

It was several months after I arrived at Palomar that I first saw Father Nunzio again. It was at the fiesta, the Corpus Christi celebration in Pala, at the base of the mountain. He emerged from a horse-drawn carriage, jowly and gray-haired.

I stood there momentarily paralyzed by the thought that perhaps I had come all this way and endured all this loneliness and pain simply to be in the presence of my tormentor. Like an abuse victim seeking the approval of the abuser, had I unconsciously sought out the source of my fears?

But then something wonderful happened. I just started laughing. In the middle of that mariachi-driven inferno of noise and boisterous colors. Looking at this old man overflowing his princely chair bestowing gouty waves to the cheering crowds, I laughed. Even that smile of his, the one that always felt to me like it gave paper cuts now seemed almost marinated in drool.

It was not because of Father Nunzio himself that I was here in Palomar.

No, it was because of the images he had held out in front of twelve-year-old minds, the ones of a mystical California mountain with orange groves and palm trees below, and a place where you could see all the way back to creation. *That* was why I was here —without knowing it until that instant. Watching the raucous throngs of Mexicans and Indians who were lining the road and the riders with flags and banners cantering through the mission in front of him the way they always did at this fiesta.

Even with all this ceremony, this fawning by the masses, he looked faintly ridiculous. The way he may always have looked. To everyone except the twelve-year-olds who perceived only fear.

I watched him holding court among the crowds around the pit barbecue and the game booths. And from afar I heard him talk of the years he had been away, first in Canada and then for five years in Ohio. And now mercifully back here.

I was at the fiesta helping one of the local contractors who had been hired to build a makeshift stage from which Father Nunzio would survey his flock that night in the grand finale. It was a job that provided me with a plausible reason for the tools that hung from the big leather belt encircling my waist as I tracked him for hours amid the throngs of revelers.

In the heat of midday I saw him slip unnoticed through the fringes of the crowd that was cheering the costumed trumpeters and head for the rectory. And then furtively slipping inside as if it was he who was the intruder in his own residence.

I waited until the trumpets were loudest, tried the door—*Mikey, I'd watch it here*—and finding it locked, walked quickly around to the side. At the back of the low stucco building I jumped a fence and moved silently across the blotched remnants of a lawn. I tried to open the nearest window but it would not yield.

The music, strident and tuneless, swelled in the heat as I hurried to the next window, which resisted in similar fashion, spitting wood chips like broken teeth where the small crowbar tried to force it with a low grating noise. But it was another noise, a rumbling noise that came from the back of the rectory, that gave the first sign of access. It was a noise that drew me toward it, toward the one open window, its curtains shimmying in little heat-blown gusts.

And just inside, splayed across a big overstuffed reclining chair, was Father Nunzio. Snoring into the heat, his big head slumped sideways at the top of the chair, with his greased and graying hair matted in dusty strands that left a faint sheen on the leatherette covering.

He was less than an arm's length away from me. And the thought occurred to me that I—armed with all those lethal weapons on that tool belt, the hammer, the adjustable wrenches and the crowbar—stood there staring down at a life. A life just like my brother's that could have been ended in a flash.

And hearing Tommy yelling a million things to me all at once.

It was not that I would have killed. Any more than I could have done to Baymer what he did to Tommy.

No, it was simply just knowing, for that one instant, that I had the opportunity. The choice. To avenge Tommy. And that I had turned away from it.

Waiting for the moment when I could do it properly. Slowly. And with infinitely more devastation.

At least that is what I told myself. But what really saved both Father Nunzio and I at that moment was the laughter that had overcome me earlier.

Pity trumps hatred.

Father Nunzio lay sprawled in the heat, making a little bubble of spit between his lips every time he wheezed out another breath.

I watched the little bubbles form and then burst. Over and over again.

The contractor who had hired me played bass guitar in a mountain band with Bob Thicksten, who pretty much ran the whole Caltech operational side of the Palomar observatory.

A month later, at the Thickstens' old bungalow after one of the mountain parties, I was offered a job as a maintenance assistant working mainly on the smaller, 60-inch telescope. I sensed that I got hired partly because of that way the self-taught have of instinctively recognizing one of their own—that Bob understood more about me than we ever talked about. And then after two years of reading astronomy books and immersing myself in the genius of the Druids' grand creation—*West Declination Trunnion, South Polar-Axis Bearing* and all the rest—I was put in charge of running the big telescope.

I was touching the face of God, peering into eternity on a nightly basis.

And realizing that I had forgotten what elation felt like.

Palomar

We are chasing the afterglow.

The gamma ray burst has now gone from a galaxy-shredding blast—all that cosmic hell of a million, trillion suns blazing through all their energy in a few seconds—and has settled into the vastly misnamed afterglow. Which is blasting out a nicely focused jet of gas and destruction that would rip through a huge star as if it was a feather in a blast furnace. Except the feather would stand more of a chance of surviving.

"10^{50} ergs at least," says Carl, peering into the monitors. It's his way of showing excitement even if he's forced to work in optical tonight. The wooden cases of his infrared equipment lie scattered around the dome. Usually he'd be complaining, but the gamma ray burst takes precedence over everything else.

Yannic's pacing the data room, working the phones and email, in contact with an observatory in the Canary Islands and the satellite guys in Europe and watching me nervously, wondering when I'm going to invoke the wrath of the Druids as out there in the dome, on the other side of the data-room doors, the telescope strains onto its side, groaning through the arc seconds, suspended on its side with gravity beckoning ferociously.

"Four hours and climbing," I tell them. Putting them on notice.

"The Ordovician period," says Carl. "That's what we have to worry about. Forget asteroids and that dinky stuff."

For the rest of the night—or at least until I shut us down due to the victory of gravity—we hear about what happened 440 million years ago. When a nearby gamma ray burst—in this case think of *nearby* as being a few trillion, trillion miles away from earth—obliterated whatever life existed on our planet. Thereby ending the Ordovician period. Whatever that was.

"That dinosaur extinction thing was nothing," says Carl, staring into the pixelated image on the screen.

"Would it erase my hard drive?" asks Yannic.

"Hah," says Carl. "Remember that gamma ray burst they thought happened last March? For a few minutes it ionized the earth's upper atmosphere."

Which is like saying we were grazed by the cosmic bullet that could have blown our epochal brains out.

And not for the first time.

I want to talk to her.

She lies there asleep, this time on the couch, not in my bed. A note explains, in the syntax of two languages, that she had chosen the couch instead of my bedroom. Saying she knew I would need the sleep when I got back from the dome at dawn.

In whispers Charger meticulously confirms what is in her note, emerging from the sunporch pleased that he has been protective, useful even, for another night. "Hard to believe that somebody wants to hurt her," he says, and when I don't answer he prods for a response. "Isn't it?"

Hurt her. Like the man nailed to the beams was hurt?

"Yes."

"I didn't sleep all last night," he says. "I kept hearing noises out there in the dark."

"What kind of noises?"

"Just noises. You know. The kind that could be something. Or nothing," he says, tiptoeing toward his old Cadillac.

And then I am left alone with her. Watching her sleep. Wanting to talk to her about—what? About the Ordovician wipeout?

When I wake up, there is noise, a quiet rustling on the other side of the door that swings open when I push at it with my foot.

The afternoon light sifts through the windows as never before. Or at least not since I've lived there.

"When was the last time they were cleaned?" she asks from somewhere beyond the bedroom, where I lie trying to wake up and focus on different parts of the transformation before me. Everything is orderly. Where once last year's Pep Boys calendar covered the stain on the wall, now a colorful old rug is hanging. And there are new curtains that look suspiciously like once, in another life, they might have been a dress with sequins removed from it.

"What happened to my place?"

She deigns to answer only with the dreaded eye roll. The kind that guys figure is some sort of postfeminist code that bookmarks an incident for telling when only other women are present.

"I went to sleep last night in a cabin filled with earth tones—"

"Mold, you mean," she says.

"—and what happened?"

"It's called cleaning."

"I cleaned." Said way more defensively than I intended.

Another eye roll. She shakes her head, her hair falling around her face in a silken cascade that she sweeps aside. "Don't get used to this. It's one time only," she says. And then looks at me and starts to smile. I have never seen that smile before. A wide Mediterranean smile that is like a gift, her mouth widening in a crescent of teasing, of beckoning.

Or maybe that's what I want it to be.

It is the photographs hung on the rough-hewn walls near the fireplace that stop me. Photos of Lightning and Mother.

And of Tommy. *Hey Mikey, getting a little watery, aren't you? I mean she's nice and all, but careful, you know what they do to you in the end, once the chips are down—*

"I found them. In that box in the drawer," she says. "They are important to you. Yes?"

Yes.

The name keeps coming back to me.

Juan Carlos.

"Were you in love with him?" I ask. And immediately want to retract the question.

Those vast wide eyes fix on me, flicker, and then close for a moment. We are in the sunporch, bathed in the warmth of the late-afternoon light.

Her eyes close again. "Yes," she says after the silence has become loud. Then softer and less declarative: "Yes."

Nothing else is said for a long time.

"Most people forget that Che Guevara was a doctor before he was a revolutionary. And that he had asthma," she says. "Very bad asthma. My grandfather knew a little about acupuncture. So he tried it on Che shortly after the *revolución.* And it worked for a while. They became close friends, and when Che was executing men, sending them to their death, choosing who would die and who would live as easily as he chose his cigars, my grandfather and he would sit and talk about how life would be now that everything was settled.

"He was everything a little girl could want for a grandpa. He was warm and funny, and to me in those days, he was the kindest man I knew. It was only years later that I had to confront what was the other side of him. The side I did not want to know about.

"My grandfather was given a psychiatric hospital to run, a huge place out near the Havana airport. Everyone was afraid of him, you could tell by the way they talked to him. He ran a lot of other hospitals too. He had enormous power. As a *comandante de la revolución* he could do almost anything. I came to realize this when I was older.

"He loved classical music. And he had decided that he would have his own symphony orchestra, but since he couldn't get in the way of the *ministro de cultura* who ran the real symphony, he figured out a way to get an orchestra all his own.

"He started having certain promising musicians declared insane. Especially if they'd made sarcastic remarks about the regime or Fidel. He'd have them thrown into Combinado del Este prison for a month or two to make them afraid and then get them transferred to Havana Psychiatric. That was how it started.

"But it was difficult finding enough flutists to declare crazy. Flutists were a big problem.

"My grandfather raised me. More than my mother after my father, who was also a doctor, died when I was eight. He would take me to those concerts at the psychiatric hospital.

"I heard Beethoven performed and loved it until one day when I saw a man from our neighborhood, a Señor Tieles, who was playing trumpet in my grandfather's orchestra. I ran over to him and asked him why I had not seen him on our street lately and I could not understand when he turned away, not wanting to answer me.

"And that was when I met Juan Carlos. His father was Señor Tieles. And it was because of Juan Carlos that I began to understand what my grandfather was doing. I loved my grandfather. But do you know what it was like having to go to hear Beethoven in a psychiatric hospital knowing it was played by captives? For a few old revolutionaries who didn't have much else to do? And any inmate who could be counted on not to hallucinate during the performance?

"I grew to hate it all. When I was old enough I started going to the nightclubs, the Café Cantante, Casa de la Musica, Palacio de la Salsa, anywhere where there was loud salsa and people dancing and no Beethoven. You could go to these clubs that were packed with men from Canada, from England and France and Spain. When Cubans made eight dollars a month these men were like millionaires. That was during the 'special period.' The whole country was out of food.

"My grandfather got very angry with me. He used to yell that I was hanging around with *jinateras*, the girls who would sleep with foreigners for money. I did not. But I didn't blame the *jinateras* for sleeping with strange men. Or going with those men for a meal at El Aljibe or La Cecilia, places that only foreigners could afford. They had to eat. Feed their families.

"Cuba was starving. Except for the tourist hotels and high-up party members. Like my grandfather. Some poor people were getting a blindness, this optical neuritis that comes from malnutrition.

"My grandfather became even more strict with me. He had decided that I would become a doctor. But by then I just wanted to quit school and go far away, maybe to Santiago, but I didn't. And the older I got the more I knew I had to get away from him. One day I announced I was never going to be a doctor like he wanted me to."

Suddenly she is sitting up and looking around. Alert. Almost tense like some creature of the woods. Sensing whatever cannot be seen. But is out there and will bring harm.

"What's wrong?"

"Green," she says.

"What?"

"So green." She is still looking all around. She starts to get up. Then she stops and sits down again.

And then she settles back onto the big overstuffed armchair and lets the sunlight play against her closed eyes. For a very long time she says nothing.

Hey hey Mikey. Not bad, I'm telling you, this one could be int—

There is a story that is told on the mountain. No one knows for sure if it is true. But that's not what is important. Because it is believed in the border towns like Mexicali and Tecate, even over in areas of San Diego. It is about the Colonel. And people in those places swear it is true.

The reports a few years ago were that the Colonel was roving the mountain like a ghost. Looking for the columns of illegals coming up from Mexico, crossing his land, following the coyotes who led them. For most of the winter there had been sightings and tracks in the snow, but no one could ever prove it was him prowling through the night.

In the summer, when the nights were shortest, his white Jeep was often seen parked at the far end of the meadow in the tall grass. And in the morning it would usually still be there. Several times gunfire was heard, and on the mountain the rumors were that the human coyotes were armed and would open fire on anyone who intercepted them on the Colonel's property.

It was said that the Colonel shot a real coyote—the four-legged kind—that had been scavenging his herd. He'd taken the carcass and hung it from the tree in the meadow where long columns of illegals would sometimes march through his property in the dark, Mexicans, Guatemalans, Hondurans and sometimes Chinese or Arabs pouring into the vast sponginess of America, saturating what had already been filled with a torrent composed of trickles.

In the clear nights the dead animal swung from the bough, a contorted threat that the human coyotes read well and guided their columns farther east, threading through meth lab territory until one of those local chemists opened fire on them and the coyotes went back to taking their chances going through the Colonel's land.

That lasted for a month or two until his cattle started turning up dead with slabs of them cut off as if someone had taken a machete to the best meat. Farther up past French Valley, campfires were found and the bones of the missing parts of the Colonel's cattle were scattered among the ashes and the discarded plastic water bottles. One night one of the fires jumped and took out a hillside as the illegals scattered and fled.

The stories on the mountain had it that the Colonel and his two grown sons were waiting for them down by Cottonwood River. They caught several of them, including the coyote, a small wiry man with tattoos across his neck and a .22 pistol in his pocket.

The Colonel and his sons took them all back to the valley where the butchered cow with the missing hind flank lay in a field. With a Bowie knife they slit open the belly of the carcass. Then they fashioned a rope into a noose that was put under the coyote's arms, which were then tied behind his back by another rope. With the Colonel standing guard, his two sons threaded the rope into the steaming carcass and out the rectum. One of them shoved the screaming man into the bloody mess while the other one tugged on the rope until the man's head came out of the dead cow's ass. Then they packed all the guts back into the carcass and crudely seared the incisions shut by burning them with flaming tree branches. After that they waited.

The sun rose against a cloudless sky and by noon the carcass had begun to swell in the heat. The man in the cow had stopped yelling threats and lapsed into grunting as the pressure of the rotting animal encircled him like a tightening vise. By early afternoon he was moaning into the flyblown stench. As the other Mexicans watched in mute fear, the Colonel's sons stood waiting for the sign to cut the man out of the carcass.

In the hottest part of the afternoon the carcass had ballooned into a ball with legs that stuck stiffly out like spikes. The man was babbling when the carcass started to make a strange wheezing sound. Then it suddenly exploded, a shower of bloody innards blasting out through the incisions that could no longer hold the pressure.

The illegals were given a nod by the Colonel, their signal to race to the dazed coyote and pull him out of the raw and festering carcass stew and flee, blood-spattered and hysterical, back to Mexico.

Like I said, no one up here on the mountain knows for sure that this actually happened. But then no one believes it didn't.

And that's what is important.

I see the Colonel standing on the crest of the hill as the smoke of battle clears around him. His men are raising tattered flags all over the place like replications of Iwo Jima as he steps over the vanquished and sees me. "Traitor. Felon on the lam," he yells, rallying the others and pointing at me. "Boy here ran the border. We got another illegal alien on our hands."

It's always the same damn dream.

The one where the Colonel finds out that I'm one of them *and turns on me after driving the hordes of illegal aliens off the mountain. I'm convinced the Colonel can sense illegals like me the way those customs dogs at the border can sniff everything from dope to a piece of contraband cheese. Which in this case is all those of us without the secular blessing of the Immigration bureaucrats: Mexicans, Albanians, Haitians, Cubans, Nigerians, Chinese, Samoans, Zimbabweans, Moldavians. And me—Canadian. Jumping the walls around America, submerging her beneath the torrent of new lives clamoring to be led.*

But the Colonel stands fast on the front lines. Holding the flag and defending the border, stalking the night, taking it back from the gale force of illegals coming up from Mexico. Rewriting history as physics, as the immovable object standing before the unstoppable columns.

And Palomar itself, only an hour from the border, is slowly becoming an island of old America rising up above the valley floor where brazen waves of Spanish fill the orange groves, the shacks and the stores along Highway 76. There's a sense of reclamation about them, like the T-shirt on the guy by the side of the road outside Javier's Taco Shop: We didn't cross the border. The border crossed us.

Think about it: San Francisco. Los Angeles. Las Vegas. Santa Fe. El Paso. Not a Hartford or Greenwich or Rochester in the lot.

Around here it all started years ago with Operation Gatekeeper, the border patrol's attempt to seal the ragged remnants of the international boundary dividing Tijuana and San Diego. It became pretty much a permanent military pincer operation, with border patrol men roaring all over in every kind of vehicle from dune buggies to horses, sprouting night-vision devices and springing checkpoints on the highways all over the area. So the congealed hordes of Mexicans, Guatemalans, Salvadorans and whatever other descendants of conquistadors and their subservient masses that could be spontaneously assembled into a human battering ram had to find a different Yanqui *door to kick in.*

And what they found was the mountainous area north of the border town of Tecate, about thirty miles farther east of Tijuana. Almost directly below Palomar.

Which meant the illegals began sneaking up through the forbidding mountains of the Cleveland National Forest that undulated all the way back to Palomar and beyond that to the San Jacintos and the San Gabriels. Mountains that could turn vengeful with a twist of the winter winds, freezing them into the earth in their T-shirts and cheap sneakers, leaving them as stiff and dead as twigs in winter. And with valleys that burned in the summers, in the deserts of El Centro where bad stream water betrayed the parched mirage of the gelatinous shroud of lights from Los Angeles off in the distance of their minds.

But still they come. The car washes and kitchens and lawns of America await.

And in its own way it is physics. A kind of gravity, the pull of one mass upon another.

I live with this gravity.

Every night in the data room I sit at the console under shelves of leather-bound books with titles like Star Catalog *and* Galaxies *and* Clusters of Galaxies. *Rows of the things. And every one is telling horrendous tales of gravity.*

Objects—which is what astronomers call stars—of greater mass exerting a gravitational pull on weaker objects. Stripping away their elements. Literally pulling the other stars to pieces, sucking their surfaces through space onto themselves, circling them in an orbit that draws the two of them closer in a spinning embrace of doom.

It's always this way—the weaker star being drawn into the stronger, where they're absorbed. Assimilated if you will. At least for a while. Until the stronger star has consumed too much of the weaker, a greedy fat man at the celestial buffet. And then it blows up. It's that simple. These type of stars just ingest too much—the precise magic number of their apocalypse is 1.4 times the mass of our sun—at which point they've gobbled up so much that they come unhinged in a thermonuclear explosion so powerful that it would pretty much test the limits of imagination. At perhaps somewhere around the total incineration of our little solar system.

Every year they figure out some new form of apocalypse that's been going on for eons but we're only just noticing it. They've just decided that stars really can smash into each other—which set someone off figuring out that a star much like our sun could actually take a hit from a smaller, way more dense star called a white dwarf and the results would be something like a trillion-pound armor-plated kid on his tricycle having a head-on collision with a transport truck, leaving the truck in smoldering ruins as he just kept toodling down the road.

It's happening out there. Right now. Somewhere. In seconds, entire suns are left cosmically mangled. And if it happened to our sun? After a few hours we wouldn't be in any shape to care.

The years in the data room watching this kind of thing on a nightly basis has a way of inuring. You sit there watching all this mayhem and after a while philosophy ceases to exist.

It's just one long food chain. Like with those cartoons of the small fish about to be devoured by a bigger fish that is about to devoured by an even bigger fish that is about to... And go all the way up the biggest of the big. Galaxies devouring one another.

Even our own, the Milky Way, is right now ripping apart smaller galaxies like the Sagittarius dwarf, sucking it in from below our galactic plane. With one hundred billion stars and now we're gobbling up more? A fat guy with a straw, sucking and slurping up more of whatever's left in the cup. Only in this case what's left are stars the size of our sun. Bigger even.

And if gluttony's one of the seven deadly sins but it's built right into the cosmic scheme of things, where exactly are we?

I have evolved my own cosmological quest to find one single case of the weaker fending off the stronger.

So far I have not found it.

It all comes down to one terrible, primitive cosmic law: The strong always attack the weak.

There are no pacifists in the cosmos.

Only remnants.

The fog sifts in from the ocean, settling around the mountain as if a kind of packing material has been stuffed into the folds of the lower elevations.

She lies beside me, stirring only slightly when the phone rings. It takes me a moment to register that it is the Colonel. The lack of context leaves me staring into the phone for a moment.

"Something happened," he says.

"Off the mountain." Which is what the people on the mountain call anything below two thousand feet elevation.

"This Charger character, the one that I hire for guard duty, he's a good friend of yours, I presume?"

In the garage big enough to hold five cars and built next to his house at the edge of the sheerest part of the mountain, he waits for me.

No one I know has ever been inside the Colonel's house. It is generally outside the realm of perceived possibility. The Colonel simply does not socialize. He is more often the phantom stalking the mountain, the legend without real corporal substance. And he is feared in the way some people are, those who sow uncertainty in others merely by their presence.

But he is now finding ways to seek contact with me. It is as if there is the uncertainty of a man who was not around for the raising of his sons, now middle-aged, loyal—and distant.

It is the vulnerability of an older man wanting a second chance.

And unable to acknowledge it. And somehow, for whatever I represent, I am that chance. Since the hotel fire, he has been inventing excuses for contact, once pointing out how much younger I am than his sons. And wanting to include me in whatever activities I could reasonably be included in.

"Something happened. Still waiting for the location," he says.

"What happened to Charger?"

"He's okay."

"Was he hurt?"

He cuffs aside my insistence. With a distracted "Uh-uh," inwardly adjusting his armor, calibrating his gruffness. Eye contact is for a later, easier hour. He turns restlessly to the controls of a digital video projector that hums to life. "Got cameras and nightlens stuff stashed all over the valley. Up on trees all over the place. Remote control. Pan and zoom. The works," he says.

"Hit the light switch," he says. As the garage falls further into darkness he fumbles with something near the monitor until an image is projected onto the wall in shades of bleached colors.

It is an image of people walking, illegals unaware that the sanctuary of the fog has been stripped away from them.

"Night and day now," he says. "A sea of Mexicans and god knows what else. Just walking into America. Makes me practically crazy."

He turns to look out the windows. The fog is shading the hills that rise up on either side of the valley. "They're down there. Right in that fog in the middle of the valley," he says. "They just keep coming. Like a goddamn human wave that never ends."

He hits the buttons again and the image changes. There are several women interspersed among the men, bundled against the damp air, leaning into the altitude.

"I mean some of this is okay. Desirable even. Just enough to keep scrambling the combination on the gene codes of the nation. Otherwise viruses come in and pick all the genetic locks. Hell, look at the Incas. Most powerful, cruelest bunch of bastards in all the Americas. But they never got any new blood. No immunity. So smallpox picked the locks and knocked 'em off like flies once they started breathing the same air as what those diseased Spaniards were sneezing into."

Another digital click and then a wide-angle ghosting image of an endless line of humanity. "We're practically into third-century Rome, you know that? Hell, Rome never got conquered. Everyone thinks the problems was the barbarians overran them. The real problem was the damn Romans just stopped being Romans. There were no real Romans left. Even had an emperor, Severus, born somewhere in North Africa.

"And then after him there was Caracalla, this other lame excuse of an emperor, and it was game over. Dumb bastard made practically everybody in the known world a citizen of Rome. Same as what we're doing right now. Twenty years later Rome'd sunk under the weight of all their damn chaos and crime and weakness. Just like us if this keeps going."

He turns to me, losing some of his natural force to uncertainty. "You get this. I know you do."

It is the taillights on the car in front us that tell me I have never really left Penetang.

They are guiding me back into that world, the ones in front of the Colonel's Jeep as we race along the bottom edges of the mountain. The taillights smear the fog-swept morning, leaving smudges on my memory like the strokes of a painter covering previous images that have not yet dried. On a canvas I have painted over again and again.

It is Father Nunzio in the car in front of us.

"It means someone's dead," says the Colonel. "Last rites. Has to be." The Colonel has a way of making possibility into certainty.

All the way down the mountain in his Jeep he had said nothing except that a phone call came in around 6 a.m. From one of the drivers of his water trucks. There was some kind of accident that he needed to look at.

And then there is silence. The permanent fierceness around his eyes is lit by the reflection of the car's headlights thrown back at us from the fog we have just plunged into.

On the winding road in front of us the taillights of the white Pontiac drift through the fog. From behind, Father Nunzio's bulky outline melts across the seat like those drivers who steer with one hand and always look bored behind the wheel.

"Damn fool priest," says the Colonel. "Like a politician. He loves it when the illegals flood in here. Increases his voters."

Around the next bend it's as if the Pontiac is sucked into the centrifugal swirl of lights that whip through the fog as streamers of redness. The lights come from a sheriff's car, parked just off the road. The same forest ranger, the one who wants to be a cop, is there unspooling the yellow plastic *Do Not Cross* tapes that cordon off part of the highway.

We pull in behind Father Nunzio's Pontiac and exchange perfunctory nods. All I can think of is Tommy. And what he would say now.

For some reason I begin counting the years. Seventeen since Penetang. And eight since the Corpus Christi celebration—and the memory of standing over him as he slept.

You had your chance, Mikey. You coulda done it.

Father Nunzio looks even older now, any residual blackness in his hair having settled into a shaggy gray penumbra around the widened jowls. He moves like a lot of heavy men, with the palms of his pudgy hands facing backwards. He carries the vestments and his Bible with the casual carelessness of a plumber holding wrenches.

"I was called for last rites," he says into the fog.

"Are goats Catholic?" says the ranger with a nervous smile. None of us know what he's talking about. He's acting like he wants to please Father Nunzio, who won't even acknowledge him.

And then it hits us, perhaps from a shift in the breeze carrying with it a stench that jolts the breath out of me. It's like something out of a sewer reaching in through your nostrils to grab your innards, yanking them against your throat.

"You get used to it," says the ranger. But he still covers his nose for a moment.

The breeze pries away the fog just enough that we can see the carnage in the steel gray wedge of faint daylight. Everywhere there are dead goats. Or parts of dead goats. As if an explosion went off in an abattoir. The pieces of goat are all over the road and on the rocks and the hillside. And even in the tree above the wreckage of a truck that looks like it had been split open by a bomb.

The deputy, the one who looks like a former leading man, emerges out of the mist nodding acknowledgements and muttering. "Mexican," he says. "Truck filled with live goats. Or at least they used to be." From across the highway there's shouting in two languages. "Damn. This is getting irksome," says the deputy, striding off toward the yelling.

One of the voices is Charger's. When I find him he and a Mexican guy are stumbling in and out of the fog trying to corral a limping goat. The Mexican is hysterical, covered in blood and bursting into screechy fits every time he sees another of his dead goats.

"*Señor! Señor!* It'll be okay," Charger is shouting but the Mexican guy just erupts in more fits of screeching every time he trips over another dead goat. Charger sees me as one of the few live goats lurches toward him. He makes a dive for it and ends up on the ground holding his knee as the goat shoots past him. Which produces another round of yelling from the Mexican.

"That poor guy. He'd had a few drinks at the casino so he decided to have a nap in his truck. Nothing wrong with that, is there?" Charger's already sounding defensive on behalf of the Mexican.

"So what happened to him?"

"He just forgot, that's all."

"Forgot what?"

"To pull all the way off the road. The back of his truck was still on the road. So the transport truck I was following came barreling through the fog and ... Those poor little goats."

"The Mexican looks okay. Except for the blood."

"That's goats' blood. He's in a daze. Wouldn't you be? Lying there asleep when all of a sudden your truck explodes? With twenty of your goats blown up? I had to stop him from trying to find pieces of goat big enough to put back into his truck. There's nothing left of it either."

Over on the highway the Mexican is yelling at the deputy to stop the limping goat. The deputy just watches it teeter past him.

"I was coming up from Rosarito Beach," says Charger. He's

emotional the way he always gets when he thinks harm has been done to the innocent. "Driving real slow through all this fog when some big truck just plows past me doing sixty. Then all of a sudden I hear what sounds like a bomb. Boom! That big transport truck—it never even stopped. I'm tellin' you, Michael—where's the justice in that?"

He's massaging his knee and shaking his head. There's something about the dead goats that I know will bother him for days to come. Charger's like that. There's no point in telling him that the goats were probably on their way to their doom anyway. At some slaughterhouse. Charger doesn't think like that.

He sees Father Nunzio and gets up, hobbling over to him. "I'm tellin' you, Father," he calls out. "It's an omen. I used to know before every game when I'd be driving up to the stadium. If I saw roadkill I knew we were in trouble. Every time I saw it we lost by at least ten points." He looks around at the goat pieces and then up at the vultures and crows circling above us in the dawn light. Black wings against a slate sky.

"Seriously. If there's one thing I know it's roadkill. And this is serious roadkill. I'm tellin' you."

He's working his way through a thought as he looks at the carnage. "Father? Do goats have souls?" he says finally.

Father Nunzio looks vaguely irritated at having to figure out the answer to this one. After a moment he says, "Animal souls," and walks away. Charger mouths the answer as he thinks about it.

"You want to know what all this is?" says the ranger, interrupting. "It's the damn casinos the Indians have built. Boozed-up Mexicans, Indians and white trash just killing each other off on the roads all the time now. Must keep you busy, Father," he says, trying to get something more from Father Nunzio than a glancing glare.

The ranger always gets twitchy around Father Nunzio. The ranger is tall, with a skinny little mustache like an old-time movie villain. He knows Father Nunzio has been mad at him since he started shacking up with the eighteen-year-old Mexican girl who works at the taco stand down in Pauma.

The ranger's probably the only one on the mountain who hasn't figured out that Father Nunzio wouldn't care what he's doing to the eighteen-year-old if he hadn't caused her to stop showing up on Sundays at his mission church at San Antonio de Pala, the one the Spaniards built two hundred years ago to convert whatever Indians they hadn't got around to massacring.

The ranger has been taking the girl to the Estudio Biblical over near Escondido every Sunday for the last month, ever since they started their serious fornication sessions in the back of his van on Saturday nights. He discovered that some heavy-duty holy-roller cleansing of sins, the kind that this Estudio Biblical specializes in, was a necessity. Otherwise the girl started getting into time-wasting questions about right and wrong. Which cut way back on the fornication time in the van.

As far as Father Nunzio is concerned, merely going to the Estudio Biblical is making a pact with the devil.

He keeps a mental scorecard, the way he has all his life. And losing one—even this one Mexican girl—to the godless Pentecostals, those counterfeit, ersatz, imposter Christians, is a defeat that sends him into the dark nights of Chianti and Pepto-Bismol.

Stepping over the goat remnants on the way back to his car, Father Nunzio dismisses the ranger with a volley of staring silence before turning away. Which is when he notices me.

For a moment he loses his tenuous hold on the scene. He is fixed on me, trying to figure out if he knows me. He's pounding jigsaw pieces of memory together with a hammer and nothing fits quite right.

"Do I know you?" says Father Nunzio. He cannot stop looking at me.

"I don't think we've met."

But this does not satisfy him. "Are you sure?"

Am I sure? Tommy's yelling is so loud within me that I can barely hear my own words. "Maybe you toured the observatory?" I say. "I run the 200-inch telescope."

"Father Nunzio," he says, reaching out to shake my hand.

Not Michael, you moron—Michel! Mikey! Hit him with Michel! Let him know who you are! It's payback ti—

"Michael Braden," I say, matching his stare.

What is it with you?

His eyes never leave me. That same fixed stare. But now clouded with accumulated decades, the stare has lost so much of its piercing luminosity that used to terrify us back in Penetang.

And now, unable to collate memories of a skinny, uncertain thirteen-year-old blond-haired boy with this darker-haired man with carpenter's arms and sharp green eyes standing before him, he falters.

"Nice to meet you," he says. Still looking puzzled.

So tell me, it says.

Old letter from Tommy. One of the last ones. From a time when we had both dreamed of California as our escape.

Is it true that there's a Mexican whore in Tijuana who's still pissed 'cause she can't find her missing stocking? Friend of mine from Penetang told me that he'd been sifting through the various bordellos down there and one night after a tad too much tequila he bedded her in ways still being tested for the revised edition of the Kama Sutra. *Persuaded her to take off one of her expensive silk stockings, the kind that hitch up to garter belts in a billion wet dreams. Seems that my friend talked his whore into tying her stocking in knots and sticking it up his ass, to be pulled like a rip cord in case of emergency—the emergency in this case being the exact instant of one world-class orgasm on his part.*

Apparently, if this method of erotic yee-hahs was being road tested in Consumer Reports *it would get one of those cherished little red circles beside it. In other words: rush out and test drive one for yourself. Only problem apparently is that there is one righteously angry whore stalking the street of Tijuana looking for her missing stocking. If you see her don't say that you're from Penetang. Remember: revenge is a dish best served cold. No telling what she'll do with that other stocking.*

By the way, did I tell you about what happened here...

It was vintage Tommy. As I read from the letter I can still see him. Love him. And right now I need to hear his voice coming off those pages. Laughing.

Maybe it is the silence that sends me searching for his voice. Or maybe it is her.

God, Tommy, c'mon, give me a sign.

Oh yeah right, like you need a sign. You got a billboard's worth of hints, clues and general revelations juicing you up worse 'n a Pentecostal on a brothel run.

I am being drawn to her and wanting to be. And like all such mysteries this one has no boundaries of reason, merely the same immutable laws of gravity that weigh attraction and repulsion in endlessly evanescent rituals, bought, sold, bartered and haggled over in the bodegas of the soul.

She does not want to leave.

"You can stay here as long as you want," I say. She nods. "You'll be safe." *Oh shut the fuck up,* Tommy's yelling. *I can't believe we're even related! Do something. Make her laugh. Throw something. Anything, for godsakes.* "I like the curtains," I say. She looks pleased. "But I miss the sequins."

There's an eye roll. And then a faint and fleeting trace of a smile.

It's as if the sun has come out for a second time this morning.

Now listen up very serious here Mikey because you're whistling through the libidinous minefield otherwise known as True Undying Love. You gotta remember the Golden Oldie rule Mikey, which is don't go screwing it all up by getting an infectious case of the dewey-eyed moist ga-gas. That *leads simple souls like you and me to trust, which is where the wheels come off because once you trust it causes no end of seriously diabolical forms of modern torture like long-term marriage counseling—which in a little-known fact is what replaced the medieval rack as a means of making otherwise brave men confess all, you heard it here first. I mean seriously, look at Lightning when he—Mikey?*

Are you listening to me?

They had already cruised past my cabin several times before Dr. Herrera phones, his calmness lying like a shroud across some sense of urgency he tries not to show. "Keep her inside. Away from anyone who might see her," he says.

"Why?"

"Especially a group of men. Young men."

"How do you know this?"

"Just do what I ask," he says and hangs up.

She sees them first. Like prey watching a hunter test the wind.

Cruising past in an old Chevrolet made before they were born that might as well have had *gangbanger* written on the side.

I will not leave her alone. She knows this and smiles faintly, a fleeting smile of the mouth, not the eyes. I phone Charger and finally reach him in Mexicali, telling him to get back here. And bring weapons, I add.

Dr. Herrera has already phoned him, saying pretty much the same thing. Weapons.

Then I look for the pistol the old couple had left in some hiding place under the sink before they became my landlords.

Later, others show up in a more ordinary-looking vehicle, a big Chevy Suburban, ordinary that is except for the side windows all being smoked.

I circle through the woods so they will not know which cabin I came out of.

Then I walk out to the road. The Suburban drives past, stops and backs up. When the window rolls down I am looking into the thousand-yard stare. A shaved head with a massive tattoo cresting above the collar of the T-shirt. And another shaved head behind him with a crescent mustache. Two Mexicans born in America. With more behind the smoked glass in the back seat.

"Hey, homes. *Hey, vaco.*"

When I just look and say nothing, the far rear door opens. Charles Atlas steps out, dark, vacant eyes under a hair net, *a hair net?* Buff. Muscled to a perfect V from the waist up, complete with a sound track from *Mi Unico Camino.* I instantly start living in my own TIVO world, deciding that this should all be happening in some different time zone, anything but mine.

"We lost a friend of ours."

"Yeah?" I say. "Who?"

"Woman," says hair net. "Bitch" echoes faintly from inside the smoked glass followed by laughing, shushing noises.

"A woman?" I ask.

"About maybe twenty-five, maybe thirty. Older woman," he says.

"That old?" I say, not knowing why.

"Yeah. You seen her?"

"Blond?"

"No, man, not fuckin' blond."

"What's her name?" I ask, industriously spewing naiveté.

"Hey man, you live up here?"

"Why?"

"Why? 'Cause I'm asking you, that's why."

"Yeah. I do." I feel the threat rising around me. Like a razor silently slitting my composure from the ground up.

"Where, man? Which fuckin' house you live in?"

"Aren't you guys asking a few too many questions?"

"Fuck this *blanco*," comes a whisper sifting out from the smoked glass. And with it some weird growling sound.

Yeah, say the vacant eyes of this hair net, who, according to the instant bio I have created for him, has without a doubt taken out his share of the less quick, the less lethal who have faced him.

"Excuse me?" I say. Oh right—*Excuse me?* as if phony indignation was going to save the day. As the closest rear door opens on the Suburban, disgorging Jabba the Hutt in human form, a fat shaved-headed kid with a pit bull, some ugly animalistic ball of spring-loaded hate shot from the cannon of its own genetic furies.

Now I can provide reams of historical interpretation on why Canadians do not own or use guns the same way Americans do; why *Peace, Order and Good Government* rings with bugles of latent Canadian decorum whereas its counterpart *Life, Liberty and the pursuit of Happiness* is shot through with Yankee frontier justice that demands plugging the sonsofbitches.

In other words I don't have a rational clue why I whipped out that pistol from under my baggy T-shirt and starting blasting away at all that smoked glass, sent the hair net and the furball cartwheeling for cover as the Suburban fishtailed off into the sunset with that woeful dog yelping behind it.

It was probably one of the dumber things I've ever done. And yet somehow fulfilling. Troublingly so.

Any remotely rational assessment would have presumed Glocks, Uzzis, Berettas and god knows what on their side. Not to mention the experience of using them. And on my side, some nameless pistol, found with its shells in a cupboard where the old man who owns my cabin had stored them.

Circling back through the woods to get to the cabin. Making sure no one could identify which cabin I was returning to. And then waiting to see if the Suburban had left. Or was coming back. Seeing her face through the back window receding into shadows.

Leaving only the reverberating moment of her eyes looming in the mist.

Inside she stands at the far side of the room. Her lips are moving as if she is trying to talk. But no sound comes out. And then: "I was afraid for you."

I put the gun down on the counter. "We're okay." We.

She nods slowly, drawing me in—drawing myself in, her eyes echoing a silence of what is there shining before us.

"The man," she says finally.

"The man?"

"The doctor. Dr. Reyes..."—she is reverting to an earlier state where forming the words is difficult—"...who was with me. When I came here."

"You mean the man who my friend—Charger—saw you with? When he found you?"

She nods. "When I ask what happened to him no one knows. But I think people do know. Someone knows. What happened to him?"

For the moment until intuition takes over I am caught between alternative answers. "He was seen running away. That's all I know," I say, not wanting to tell her the truth. And not knowing exactly why a lie is necessary. Fighting images of what once was human, nailed, faceless and crucified in the flames of the hotel.

She looks at me, through me, as if waiting for some kind of irony.

Something gives way inside her, some fear or fury that sours into uncertainty. "I am not going to run away from here," she says.

I wait. "I need you to know something," she says. "In case anything happens to me."

"Nothing will happen to you."

"You don't know that. I need to tell someone—tell you—why I am here. For me. Just to say it. To have it come out. In case ..." She trails off and sinks into the old overstuffed armchair with the pile of books underneath where one of the legs used to be.

"I only wanted to make up for what was wrong. I was privileged. Safe. In Cuba. Because of my grandfather. With all his power." She stops and looks around. "Can we go outside, please?"

Out behind the cabin, she circles the clearings in the forest, staring into the light and then up at the massive cedars until she finds a place that fills whatever need has woven itself within her. "Here," she says, settling onto the blanket she brought with her.

"Green," she says as she has before. She lies back and closes her eyes

"It's green here. In Havana. As a little girl I used to play in the most green—greenest?—place in all the world. That's what we told ourselves." Her hands roll up into fists for a moment.

"Are you okay?"

"This place is like it. A little. Maybe more than a little." Filigreed silhouettes of the leaves flick across her face in sharp shadows that sometimes part, showing her eyes still closed tightly as she talks.

"It was called the Bosque de la Habana. Our house looked down over it and the Almendares River. I remember our house and the gray stone wall on the edge of the hill. And down below was a house for the boats?—a place where they repaired small boats. Everything was green. More green than anywhere else I have ever been in my whole life. Magic. Like a little jungle. It was my place of fantasies. My place of dreams. I loved it.

"Until one day down there playing our fantasy games we watched a man running through the trees and underbrush. There was yelling behind him. He was dirty and ragged like he was a prisoner. Which he must have been. He had terror in his eyes and he ran straight toward us not knowing we were there playing our children's games. He saw us as he was running and in one terrible instant he waved us away, shouting at us to get away. He was saving us from what was to come. But we didn't know. We were only eight, maybe nine years old.

"There were soldiers chasing him.

"He waved us back into the trees in that beautiful place, that place of our childhood fantasies. And then he ran in a different direction, into the open so that when the soldiers fired they would not hit us. We saw him hit. Die. And bleed into the grass.

"My childhood ended at that moment. I wanted to run out and make him better. But I was too terrified. I could not. No one can know what that feeling is like, that kind of anger at yourself for doing nothing and just letting something terrible happen—

"But I could not stop it. Could I? I wanted to go out there and stop his bleeding. But what could I do? At eight years old?

"But I have spent my whole life telling myself that I could have stopped it. Should have stopped it. Somehow it became my fault. That will not make sense to you."

It does, oh yes it does.

"And that night when I was crying and my grandfather wanted to know why, I told him. I was shocked and terrified by his reaction. He was pleased that the man had been shot. And died. My grandfather even knew the man's name. An enemy of the revolution, he said. A man whose family had once owned three houses. And who had been organizing *bolseros* to get out of the country.

"And when I started yelling at him he put me over his knee and hit me. On my back parts. It was the moment I first feared, or maybe hated him.

"And many years later as a student at the medical school in Havana, I realized why I was there. Not because my grandfather wanted me—ordered me—to be there. But because of that man. The one I should have saved."

The one I should have saved.

"When I was watching my first operation and wanting to run in horror from all the blood, it was the image of that man that kept me there, telling myself I had to be brave. It was only then that I knew why I was becoming a doctor. For the sake of that man who died. While I watched."

Her eyes open. She is staring straight up into the clearest sky imaginable.

The exhaustion of the previous nights is regrouping and rushing over me in waves now. Pulling me under as her words have grown more distant. And my own words echo in my head.

"Tell me who that man was. The one you were with on the night Charger found the two of you in that storm."

"He is *el Diablo*—the devil?—in the body of a human," she says. "I don't want to talk about him any more."

El Diablo nailed to a cross.

At the height of the Vietnam War, American Secretary of State Henry Kissinger uttered what may remain his legacy: "Power is the ultimate aphrodisiac." Henry, you're wrong. Not power—danger. Danger is the aphrodisiac. Up to a point at least.

It slips the surly bonds of propriety, shredding social niceties, hurtling right into the roiling silk 'n' musk of lubricated body parts conjoined in steaming tangles. Firing lightning into whatever overheated psyches are suddenly centrifugally attached to those parts. Local legend has it that women get a heightened state of eroticism not from the danger itself but from the men who personify it, who handle it, who tame it. Who are it. And it is this heightened state that gives the spark.

This, I now tell myself, I know for sure.

It is a dream or maybe not. I cannot tell at first, the way this other Suburban sifts through the shimmering remnants of consciousness, past trailing fumes of danger and excitement on the road way out there. Far, far away in some other life. But I am climbing up through layers of exhaustion, trying to awake from the sleep that has overwhelmed me … *and I see her—Annie—sitting with Grandma. I reach out, to let her know that it's okay, she will be saving others. Helping. Annie the doctor will be helping. As she had wanted to do so much when she was young.*

But it is someone else who I am trying to make understand. About Annie. Mother. But my words glue together like a low horn running out of power.

It is the sound of a name being called out.

Elena Garcia Molina.

"You were saying my name," she says, looking down from the edge of the bed. Reading. Or maybe watching over me. As I sit up I brush her hand. Then neither of us moves. For what seems like the length of another dream there is only stillness.

Until I kiss her. A soft, gentle kiss that is met first with a flash of stunned incomprehension, her eyes searching me quickly for some clue, some translation of what I have just done.

And then with a fierceness that comes from somewhere beyond what is her, some tumbling headlong collision of souls given form in flesh, she presses up against me. Our lips against each other. Tumbling into the falling, the soaring, across the back of a couch. With hands probing and tearing. As somewhere the sound of cloth ripping may be heard in a different faraway life of other moments.

Falling across the back of that couch, pressing against all that is naked in me as we spin down, my lips brushing that white strap straining across her shoulder. Until I reach behind her and, released, it yields and drifts through the air like a falling dove in all its whiteness, her breasts spilling out above me as some distant calliope blasts anthems of breathing.

Spinning, floating, we reach the floor. Her hands and mine guided by the force of the fevered orchestration, lunging into that floor until

I am above her circling fears flung from her eyes. As she reaches down and draws me into her.

Crying out something in Spanish that careens in echoes. In the maelstrom of the moment I lean up toward her. Into her. As she tries to push me back down pounding with her thighs wrapped around mine. Flailing tears that somehow lash as she sinks her mouth onto me. My arms pinning hers. And then hers mine. We crash onto another part of the floor. It stings with a coldness. And then out into a blinding daylight. That for one instant hurls consciousness at us. In a gasping finality …

We hurtle into the only instant of eternity we ever glimpse, that one moment where past and future never exist. And the flash of a present goes on forever.

And then there is only the sound of our breathing like waves on some far-off shore. Lying there. On the earth beside the front porch. With the leaves and dirt clinging to our nakedness. The sky above us slowly rights itself and steadies. She rises up, reaching out to take my hand.

Her mouth forms and re-forms words without sound. Until finally she says simply, "Yes."

"Yes?"

She nods, looking down at me, and I'm sure she's laughing as she says it.

Until I feel tears running across my cheeks as if they were my own.

I dunno Mikey this is getting out of control for godsakes get a grip I mean doing glandular calisthenics is fine but getting damp around the extremities is just too much for a card-carrying innocent like yours truly to fathom so watch out for this one because—

We're back to gravity.

Charger shows up a few minutes later. He looks around at the wrecked furniture, at the carpet piled into the corner and the plate rack lying on the floor with the smithereened remnants of its nice little old lady plates scattered all over.

"Somebody break in?"

"Sort of," I tell him.

He stands there filling the doorway as usual, his haystack of hair in silhouette and ingesting confusion with a dignity for which I treasure him. "Huh" is the sum total of his analysis.

"Know what Marilyn said?" he inquires.

"What?"

"She said, 'Sooner or later gravity gets us all.' I just heard that. Just like your guys in the dome—she was into this gravity business too."

And she was, bless her. Marilyn Monroe—astronomer. Exploring gravity with the same intensity as the Druids and the worthies and the High Priests who would never hand out PhDs for her personal treatise on falling breasts and sagging faces. But to hell with them, what do they know that Marilyn doesn't?

Elena comes out of the bedroom. She nods to Charger with a faint smile. "Hello," she says softly, the sound of her voice sending his eyebrows arching. And then mirrored by that big dopey smile he sometimes gets.

Yes—sooner or later gravity gets us all. As it has gotten me, exerting the unseen attraction that hurtles one object into another.

And somewhere out there, out in the eons and megaparsecs beyond the curvature of time, beyond that convolution of physics where time swings backward on itself, is the ultimate gravity that Marilyn might just comprehend in her own way. For this is where our telescopes and satellites have no choice but to merge faith and science—say where a pebble dropped from waist-high would be sucked toward the ground at five million miles an hour, the ground in this case being the surface of a neutron star, those weird tiny stars made out of stuff that weighs billions of tons per teaspoon.

Enduring their final, excruciating struggle with gravity.

And for some of them the struggle is indeed terrible. The pitiless forces are at work. With death throes shrieking of cosmic agonies, they labor to withstand gravity, that crushing pressure of their own neutrons, once the proudest, fieriest stars of them all *Marilyn!* imploding in on themselves because of gravity that gets us all until they become black holes. Where not even light can break through the event horizon encircling them—the point of no return where gravity allows nothing to escape. Not even other massive stars that are pulled in and devoured in that instant of dismemberment when they vanish past the event horizon.

And on the night she took the pills and became that candle in the wind, Marilyn would in some way have understood this place where faith and reason collide as she crossed an event horizon of her own. Einstein and Marilyn, the two towering figures of relativity, both in intuitive harmony, both understanding the infinite tragedy of what is out there waiting for us at the event horizon.

For that is the place where reason and faith are locked in the struggle that neither can win as the laws of reason break down and faith becomes a desperate necessity.

It is where God resides in those of us afraid to be in the ultimate loneliness.

And I think about this watching Father Nunzio driving back and forth along the road in front of my cabin in his white Pontiac, his bulky form, settled across the seat like it was an armchair and his head rotating slowly as if it was on a spindle.

It is early afternoon. Charger is busy telling Elena about Marilyn in that way he has, like people from very small towns who do not need context for a conversation, presuming that all experience is shared, relevant. Without any explanation Charger is telling her about Freddie lying there right above Marilyn, not sensing the difficulty she has in understanding what he is talking about.

He remains so preoccupied that he doesn't notice Father Nunzio's car cruising past for the third, maybe the fourth time.

I reach the road as the Pontiac comes into view again. He slows to a stop beside me and overflows out the side window as it rolls down.

"I saw your car driving back and forth."

A moment of weighing. "Yes," he says. "Yes." Another moment. "You haven't seen a group of boys up here on the mountain, have you?"

"Boys?"

"Not boys exactly. I still think of them as boys. Or at least Gilberto. His parents came to see me at the mission this morning. They thought for some reason he might be up here on the mountain."

He waits for some response from me. Which does not come.

"Terrible shame," he says. "The boy got in with the wrong element."

"What kind of element is that?"

"Bad. Just bad," he says avoiding details. "I used to know his parents when I was in San Diego. Years ago. Such a sweet little boy he was."

And Tommy? Would you say the same about him? Sweet little boy.

Squinting through his thick glasses: "You're from the observatory, right?"

"Yeah. We met yesterday."

"Of course, of course." But he is still looking for that part of the puzzle, the piece of his memory that does not quite fit. The piece of a thirteen-year-old boy who kicked in his office door and yelled at him for being a fat liar. He cannot make the connection to the man he sees before him. Yet something echoes.

"What does the boy look like?" I say.

"A little heavy, perhaps. With a shaved head."

"Anything else?"

"He loves his dog."

"His dog?"

"His dog."

"It wouldn't be a pit bull, by any chance?"

"You've seen him then."

"Why are you looking for him?"

"His parents. They are good people. They asked me to help." As I once asked you to help? "Their son went off in a car last night driven by some gang members from San Diego. Somehow their son is connected."

"What are you going to do if you find them?"

"I will do whatever I can. The boy is a good boy."

I am not aware of Charger standing behind me, still in his own set of concerns. "She really talks okay for someone who couldn't even speak," he says.

Father Nunzio looks confused. "Who couldn't speak?"

"No one," I say, throwing Charger a look.

Something steers him into the path of Elena's gaze that has locked onto him from beyond the doorway. He gets out of the car, never letting his gaze leave her. And murmuring something to her in Spanish. We can make out neither his words nor the fragments of her response.

Elena vanishes inside the cabin. He follows her and then turns back to me, his eyes different than they were a moment ago. "She?" he whispers in disbelief. "*She* is the woman?"

"What woman?"

"The one they are looking for."

He takes my arm and steers me to the side of the cabin. "She is the Cuban, yes?" he whispers again with urgency. I have never heard Father Nunzio sound nervous. It does not fit any of the memories I have of him. "If the gang members the boy was with—the ones from Mexico and San Diego—found her…" His whisper trails off. "The boy's parents are afraid."

"Afraid of what?"

"Of what would happen if they find her. Of what their son will do."

"What will he do?"

"Kill her."

I just stare at him, not quite in command of what I'm being told. And then out to the SUV out on the road, sifting slowly past. It is the same one, but now with all the heavily tinted windows rolled up it looks to me like a black slab, a machine of vengeance seeking out what it has been programmed to hunt.

For an hour, maybe more, we wait. The SUV does not return. From the shadows of the cabin I watch with Father Nunzio. "They seem to have left."

He starts to leave, moving toward his car, which has been sheltered among the cedars. But it is Elena who stops him.

"No," she says.

He looks confused.

"You remember me, don't you?" she says. Her voice is barely audible. It is her eyes that say more.

The confusion drains away from his face. "That was you?" he says quietly, in muted astonishment.

"You left us there. We could have died."

"No. No," he says again. And then again.

Tijuana

"All I knew for sure was this: I knew that Ramon's brother, Antonio, would have me murdered at any minute. Shot in the head the way I saw them shoot a man who displeased them, bellowing blood like a bull being sacrificed. I saw this. Or even worse. When I was being held prisoner in that house, that clinic somewhere near Tijuana, I heard the screams from somewhere below us, somewhere in the basement where the unspeakable happened."

She will not even look at Father Nunzio as she talks.

Looking only at Charger or me, or out the window with a flat gaze that sees somewhere to the coastline of Havana or farther as the sunlight circles her and casts changing shadows during the time it takes for her to say what she wants to.

"It was Antonio who was a ball of human fury, an evil man who loved to watch fear in other people. He was a genius at creating terror. That's what they all said—that no one was more brilliant than Antonio. Or more cruel.

"The guards just called him *El Señor*. The Mexican term for God. Even Dr. Reyes called him *El Señor*.

"Antonio was the one who made it so terrifying there that I felt I was breathing acid. It was fear, the kind I have never known before. Even his own men were terrified of him. They would pretend that the cries from the torture downstairs did not affect them. But it did. I know this. Because I saw their hands shake when they were playing cards and acting macho.

"Antonio was like a ghost. I never once saw him. This was because he had been the first one to have plastic surgery, about a month before I was taken there. I had heard that with his real face Antonio always looked angry. So he told his plastic surgeon he wanted a new face that made him look like someone who was happy. A new face that people would not think could have done all those tortures, those murders.

"No one was allowed to see his new face. There were stories that one of his cholos made a mistake and came into his suite upstairs to clean it while Antonio was in there with no face mask on. The cholo was supposed to have been shot in the head before he could even back out the door.

"Sometimes at night I would hear the whole place fall silent. The guards would stop talking. Even the dogs seemed to stop barking. It was Antonio. *El Señor.* Walking around in the darkness, his head covered over in white cloth. A ghost. He was really some kind of terrible ghost.

"If Antonio was a genius, his brother, Ramon, was just stupid. Behind his back I heard the guards call him Fredo—after the stupid brother in *The Godfather.* And since Antonio had a new face, Ramon decided he needed one too.

"But he wanted to show he could do it on his own. He didn't want the same doctors Antonio used. He thought it would make him look like he was a copyist? copier?"

"Copycat?" says Charger. She nods.

"So that's why I had been kidnapped, taken there to do plastic surgery on Ramon Cabrera. To make him handsome. This ugly little ... pustala? pustule? of humanity had demanded to be made beautiful. We were being told to build a palace from a pile of shit.

"And as long as I stayed as the good luck charm, Ramon's Cuban link to Che, I might survive. Might. But if anything went wrong, if his mood changed or if Antonio grew tired of me being around, I would be killed. And no one, not a soul, would ever know what happened to me. For my mother, my grandfather, my friends, I would have simply vanished off the face of the earth.

"I spent hours alone in my little cell of a room angry at myself for being in this situation. For ever believing Dr. Reyes. Who I had come to despise as much as Ramon. Dr. Reyes thought only about money. He had three houses and a lot of big cars. But always he wanted more. In a way that made all the things money can buy seem not just uninteresting, but repulsive. Dr. Reyes' briefcase was full of advertising for the cars he wanted and the houses in Miami. He talked to me like I should know what they were. These Ferrari. These Bentley cars. All he could think about was how much money he was getting from working for the Cabreras.

"He was an empty shell in gambler's clothes. And now I was dressed the way he liked his women to look—in these shiny clothes. The only clothes I had there. For so many nights my only way of not going insane was to spend hours in my room taking the *lentejuelas*—sequins, yes?—off the clothes he had bought for me.

"I would sit there with little scissors and a needle and thread to repair any tears in the fabric. Every sequin I removed was a little victory. My only victory. The rest of the time I lived with the tension. And with fear.

"Dr. Reyes was like a child who would throw tantrums if everything was not exactly the way he wanted. Every detail. If the lights weren't turned on exactly the way he wanted them he would get angry. His wife had left him. She was afraid for their children. She told him that she would say prayers for him. That's what he told me. Even after I made motions for him not to talk because I knew Antonio and Ramon had microphones everywhere. His mind was going strange. It was like a wire strung too tight.

"One day Ramon said he wanted to see for himself what we would do. So in his own stupid, brutal way he gave us a test.

"He brought one of his mistresses to us and told us what he wanted. She was a little bit fat with small breasts. He wanted her thin with big breasts. We started one morning at seven and kept her on the operating table until almost midnight. I was somewhere between a scrub nurse and the surgical assistant. There was another doctor who did the anesthetics. He was Dr. Reyes' partner, Dr. Navarro, he was young, from Sinaloa, and drove a Mercedes Benz sportscar. He was *el anestesista*, the anesthesiologist? He was always wanting to please Dr. Reyes. He was not what you would call strong. In personality I mean.

"There was just the three of us in the operating room, which was difficult for me because we really needed a circulating nurse who would be non-sterile. As the scrub nurse I had to be sterile. It meant that all day I had to change and make myself sterile several times. But by the end of the day Ramon had a different mistress—not exactly thin, but less fat. And with enormous breasts.

"It was horrible. I slept that night having nightmares that I had become a doctor to harm people. I kept dreaming about the operation. And Beethoven was playing all through my dreams.

"I had already told myself that I would have to escape before we gave Ramon a new face. I could see that they were becoming tired of me. One day, when the guards were busy stacking money, huge piles of it that got put into special boxes and shipped somewhere, I climbed to this little roof, up through some door that I think was built for them to go up and shoot at people who came too close. The door had an alarm system but the wires had never been connected so there was no problem opening it. The place was sloppy that way. Except for the operating room, the house was never properly finished. There was construction things—junk?—all around.

"From the roof I could see that we were on a hill. And all around that hill were other, smaller houses, all in a big jumble at the bottom like no one had planned anything, they had just been dropped there. I began to learn the roads around us. And which small roads went to the bigger roads. And which bigger roads went north.

"North was where America was.

"Then one morning last week, Monday I think, Ramon arrived with no warning and said he wanted his face-lift the next day. And then he held up a picture of Che. 'I want to look like this,' he said.

"I remember Dr. Reyes being nervous, almost terrified. After Ramon left I thought he was going to break down.

"'Che? That little turd wants to be Che? Madness!' he kept saying like he was hysterical or something. 'Madness!' When things upset him he would either become vicious or he'd almost start to cry.

"But it got worse. The next day when Ramon came in for the operation you could smell the alcohol on his breath as he was yelling orders to the three guards. I said to him, '*Voy a prepario para la operacion,*' and he laughed and took another drink of whiskey. It was like he was saying he had prepared himself for the operation in his own way.

"Even Dr. Navarro could smell the liquor, and his hands began to tremble. Alcoholics like Ramon need more anesthetic and this can be dangerous. These anesthetics are like cocktails of painkillers and other drugs. And for someone who is in bad shape like Ramon was, it can be dangerous.

"I don't know what went wrong. I don't think it was the liposuction that did it. Although a fat embolism was what I kept thinking about because both of them, Dr. Reyes and Dr. Navarro, were so nervous. One puncture of a little vein and the fat could get into the bloodstream and kill Ramon. Dr. Reyes' hands were not steady like they usually were. When he made the incision near the groin and put in the cannula to suck out the fat, I watched him shake.

"Dr. Navarro was having difficulty regulating the heart rate because the amount of adrenalin he was giving to constrict the blood vessels was not stopping the bleeding. It was something about him not giving Ramon enough Xylocaine. Xylocaine can weaken the heart but adrenalin speeds it up. Pretty soon they were arguing about how much Xylocaine to use. I'd never seen them argue before.

"The heart monitor was shooting all over. But we got through to the face-lift. And after an hour, maybe two, I knew something was seriously wrong. Dr. Reyes had made the incisions all around the face. Then he would stop and stare down at Ramon lying there unconscious, like he was talking to him, muttering through his surgical mask. Then he did something that horrified us. He was stitching Ramon's face in a way that gave him a big stupid smile. On that horrible scowling face. 'Perfect,' he kept saying.

"Dr. Reyes was having a nervous breakdown.

"Dr. Navarro was almost yelling, 'That's not what Che looks like!' but he was having a terrible time with his own work. The machines were going crazy, the heart monitor was doing something I'd never seen before, and he was sweating and shaking as he kept adjusting the dosages.

"And then suddenly Ramon was dead.

"Just like that. All the machines went flat. Or sounded alarms. It was over. And Dr. Reyes stood up. Everything was still for a moment. Then he started to laugh. Or maybe cry. I couldn't tell which.

"There was no choice at all now. I had to get out of there. Or die. In some terrible way.

"The strange thing was that getting out of there was the easy part. After all these months of wondering how I could escape, I just went out to the kitchen like I did several times during every operation when I got water or juice for Dr. Reyes or Dr. Navarro. The three guards always drank from whiskey or rum bottles that were open on the counter. It was midnight, which was when they always drank a lot. I poured Dormicum into those bottles. And then we waited. I put on the only other clothes I had, a dress with most of the sequins cut off and the shoes. Every minute seemed like forever. But an hour later we just walked out as the guards lay on the floor.

"Except for one moment Dr. Reyes was helpless just like a baby. We were leaving through the guards' room and there were what they called sausages—you know, condoms? stuffed like sausages. With cocaine. We sometimes saw them there, lying around to be given away. Maybe to mistresses or *pequeños narcos*—small-time gangsters. Dr. Reyes grabbed a lot of those cocaine condom sausages as we were leaving. That was the one thing he did.

"Dr. Navarro was so hysterical it was impossible to know what he was saying. He was giving off screeching noises that were supposed to be words. He drove away before I could understand what he was saying. Dr. Reyes was just standing there like he didn't know what to do, where to go. I made him leave his car behind; it was too big, too fancy. Instead we took an old truck that no one would notice. I drove. I knew the roads out to the highway, I had memorized them. And the most important thing of all, I knew from watching the news on San Diego television that the border there was not a good place to go through. Too many of *la migra*?—the border police, yes?

"So we drove east to Tecate. Every time I would ask him how we would get through to America, Dr. Reyes would start crying. So I did the only thing I could think of. I stopped the car and as hard as I could I slapped him in the face. This big spoiled rich baby. He calmed down. He said he had a driver who could arrange for someone to get us through. I made him phone this man.

"An hour later we met the driver and another man, a tall, skinny coyote, a man whose nickname was Chuco—I never knew his real name—on a road outside Tecate.

"Chuco was scary because he laughed a lot but only with his mouth, not with his eyes, you know the kind? And he had a long mustache that hung like string around that mouth that was full of bad teeth. The driver was more like a *pequeño*, a small-time gangster. The first thing I noticed was that this Chuco had a *cuernos de chivos*, you know, the goat horn gun? The AK-47, I think. He kept it in his car.

"It was three in the morning. I did most of the talking. Chuco knew we were desperate when we told him we wanted to be over the border before dawn. He wanted to know what we would pay. The only thing we had were the condoms of cocaine. He started to laugh when he saw them.

"The driver, this *pequeño*, took us up to a place very near the border. He and this Chuco were fighting over the condoms. They both wanted them. Chuco made the *pequeño* stop at a house. When he came out again Chuco was holding a small bottle and a pistol. The bottle was cooking oil. He told the *pequeño* that if we got caught by the *migra* while we were crossing the border, we wouldn't get arrested for drug smuggling if the cocaine was inside him. He gave the cooking oil to the *pequeño* and said, 'Start swallowing.' He pointed the pistol right at the man's head and made him swallow the condoms while drinking cooking oil so they would slide down his throat. Chuco threatened to kill the *pequeño* if he didn't do it.

"Chuco had a cell phone. He was talking in code to someone on the American side about where *la migra* were patrolling. When it was clear, we crossed over.

"We just walked into America. A truck met us about a mile inside the border and we were put in the back. I saw America for the first time through the back of this truck that was carrying flowers. There were bits of flowers everywhere. I didn't know which way it was going. But at dawn we'd been driving for about an hour. Always on small, bumpy roads. Soon all around us were flowers, it was like we were in a flower farm, and off in the distance was the mountain, this mountain we are on now. We stopped at some cabins a long way off a highway. Just wood cabins. With no water, no bathroom and one window covered by a rag. There were about ten other cabins with people in them, all Mexican illegals from what I could tell. They were workers in this place, this flower farm.

"Chuco knew a lot of people there. It was obvious that this was a place he used for smuggling people. He told us we would stay there until it was late afternoon. Then we would walk across the mountain and wait beside the highway going to a place called Temecula. Someone in another truck would meet us and then take us to Los Angeles.

"The cabin smelled terrible and there was nowhere to sleep but on the floor. This made Dr. Reyes almost hysterical because of the filth. But I was too exhausted to care. I passed out listening to him demanding clean sheets.

"When I woke up it was mid-afternoon. There was an argument going on outside between Chuco and some other men, some Indians who wanted money for renting us the cabin for a few hours. And when they saw the way Dr. Reyes and I were dressed they wanted even more money. They knew we were not the usual kind of person being smuggled into America.

"The yelling got worse, with Chuco's long mustache flying all over like string as he got excited. The Indians had guns too and I thought something bad was going to happen, but then Chuco kicked the door to our cabin. He came inside cursing, grabbed the *pequeño* by his shirt and dragged him outside to a pail. Chuco pointed his gun at him and told to pull down his pants and sit on the pail until one of the condoms came out of him.

"'But just one!' he kept yelling. And then he'd yell at the Indians, 'You're just getting one condom.'

"But nobody got anything because the *pequeño* just sat on the pail looking terrified and cried. He stayed sitting on the pail crying for a long time, with Chuco on one side of him and the Indians on the other side, everyone pointing guns and yelling. All waiting for the condom of cocaine to come out of his rear end.

"And all around were these Mexicans who were also illegals, coming and going from the fields where they were picking flowers. Everyone was yelling.

"And that was when I first saw you."

Elena turns around, not stopping until her gaze locks onto Father Nunzio.

"I thought *you* would help us," she says, her words sounding like something falling onto thin metal.

Back in Penetang, whenever Father Nunzio was challenged, he would rally behind that awesome stare he had perfected. The one that terrified all of us, all except Tommy.

And for an instant the old Father Nunzio is here again. With eyes that flash to their target, the source of this challenge. And the wide mouth cinched tight by faded grandeur. Old reflexes limbered by anger, ready, greased and unshackled by the quelling of heresies wherever they may be found.

But he cannot sustain. Like a leaky vessel of absolute certainties, he slowly sits down and stares at the floor.

"Do you believe," he almost whispers, "that I have any real authority over anything that happens there? Over those Indians? We have been here for two hundred years and none of us has converted the Indians. The Franciscans whipped them like dogs for a century before my people got to them. They even had a post in the mission they tied them to. And what good did it do? None! And now they have even found their own exquisitely symmetrical form of torture—they let us think we have converted them. They take the sacraments. They toy with us.

"Now we are the ones at the post."

She is driven by truths simpler than his. "But you just got back into your car and drove away," she says. "Leaving us there."

"No," he says, summoning up the remnants of that anger. Which now seems emptied of its power. "My presence at those flower farms is barely tolerated. I go there every week to minister to those who come across the border. And on that day I exercised the only power I have over those armed men there—I made them lower their guns. And that is the full extent of my power," he says.

Elena remains silent. Charger is about to say something, but he can't think of what to say so he lapses back into his pondering uneasiness.

"Let me tell you something," Father Nunzio says. "The Indians at Rincon have been robbing the Mexican illegals long before I came here. And I can't even stop that. I've already lost most of them anyway, to this new casino of theirs. They're obsessed with greed now—the moneychangers have risen from the dead and taken over the temples again. The only hope is to keep them belonging to a god—to God. That is the only hope."

He turns and walks toward his car. More in humiliation than anger.

As he is about to drive away, he cranes into the windshield as if pulled in after that milky stare. He is staring at me. He rolls the window down.

"Where do I know you from?" he says. "Not from here. From somewhere else."

All I can do is shrug and shake my head. Which is like smothering him in quiet confusion as drives away.

Nuthouse Looney Bin Rubber Room

Tommy, Tommy.

Talking through the Plexiglas screen in that jail. "He told her she'd fry in hell if she didn't have the baby."

My fourteen-year-old sensibilities had no precedent, no buffer to grasp even the edges of what I was being told. "What are you—crazy?" I was talking too loudly. Almost shouting. The guard was looking over at me.

"Father Nunzio." He whispers.

"What about Father Nunzio?"

"He was the one who told her. That she'd fry in hell."

"*What?*"

"She's going to have a baby."

"*What? What baby*? You're full of shit."

"Mikey. I don't know what else to tell you."

"Fuck you, Tommy."

"Listen to me. I'm the man of the family now. But I got my problems in here. So you gotta be the man—"

"Lightning's the man."

"Lightning's dead."

"Yeah! So then how can she be having a baby? They don't just happen, stupid. You gotta screw to have babies."

And Tommy just looked at me through the Plexiglas that might as well have been as thick as an iceberg. "You gotta be strong, Mikey. You gotta be strong for all of us."

I was only allowed to be there for parts of Tommy's trial.

But Mother sat through it all, in the front row of the public section, her stomach bulging through the maternity dress like a beacon. Or maybe like a scarlet letter. She stared straight ahead and never deigned to acknowledge the looks and, once in a while, the stage whispers from the visitors gallery. Oinky's mother had appointed herself the unofficial crime reporter for the town.

The trial went on for nine days but it was probably all over in the first few hours. Of course I didn't know this. But I suspect Mother did. All kinds of things were said about Tommy. Any one of them might have meant simply that he was just this crazy, rambunctious son of a man he worshipped. But there was a Gestalt quality to the evidence, the sum of the parts slowly destroying him. His legal aid lawyer did not even bother contesting the arson charge for the fire that destroyed Grew Boats, the fulcrum of the Crown attorney's case. What sank Tommy were the details: an old bar fight when he was defending Lightning and sent his tormentor to hospital; the *yupokiedoke* cop who testified about Tommy's penchant for digging enormous holes in public roads, thereby, it was added with duly noted solemnity, endangering the public at large.

And the damning remarks from Father Nunzio read to the court by one of the OPP officers and not challenged by Tommy's lawyer.

And finally the draining of the last drops of hope from Tommy's life —the court-appointed psychiatrist sitting up there and recounting Tommy's answer to the question: Do you regret what you have done?

Even at fourteen I knew the only response—*Well of course not, you idiot!* Tommy was not about regret. Pain, maybe. Heartbreak, yes. Loss, always. Ask *those* questions. But regret? Tommy was about exuberance and laughter riding some unicycle of mischief, even outrage, on the fraying wire of propriety. Lurching over the abyss hearing his own wild echoes come yodeling back at him. But regret? Never!

And then the verdict comes in.

Not guilty! By reason of fucking insanity.

I went home. Or at least to the place that had once been home. It was a cool, clear night. I went up behind the empty house to the ground that had not been cleared for months. I sat and stared up at the stars and wanted to be up there, far, far away in some other universe, galaxy or whatever was up there, somewhere a million trillion miles away from where I was because I hated it all.

But right across the harbor, just up the bay to the east, was where Tommy was now. In the most hideous of ironies Tommy, the freest spirit in all the worlds I knew, was confined behind the walls of Oak Ridge, the scary old Victorian compound on the water that we used to bicycle past at double speed, *nuthouse looney bin rubber room* for the criminally insane that they were now trying to palm off as the Mental Health Centre. Would Tommy ever have fun with *that!* Mental health? Is that like saying the Nazis were just politically incorrect?

I sat there all night wondering why the northern lights had not come back, why something so beautiful and mysterious should be granted to us so seldom. I sat and wondered about beauty and why you can almost never see it when it is there.

And by the way I thought, Fuck you, Father Nunzio.

In the morning I walked through the shell of a house that had once rung with voices and now was silent. In every room I saw Mother and Lightning and Tommy. And simultaneously I saw emptiness.

In sequence I sat in each of the rooms, like a gambler playing a hunch that this would be the lucky room, this would be the one that would bring them back and make it all normal again. I could not have remotely begun to define normal, but whatever it was, I wanted it back. Just for a while.

Finally, in the garage, I seized upon the only chance for permanence as I understood it at that moment. I took Lightning's hand tools—beautiful wooden-handled chisels, planes, miters and levels, the ones that had been passed down through the generations and whose handles were darkened and worn smooth with the toil and the sweat of men long gone. I wrapped them as if they were a newborn. With all the care I possessed, I enveloped them in layers of cloth, swaddled them in protective coatings of grease. And then in a metal trunk, I carried them up to the ground up behind the house.

Cutting through the glass, I dug into the earth in a kind of frenzy. And then gently lowered the trunk into the ground before throwing earth on top of it.

It was a burial of another kind.

Tommy stayed Tommy. For a while. As much as anyone possibly could. While locked in a fearsome place that, except for heavy metal grates over the windows, looked like an ugly suburban high school built on a hill behind the forbidding old Gothic building.

A kind of campus for the criminally insane beside a beautiful bay.

Kesey would have loved it. He'd have volume two: Two Flew Over the Cuckoo's Nest. *Here's the deal: I'm trying hard to get myself declared a sexual wacko. Those guys are the happiest droolers in this place. They have way more fun than the rest of us. Actually some of them look so fucking normal it's causing me to re-evaluate the outside world. In other words check out the next bank manager or accountant you deal with. (In your case you're too young. Make it your next hockey coach or teacher.) Some of these sexual wackos are so normal-looking it's scary. Hardly a drooler in the bunch. However, there are definitely a few of them you don't want to do conversational archaeology with. You dig down below the surface of their normalcy and the (literal) skeletons are all over the place.*

Anyway these happy perverts get to sit in an easy chair staring at amazing porn for hours at a time. The only catch is that they have to be hooked up to wires; they wear some kind of mercury-filled ring around their ying-yangs and are told to jerk off like sex-crazed chimpanzees on an assembly line. While a researcher or therapist or whatever they call him is sitting in the next room, his tongue presumably sticking out between his lips and measuring your hard-on on some graph. All in the name of research. Or maybe therapy. Or maybe just keeping the researchers employed. Anyway a good time is had by all.

Needless to say I've volunteered over and over again. But somehow I never get to sign up for active duty. Guess I'll just have to practice until I'm called to serve my country in its hour of need. In the meantime the bastards have got me making baseballs!! We actually sit and sew Cooper baseballs. Fucking slavery. Wackos unite. I'm being very subversive about it though. I'm winding the thread so loose that even Babe Ruth could never get the damned thing out of the infield.

News flash: You heard it here first. Paranoid schizophrenics have just become the majority here. Psychopaths used to be the majority but we're losing ground. And psychotics? Forget them. They're bringing up the rear, 50 to 1 long shots at best. Oh by the way—we are now "patients." And the guards are now "nurses." Nurse Ratched in this place has a beard, drinks a lot of beer and knows exactly how many months and years before he and the missus retire in Florida.

I WILL get out of here you know. One looney just did it last week. Word is he's going back to politics. Or maybe robbing banks. From in here it's hard to tell the difference.

Your loving etc. etc.

Mother had been fired from the Atwater campaign. There were so many reasons you heard: He had tired of her. She had argued with him. Her expecting a baby was just too weird. Especially when *A Candidate for Our Times* was widely suspected of being the father. Oinky's mother definitely took care of that.

We never knew the real reason why she was fired. Nor did we want to. It just didn't matter any more.

After the trial, I could not stand the fighting and name-calling I had to go through at school. So I stayed home so much that they threatened to throw me out. I didn't care about that either.

One weekday morning I was at home when Mother announced we were going somewhere. She drove with the seat pushed back in the car because of her stomach. Like always, I pretended not to notice, but that was getting difficult because she was very pregnant. It was a mutual suspension of the obvious because she pretended not to notice me pretending not to notice. It made for a lot of silences and talk about things neither of us cared about. But on this morning something was different. She was so nervous that she lost her keys twice before we got out the door.

"Where are we going?" I asked as she was almost backing into the ditch.

"I need you to be good." *Be good* was the code for her trying not to panic. Whenever she was on the verge of losing it we were always instructed to *be good.* And if she did actually succumb to a bout of hysterics it was because we had not been good.

"Are you okay?"

"Why? Don't I look okay?" she said, grabbing the rearview mirror in a stranglehold and hurriedly checking herself in it. I had to yell at her because she almost drove us into an oncoming car. When all the horn honking was done she sat there with her foot on the brake and her eyes closed. "I'm fine," she said quietly.

Gripping the steering wheel like it was a life preserver, she got us around the harbor into Penetang. Crossing Main Street and then somewhere on Church Street we stopped in front of one of the oldest houses on the street, an old brick place built a hundred years ago with a white picket fence around it.

It was the house that the last of mother's aunts lived in, the ones we had seen less and less over the years.

Sitting on a scalloped metal lawn chair by the side of the house was an old woman who was obviously not from our town. It was her hair that told you. All the women I ever saw over the age of fifty ended up with short tight little hair styles—usually dyed faintly blue—that made them look as ridiculously plain as possible. But this woman had long silver-gray hair that flooded down across her shoulders and flowed like a mane when she turned her head.

I had never seen this old woman before. And yet in that one instant I knew exactly who she was.

And I also knew why Mother was terrified of getting out of the car.

"That's Grandma, isn't it?"

She answered with a nod that was barely more than a twitch.

Her mother, my grandmother, sat there blinking into the sun that shone directly onto her face. She had aged in the way only a few people do, so that you can still see the young buried within the old. Whatever had been pretty about her was still there, encrusted by the years. She was slender and inscrutable in the way that someone who has survived what can never be explained to others learns the preciousness of silence.

A tiny, mysterious smile crept onto her deeply lined face. "You must be Michel," she said.

"Mikey," I said, realizing that my mother was hurt that her first words were to me.

"Mikey." She smiled and rubbed my hair. "Honoring the French-Canadian side of the family. That's good." Only then did she look up at Mother. Or maybe at her stomach. I couldn't tell.

"How are you, Annie?"

Annie. It had been so long since I'd heard her called anything but the usual Mom, Ma, Mother, or Lightning's "honey" that I'd almost forgotten she had a name.

"Okay, I guess."

There was no mistaking her look this time, right into Mother's stomach. "I have a feeling we have some catching up to do." And then Grandma shook her head, looking into the ground. "Oh god, Annie..."

They sat in silence, neither looking at the other. My grandma's hand on top of my mother's.

"I had wanted to be a doctor once," my mother said, her voice empty and sad.

"I heard."

"God," said Mother. "I could have helped people."

She started crying. You couldn't hear it but you could see tears that she quickly wiped away. "Go and play, Michel," she said.

Go and play? That was another code, one that adults used for *get lost.* I couldn't believe it—I was the decoy. I'd been used. To get Mother through her heebie-jeebie nerves, and now I was told to go play? Little kids played.

"Michel!"

"Oh he's okay. Aren't you, baby? You can stay," said my grandmother coyly, ruffling my hair again, and in that instant I understood on some barely conscious level that there was a struggle for power, for control, that was going on between mother and daughter. It was an instantly resumed competition begun in the womb, and fueled by guilt and resentment. And I was the weapon of choice, being used by my grandmother who had a lifetime of pleasing men, but never enough. And who now needed to know that the old skills were still somehow intact, even at the expense of her daughter whom she hadn't seen in thirty years.

"I gotta go and play," I said.

I went inside the house, where grandmother's sister, Aunt Celia, was sitting with her cat asleep on her lap and reading a missionary book. She offered a withered cheek to be kissed and said approvingly, "It's best that you stay out of the way."

I listened through the open window. This time I heard the tears. And the story of how Grandmother couldn't care for her—the problems with drugs. And other things. All the different men. The struggle to regain custody. Interrupted by more drugs. And more men.

"I tried, Annie, I tried."

"Did you?" asked Mother, and that set off the anger that flared back and forth. *Are you crazy enough to want to be pulled into the life I was leading?* mixed in with *You never gave me the choice.*

And when it was late afternoon, there was the story of the baby that was due. Steven Atwater's baby. And the question: Why didn't you have an abortion? The priest, Mother says, this Father Nunzio. I needed him to help Tommy.

Him help Tommy?

He said that an abortion would be a sign that we were damned as a family. That we had turned our back on God. So I did not abort. For God and for Tommy. But he damned Tommy anyway with what he said to the police. And then he left for California.

I jumped up and ran outside.

Yelling and crying about that fat prick Father Nunzio if I ever caught him I'd—

Grandmother stopped me. "I was going to have an abortion once," she said serenely.

"What happened?" I asked.

"I had your mother," she said.

Tommy's letters began to get more erratic.

Hey! We had a Code Blue yesterday. Great fun. Truncheons, handcuffs, leg irons, leather restraints. Hah. Good luck to that asshole Dr. Baymer—check that (in case this letter is being censored), this genius, wonderful human being Dr. Baymer—you get the idea.

Hey Mikey, you heard it here first. I've come up with the way the Leafs or the Rangers or the Red Wings or whichever hockey team has the guts to go through with it can win the Stanley Cup: get themselves declared lunatics! Why, you ask? Wellllt—get a load of this: We got our very own nuthouse hockey team. We play in a rink they have in Yard 2. And we actually play outside teams from Barrie and Collingwood and other reputedly sane places. (Ha!) But because we are the psycho-looneys we cannot be let out. So all of our games are home games. The other teams always have to come here to play us. So here's where Yours Truly is going to be named Coach-of-the-Year. It's a well-known fact that every team in the world wins more home games than away games.

So my plan is this: Tell the Toronto Maple Leafs to get themselves declared psychotic and therefore have all their games played under armed guard at home in Maple Leaf Gardens. Presto. Championships every year!

Then I move on to the New York Yankees and get them to stand up and declare they are deviants, schizos, pervs, psychos and all the rest. Yankee Stadium won't have room for all the World Series banners. Of course the ticker-tape parades down Broadway will have to be done in leg irons. But hey—What price glory?

signed

Your genius brother

P.S. After every game the "Nurses" count the hockey sticks and skates about ten times. Because they could be used for weapons by us lunatics. Don't tell anyone but they move their lips while they're counting.

P.P.S.S. Was it my fault the Collingwood player wanted to pick a fight with me right in front of his own goal? Fuck Dr. Baymer.

I read it over and over with a sense of dread I could not ever define.

Mother had the baby, a girl who was later to be diagnosed with autism.

No longer able to withstand the withering silence of Oinky's mother and all the other custodians of moral probity, Mother rented our house to the first people who inquired about it. She went to live with Alice Sanders, and it was more or less understood that it was okay if I went with her. I knew she was not really the same person I had known as my mother. She was just a frightened woman doing her best to smile without being buried under the memories and the guilt that hung over our days like a shroud.

Alice Sanders was the only person mother knew who would never, could never, pass judgment. Alice Sanders—the most popular and beautiful girl in Tay Township back when Mother and Lightning had been in high school—had just got divorced from that fool Calvin Barker. She kept the house over on the concession road because it had been in her family long before she got married, but Calvin got his revenge.

Years earlier, when they were just married, he'd taken Polaroids of her down on her knees giving him a blow job. He took those photos and had them made into posters, which he tacked up on telephone poles in three townships.

Thanks for the Thorazine
I'd rather read a magazine
And as for the Largactil
It's as old as a pterodactyl
And surely not that old Trilafon
You must simply be having me on
But now baby that cool scopolamine
Must mean I'm Baymer's Valentine
As he jams me full of LSD
To see how fucked up I can be.

Shakespeare? Yeats? Dylan Thomas?
Oh pshaw. Okay it's me. Bet you never would have guessed.

Bad, Mikey. It's getting bad. This is like some mental cluster-fuck. Literally. Dr. Baymer has got all these new theories. I'm not kidding, fucking Mengele would have felt right at home. It's fucking Cool Hand Luke *in here with Baymer telling us that mental illness is all a problem of communications ("What we have here is a failure to communicate"). No shit! How can this happen when fucking Chief Broom has already escaped? We get locked into the fucking Sun Room for 80 hours at a time. The Social Therapy Unit he calls it. For 100 days a dozen lunatics locked in together yelling at each other. Like a bunch of monkeys trying to fuck a football. I got sleep deprivation craziness last time. Insects were crawling out of my skin. Then this fucker gives me scopolamine!!! and my throat instantly goes to the size of a fucking pinhole while my heart is beating the shit out of my chest.*

Scopolamine by the way was used by the fucking Gestapo. HOW CAN THIS HAPPEN? Send fucking Ken Kesey quick.

P.S. This letter is being smuggled out in the jock strap of—oh never mind, some details you don't need to know. Air it out though.

The night after he tacked up more posters showing his ex-wife, Alice, on her knees, that fool Calvin Barker went out and spent hours drinking at the Brûle. Then he went over to the house he had once shared with Alice and started the engine of his one remaining old bulldozer that the bank had not yet seized, a Caterpillar D6.

When he got it going he sheared the screened-in porch right off Alice's house.

Normally I would not have known the details of this shearing, but it happened that I was sleeping in the porch until moments before it was obliterated.

And then he stood up on that Cat, screaming at Alice, who was huddled in the doorway with me and Mother. And then that fool Calvin Barker put a shotgun to his head and became a geyser, blowing his head right off the rest of his body.

LSD, man, the goddamn White Rabbit is really in for it now. They jam us full of fucking LSD. I thought people got busted for LSD but oh no—Dr. Hitler and his protégé Dr. Myner (aka Dr. Mengele) pump us full of that shit and all of a sudden the windows are where the doors used to be, Mikey.

I've been in the Capsule—that's what it's called, no windows, eight feet wide by ten feet, the size of your goddamn car—with four other lunatics and when I said fuck you sir, Baymer that asshole sprayed me with Mace, let me burn for a day, and then had his flunky Dr. Myner pump me full of LSD and throw me inside. I'm going crazy, Mikey. I swear I am. Naked in that fucking box, all five of us naked because of his fucking theory that naked people come out with naked thoughts. I yelled at him wanting to know why he was always in a three-piece suit, that diabolical little piece of shit. We're locked in there together, stinking like crotch rot in that steam bath. Lights burning all the time. Eight feet by fucking ten feet. Total. And one of the other loonies wants to talk about why the Mafia has him on a hit list his own mother had given them while another one keeps washing his hands over and over in the tiny sink.

Bad, Mikey. Bad.

I was almost eighteen when we got the call from Oak Ridge saying that it might be an idea if I came down for a visit. Me, not Mother. Tommy had wanted me.

In the past it had not mattered what Tommy wanted. But his last letter, rambling, incoherent and filled with rage, kept saying they can't win, and something about that letter seemed different.

I left school early on a Friday afternoon and bicycled over to what was now officially known as the Mental Health Centre, Penetanguishene, coasting along the treed end of Church Street, through groves of birches and maples that lined the water below. It was as gentle and as beautiful a place to ride as there was in the township. The complex of buildings appeared through the trees, the more benign ones visible first in the beautiful treed setting. Farther into the grounds was the original building, looming above Penetang harbor, the massive cut-stone institution built in the 1860s and now renovated to the social specifications of a less categorical age. But all the softening touches, the lighting and landscaping, could not hide its origins as the Upper Canada Reformatory Prison housing criminals when Queen Victoria ruled the colony.

Bristling with cheeriness inside the brightly lit offices, the building filled with ghosts seeping up through the newly refinished floors and the drywalled corporate design blandness.

Dr. Myner would see me, I was told by a nice older lady dressed all in baby-blue polyester. She quickly bustled back to her post from the waiting area where she had deposited me,

I looked around wondering if I was the only one who felt the ghosts that seemed to be coming out of the walls.

"Are you the brother?" a reedy voice called out of nowhere.

I looked around, wondering if the walls were actually talking to me. "In here," the voice said, ricocheting off the shiny surfaces of the hallway. I walked past several offices, file laden and bright, until I came to one where the curtains were pulled and only the faint light of a small lamp illuminated the dark oriental rugs that covered the floors and the walls.

A rumpled, bearded man sat on the floor in the lotus position, his little pink hands resting, palms up, on his knees.

"Dr. Myner?" I said.

He opened his eyes as if the burdens of the world were pressing down on him. "I spent a month last year at an ashram in India," he said. "You might consider it some day. Utterly purifying."

"Is Tommy okay?"

"Tommy." He said it while ingesting a little belch. He stared at the floor distastefully. "Tommy," he said again, shaking his head. Then he struggled to his feet, put on his shoes and walked out the door. I presumed that was my sign to follow him.

He waddled through the rear door of the old building and headed up the hill toward the two-story high-school-looking building that I knew as the Ridge.

Suddenly he turned to me. "Furniture is very overrated. You know that, don't you?"

"I guess so."

He kept on hurrying up the path, moving from side to side as much as forward. He had one of those bodies where everything seemed to be in centrifugal motion in some vast wheezing expenditure of energy for even the simplest of movements. "I will be taking over next year from Dr. Baymer. So Tommy will be my problem."

I wanted to kick this wheezer right in his big fat ass that was bobbing in front of me. "Oh get off it," I practically barked at him. "Tommy's never been a problem."

He turned, huffing and pushed his glasses back up on his nose as he looked at me like I was some kind of child. "You've obviously never taken LSD, have you? You're a candidate, trust me. It would help you."

Inside the Ridge, I was searched by the guards or nurses or whatever they were, two big men wearing blue shirts and gray pants. Lunch-bucket guys. The opposite of Dr. Myner. You could tell they thought he was some kind of freak just by the way they looked at him. I was given a clip-on laminated badge saying *Visitor* and was escorted through a second heavy steel-barred gate and then downstairs into what looked like a big recreation room with couches and pool tables. Dr. Myner vanished, leaving me there alone. I sat and waited. I opened some of the Reader's Digest Condensed Books that were all there was to read. But I couldn't read. So I sat there and waited some more.

Finally a door opened. A man entered, a man in a blazer with the preoccupied look of being late for something more important than meeting me. Slim, maybe fifty years old, with steel-gray hair that fell flatly on either side of a meticulously straight part on the left side of his head.

"Now then ..."—he quickly glanced down at his notes—"Michel. I'm Dr. Baymer. Let me get right down to the reason why I wanted you here today. Your brother, Thomas—we have been enormously encouraged by the treatment I've put him on. Until recently, that is." He leaned over at a sharper angle and lowered his voice, giving the effect of making us co-conspirators in Thomas's encouraging treatment. "Of course there were a few little rocky patches, but that is to be expected with the kind of symptoms we were dealing with. But in the past, oh maybe month or so, we've seen some rather regressive tendencies. Disturbing even."

"What do you want me to do?"

"Ah. You might be the key to saving your brother."

"Saving?"

"Yes. Saving," he said with that piercing hypnotic look that you just knew he'd discovered would make people look away. "That's the only word for it. You see, we know he values you, that you mean more to him than anyone else. So we're hoping you can convince him not to do what he's doing."

"Me? Convince him? You're the guy who's got him locked up."

He looked like he urgently wanted to rid me of any illusions that it was he who was responsible for locking up poor Thomas, and surely I must realize he was merely carrying out the will of the court... and all that crap. But instead he stayed ever focused: "You can convince him. You will be helping him."

"Convince him to do what?"

The question had been anticipated, and like in any good theatrical production it served as a cue. Dr. Baymer raised his hand in a casual little beckoning motion. At the far end of the long room a guard opened a door.

And in that instant the only safe place within me, my little hidden nook of refuge, the one sanctuary I had, burned to the ground dissolving beneath it. Because whoever—whatever—came through that door, it was no longer Tommy.

"Tommy? What the hell?"

It was Tommy? It was not Tommy.

It was a woman. Sort of a woman.

A crazed, flamboyant drag queen woman that used to be my brother, Tommy, standing there shimmy-hipped and full of grande-dame gestures with that great grinning mouth of his grotesquely lipsticked into a kiss-blowing smile.

"I have found my inner female!" he announced like a diva, throwing his arms straight out, snapping his head down in a devilish grin and flinging his hips back and forth.

"You see what I mean?" said Dr. Baymer with a kind of grim vindication.

"Tommy?" It was all I could say. Words just weren't forming.

"Mikey, Mikey, they dragged you into this, did they?" And then, shaking a nail-polished finger at Dr. Baymer, he cocked his head. "Naughty, naughty," he said, flipping his long hair back with his hand.

Pointing to his lips, he unfurled a smile. "Crayon," he said. "These nasty men won't let a girl have lipstick. Sexists," and then holding out a manicured finger with a colorful nail, "Red paint."

He slunk around the couch like a silent-movie starlet. "Poor Dr. Baymer," Tommy lisped. "This one's out of his control, Mikey." Then he blew a kiss and sashayed over to Dr. Baymer, who sat thin lipped in swallowed fury.

"I need to talk to Tommy—Thomas," I said.

"Thomas! Ooooh, Mikey! So formal! My, my!" trilled Tommy.

"Feel free," said Dr. Baymer with a permission-granted wave.

"I can't talk to him in front of you," I said, feeling both angry and intimidated.

"Well you'll have to." Dr. Baymer's eyes were flashing between me and Tommy.

"My bra's too tight," said Tommy, puckering his lips and looking at his reflection in the window. "Puts a crimp in playing hockey, wouldn't you say? A girl just can't throw a punch like she used to."

"No," I said, trying to make my lips as thin as Dr. Baymer's.

"You have no choice."

"Okay," I said, getting up and walking toward the door.

"Ooooh, a showdown!" fluttered Tommy, clapping his hands. "I do love a showdown. Big brave men. Biceps clenched. Thighs rubbing together. Tumescent members ready for battle—"

"Five minutes," snapped Dr. Baymer as I got to the door. I stopped and went back to the couch. Dr. Baymer stood up and walked out. I sat there watching the closing door and then turned to Tommy.

He remained frozen in that diva pose, batting his eyes. And then he vaulted over the back of the couch across from me and lay across it. "Hey, Mikey. How's things?" he said. Grinning. The same old Tommy grin. "Had you worried, didn't I?"

"What the hell are you doing?"

"Good question." He kept grinning.

"Tommy, c'mon! We got five minutes."

"Mikey, we got a lifetime."

"Oh yeah?"

"Yeah. We've taken over. I'm serious. We—the lunatics—run the world now. We're like the pod people. We look the same, talk the same. But it's us in the government. In the colleges. The media. No kidding. I found this out a month ago when ..." He looked around for dramatic effect. "I became a client. I'm serious. Some guy from the Ministry of Health showed up and announced a new government policy to Baymer and Myner and all the others. We arc now to be called clients. Clients? Like that'll make us any less looney? Like we're buying a new car? Hiring them to torture us? Having them do our tax returns? It's ... what's the word, Mikey? ... C'mon you know the word ... it's *insane!* That's what it is! And that's when I knew! The Ministry of Health is as crazy as these looneys in here. They all are. They've become us! We're ruling the world now."

I was feeling desperate, like he wasn't even seeing what I sensed lay ahead. "Tommy, c'mon! This is serious!"

His eyes narrowed as I'd never seen them narrow. Something in him was so fierce I felt a chill. "Oh you bet it is, Mikey. This is so fucking serious you have no idea."

"Yeah, so why are you dressed as a woman?" I hissed.

"I've already explained it—because they've become us."

"Aw god, Tommy." I was almost starting to cry, I felt so helpless.

He got up and sat in front of me. "Okay, okay, listen up." He talked in a low, calm voice. "I found out that under this new official policy, sex change operations cannot be denied, okay? Human rights and all that stuff. So all you have to do is stand up and say that you've really been a woman all along. And they—the great bureaucratic they—are so terrified of being called sexist or racist or any other *-ist* that they'll let you do it. Pay for it, even! It's government policy, Mikey. Even in here. It's the one thing Baymer can't control."

"You moron," I said, almost yelling at him. "You want to get your dick chopped off?"

"Mikey," he said soothingly. "Think carefully—skill-testing question coming up: This is a lunatic asylum—oops, sorry, mental health center—for *men*."

It started to dawn on me. "Oh Tommy, no—"

"Guys grow old and rot in here. I could be here till I die. Twenty years at least. But *this* is my ticket out of here. See, the government doesn't have one single criminal nuthouse—sorry, mental health center for women. I swear to God, Mikey, there ain't one single lady-type nuthouse in the whole damn province."

"What's that got to do with anything?"

"A loophole, Mikey. The law says that if there's no appropriate place of incarceration they have to let the designated about-to-be-female nutcases, namely, me, go free."

"No!"

"Yes! It's the law. I read all the statutes. If I become a woman they *have* to ship me out. And you know what? I knew I was right when Baymer started losing it. He can't do a fucking thing about it if I become a woman. And for a control freak like him that is the worst thing he can imagine."

"The operation—are you really going to ...?"

"Of course not. I'll mince around. Take a few female hormones. Just enough to grow tits, maybe. Which is when they'll have to transfer me out of here. And then after that I'll improvise."

I took a deep breath and looked somewhere far off into space. "It wasn't supposed to be like this, Tommy."

"Well it is. And what are we gonna do about it, huh?" He gave me a knuckle punch on my arm, the kind that used to drive me crazy when I was little. "'Melica," he said. "How about we take a trip to 'Melica?" I laughed and he laughed too, neither one of us knowing exactly why we were laughing. Except that it was what we used to do when we were little whenever he said that dopey word. And somehow it just felt good.

And then the door opened and Baymer entered.

"Well hello, big boy," said Tommy in his most seductive voice.

Two months later Tommy died from massive trauma to the head caused by repeated blows from a lead pipe wielded by one of the most dangerous sexual psychopaths in Oak Ridge.

The autopsy report entered as evidence indicated that other patients stated that the killer had become sexually excited when he saw Tommy. After overpowering him, the killer had attempted to rape Tommy while he was still alive. The killer, who had been confined to Oak Ridge for murdering three women, was enraged when Tommy showed no fear. According to psychiatric reports on the killer, fear in his victims was what gave him his gratification. Once Tommy was unconscious, the killer attempted to rape him but could not get an erection. So he beat Tommy some more.

There was an official hearing that lasted less than three hours.

There were questions put to Dr. Baymer regarding the advisability of locking Tommy in a confined space with the killer, particularly in light of his "state of gender confusion."

Dr. Baymer, in his testimony, explained that there was no way of predicting the killer's actions.

Three weeks later Dr. Baymer was entering his large log home on Georgian Bay when his nose was blown off by a bullet fired from a high-powered rifle.

And then I ran.

Palomar

I dwell too much on Tommy's smile and why it was extinguished.

When the nights are ending and the dome falls silent in those moments of first light, I sometimes hurl stillborn questions into that silence. I want there to be some old guy with a white beard sitting up there in Orion or Sagittarius or Ursa Major, the kind of God we all thought existed when we were getting hammered by the priests, some old God looking down on what He created. I want Him to exist so I can demand an answer: Why? Why it was allowed. Why Tommy had to die.

Ever since he was murdered, I cannot stop thinking about why He permitted it. Where's this All-Loving stuff?

It is perhaps the real reason that this place, Palomar, was out there waiting for me all those years when I was drifting through America. If there are answers, any answers, to be had out there, then this is where they will be found.

Here.

In the data room. Where we are like code breakers laboring over the intercepts.

Omega.

The end. Our end.

The current news from God is that omega appears to be less than 1.

Or perhaps more accurately that is what we are currently able to translate from whatever He's telling us.

For years I've eaten dinner with the astronomers at the monastery and listened to the omega debate being played out in various guises intermittently over the meatloaf. It is nothing more or less than an inquiry into the end of the universe. The end of life itself.

It has to do with the mass density of the universe, and a whole lot of physics gets churned into midnight talks in the data room, but what it all comes down to is a number. And all you really need to know about that number—omega—is whether it is:

(a) more than 1, or

(b) less than 1.

If (a) is right it means we've got problems. It means that the universe is going to start falling in on itself. And in a trillion trillion years we are going to get so squeezed that Jupiter and Pluto will be coming through the back door. The earth will be squashed like a bug. The Big Bang will be reversing itself and the whole universe will be scrunched into the head of a cosmic pin. Literally.

But the good news—for the moment at least, until the High Priests come up with yet another contradictory conclusion—is that (b) is the winner. In other words, Hurrah! the universe is expanding. And that's not all. This expansion is speeding up all the time.

Of course astronomers are flinging other theories around like some academic food fight. There's been everything from some mysterious parallel universe colliding with ours to cause the Big Bang, to some kind of invisible dark energy that is overpowering even gravity, flinging everything apart.

At least that's the word according to this year's theories. Next year, who knows? But whatever—you'd think it would have all the trappings of really good news. We're not going to get squeezed onto the head of a celestial pin in the Big Crunch!

But it's not such great news after all.

What it really means is that our universe will keep flying apart so that in untold trillions of years, the planets will have been flung away from stars like our sun and everything will be drifting in the black void of space. There will be no galaxies. No stars even. Just subatomic particles in a dark, infinitely cold and empty nothingness.

In other words, there will be no life of any kind. Anywhere in the universe.

And just for an added twist, the High Priests are now pretty sure that ever since the universe was roughly seven billion years old (in other words, about half its lifetime ago) its rate of expansion has actually been speeding up. So we're like an 18-wheeler barreling down a steep grade, headed straight for oblivion with deeply suspect brakes.

So this is the point where I always want to sit down with God and say: Hey, what exactly is it with You? And this morbid sense of humor of Yours? I mean, so You give us consciousness and a rulebook You want us to follow. And what good's it going to do us?

We've just spent a millennium or two trying to change this mess, and now we learn that You're going to turn out the lights on us. Well hardy-har-har.

Forget the snail darter or the peregrine falcon. You turned *us* into the endangered species.

... and tell me again exactly why it was that Tommy had to die? There was no need for it. None. He was the most decent person in my life, the one who looked fate in the eye and laughed at it no matter what hand he was dealt. The one who cared least for himself and most for the others he loved...

All these opiates they've concocted in place of religion, things like grief counseling, serious shopping and big-league sports, are there to ward off these big fat cosmic jokes of His. Breaking our lives down into component parts that can be polished and repackaged in shiny new wrapping until it becomes a facsimile of hope.

Which might just be the best we can hope for.

Or am I missing something? Is God just a joker with a warped sense of humor? Tell me where I'm wrong. I mean, even with what we take for granted—our sun. That nice dependable orange thing that comes up in the morning and gives off those travel-poster sunsets like clockwork every evening.

Well right now our sun is throwing a massive tantrum, blasting out a solar flare that has the planetary guys glued to optical and X-ray telescopes all over the world. They're talking about how it's in the X-20 class, which means that a couple of days ago the sun belched out a billion-megaton ball of fire. Which, to put all that in perspective: those pretty mushroom clouds that vaporized scenic little atolls in the Pacific back in the 1950s had a dinky ten megatons, more or less. So here we've just had the sun firing off a billion of them over a 90,000 mile-wide area—eleven times the diameter of the earth. It's blasting bits of itself out at around five million miles an hour. But great news: because of the angle, it'll miss us—this time.

Or an even better cosmic whoopee cushion: what some of the High Priests are now calling the Big Rip (everything's Big as in Bang or Crunch or Rip). If these guys are right, we get to sit through this spectator sport in about twenty-one billion years and watch every galaxy, star, planet etc. etc. all the way down to molecules and atoms being torn away from one another. In other words, our little earth just drifts away from the solar system and, about half an hour before the Big Rip, it literally falls apart. The whole damn planet. Just turns to ashes in space. Actually less than ashes because at precisely one ten-thousandth of a second (10^{-19} for those who are planning to clock it) every molecule on the planet would disintegrate, *Poof!*

This has to be why God invented comedy.

But is that part of the joke too?

Or is God just making us crazy? By giving us intelligence? Just enough to know another fun scenario: when the sun runs out of hydrogen in a few billion years it will start to swell, the cosmic fat man eating its own planets. It'll get so huge that the earth—us!—will end up fried and inside the sun. It'll be bloating all the way out to Jupiter. But we don't even have to wait around for that thigh-slapper. Because way before that, maybe even a mere half billion years from now, the sun will have gotten so hot that it'll boil off our oceans. And forget sunblock. We'll have been cooked eons ago.

So then who cares about the Big Rip, omega, gamma ray bursts—whatever? It's like sending a polite note to the condemned innocent: *Electric chair or garotte?*

The tribulations of Job is one thing. But this? Urging us to get it right, to shape ourselves into beings of infinite worthiness in His image, and then pulling this?

I mean, in a puny couple of thousand years—a cosmic nanosecond—we've actually come up with the Taj Mahal, Mozart, representative democracy, Goya, Gutenberg, the '67 Leafs and Einstein. Okay, so there's been a few bumps along the way, like the Nazis, Pol Pot, British cooking and urban sprawl. But generally things have been looking up. So imagine what another million or so years might achieve.

But what's the point?

That's what I want to ask Him. When He has given us the wit and the tools to know what's coming, why not just leave us in ignorance?

Instead of playing it for laughs, using us for batting practice? Firing off all these garden-variety asteroids at us. Or the comets in the Oort Cloud that routinely pound us and the moon every few millennia.

Or the Andromeda galaxy. This gorgeously soft blur of light deep in the autumn skies. Is this God's idea of irony?

Because Andromeda is a monster. And our neighbor.

Bigger than our own Milky Way. Us—the two biggest galaxies in our little corner of the universe. And it's barreling along at 300,000 miles an hour, one big blue shift, which is astronomer talk for something hurtling straight toward us. So while the rest of the universe is flying apart with red shifts all over the place we've been conscripted to be cosmic blue shift crash test dummies.

But why? This is what I want to ask Him. Why wreck it all when merely creating life—our kind of human life—is almost impossible in the first place? When only infinitesimal parts of our own galaxy even have the metallicity needed for life to exist? And the rest of the universe is even less hospitable?

In other words, we are precious. Rare. So why create us just to destroy us?

Tommy would get it.

He would seize on the absurdity of it all. It was his genius.

On behalf of Tommy, that is the question I've wanted to have answered ever since I was seventeen years old.

And the answer never comes.

But for me the real joke is that ever since Tommy's death, after all those years of being sheltered in some nihilistic warmth, I am in danger of losing it. Very simply, love and nihilism just don't mix. The former corrodes the latter.

And I am being corroded. Gently. Magically. *Oh god no no don't go and blow it all now, Mikey.*

When I leave the cabin, her hand brushes against mine and the physical echo stays with me all the way to the dome.

The mountain is seething with fears. You can almost convince yourself you feel it, like something that shudders at the touch. And the tinted-window vehicles are all over the mountain.

Twice before I reach the dome I phone the cabin just to make sure everything is okay. Or maybe it's just to hear her voice. The second time, she answers, not Charger, and the teasing in her voice makes me feel foolish for having called.

And hanging up I realize why this sense of low dread is seeping through my thoughts: it is that I am afraid of losing someone.

Again.

Precisely! See now, doing the same lousy thing over and over and expecting a yeehaw result—now that's madness. And trust me, I'm an expert on that topic now. By the way, the next federal election has just been called out there in the World so I thought the least I could do was organize this nuthouse into political parties. I had the psychopaths making speeches on the Liberal platform, the psychotics playing the Conservatives, and various droolers, paranoids and schizos playing the splinter parties. My finest hour, Mikey! The oratory was Churchillian if I do say so myself until the fucking psychopaths pulled a fast one and staged a coup, I should have known they had totalitarian tendencies that would bring in the Nurse Ratcheds, complete with truncheons, leg irons and other paraphernalia of the democratic process.

So now we're back to watching the droolers pounding away in their armchairs choking the chicken with those form-fitting mercury-filled rings around their—oh never mind. It's all just too yucky for words … think pure thoughts, Mikey.

The storm clouds taunt the mountain again. Flicking at its edges, they ebb and surge. Finally, just after sundown, seeming to yield, they settle sullenly for the lower elevations of the mountain.

In the data room we renew the chase for the gamma ray burst, wrestling with the telescope over again on its side at 5 hours, 30 minutes, which is making me nervous. You can almost hear it groaning through all the chatter as everyone's talking on the phones. Carl's on with an astronomer at Caltech up in Pasadena who's co-coordinating everything with the Keck telescope over in Hawaii, and Vikram, the Indian astronomer who's one of the Highest Priests of Caltech, is musing over what has just come out of the laser printer—black smudges on a gray background. He holds it up next to the image on the monitor.

"This is that star. Plus-minus 15 arc seconds."

"You sure it's not a K star?" Yannic asks.

"It's got to be an M star. By definition," says Vikram. He's a small man trailing genius dispensed through a slight Indian accent flavored with droll subversions of irony.

Vikram instantly changes mental gears, the way he often does, and is telling a story about growing up in India as part of the Brahmin caste—about how as a little boy he got in trouble when his very formal aunt came to visit while she was menstruating. Among the Brahmins, women in this condition must be kept away from everyone else.

"Exposure's finished," says Carl.

I listen to this story but I'm only vaguely hearing about how his aunt had to eat her meals away from the rest of the family. And how no one was supposed to touch her, so of course he wanted to do it, but with his six-year-old's semblance of tradition, he tried to touch her only with a small stick. When she shooed him away, he jumped and fell against her. Then he ran around giggling and touching everyone else in the family, which caused a huge uproar. He was scolded and told that the Brahmin way to counteract this sacred outrage was to sprinkle cow's urine all around. So he was swatted on the rear and sent out with a pail—

I'm listening, half listening, not listening, riding the beast but I'm somewhere else.

—to collect cow's urine. But being terrified of cows, Vikram peed in the pail himself and tried to pass it off as being from the cow. And got thrashed because his uncle had seen him.

I should not be here.

Yannic is asking something about the difference in the violence created by two neutron stars colliding compared to a collision of galaxies. Vikram thinks about it for a moment as if he's in some minor trance and then bustles over to the chalkboard and starts scrawling:

GM^2
R

$6.6 \times 10-8 \times (1011 \times 2 \times 1033)^2$
$3 \times 10-7 \times 10$

$= 10-7 + 22 + 66-22$
10^{59}

"Ah," says Yannic. "Of course." And then goes back to the smudges on the monitor. This is what passes for conversation on some nights up here in the data room.

While Vikram is writing all this I'm fixed on the digital windspeed indicators. Something's going on out there. And so I go outside to the catwalk, where I'm leaning into a wild wind coming out of the west.

The clouds are churning again, hovering low like attacking forces. The storm is regrouping.

Back in the warmth of the data room Yannic looks over. "Phone call came through for you on the private line," he says, brushing the curls away from his forehead the way he does when he's concentrating. "Said his name was Charger. I wrote the number down."

The number is my own home phone. When Charger answers my eyes are fixed on the Speed/Instantaneous readout, which is going meteorologically crazy. "You okay?" I say to him.

"Guys with guns," says Charger. He's whispering.

"I see. You want to explain that a little more?" I say, trying not to be too intelligible to Vikram, who is hovering behind me, forming thoughts on some logarithmic plane.

I can hear the confusion coming through the phone in volumes of silence. "Hold on," Charger says. There are muffled voices and then: "Hello?"

"Dr. Herrera?" I say, feeling an onrush of dread.

"Michael," he says in that undulating Spanish accent. "I came back here believing that you would have gotten her off the mountain."

"Hey, Doctor," I say in a seething whisper. "Pretend you're doing brain surgery and someone wants you to evacuate the operating room."

"I don't understand."

"I have a gamma ray burst on my hands. This won't mean a damn thing to you, but consider it brain surgery by astronomers. *I—can't—leave!* And she doesn't want to. Do you understand?"

An angry silence. "Then take precautions," he says.

"What precautions?"

"You haven't seen the news?"

"I'm inside the observatory. I haven't seen anything."

"The revenge has started in Tijuana. It will spread here."

I am trying to act nonchalant as Vikram peers into the digital readouts next to me and then moves on. "The other brother?" I hear myself echoing Dr. Herrera.

"Yes. Antonio. He's got them killing everyone they can find."

"Who is they?" I whisper.

"The *sicarios* have been turned loose."

"The what?"

"Professional killers. They're very different from the street-gang punks he's been sending up here. These are the best killers he has," he says. "The woman, Elena, cannot stay where she is."

Vikram has drifted over to the computer screen. Carl and Yannic are looking at whatever has just been printed.

"Give me half an hour," I whisper. "Then come over here to the dome."

"Why there?"

"It's the safest place on the mountain. The place is a fortress."

"Aren't you working in there?"

"Let me take care of that."

On the console in the data room are two recently installed green buttons. They nestle innocuously above the aluminum pad that moves the telescope. Just two little buttons among a cluster of servomechanisms, controls, dials and gauges. But these are different.

These little buttons are avatars of demise.

They are the newly installed controls for the smaller dome, where the 48-inch telescope is housed farther over on the mountain. Now, instead of the generations of astronomers and night assistants who have worked the countless nights in that little dome, it is empty. Eerie, automated and silent, obeying my commands to open or close when I hit those green buttons.

The dome is turning in the night as the astronomers using it sit in their homes or their offices hundreds, thousands of miles away. Typing requests and instructions into their computers.

The human component is being removed from the domes of the planet. They are becoming mere tools.

And even this, the 200-inch Palomar dome, the most fabled telescope of them all, will turn in silence, unaccompanied by human voices within it. Ever since the astronomers left the freezing heights of their prime focus capsules and descended into the warmth of the data rooms below, the end has been in sight.

The need for any of us to be on the mountain is vanishing.

From their catacombs, I can hear the Druids gnashing.

Within minutes I have peered gravely into the gauges and announced with all the regret I can marshal: "Gotta button it up, guys!"

And then I close the dome.

Carl, Yannic and Vikram cluster in collective hopes and unspoken groans, astronomers staring into these digital readouts and acknowledging the reality of the weather.

Outside, the storm is gathering in surges of wind that churn the trees as if they were waves in search of a shore. The sky has been coated in clouds, sending Vikram, Carl and Yannic off into the night. I wait until they leave and then descend in the tiny, ancient elevator, open the heavy metal door on the thick outer wall. The blackness outside is absolute and not even outlines are visible.

A car approaches.

Elena, Charger and Dr. Herrera walk through the ground floor of the observatory, two stories below the telescope. I lead them up a few metal stairs and into the looming murkiness of the floors below the telescope past windowless rooms that are suspended somewhere in the 1940s, which may be the last time they were used. It is the Druids' domain, a long-unused world of shadows and hallways and old empty offices like some noir movie set where you almost expect Humphrey Bogart to step out of the dark-paneled room.

It is Charger who speaks for the three of them. "Aren't you going to show them the telescope?" he says.

Up on the floor of the dome they emerge from the old elevator and make me aware of familiarity's losses. What I have become used to renders them awestruck. As I always used to be. "I had no idea," says Dr. Herrera, staring up at the immensity of the telescope. It takes me a moment to figure out why he looks so out of place: he is well dressed. As always. I have grown accustomed to jeans, plaid, sagging cotton pants and breast pockets stuffed with pens. No astronomer I know will ever make a fashion magazine.

Charger is looking around, pleased by the solidity of it all. "There's no way these *sicarios* could get in here."

Elena is like a cat dropped into uncertain surroundings, inspecting everything from a distance with tentative steps and her eyes doing all the work. She catches me watching her. "You feel small in here," she says, her voice echoing into the cavernous depths. And then she shudders.

Dr. Herrera takes me aside and whispers, "The Mexicans are full of horrendous stories. Only a few of them are reported on the radio and television in Tijuana. The rest I hear from my patients. Do you have a television?"

In the data room, the small television tuned to a Tijuana station eventually yields lingering images of men lying in the streets, gunned down in what the reporters say is the vengeance of Antonio Cabrera. For the death of his brother, Ramon.

"Antonio," whispers Elena, reaching for me, closing her hand around mine.

She flinches at the televised image of Ramon—more accurately the grotesque remnant of Ramon's corpse shown lying in that coffin. It looks as if a horror film mask has been sewn around the face in a mummified rictus of death, shriveled and leathery, with the mouth stretched back revealing the teeth bared in a frozen snarl.

"Jeeze," says Charger, fixed on the screen. "They show a lot on Mexican TV."

Elena's hand closes around my arm. She is trembling. "I did that," she says, looking away from the television.

"No. It's not your fault."

I can barely hear her whisper, "*It is, it is, it is.*" On the television screen are the assembled relatives, Ramon's mother, his wife and other family members, all redoubtable in their stoicism, which suddenly crumbles when his mother sinks to the floor wailing.

And there is a final horrendous image: at the side of a highway, a geometric tangle of charred limbs improbably affixed to an obliterated body.

The blackened tangle is being shoveled onto a stretcher. Dr. Jose Navarro, the reporter says. Or what is left of him. He had been mutilated by a blowtorch and had all his fingernails pulled out before he was strangled and set on fire. And then stuffed into a filthy oil drum.

Elena gasps, gets up and walks through the double doors, out into the blackness of the dome. I follow.

"Please," she whispers, passing through the shaft of light into the darkness until she is just a faint outline.

When I return to the data room, Dr. Herrera is on the phone looking intense while Charger is telling him how the Colonel and his sons are patrolling the roads. But nothing Charger says is getting through.

"You must have friends who stay up late," I say.

He stares right through me, listening to whoever is talking to him. Dr. Herrera is one of those people who can look at you and nod in all the right places while you're talking, but you know he's not hearing a thing you're saying. I'm always weighing my response to him, and the scales are constantly shifting.

"A news broadcast?" I say when he hangs up. "*That's* what made you drive here all the way from San Diego?"

"No," he says.

In shards of memory and reason I am groping for what still does not quite make sense about him. Or what he says. "Why was it so important that you come rushing up here a few nights ago?" I ask.

In so many ways he signals that he doesn't want to answer the question. It's like his self-control is all of a sudden overridden by some auto-correcting mechanism that shifts his voice, his motions, his gaze to adjust to the turbulence he's just hit. "When we first talked on the phone I knew that it would be a desperate matter to protect her. The Juniors and the Calle Treinte had already been given orders to kill her and the doctor."

"You didn't say anything about that when you came up to see her."

He looks at the floor, shakes his head and then walks away. "I couldn't," he says.

For minutes there is silence. "These Juniors are terrifying. They are the spoiled rich young men who exist in a world of discos, money and blood. Just go to the parties at Caliente and you see them."

"And that's why you didn't say anything?"

"Maybe I did. And you didn't listen."

"I listened."

"There are some things I can't do. Can't say."

"What?"

Again, nothing. He gets up as if he's leaving and then turns, his voice trembling. "Please," he says. Silence. And then: "Please. I have my own problems."

After a while, when the stillness and the blackness have merged, he begins again. "These Juniors, I had some of them brought to me as patients when they were just boys—ten, eleven years old. Even then they could give you nightmares beyond anything Freud ever imagined. It is as if any trace of morality has been bred out of them. They went to school, some years in San Diego and some in Tijuana. They live and kill on both sides as if it was just one big city. There really is no border any more, you know that, don't you?"

"That's what the Colonel keeps telling everyone," Charger says, frowning as he always does when juggling more than one thought. "Huh. Taking revenge on a woman." He thinks some more. "I'll bet your Freud would have some theory on killing a woman." Charger looks over me indignantly. "Linemen know about Freud, you know. Defensive linemen anyway."

"Freud," says Dr. Herrera, as if talking about an old friend who had betrayed him. "I envy those who kept the faith. I used to believe what we were taught, that mass violence in the modern world is because certain individuals don't manage the conflicts in their own psyche."

"Sounds like Antonio. Maybe you still can have your faith."

"That would be comforting. For old times' sake. But unfortunately for Freud, maybe Antonio's just a Tg8."

"We had a play we called TG-8," says Charger. "The tackle and the guard pulled to the right on a fake reverse."

"Tg8 are mice. Genetic freaks bred in a lab, born with an excess of serotonin in their brain. They are aggressive, bad-tempered little killers who will tear apart any other mouse they encounter. And there are people like this, born without an enzyme needed to break down serotonin. In effect they are human Tg8s. Freud was long dead before this was known. It would have destroyed him."

"Denver Broncos must have been full of those Tg8s," says Charger. Then he goes back to thinking about the mice. "Those poor little things," he says. "It's not their fault. Maybe they just have too much of this serotonin. Maybe they're like this Antonio."

"Antonio's on his way here," says Dr. Herrera.

"How do you know that?" Charger asks.

"One of my sources."

Reporters have sources. Cops have sources. Psychiatrists do not.

"He's really trying to kill Elena?" Charger can barely believe what he's hearing. "But why?"

"Maybe it's nothing more than power lust," says Dr. Herrera.

I am suddenly aware that Elena is in the doorway. She has been there for longer than the rest of us know.

"No," she says. "What Antonio is doing now is far more than that."

"What can possibly be more?" asks Dr. Herrera.

It is her hands I watch as she talks. They give her away.

They clench and uncurl, silent indicators of whatever furies or fears are at work. Everything else about Elena is still, serene even, as if she is remembering a picnic.

The acoustics in the dome send her words circling around it, a centrifuge of overlapping sounds. I can hear her from over near the massive yoke of the telescope as clearly as Dr. Herrera and Charger can from a few feet away.

"The *pequeño* could not get any of the condoms out of himself. They kept him sitting on that pail for hours, until someone said the *migras* were setting up a roadblock down on the highway. Then the coyote, this Chuco, panicked and had two men hold the *pequeño* while he poured more cooking oil down his throat and yelled at him to shit the condoms out. It was still no use, so he took some money, hundred-dollar bills, out of his pocket and threw them at the Indians as the money we had to pay for staying there. Then he started kicking the *pequeño*, who was pulling his pants up.

"The Indians made us leave, ordering us to head north toward the mountain. We ran across the highway and then through all the orange trees. We started to go up the side of the mountain when the storm was coming. We kept going up and Chuco had this pistol pointed at the *pequeño* telling him that if he didn't shit out the cocaine he was going to kill him. The *pequeño* was holding his stomach and had *espasmos*, and I thought he was going to die anyway. But Chuco was like a crazy man, shouting that he wanted his cocaine. I kept asking Dr. Reyes to explain to Chuco that the tension was just going to make it worse for the *pequeño* to have a bowel movement. But Dr. Reyes was just like a baby. He was more terrified of getting attacked by … how do you say? *El alacran*? Scorpion, yes? Or *el gato montes*.

"It got very dark. Like a storm was going to happen. We were tired and somewhere up on the mountain. I could see the dome of this place we're in now—Palomar, yes? It scared me, like something from some other world in the middle of nowhere on a mountain. So white. So big.

"We came to a kind of arroyo and then Chuco's cell phone rang. Right there in this place with trees all around. It was someone from San Diego phoning him. I watched his face while he was talking on it, telling them about us. Chuco was suddenly so cold he made me scared. And right then I knew he was going to kill us—when he stopped talking on the phone. His whole face changed.

"He started screaming at us, 'You killed Ramon? And you didn't tell me? And I get you into America? Now they're going to kill me. For helping you! Fuck you!' he kept yelling. He pointed the pistol at me and *yo le dije* and something stopped him. He turned and hit the *pequeño* in the face and then jumped on his stomach, yelling, 'Give me my cocaine. Shit it out! Now!' But the *pequeño* was just crying and moaning, so Chuco shot him somewhere in the stomach. To get the cocaine.

"All of a sudden we saw these soldiers. American soldiers. They were up above us on the hill and they were carrying one of their men like he was sick. They looked surprised to see us. Just like we were. They started yelling at us. But Chuco just pointed the gun at them and started firing. He hit an American. The other Americans opened fire on him and Chuco was almost cut into two pieces.

"Everyone was running all over. It was crazy. I saw Dr. Reyes run away. I followed him. But then I went back and got the *pequeño* and helped him get away. He was leaning on me as we went down through the trees into the valley away from the soldiers, who were waiting for a helicopter to come down. The *pequeño* was shot. At first it didn't seem to be bad. But then he started holding his stomach and *sangrar por la boca*, you know, blood? through his mouth? I tried to help but it was crazy he was so hurt.

"Then I saw Dr. Reyes again. He came back, at first I thought it was to help. But he was yelling and saying that without money we were nothing in America. He pushed me away and took out a small knife, the kind you fold. And he cut the *pequeño* open. A big cut with his knife. To try to get the cocaine.

"I tried to scream. But no sound came out. No sound. No word. Nothing. That was when I lost how to talk. When he cut that poor man.

"Dr. Reyes was acting crazy. He kept saying that I shouldn't worry, that we would share the money from the cocaine. That's the way he thinks. But then he stopped with this look in his eyes, like he was looking at something behind me. He was. It was *el gato* … a mountain lion? Because it smelled the *sangrar*—the blood—which was making it crazy. It jumped onto the poor *pequeño* before Dr. Reyes could even get the cocaine.

"Dr. Reyes ran like a thief. I threw rocks at the lion. But it was crazy too. I hit its head and then it turned to me. I thought I was going to die. I ran. I followed, going where I thought Dr. Reyes had gone. And then you found us." She's looking at Charger. "Thank you. You saved us."

"Oh, you're welcome," Charger says and he smiles. More accurately, he beams.

"But on that first night when Dr. Reyes and I were taken to your home, he would not stay there after you left. He insisted on running out the door. Saying he was going to go to Los Angeles." And then almost as an afterthought: "Do you know if he ever got there?"

Charger looks over at me, uncomfortable in the moment of silence that follows.

"You know something. Don't you," she says. "About Dr. Reyes."

The time for protective lies is over. Finally I say, "He's dead."

"How?"

"Does it matter?"

"In so many ways no, it doesn't matter. I really would like not ever to think about him again. Not after all that he..." Her voice trails off. And then regroups. "But in one important way, yes, it matters."

"What way?"

"When you tell me how he died I'll tell you why it matters."

Charger's welling up with awkwardness. He won't look her in the eyes, as if he's done something wrong. Which leaves her looking at me.

Charger intervenes. "You know, I think maybe we shouldn't talk about it."

"You don't understand. I need to know," she says, reaching out and touching his arm. Charger can't take his eyes off her hand lying gently upon him. "Antonio has methods of pain and death. Refined methods of terror that Ramon in all his brutality could never have thought of.

"Antonio's methods of torture are like another voice to him. How he kills tells how he is thinking. I used to hear him sitting around with his men laughing and telling stories about how his victims died, the ones he tied to anthills in the sun and left to die.

"But then he saw the movie *Gladiator* and he loved the way the emperors sat up there and gave the thumbs up or thumbs down to any slaves who survived the lions. So Antonio had a pit dug beneath the house I was kept in. This was before I was taken there. In the basement. It was like a small round gladiator ring with some seats going up around it. Around the ring he had cages. In some cages were huge dogs that had been starved and beaten all their lives. These dogs were killers. In other cages he kept men, the men who had displeased him or betrayed him and Ramon. When a man had been driven almost mad by fear he would be drenched in pails of meat sauce dumped on him through the top of the cage. The starving dogs would smell the meat sauce and go wild. Then Antonio would signal for the cage door to be opened.

"In the center of the ring was a knife. It was Antonio's idea of being like the emperor in *Gladiator* so that when two of these huge dogs were let loose in the ring it would be the man with a knife against the dogs. Then Antonio and his men would make bets how long it would last. The dogs always won. All except one time.

"One of the Juniors who had gotten older, a man in his thirties was kidnapped from a parking lot in the middle of the day by Antonio's men. He was a man who lived most of the time in San Diego, and Ramon and Antonio knew he was betraying them to the Mexican Anti-Drug Institute. They knew this because the big general of the institute was secretly working for them. So this Junior, they wanted something special for him. Before the dogs, they dumped scorpions into his cage just to make him crazier. Then they had men hold him down and they put the meat sauce only on the area between his legs—down here. Then it was time for the dogs, and they were all watching from the seats, Ramon and Antonio and their nineteen-year-old brother and all their men. They were laughing and drinking.

"The Junior was pushed out of the cage just before they let the dogs out. He grabbed the knife and instead of doing what all the others had done with it he looked up and threw it right at Antonio. He missed, but he hit their brother, the nineteen-year-old boy. Right in the heart. And then the Junior started laughing. Antonio and Ramon were screaming and going crazy. The dogs had just been let out. Antonio took out a gun and shot the dogs dead before they had done any more than rip at the Junior's hands. He wanted to think up the worst death anyone had ever had. Worse than what the dogs could do.

"All this I heard from listening to the guards talking while I was a prisoner in the house. Either to themselves or sometimes on the phone. When new guards came in they would tell the story all over again.

"In those days while we were waiting to do the operation on Ramon, I could hear the screaming coming up from the basement. There was no soundproofing, no concrete that could keep out that terrible sound this Junior made before he died.

"I lay there with the pillow over my head not wanting to hear these sounds that I still hear in my dreams, even now. But one night when I was in the kitchen I saw something. I saw them pouring something for this Junior to drink, something that looked like water but it was not. It was vinegar. To make his thirst even worse. Antonio was the one who had ordered it.

It is Dr. Herrera who speaks. "Yes. The Romans gave Christ vinegar. On the cross."

"Antonio had crosses everywhere," she says. "And you know that Antonio ordered that the others call him by his nickname—El Señor?" she says. "Which sometimes is what they say when they mean God.

"This is why I have to know how Dr. Reyes died."

The silence afterward unnerves Charger. "Dr. Reyes was sort of confined," he says. And then he adds reluctantly, "In a burning building."

"Confined?"

"With nails."

"With nails?" she asks.

"He means we saw him crucified," I say. She is looking at me, into me. Her face as motionless as a painting. "Like on a cross."

"That is all?" she says.

"No."

"They cut him."

"Cut?"

"Mutilated."

"Where? Which part of him?"

"You want us to get that specific?"

"Please."

Neither Charger nor I say anything.

"His face," she says. "It was his face, wasn't it?"

And then the moment it takes for our silence to register as confirmation. "Of course," she says. "It's Antonio's way. He would like that. His own kind of plastic surgery. Having them take the face from the man who made new faces. It would amuse him."

The phone is ringing, the private line known only to a few of the astronomers. It is Yannic, slurring through jukebox music that a priest—*your* priest—is over there at the Lodge wanting to know my last name. And then Vikram comes on the line. "A charming guy, this Father Nunzio of yours," he says. "He thought he'd find you over here. Because of the storm. Wait, he was right here, where did he get to? He said it's urgent—"

More slurring and muffled remarks. Until Vikram comes back on the line and says, "This priest of yours, he claims to have something to tell you."

Rich, Mikey, rich. Lemme understand this ... Torquemada *here has something to tell you. About what? About sending yours truly up the river to the Drooler House? Or—*

Charger wants to come with me. Or even follow in his car, the rifle cradled across his lap. But carefully, patiently, I go through the scenarios with him until he agrees that it is best he stays with Elena. Even though the dome is a fortress all its own, this is where he will be most valuable. Protecting Elena.

Yeah. Uh-huh. Elena. He's working through his own equations, convincing himself. It is the idea of protecting her that tips the scales. So Charger sets himself up near the creaking elevator, content in his role as guardian.

"Half an hour," I tell him. "An hour at most. That's all I'll be gone." He thinks. Then nods.

Still replaying Vikram's words as I'm leaving the dome for the Lodge, I see Elena hurrying after me, reaching out through the perfect darkness that erases the shaft of light when the door behind her slowly closed. Asking me—telling me—not to go. Not out on the roads tonight. And then whispering the same words over and over.

Words and phrases tumbling out in Spanish. And when I ask what they mean she is silent and for a moment she is close to me, my arms around her, whispering what sounds like a chant. Or maybe a prayer.

The old Lodge sits back off a small road, deep among the trees with its wooded, Gothic sense of the unimaginable shining faintly from latticed windows set deep in its massive log walls.

Only a few miles from the dome, it always seemed to me as if it was somewhere else entirely, like maybe on some Transylvanian part of the mountain. I always see a spooky, low-lying mist around the place no matter whether it's there or not. It's just the way your mind rearranges the mental architecture when something like this place whispers to you in a frequency not audible to your normal senses.

And yet we've had some of our best times in its dark, cavernous bar, all wood and stone and yellowing framed photos. On the nights when we get rained out or clouded out, more than one astronomer has been found testing the limits of closing hour at the Lodge. Which is the situation tonight.

When I enter they're all sitting in the gloom of the far corner in front of the big stone fireplace. Under the ever-vigilant elk and deer whose heads are mounted on the walls, Vikram, Carl, Yannic and Father Nunzio are on the overstuffed couches. Father Nunzio is facing away from the entrance and does not see me approach.

The manager, Louie, and the black cook also named Louie are the only other people in the place. Louie the manager has the haunted dark look of a Gypsy who smokes too much and is walking around with a bandage on his head complaining about a bad spider bite on his arm that no one can see. No one bothers to ask why he has a bandage on his head if the bite is on the arm. It's just the way things work at the Lodge.

Vikram is deep into the mysteries of the Star of Bethlehem as seen through the filter of his Hinduism and the suspect cognac he drinks badly and often. "This Star of Bethlehem, it was not some miracle. It had to be a supernova," he says.

But Father Nunzio will have none of it. "It was God's will," he says, fueled by the wine from the cardboard containers stored in a refrigerator.

"You say God, I say Krishna." Vikram is getting up unsteadily. "But as you wish. If you want God, fine, it can be God," he says.

"But it was probably a supernova in Orion. Or maybe Hydra."

"The Wise Men were following a sign from God."

"Statistical probability would lay bets on them following a red supergiant that blew itself to bits."

"Then God chose the supergiant and blew it to bits himself."

"As you wish. But Krishna would have to have chosen iron above all." Vikram's holding up his glass signaling for more suspect cognac.

"Iron?" says Father Nunzio, now belting down Mexican beer. He leans over to one side, like an old freighter listing badly, and I know what's coming. Next to him Yannic is suddenly jolted and looks like he's just had something dead passed under his nose. He stands up quickly, sniffing the air and making a face.

"Iron!" says Vikram. "Your Star of Bethlehem burns through everything, hydrogen, helium, even puny silicon, trying to keep itself from exploding until it gets down to iron. Iron is the last. The most merciless. Iron never yields, never burns. So your God would have given this star the signal to reach iron by the time—"

"*My* God?" says Father Nunzio, who does not notice Yannic lighting matches and fanning the air.

"Michael, show him!" says Vikram, extravagantly waving to me. "Take him into Palomar and show him what his God will do."

Father Nunzio turns, looking surprised that I have been listening to it all. "Ah, Michael! My boy," he says with an uneasy smile. "We have something to discuss."

"Yeah. We do."

And then the smile on his face suddenly withers.

And Carl, Yannic and Vikram are all staring uneasily at something behind me.

I turn, looking into an array of shaved heads. Hair nets. Fu Manchu mustaches. Tattoos. Coming through the door. Clustered at the far end of the room near the entrance. Spring-loaded in jittery, sullen fury and grappling with whatever weapons are in the pockets of their baggy pants.

"Well hello... boys," says Father Nunzio.

He turns back to look at me, and the slight arching of his eyebrows says whatever is needed.

It is Father Nunzio, in his own shambling way, who takes charge the moment the door opens again and Jabba the Hutt, *such a sweet little boy,* pokes his shaved head through the pack with a dead-eyed stare that impales.

He is staring directly at me.

"Ah, Gilberto!" booms Father Nunzio, breaking a deafening silence. "I just talked with your *parents.* I am taking them to meet the *bishop* next week," he says, pounding emphasis into the word. Already he is nudging me toward the door.

The dead-eyed stare falters for an instant. And I realize I am taking refuge behind the thin diameter of the clerical collar he is not wearing. It is the only shield I have.

"Adolpho!" he proclaims into the gale-force blankness of two eyes above a Fu Manchu. "I *christened* Adolpho," he says to the others in the room. Grandly. Pointedly. "His *mother* still comes to me for confession." Father Nunzio's doing a Moses, parting the dead stares, his hand at my back as we walk straight into the assembled menace.

"My friend here is taking me to Palomar," Father Nunzio says, motioning to me as they part. "To show me what *God* can do."

The dead stares flash and ricochet for instants of fevered calculation, weighing the downside of carnage in front of a priest, their priest. Vestigial respect for that clerical collar is overloading the circuits. "Ah. Javier. I remember baptizing *your sister.* Such a sweet girl."

We are outside, walking casually toward his white Pontiac, hearing the seething rustle of receding whispers at our backs.

"This is why I came here. I was afraid of this. I heard these boys were looking for you," he whispers, looking around nervously "Did you really shoot at them?"

"I'll drive," I say, taking the keys from him before he can protest. It is a mistake. The instant I take the keys from him, in their eyes I have somehow removed his control over the situation.

"Hey!" comes the yell from the door of the Lodge and I don't wait to turn around, getting into his car, starting it, reaching over and pulling him inside as the voices behind detonate like a profanity grenade with fragments flying all over.

Before we've even cleared the parking lot I've got the tinted-window Suburban racing after us. By the road it is almost on our rear bumper. I floor it and the Pontiac lurches ahead. The Suburban stays right with us. Its headlights are blinding, like magnesium burning inside my eyes.

"Stop the car," says Father Nunzio. "I'm going to talk to them. I know most of those boys. Since they were infants. I know their parents."

"It's too late for that," I tell him.

"They're really nice boys, you know."

"Those nice boys have been given orders."

I'm driving as if I'm strangling the steering wheel and what I see before me in the darkness of the road is Elena's face. I look around and then I know exactly where I am.

I've never been a great driver, not even on the frozen roads back around Penetang, but right now I have no choice. I yank the steering wheel to the right and fishtail into the brush in a shower of dirt spun out from the back wheels, sandblasting the wildly weaving Suburban that tries to follow. For a moment I lose them, swerving around a tree and stopping right behind a broken-down off-the-grid shack. Big oil drums are lying all around it.

Then I practically lay on the horn.

From the screenless screen door at the side of the shack a desiccated head with wild bug eyes and a stringy mustache flailing all over shoots out behind the barrel of a gun.

Vern!

And this time it's not just some Sunday-afternoon dentist in an ultralite buzzing around overhead until relieved of his airspace by a load of buckshot. No, this is the real thing, a full-blown Waco-type assault by the dark-windowed SUV forces of the Feds out to get any mangy-haired, meth-making, freedom-loving survivalist who—

Vern raises the shotgun and with bug-eyed accuracy and a double-barreled roar he obliterates exactly where we were an instant ago.

And where we were an instant ago is where the Suburban is now. Its windshield explodes.

Over the pounding of my heart I can hear glass and metal getting shredded. And in the rearview mirror I see the SUV careen into a tree. And after more gunfire something back there lights up the night in a fireball.

Which is what meth labs have a habit of doing when hit by volleys of automatic-weapons fire.

"We have to go back," says Father Nunzio when we get to the crossroads. He has remained silent, almost stunned, all the way up to the South Road.

"What was it you wanted to talk about?"

"This is not the time to—"

"It is. What?"

"It was about using the telescope to show His works. But please—"

"*That* was what was so important?"

"It seemed so," he says. "At the time." His voice trails off as if he's trying to figure it out himself.

"You were drinking."

"An aspersion I shall disregard," he says indignantly. "What is your point?"

"Nothing. Obviously."

I don't slow down until long after the sheriff's cars race past us going in the opposite direction. There's no way I'm going to double back into the teeth of what we have just escaped from.

"What you did back there was not right," says Father Nunzio, becoming more agitated.

"Thank you for saving me," I say.

"I want to go back there! Did you hear what I said?"

"I heard you. They're a bunch of killers trying to find Elena."

"Stop. They need my assistance."

My assistance?

I start laughing. *Assistance? Like you assisted Tommy?* I can't help it.

Since when have you ever . . . ? It's as if Tommy's voice is mine. And I'm laughing on his behalf. *Or is it really laughing?* I blurt it out. Almost yelling. "Father?" Utterly without planning or pretense. "I need you to hear my confession." Maybe it comes out because of that image of Tommy. Only Tommy would do something so insane.

Insane? Oh please, Mikey. Cerebrally challenged, por favor.

He looks as if he hasn't quite heard me. "Confession?"

"Yes." We're racing past the intersection in front of Mother's Kitchen, turning onto the Palomar road, the sound of sirens pumping through the stillness from somewhere behind us down on the East Grade.

"Well come and see me at the mission and—"

"No. Here." At 50 to 80 miles per hour—*Mikey, I love it!*—veering all over a mountain road.

"This is not the place."

"I shot a man," I say. I have never spoken those words before. They are as chilling to me, hearing them out in the open, as they seem to be to him.

"You . . ."

"Shot a man." I complete what he does not. "In the nose. I blew his nose off."

"I don't understand."

"He was a psychiatrist. In Penetang."

The compartments of his life have been precariously stacked and I have just pulled one out from the bottom. He leans forward, urgently peering through me like he's putting together all the fragments of a cluttered puzzle that has suddenly spilled out from that compartment. His head is shaking back and forth and for a moment no sound emerges even though his mouth is moving like something hinged has broken.

"*Penetang?*" The word explodes. "Oh God no." For a moment I think he's about to open the door and leap from the car.

"I had nothing to do with what happened to your brother!"

He is almost bellowing as he says it.

A few thousand feet below the dome, Father Nunzio's rectory stretches into the encroaching darkness of the Indian reservation, joined to the mission by low plaster walls built by Indian slaves back when Spain ruled much of the discovered world. A few desultory lights fray the darkened stillness, broken only by a three-legged dog that limps and howls in sequence on the tattered asphalt road.

Under a swaying and naked lightbulb scattering the night in patches, I stop the car in front of the rectory

—and see Antonio. Everywhere. In every shadow, in every headlight that flashes past ripping away the night, blue shifting the fears that hurtle in, unstoppable. And in the lumbering motions of this old priest, who talks of telescopes and God with urgency as if he alone had made the connection. Is he Antonio? With this new face? Whose face am I looking for? Mine? Whose face? Yours? The description of the Wanted is presently infinite.

Father Nunzio has barely paused in a jumbled torrent of indignation and uncertainty for the last two thousand feet of the descent. Which I meet with a wall of silence, constructed years ago by Tommy. Brick by brick.

"I keep records, you know," he says. Almost pleading. "For years. In my trunk. You *will* see the trunk."

"Fuck you and your trunk."

"It's important!" Tugging at my sleeve. "You need to know!"

"I've known since I was thirteen. When you destroyed my brother."

"No! The truth. I did not destroy your brother." He turns on the interior light. "I tried to help him. But he was not suitable!"

"Why are you yelling?"

"Are you listening to me? He was not suitable!"

"What are you talking about? *Suitable?*" I say. "Suitable for *what?*"

"For what he wanted to be."

"What do you know about what he wanted to be?"

"I know!" Father Nunzio is almost hissing now. "He wanted to be a priest."

I laugh. It is the only possible response.

"No!" he says. "It was the only thing that could save him from all that!"

"Save him? From what?"

"From what he feared most about himself," he beseeches, searching my face for signs that I understand what he is saying.

"Tommy wasn't afraid of anything."

"Oh yes," he says. "Oh yes he was."

"Of what?"

"The fires," says Father Nunzio. And then realizing I don't understand: "*His* fires."

Father Nunzio fumbles with his keys in the heavy wooden door. He pushes quickly past the tiny office and into his living area with its heavy wooden beams and piles of twigs stacked against the side of the fireplace. From a corner, a television fecklessly flings images of a European soccer match into the gloom. The faint odor of cigar smoke hangs in the air like a clue. Father Nunzio lumbers over to a steamer chest. He heaves it open and pulls out the recorded sum of his life—documents, letters and clippings that spill around him in some unspeakably sad cascade of paper.

"I actually withheld information from the authorities—information harmful to your brother that the police were hoping to find when they came to see me. I prayed for guidance, I did." He turns to me with a stricken look, magnified through his thick glasses.

He holds up a weathered file folder and shakes it in front of me. “You’re going to look at this!” he almost screeches as the old letters tumble out.

Dear Father Nunzio, please believe me, setting fire to the tool shed behind the Shrine wasn’t exactly my fault, not totally at least and oh god, Tommy *Dear Father Nunzio, You have to let me become a priest. Otherwise I am afraid of what is inside me* because of all those fires up where the glass comes out of the ground? When Lightning and Mother and you and me were sitting around in as perfect a family as we ever got to be. They were just cute little bonfires, weren’t they? The same with the Robillards’ old car? And… Tommy, no, no *Dear Father Nunzio, I had nothing to do with that fire that burned through the Ukrainian Shrine. Actually, okay so I thought that maybe lighting a few extra candles up there would look good, it’s not like I have anything against Ukrainians, it’s just that the fire looked so pretty, which is the thing—people don’t really see them for the pretty things they are. I mean fires can be pretty if you stop to really look at them* Tommy, Tommy, I love you.

Tommy, Tommy. Why did we never see?

Because we could not. Can not *and I’m sorry the handyman’s arm got burned by the fire but I didn’t intend for it to get so big, swear to ~~god~~ God I didn’t*

Pretty fire.

I read and reread his letters. And the reports about Tommy.

Before the haze of exhaustion settles around him, Father Nunzio murmurs, “You know I am telling you the truth.”

I do. And I know too that I must have seen this all along.

Without allowing myself to see it. Dousing it in darkness the moment it dared hover before me.

As I have done with everything that is filled with pain. It is how I survived.

But now a searing light is being shone in this darkest of places within me.

Because I have followed Tommy. He has been my guide. I too have been drawn to the fires, not Tommy's pretty little blazes but ones that destroy and give life as *I look for it out there in the cosmos and I have come to worship it at the altar of…*

And Father Nunzio. I have needed this man, this fearsome priest.

I have needed him to remain fixed in my mind because he alone is the reason I could clasp together the drawstrings of what I have woven, this covering that has allowed me to lie in the darkness of night under those stars, without being cut by the shards of broken memory as they pushed up from below.

I needed—so very much—not to know what Tommy really was. Because I loved him.

Love him.

So now, instead of the incarnation of God's wrath, images cast in Penetang in the mind of a child and hardening over all these years, all I have is the reality of a bulky, awkward old man, an obsolete priest settling into lonely uncertainty.

Wheezing and drooling in his troubled sleep on a ragged couch.

I feel a low dread that I have not felt in years.

I know in an instant the source of this dread as I see them all off in some darkness of my own—Lightning, Tommy, my mother, all those whom I have loved and should have saved. But could not. Did not.

And Elena?

Quickly I wake up Father Nunzio, who, when pulled from his sleep, is as lost and confused as a child.

Even before the volunteer fire department has put out the flames, the shootout at Vern's and the fire are destined to be relegated to the annals of the endless drug wars. With the outsiders being blamed for trying to encroach on the mountain meth labs. Vern, who will be convicted on drug charges, will eventually recover from his wounds. One of the Calle Treinte will not.

On the way back up the mountain I push the mechanical limits of Father Nunzio's car, racing against that same low dread that etches images—faces—into the night in front of me. The faces of all those I have loved. And every one of them is gone. Loss is the one constant I have.

Elena.

I press even harder on the accelerator and the car is filled with an urgent silence interrupted only by the shriek of the tires on the hairpin turns. Exhaustion and vigilance war within Father Nunzio, his drooping head snapping to attention whenever the car lurches.

For the last couple of miles before we arrive, the dome strobes into view through the palisade of cedars that lines the mountain. A flash of whiteness against the singed coldness of a crystalline night ablaze with stars. Even these glimpses give me comfort. The Druids, when they built the place back in the 1930s and '40s, had an almost medieval sense of design. Against the shimmering darkness it now seems like a fortress, so massive, so solid, and with walls thick enough to sustain images of boiling tar being poured down onto any invaders foolish enough to attempt to conquer.

"The boys would never be foolish enough to try anything harmful at the dome," says Father Nunzio, pulling my thoughts out of the tension in the car. *The boys.*

It is 3 a.m. when we return to the dome.

Charger has found a place to sleep in the windowless offices in the floor below the telescope. Dr. Herrera is prowling the darkness, remote and unapproachable. But Elena waits for me up in the data room, her head resting on the desk next to the monitors. I am even more afraid for her, that same low dread making me hold her tighter, swaying in the darkness.

In these last hours before dawn the inside of the dome is as still as it has ever been. Father Nunzio almost gasps as he looks up at the immensity of the telescope silhouetted against the fierce tiny beacons of starlight blazing through the opening in the dome.

"I had no idea," he says, leaning backwards. "May I?" he asks. "I want to see what you see."

But in the data room, when I dial in the coordinates for M 31—Andromeda—off in the northeast sky and the monitor fills with its image of those billions of stars whirling toward us, he looks appalled. "A computer screen?" he says. "I thought you looked through the telescope."

"They used to. Decades ago. This is how it's done now."

"But I want to see through the telescope. I want to be closer to His works. Your friend Vikram said it was possible. You heard him."

It's almost not worth trying to explain. About all the painstaking adjustments and how the optical camera would have to be reconfigured and removed. Back in the sepulchral stillness of the dome I point through the darkness to the top of the telescope high above us. The clouds have gone and through the huge slit the starlight is bright enough that he can see the outline of my arm. "I can get you up there."

We ascend in the prime focus elevator, which is kind of a gated gangplank that rides the inside of the dome's curvature up to the prime focus capsule at the top of the telescope, where decades ago astronomers spent entire nights making photographic plates no matter how cold it was.

The floor vanishes into the darkness beneath us. When we jolt to a stop high above the floor of the dome I help him climb down into the capsule. “I’m sorry,” he says, sounding very old, his accent thickening. “I’m afraid of heights.”

I leave him up in the capsule and descend to the floor of the dome. I hear him high above. But I can’t tell if he is laughing or sobbing. It is an indeterminate sound of nearly unrecognizable origin. “God is up here,” he calls down. “I envy you! You live so close to Him! A few more minutes, please. Oh *marvelous!*”

A wedge of light widens when the door to the ancient elevator fully opens. The faint light reveals Dr. Herrera looking haggard and strangely vulnerable.

“Magnificent!” bellows Father Nunzio from on high, his voice circling the dome in echoes.

Dr. Herrera mutters, “What is that old fraud doing up there?”

“I can feel *Him!* In the stars!”

“People suffering from intense activity in the temporal lobes of the brain see God in everything,” says Dr. Herrera in a deliberately louder voice. “The condition creates fervent spirituality. God may well just be an overactive temporal lobe.”

From high above us there is a silence. And then an accusatory roar: “Who is that?” It is the old Father Nunzio, the one I remember.

“Do you think it would bother him if he knew most of the saints were probably bipolar?” says Dr. Herrera.

“Who are you calling bipolar?” Father Nunzio yells, peering down at Dr. Herrera. “Not him! Not that charlatan!” His voice echoes around the dome with fury. “Get me down! At once!”

Like dice spinning on the crap table, sometimes the answers we seek turn out not to be the answers we wanted. And so we force the dice to roll the way we want them. We ward off the laws of chance and the exigencies of reality by fusing incompatibles together. Even if it renders us mad, children with hammers pounding at the pieces of an existential puzzle until they fit, damn it they will fit!

The easy incompatibles—political views, marital strife, revolutionary dogmas, etc.—get solved by the usual run-of-the-mill manifestations: talk shows, over-

paid lawyers, firing squads, etc. But out in the cosmos the oxymorons are, as the scientists say, of a different order of magnitude.

And no order of magnitude was greater than the 20th-century scientific food-fight between Einstein and quantum mechanics.

Einstein's theories of relativity blew all that came before it out of the class-rooms. Suddenly space and time were not fixed measurements. They were vari-able, fusable even. And light was found to have a constant speed relative to everything no matter what speeds the other objects were traveling, toward or away from that light. More than that, said Einstein, light was actually bend-able. By gravity.

In other words, astronomers suddenly had all their tools rearranged. Everything was now subject to Einstein's relativity theories. All that was infinitely big—stars, galaxies, the universe itself—began making a kind of sense.

But the simultaneous and bizarre problem arose because quantum mechanics had just been discovered. And its laws governed all that was infinitely small—molecules, atoms and all the way down to particles, the neutrons, protons, pho-tons, gluons and the like. In other words, the small stuff that made up the big stars, galaxies and the rest of it

Quantum mechanics was like science on acid. With wild theories of little sub-atomic particles that could be in two places at once. Or so it seemed.

Eimstein's relativity and quantum mechanics should merge together like two superhighways at an interchange. One theory for infinitely big objects merging with another theory for infinitely small objects.

But they didn't. Not even remotely.

The mathematics of each created incompatibles so great that they caused a sci-entific wreck of enormous proportions when they met. Nothing fit together. It threw astronomers, physicists, mathematicians and the like into what passes in the pro-fession for turmoil —because each theory was proved to be mathematically cor-rect, yet each canceled the other out.

Where was the Answer now?

The only way astronomers could lessen this turmoil and keep going was by embracing an alien concept from another discipline:

Faith.

They simply had to believe.

And then get on with life until someone figured out a way to reconcile these Great Incompatibles.

Feverish attempts to discover a Unified Theory resulted in a series of strange round-hole/square-peg reinterpretations of the cosmos. Like the superstring theory, which demands we accept not a mere three dimensions in the world around us but instead eleven—or more. But none of these new dimensions can be seen.

Ever.

Or even verified as to their existence.

So these eleven dimensions require faith. In the hopes of leading to the Answer.

So great, so urgent, is this quest for the Answer that at one point, a British physicist decided there had to be some subatomic particle no one had ever proved existed. This particle would explain away all these irritating incompatibles. The lion and the lamb—Einstein and quantum mechanics—would lie down together once this particle was found to exist.

But not seen—it could never be seen. All we can hope for, supplicants ever, is merely to know that it's there. Somewhere.

Decades of scientists set off, scientific hounds on the chase for the mere existence of this particle! Building massive underground scientific structures and spending amounts of money that would arm a modest nation at war.

They gave an informal name to what they were trying to prove existed.

They called it the God particle.

Like all the other quests for The Answer, it was religion and science fusing in some cauldron, stirred together even as they dissolved the ladle.

And so now in the finest tradition…

… Father Nunzio steps out of the prime focus elevator, ready to confront his attackers. "This man believes in nothing." His voice echoes in its wrath throughout the dome. "I know him!"

"He should," says Dr. Herrera. "We have both been taking money from the same drug lords."

"I beg your pardon!"

"Ramon and Antonio Cabrera—our benefactors," says Dr. Herrera, his voice as hard as a scythe.

"I did not take money," says Father Nunzio, his accent thickening the way it always has under the weight of indignation.

"Of course you did. As did I. For treating their wives. Their pathetic mistresses. Their mother," says Dr. Herrera with a theatrical little flourish. He has been waiting for this encounter. "Do you know the most damning three words in the English language?" He doesn't wait for an answer. "Character. Is. Destiny! Neither of us had it, *Father!* We had Freud, medicine and, yes, *your* God. But not character. Neither of us left the brothel we all live in, you and I."

"Blasphemy."

"My wife, Sonia, she had character. She saw. But I did not. Nor did you." He laughs. At least it seems like a laugh. "But I was so close."

"Close to what?"

"To a breakthrough. The wives. The women. They were tormented by what Ramon and Antonio were doing—the mother especially. I thought that through her, the violence could have been lessened. Not stopped. But maybe lessened—"

"Lessened? With what? This—" Father Nunzio is practically spitting "—this *therapy* of yours?"

"Maybe. It's a miracle, you know, converting outright misery into mere ordinary unhappiness."

"*That* is your idea of a miracle?"

"Nowadays it's close enough. I actually had Ramon coming in for a session. *Ramon* of all people!" says Dr. Herrera. "But then the Church here stopped it—"

"By the time I got Ramon into the confession box," erupts Father Nunzio, looking at me but pointing to Dr. Herrera, "the doctor here had managed to transform sin into mere neuroses."

"*Sin?*" Dr. Herrera curls the word for effect. "So evil is not in fashion any more, is it? Satan is just for Pentecostal churches with pickup trucks in the parking lot?"

"What would you know about evil? To people like you it's all just a mere chemical imbalance."

"Really? So where was your God after you heard confessions from Ramon? If there is a God why did He not stop all their murdering and torture?"

"Free will is His gift to us," says Father Nunzio, "and with it, the bad must come with the good. Or would you rather He had made us slaves? With no free will?"

On the mountain there is now a story passed among those who knew the people involved. According to the story the two Cabrera women—the mother and one of the wives, probably Ramon's—were said to have approached both of these men separately, Father Nunzio or Dr. Herrera, seeking whatever solution could be found from either of them.

Each of these women had come to believe in her own way that redemption, or cure, whichever came first, would be of equal value. As long as it healed Ramon and Antonio. And maybe themselves too. At different times and with varying levels of conviction, each of these women, the mother and the wife, had believed that a miracle was possible.

Whether it was from God or psychoanalysis, they didn't care. One of these two men must surely know how to make this miracle happen.

But the women became confused trying to follow conflicting advice. Their confusion grew after Father Nunzio, learning of what he considered competition from a mere psychiatrist, ordered them to disregard whatever was told to them by this practitioner of secular dispensation,

When the wife summoned up her courage to ask why they should ignore the psychiatrist, Father Nunzio replied that such men destroy absolutes. They make everything relative.

And that is one step away from the devil.

The women thought about it.

And then, for many months, they ceased regular contact with both the priest and the psychiatrist.

Before dawn the phone call from the sheriff's office comes in to the dome.

My cabin has been destroyed. Ripped open like a can of bad beans left on a stove is the way the deputy describes the damage. Someone must have really had it in for you, he adds.

Father Nunzio leaves. Scuttling out into the darkness, admonishing me not to be taken in by charlatans like this one, this mere psychiatrist. And to be careful. He does not add: *of the boys.*

His taillights recede into the enveloping darkness of the mountain. And then there is only stillness and the stars.

Dr. Herrera sits under the telescope staring out at those same stars. "My apologies," he says in a voice emptied of any power. "I should not have involved anyone else."

"Right now I have other concerns," I say, packing a large hunting knife into a duffel bag.

"A knife won't get you far."

"I'm really not so good with automatic weapons. So it'll have to do."

He gets up and walks toward the huge aperture, looking up into the points of light. "For the past two years that priest and I fought over the minds of two murderers. Or their souls, if you must."

"Who won?"

"Let me tell you something," he says. "When I was in the jungle towns of Peru I was a young doctor, very radical and convinced of my own righteousness. There was an old priest there who was a tyrant. He reigned with fear and no one dared contradict him. And one day an Indian from the town died of tuberculosis. I said that the man had to be buried immediately to prevent contagion. The priest heard about this and ordered that the man not be buried until the next day in a proper Catholic funeral. I went to the police chief and said, 'Do you want your sons to die from this disease?' The Indian was buried that same night.

"The next Sunday I was denounced in the church.

"The old priest had pigs, his own pigs that wandered free all over the streets. Pigs can spread fatal diseases to people by contaminating the food and water supplies. I asked the old priest to build a pen to keep them in. Again he denounced me from the altar, this time for challenging God's will. So the next day I went to an army officer, Colonel Zileri, an educated man who was stationed in the town and was always grateful for the books I brought him. I explained what diseases were being spread to the people by the pigs wandering free.

"Colonel Zileri sat under a bare lightbulb in a small room where the walls were taller than the floor was wide and said to me, 'But what do you want me to do?'

"I said, 'Shoot the priest's pigs.'

"Colonel Zileri was horrified. But he thought about what I said. And then the next day he gave the orders and two of the priest's pigs were shot dead on the streets by his soldiers.

"The priest quickly had a pen built for his pigs and denounced me again.

"When I saw this old priest again he was raging. He said, 'This would never have happened before Vatican II.'

"I didn't know what he meant. But now I do. Vatican II. Their *Aggiornamento?* In the mid-1960s their old pope and his council had given away all the Church's power. All the absolutes. Their Church was suddenly afflicted with a terrible need to be loved instead of feared.

"And it is still withering from that need. The old priest with his pigs knew that. He knew it when the army shot his pigs instead of shooting me.

"But then so am I—withering, that is. Like all Freudians. We died a kind of death around the same time. Beginning when research showed that depression was organic. Not as Freud said.

"And now?" he says. "We are a band of brothers, Father Nunzio and I. He would never admit it, of course. But we are a confederation of those who have learned the fine art of listening to tales of rationalized evil. I dispense pills. He dispenses blessings."

And suddenly, as if remembering something that had been on his mind long ago: "I do not envy Sonia. She was there on the entire descent from certainty down into the wilderness."

For a moment he's as lost as a child. "She was right." And then something snaps back within him.

A kind of collapse is happening. Dr. Herrera is becoming pale, haggard-looking, and grows more so as the call goes on, talking into the phone in a low, urgent voice. The electrical hum of the data room masks what he says except for the fragments of Spanish that slice through. Something tethers him to the phone even as he looks as if parts of him are being eaten away by it. When he hangs up I ask him what is wrong.

"Nothing," he says. "I have to go."

"What was that call about?"

"Please" he says, embattled and uncertain.

He rushes away and then stops. "I can't expect you to understand," he says, "until you too find yourself explaining away some terrible violence of others."

"I don't understand."

"Really? It's a skill you will acquire soon."

He hurries out through the heavy door. The light is bleaching away the night.

I return to my cabin with Elena, followed discreetly by Charger, who parks his old Cadillac at the end of the lane and waits, the rifle lying on the seat beside him.

The deputy's cruiser, bristling with aerials like steel whiskers, is also waiting outside. It's the same leading-man deputy who showed up when the mountain lion jumped through the Baileys' window a couple of mornings ago, but now trailing a look of exhaustion around him.

"You have any clue what this is all about?" he says, looking from me to Elena, whose hand tightens around my arm as she stares at the destruction.

It is not merely wreckage, it is a statement. The door is ripped in two, everything inside is scattered across the floor, and there is what looks like blood smeared all over.

"I'm getting run off my damn feet," he says. "It's like the mountain is having some kind of breakdown. Fires. Shootings. All of a sudden. Every damn thing you can think—"

It's the little gasp from Elena in the doorway that interrupts him. She stands looking around with words forming and falling inward unspoken. Her dress, the one she wore when she fled from Mexico, is nailed to the wall.

And above the dress, where her head would be if she were wearing it, the wall is smashed in.

"Damn" is all the deputy says. "Talk about weird."

Elena shivers under my touch. "Antonio," she whispers.

"Excuse me?" says the deputy. Elena just shakes her head slowly.

"I haven't seen you around here before, ma'am," the deputy says, his own personal form of mountain radar picking up stray signals.

"This is a friend of mine—Ellen. She just arrived."

My answering for her sends even more signals. He never looks at me. "Hello, Ellen." He wants a response from her.

"Hello." And even this one word has the hint of an accent that gets filed somewhere behind that impassively tanned face. Definitely not an Ellen accent.

"Where are you from?"

"She's just moving here. To be with me."

"That's nice." His eyes never leave her. "Where you from?"

"Cuba," she says.

"Well now, that's a change. Never had a Cuban up here. An OTM." Other Than Mexican. The deputies on the mountain see their world as a kind of jigsaw puzzle where all the pieces are more or less known. When one of the pieces suddenly seems to be from a different puzzle they start acting like the game's being played on a table with one leg shorter than the others. Pretty soon they're crawling under everything trying to see where the problem comes from. "Where in Cuba?"

"Havana."

"Havana! Well now. Great cigars." He's scanning the puzzle in his mind.

"That's just where they're rolled," she says. "The tobacco comes from Pinar del Rio. A province."

"Ah," he says. "Yeah." The puzzle is losing interest as part of his attention span is sucked into the chatter on the two-way radio in his cruiser. "Yeah," he says again. "Sorry 'bout the damage. Our guys'll be back to run the chemicals and the tire-track tests. So I'd appreciate it if you'd just sort of ease out of here for a while." Retreating to the cruiser he calls out, "Nice to meet you, ma'am."

Exhaustion is pounding at me in waves as if all that was shored up is crumbling. Elena is staring at the obliterated wall above the dress.

"Where do we go?" she asks.

"Wherever they won't find us." I feel the fatigue rise around me. "Get in the car. We'll go somewhere else."

"No. I told you. I don't want to go anywhere else."

"That doesn't make any sense. Not now."

"Yes, it does. How many roads are there going down the mountain?"

"Two."

"And you think they won't be watching both of them? Just waiting for us? Any of us? They have guns that can blow a car right off the mountain."

"We can use one of the observatory trucks. No one suspects them. They go down the mountain all the time."

"I have run enough. No more. I want to stay." She looks around. "Here." She points toward the woods behind the cabin and then picks up blankets from the floor. Taking the binoculars that hang by the door, she moves through the underbrush. I stumble after her toward a place down near the stream that flows out of the higher ground.

It is where the sun breaks through as if the trees are a veil. Sinking into the folds of the blankets, shielded from the world by the ferns that unfurl between the cedars, I drift into some state so altered by fatigue that consciousness ebbs and flows.

Elena—her name stretches and drifts too as I whisper it, in waves across whatever zone of understanding is now narrowing within my mind. "We can't stay here."

"It's green here."

"What has that got to do with anything?" Almost like being drugged, I am reaching for her and she for me.

I feel her hands on my shirt and mine on her blouse. Clothes fall into a slow kaleidoscope forming on the long grass beside the stream. I start to say something.

"Shh," she whispers, rising naked above me, leaning into me. Slowly raising and then lowering herself onto me. Her hands and her breasts brush my lips. Cradled amid the undulations of her thighs, I drift through the dream under the flowing canopy of her hair that hangs down around me.

She shudders and gasps, clutching my arms.

I am floating through the fatigue.

It is all happening so far away. In this place of dreams where she settles down onto me as her breathing lessens and her words weave through a serene and jumbled tapestry, this *Bosque de la Habana* she talks of, this beautiful faraway sanctuary, this green place below where she lived by the Almendares River where we play now, she and I surrounded by green, everywhere lush and verdant in this little rain-forest kingdom where the noise of the city comes from so far away...

So far away.

The noise is metallic. Elena is shaking me from this grove of dreams and I blink into mottled afternoon sunlight filtering through the trees on the western side of the mountain. Untroubled and naked we have slept, are sleeping, through much of the day.

But now there is the tautness of fear.

And this curious matter of a car door. It slams again and again in the reverberations of my mind until the tremble in her voice jars me loose from the fog of sleep. "They're here," she's whispering again and again.

Through the binoculars I refocus from one to another. Three of them, not in a dark-colored SUV this time but an older American car, the kind of decommissioned taxi or police car that is repainted cheaply and sent out to progressively disintegrate on the roads. They are in their twenties, maybe late teens, with shaved heads. One of them is Fu Manchu. Another has a large tattoo on the side of his neck. Only when he stops moving is the tattoo visible as the form of a woman with large breasts and long hair. And under his left eye is the tattooed outline of a tear. He is the one who takes out a large pistol as he approaches the back of the house.

They talk in Spanish and fragments of what they say reach us down near the stream.

"I think they're saying we still haven't returned," Elena whispers.

I pass the binoculars to her. "None of them could be Antonio," she says, not taking her eyes from them.

In a belch of exhaust smoke, they start the car and are about to leave when another vehicle cruises up, partially obscured by the trees. Words are exchanged before the old American car drives away.

The second vehicle pulls in between some trees hidden from the road. A man gets out and walks through the trees. He comes into the clearing and looks at the cabin, walking slowly back and forth. He is about my age, with black hair combed straight back and a look of someone troubled or angry.

Beside me Elena tenses. She tries to speak but words without sound vanish from her lips.

"What?" I whisper.

"It could be...," she says finally, "it might be...I don't know..."

"Antonio?"

She says nothing.

"Are you sure?"

"I don't know... I don't know what he looks like now. With his new face ... Maybe... *Yes!*"

"Antonio?"

She nods.

I look from Elena to the man who now becomes Antonio. He vanishes behind the far side of the cabin. There is really no decision process.

What needs to be done will be done.

I dress quickly and move silently, circling around toward this second car in bare feet. Over to the tool shed on the edge of the forest, where unused implements are frozen in rust where they have remained since the old couple left the cabin. There are rakes, shears, a lawn mower, shovels—and one massive old wooden-handled knife, hand-sharpened so often that its blade runs in uneven waves from the handle to the tip.

With the knife I race through the trees toward the road and the car. The man is circling the cabin and moving almost parallel to me on the other side of the trees.

I am closer to the car, ready with the knife. He stops and checks something on the ground. He is well dressed, not expensively but with some semblance of style. And powerful, with arms that even under the dark silken shirt reveal a kind of definition that comes from some physical life.

If I knew how to throw a knife it would be over already.

Through the trees I see him picking up unopened mail that had been scattered. I think—I know—there is a darkness, a fierceness to what I can see of his face. And for a moment there is the terrifying flicker of the men he tortured, mutilated, seeing this face as their last image.

And then I remember it was not this face—this is Antonio's new face. And I wonder what the old face was like.

If there are tattoos I cannot see them. And then on one arm, coming out from the bottom of a rolled-up shirt sleeve, there is something. A dragon, perhaps? It is too hard to tell.

The vehicle is revealed between the low, young cedars. Of course—an SUV. Black, with tinted windows. It, more than anything, fills me with dread.

I rebalance the knife hanging loosely in my hand, gripping it so that it can be either thrown if absolutely necessary or, more likely, thrusted.

He takes out a cell phone and talks into it, pacing in front of the house, his eyes darting all over as he talks. Something is making him agitated, maybe angry, I can't tell. As he stalks the side of the cabin, his left arm jabs the air.

I sift through the trees waiting for that moment of intersection, feeling my heart pounding into me. I am close to the black SUV. He is approaching, talking angrily into a cell phone that keeps cutting out, and staring into the ground as he walks.

"He's not here," he says into the phone. And a moment later: "We're going to get to him, no problem."

He is walking closer and the plan takes hold of it own accord: let him pass and then attack him from behind.

But something spins him around, startled. He is frozen, holding the phone by the side of his head. "Hold on," he says into the phone.

And then lowering it slowly, he stares straight into me. Through me.

His face—*the* face?—composed in complete certainty. "You scared me," he says.

I say nothing, standing, waiting to move the knife behind me, shielded from his view.

"I'm looking for the man who lives here. Mr. Braden."

"How do you know my name?"

He changes. His face widening. Into a hint of a smile. Then a big grin. "I found him," he says into the phone. "Make sure that couple are confirmed at the condo in Temecula. Eight o'clock tonight. I'll get back to you."

He puts the phone away and holds out his hand for me to shake. "Don Williams," he says.

For some reason I can't absorb what is happening.

"Don Williams," he says again.

I hear only part of what he is saying as he opens the door of the SUV to get one of his business cards. On the door is a white magnetic sign: *Don Williams Realtor—Two Decades of Service in Escondido.*

"We always look for abandoned houses that people might want to sell. I got your name from the letters scattered over there and I thought if you're looking to list the property—most of my listings are in Escondido, but ..."

And I am struck by how ordinary, how uninteresting, the black SUV with the tinted windows is. And how his face has a kind of simple sweetness, maybe just exuberance that makes him seem eager for acceptance.

As I try to shield the knife that hangs in my hand behind me.

The Colonel's

Already I am late.

I should be in the dome working the instruments, setting up like a pilot doing visuals before the passengers board.

But Elena and I are sitting in the fading warmth of the sun. Her head against my shoulder. As she talks of what could have happened, how it would be her fault if I had killed Don Williams Realtor.

And how everyone could be Antonio now. Everywhere she turns, everyone she sees. Everywhere.

Everyone.

Words tumble out, some in Spanish, some repeated.

There is only one sanctuary now, only one place on the mountain where she will be safe, protected day and night.

Around the side of the big house on the crest of the mountain, I see him. He is staring at the ground as if he's been hypnotized.

"Colonel?"

His hand slowly rises toward me like a traffic cop's, palm out in a Stop motion. He never looks up.

Something on the ground explodes in a little puff of dust. A squirrel. It has darted to a stop. Tail straight up and waving stiffly in a flurry of twitches, it leans straight in to something on the ground. Then another flash of motion and a puff of dust as the squirrel materializes in a quantum flash somewhere other than where it was an instant ago.

It is a snake.

The squirrel is taunting a rattler, like something shot through with electricity, twitching and jumping in front of the snake.

The Colonel's voice unfurls quietly, calmly, barely audible. "One of the great sights in nature," he says, still watching the ground. "Fair fight going on here. The ground is warm so the snake'll be extra quick. It's speed against the squirrel's craziness."

There is a rattle, sounding like a sprinkler system starting up And then the snake flashes as if both it and the squirrel are fired into the air. The squirrel flips sideways and sprays dirt into the eyes of the snake.

The Colonel chuckles. "Those damn ground squirrels are a miracle. They'll taunt the rattlers like crazy. Even get bitten bad enough that it would kill a human. Squirrel'll just laugh it off and go back for more. They can actually do damage to a snake."

The snake fires forward again. "Rattlers go after the squirrel's babies thinking they'll get a free lunch. And end up getting the fight of their lives. Way it should be."

"I need to talk to you."

"Know what we're witnessing?"

"I'd say it's a fight to the death."

"More 'n that. This is genetics. At its finest."

The snake lunges and the squirrel flips in the puff of dust. Then it is the squirrel that lunges for the snake's neck and the air explodes with a tangle of fur and scales. "See, these squirrels have developed an immunity to the snake's venom. Any of them that didn't got weeded out of the gene pool.

"But take this same snake a few hundred miles north of here and it'd be dining out on squirrel till it got fat. Squirrels up north don't have many rattlers, so they never developed the immunity to the venom." The Colonel allows himself a chuckle. "Damn. Amazing, those squirrels." For the first time he looks at me. "Like with people. Things get bred in. Or bred out."

He scans the surroundings. And settles on the car where Elena waits.

"She's in danger," I say. He waits for what is to follow, his eyes narrowing like he's an auctioneer waiting for a bid. "I need to get you involved."

"Involved? *Involved*, boy? Talk like that always sends my hair standing up on edge in all the wrong places."

"Someone wants to kill her."

"Who is she?"

I tell him. Everything.

Except that I am in love with her.

His eyebrows arch, enhancing the normal ferocity of all that is below them. He says nothing when I finish, his mouth tightening and working in knots. "You kidding me? Cuban?" he says finally.

I nod.

"An illegal? Jesus, boy. You want *me* to take one of 'em in? Do you know what the hell you're asking?"

"It gets worse."

"Oh yeah?"

"Whoever protects her will come under attack."

"This Antonio character? The one always on the Mexican news?"

"Yeah."

"Is she the reason for all craziness going on on the mountain?"

"Looks like it."

"They're after her, huh? Because of that dead brother?"

I nod.

"So she's the magnet pulling all those bastards up here?"

He thinks about this for a moment.

"That son of a bitch doesn't intimidate me one damn bit."

"He's got his *sicarios*—"

He hasn't heard me.

"Matter of fact," he says, "it's about time we found a way to bring things to a head."

He seems somehow pleased.

A few hours after Elena has moved into the Colonel's house, one of his big shiny water tankers is pulled across the entrance, blocking the end of a long circular driveway still unfinished years after the house was first occupied. The tanker is not merely a barrier. In convex distortions it is a huge mirror reflecting the traffic approaching from either direction. And behind it, men from other parts of the mountain are gathering, summoned by the Colonel, in the big garage where guns and military paraphernalia are quietly unloaded from trucks and cars.

The Colonel's big white house overlooks the valley below. And far beyond that, the hills sinking toward Mexico below the gathering clouds as the weather nuzzles the mountain, a fog-strewn drizzle rolling in quickly from the east.

It is as if the house had been positioned as an outpost on the edge of America.

On my way over to the dome I make a detour to the wreckage of my cabin. Amid all the debris, all those possessions I could walk away from in a moment, there is only one piece of me I cannot leave behind.

First, I watch from the car. No one is around. The stillness has a motion all its own. The strewn debris is a collage of clothing, sodden flecks of color against the surrounding forest as it recedes into misting grayness.

What I am looking for is not among the piles of clothing from overturned drawers that were hurled through the back door. Nor on the shattered flooring of what had been the main room. And is now dusted with plaster across the debris that once had some kind of place in my life. There is no possibility of mending what is broken, no way to reassemble any kind of order. It is a process of kicking and rummaging through congealing possessions that are now mere things. Until finally, when the old stove, lying on its side now, is rolled aside.

Underneath is the small wooden box with the hand-carved image of a bird, a kind of duck swimming in water—*a loon! Get it Mikey!*—under a big full moon—*First clue: Sounds like June. Dune. Lune! You got it Mikey!—Lune, which to the French, sorry,* français *side of our ancestors means … moon! Hence Looney!*

It is the box Tommy made for me in the Oak Ridge woodworking shop in the month or so he was allowed in there—*Okay now—a loon under the lune. Get it?!* until Dr. Baymer decided he was too much of a threat handling woodworking tools. *Okay, okay already, so it's lame. But what's a nut to do? Because they really don't like you using the C-word. No one is Crazy in here any more. Now they tell us that all the Wackos in this place are DISTURBED!! We've gone from the C-word to the D-word.*

The clasp on the top of the box yields. Inside is all that matters to me now.

His letters.

I'm very DISTURBED about this, Mikey.

The ones that made me laugh.

The drizzle keeps the dome closed, sitting in stillness with its aperture facing north as the last light is leeched out of the day. By ten o'clock we have written off the last night of Yannic's run.

Heading down the mountain toward the Colonel's house, I see phantoms. The forests are seething with creatures that do not exist. My mind is filling in the voids in the darkness just beyond the headlights. Antonio is everywhere. Obsidian evil has been sprung loose, galloping through this night, racing me all the way from the dome.

I pass a car parked on one of the parking vistas at around 5,000 feet. Like cars often are. But on this night it instantly takes on demonic powers, filling my thoughts with *sicarios* emerging from the mist.

The car remains, harmless and still in the rearview mirror, momentarily lit by the red bursts of brake lights in some kind of code.

It is one of the Colonel's men, guarding the mountain.

Guarding me.

The Colonel's house has become even more of a fortress. There is almost a platoon there now, men from various parts of the mountain sleeping in tents scattered through the wooded areas beside the big house. Some of them work for him, but others are those whose lives have grown out of the mountain, a society of 4-wheel-drive vehicles and loosely shared interests: Living away from cities.

Weapons. Parties. Holiday feasts in the meadow. Hunting. Trailers. And a sense of flags flown privately but fiercely.

Several men come out of the shadows. I have seen some of them at parties on the mountain, the ones where concealed-weapons permits are marginally more prevalent than the guitars that come out after the liquor starts flowing.

"Hear you sorta got your place involuntarily remodeled." Doc grins. Doc is one of the Colonel's sons, the one who runs his water operation. He's with the sentries peering out of rain ponchos over the barrels of sawed-off shotguns. He steps out from behind the tanker that gleams in the headlights. "Trashed you up pretty bad, huh?"

"Yeah. They weren't too big on housekeeping skills."

"Damn. Some days when you wake up it just ain't worth chewing through the restraints now, is it?" Doc has a handlebar mustache over a sun-etched face that encases liquid eyes glinting with his own brand of mountain irony. He looks like he stepped out of a sepia photo of Old West outlaws.

"Everything okay here?"

"Don't it look like it?"

"What happened tonight?"

"Just look," says Doc, pointing to the tanker. The shiny front of it is stitched with bullet holes. And just beyond it, a cedar tree has been strangely decapitated. "Drive-by," he says. "Some of San Diego's finer citizens from the lower altitudes felt the need to do a little tanker decorating and tree trimming with their Uzis."

"Elena?"

"The woman? Old man said she's asleep."

Harry, the Colonel's other son emerges out of the darkness. Bulkier than Doc and without the ease. "Any trouble on the way here?"

"Nothing."

"Hear we're looking for one of the Cabreras. With a new face," Harry says.

"New face don't seem right," says Bill, a sinewed carpenter whose arms stick out of his T-shirt like drumsticks. He lives off the grid on the east side of the mountain, taking what electricity he needs from a small generator and solar panels. "Least you gotta know who's trying to kill you and who ain't. I mean that's a lack of basic fairness. Like with those sonsofbitches tonight. Uzis just ain't a fair fight."

"You seen Charger around?"

"Yeah. He's down in the valley. Probably manning a howitzer or something." Doc grins. "Or whatever the hell the Colonel's got him on. Bad shape though."

"What's wrong with him?"

"Running to the can every ten minutes. Squawking like hell about what those damn pills are doing to him."

"The Vicodins?"

"Must be. Looks like he's got a terminal case of a fart stuck sideways. Pret' near leveled the portable toilet. Sounded like a grenade in an echo chamber." Doc just loves talking about things like this. One night at the Lodge he ranked bathroom graffiti in every bar in the county.

Harry suddenly cups a hand to his ear, straining to hear through his earpiece. He looks up. "Colonel wants to see you," he says with the kind of urgency that usually accompanies such interpretations of his father's intent.

"Better watch out for your girlfriend there." Doc grins. "Ain't seen the old man so frisky in years."

He laughs.

No one answers when I knock. The door is not locked. Inside, the house itself is unremarkable, built with large amounts of money but not ingenuity or taste. Drywall and right angles predominate. But what surprises me walking through the darkened rooms toward the light at the back of the house are the mountains of books. Everywhere there are books. After the Thomas Mann, the Goethe and the Gunter Grass collections are the Prussian helmets stacked on top of Dante, with Machiavelli leading to piles of books on war. Clausewitz and Sun Tzu in several different editions shore up the battles of World War II and Vietnam.

But beyond the Balzac, Victor Hugo and Dickens are the books on genetics, hundreds of them.

"Damn books just plug the leaks in our ignorance," says a raspy voice from behind me. The Colonel stands in the shadows of the room at the end of the hallway. "Never stopped feeling that we just keep bailing in a leaky boat. Best we can hope for."

"I've just gone from Tolstoy to Mickey Mouse," I say, skimming his bookshelves, settling on a huge illustrated history of cartoons. "Sort of a jump."

"No jump. Always thought what those Warner Brothers cartoon guys did after World War II beats the hell out of Aesop and all his damn fables. And if they're teaching seminars on the Roadrunner and Daffy Duck a hundred years from now, all the gurus of the art world as we know it are gonna be raging in their abstract expressionist graves."

"I didn't mean to snoop."

"Don't bullshit me, boy." He grins. "'Course you did. Nothin' wrong with that. All gotta do our due diligence."

"I always check out people's bookshelves," I say.

"Careful," he says, vanishing into the front room. "Literature gets bought by the pound these days. Gotta watch out for Philistines trying to impress you."

I follow him and enter a large living room, with floor-to-ceiling windows. "I'm not worried about that right now."

"Yeah? Why not?"

"Get a feeling you probably haven't invited anyone else in this place since it was built."

"Probably," he says. "Probably. Not too good at playing host. Ain't got the skills for it." And for the first time I see him falter momentarily. "Wasn't always like that though."

In that split second before he recovers his reflexive gruffness I'm almost embarrassed for him. "Good woman you got," he says as his way of recovering. It takes me a moment to realize he's talking about Elena. "Wonderful. Charming. Funny," he says, walking past maps of the Roman Empire that are tacked on the wall.

"Where is she?"

"Waiting for you. Asleep," he says. "In the guest bedroom. She's a doctor," he says with a trace of awe.

"I know." And Cuban. Illegal. One of the people from out there in the dark.

"Of course you do. Had an amazing time with her. Ain't laughed so hard in a long time. Not in a real long time," he repeats, catching me looking at the wall where photos are hung.

A long time. As in the time with the woman in the old color print? Showing her laughing, young, dark haired and made more beautiful by her smile. Seated at what looks like a nightclub table and a young man's arm around her. The young man is the Colonel, lean and smiling.

"Who is she?"

"Someone I used to know," he says without looking at the photograph.

"Used to?"

"Deadly goddamn words sometimes, ain't they?" he says. He turns and keeps staring out the window. "You never know what you have until you don't have it. Basis of economics. Value comes from scarcity." He does not turn around. "Good woman you got," he says again.

It is his way of saying he doesn't want to talk about the woman in the photograph. But he does. "And that's when you're all of a sudden old. And you never know when…"

He trails off into a silence filled with what is not said. As I am showered with silent echoes from somewhere else.

He's looking out through the huge windows. "Antonio—we need more Antonios," he says. "Get it all over with before it's too late. So bring it on. Let him attack the mountain.

"Nobody attacks the mountain and gets away with it," he says.

In the bedroom Elena is asleep. A small light casts a faint and warm light in the corner of the bedroom. When I undress and get under the covers, she curls around me for a moment and then, still asleep, sits up and takes off the long T-shirt she has worn. Murmuring something I cannot decipher, she collapses back around me with a flicker of a smile. I lie there, my hand slowly tracing the contours of her nakedness, and listen to her soft breathing.

From somewhere a long way away I can hear Tommy whispering. I can't quite make out what he says but I see his face and that smile of his has vanished.

I have never seen Tommy serious like this.

In those later hours when sleep is no longer possible, I am not even aware that she is awake too. Watching me as I sit in the corner reading those letters. Hearing Tommy and talking back to him in some silent universe we all have, filled with the lost chords of music yet to be played.

She stares, even when I put the letters down. "What?" she says finally.

Which hurls me into a moment I have never had to face. Sharing that part of me that has existed pure and untarnished. Tommy, Lightning, Mother. Shielded from anyone I know, treasured behind the protective walls of my aloneness over all these years.

I tell her. At first with difficulty. Only fragments. But then when the questions come, I tell her everything. *Tell her the good stuff—*

And then after a silence, she looks at the wooden box and the pile of Tommy's letters. "Will you read me one of them?" she asks.

Atta boy, Mikey! Yeehaaw! Yesss! One big happy family. Yabbadabbadoooo!

I begin to read the letter out loud. And by somewhere a few sentences into it, I feel the breath leave me. I realize I have no consciousness memory of it... *and Mikey, I know you were helping me in your own way.* It has remained among all the other letters I have saved, the ones from Tommy, and it is opened and crumpled in a way that shows it must have been read and re-read. *I know that you saw me light that fire, the one in the Robillards' old car …* But I can remember none of it. Nothing.

… and hey, so it sort of got a little messed up what with you having to cover for me with that firecracker story that you came up with—and suddenly I cannot keep reading.

"Are you okay?" she asks.

I look away *and how was I to know you were such a great ~~liar~~ um strike that—fibber (love that word!!) when you covered for me that time when* She reaches for me and for a moment I don't even want to be touched. But she does not let go. And then *Mikey, you're a real talent, you know that?* We are sinking back across the bed. Suddenly I do—I want desperately to be touched and feel what I have fled from for all these years.

And when she touches me, for the first time I am home again.

Mikey? Mikey hold on now, where are—

I cannot imagine being without her.

Oh for godsakes be careful 'cause you don't want to turn out like—

I am dreaming. Or I think I am. I hear laughter as a kind of music.

The laughter pulls me into consciousness. It comes from somewhere beyond the door.

In the kitchen they are laughing like children with a secret. The Colonel is stirring something in a bowl as she pours a sauce into it, scolding him for not blending it properly. "I'm trying, I'm trying!" says the Colonel with a chuckle of mock exasperation that I'd bet no one's ever heard from him before. Elena looks up, wide-eyed and, seeing me, spills the sauce over the Colonel's hands, which escalates the laughter. "I'm making lunch," she says.

"We're making lunch," corrects the Colonel.

"*Masas de puerco fritas.* And other dishes my mother used to make in Havana."

"You got two cooks in the kitchen working for you, boy," says the Colonel. "Actually only one cook. I'm just the hired help around here." He laughs.

"You've got to stir the lumps out," says Elena.

"Sorry," says the Colonel, looking contrite and stirring furiously. He glances up at me and chuckles again. "Damn," he says, this time beaming.

Outside, at the front of the house, Doc and the others have set up sandbag walls between the trees. Camouflage-covered tents have been erected farther back in the woods behind a chevron of piled logs barely visible from the terrace, where a year's worth of dust and pine needles are swept off the patio chairs. And then brunch is laid out on the old log table overlooking the valley.

From the kitchen, there is the spectacle of watching the Colonel's conspiratorial delight at having Elena around. "Except for when Doc's house burned down eight years ago, I've never had anyone stay overnight here," he whispers. "God, I've missed some things. Amazing what forces you to realize it."

"I don't understand something," I say. "She came in over those hills just like all the other illegals traveling north every night. And yet you—"

"Great woman," he says pre-empting me, rising from the table to his full height, his blue eyes firing imperatives above the stern smile that has ceased to be stern at all. "You're a lucky man." He looks out over the valley as if he's trying to figure out how to say something.

"No need for you two to rush off to find another place to stay now, is there?" he says, almost child-like in his awkwardness.

At the small stable behind the Colonel's house he shows us the two horses he rides, bringing them outside with more pride than he wants revealed, and then lapsing into memories of boyhood adventures, herding his father's livestock at the age of nine. He is talking only to her, not to me. More in innocence than offense.

The stories tumble out as if she has unlocked something in him, some trove of gentleness, some awkward need for human contact, and once, when she touches his arm, he is reduced to an old man's confusion. Until a blue jay suddenly starts squawking.

The two horses instantly bolt and tear at their reins in a swirl of dust and confusion. "Rattler," he says, whirling to find the blue jay. It is fluttering and diving over an open patch of ground not far from us. "Blue jays always screech when they see snakes." I grab Elena as the hooves pirouette around us. But the Colonel storms straight into the dust-blasts that whip and surge as I yell at him to get back, my words vanishing into his laughter.

And for one moment he is back herding his father's cattle.

And then they are gone, the snakes and the blue jay; the horses are still; the clouds of dust sifting toward the earth. And he turns toward us in sheepish exhilaration.

"Sorry," he says breathlessly. "Got carried away."

"I don't know about that," the Colonel says, suddenly sounding paternal.

"If it's only for an hour I can probably make it safe," Doc replies.

"It's the *probably* part that I don't like," the Colonel frets, looking to me for support.

Late that afternoon, I take Elena to Mother's Kitchen as she had wanted. Insisted. Anything to be away from the fortress. Even for a while.

Her request had convened a meeting she never knew about, with the Colonel, Doc, me and two of Doc's men figuring out how to protect her. Elaborate plans are set in place for a simple hour-long visit to the low-slung country café.

We sit in a window booth overlooking the gathering locals, who cluster outside on the covered porch.

I'm fairly sure I am the only one there who notices Doc sitting in his pickup truck over near the little post office, pretending to read something that never holds his attention for longer than a moment. He and the others have left their normal jobs and become guards, silently patrolling. Protecting us like some mountain-style Secret Service, threaded throughout the woods around Mother's, blending in like foliage. Or strolling across the parking lot like tourists. Or careening around the curve with the rest of the racing-bike crowd, their Kawasakis and Hondas lined up like angled sentries, peeling off their form-fitting leather racing suits like invertebrates shedding skins.

Up near the intersection a black SUV slows down and stops, idles for a moment and then, as one of Doc's men emerges out of the woods, screeches away in a cloud of sprayed dirt.

Or perhaps it merely cruises away, a family of sightseers meandering across the mountain, having taken a tour of the observatory.

I am no longer sure exactly what I am seeing.

Elena does not notice them and I do nothing to draw attention.

"I needed to get away from his house. Even for a while. Because I feel…," she says uncertainly, as if grappling for translations. "I don't know, maybe… unclean."

"That's not the word I expected."

"You might not understand. Maybe no one would."

"The Colonel?"

"Yes," she says. "I am the same age as the woman in his photograph."

"Yeah. And there are moments when you become her. In his eyes."

"I know. And I'm happy to be her. For his sake. But I feel unclean because I know how to make him react. I am playing him. Like an instrument. It is a skill little girls learn growing up among strong men in societies like Cuba. I learned how so many strong men like my grandfather crave a mixture of love and defiance from a woman, even from a seven-year-old. It amuses them; sometimes they are even attracted by it too. The ones who are sure of themselves."

"Is he one of those?"

"He is more complicated. Sometimes he is like steel and he scares me. And other times he is helpless."

"Most people only see the steel."

"The woman? The one in the photograph? She was from Argentina, his wife. She left him. He spent years trying to find her. And this morning while you were asleep he told me about her. He has never gotten over her leaving him."

All around us are men wearing baseball caps with heavy-equipment logos on them. CAT. John Deere. Mack Trucks. Gnarled hands cupped around coffee cups as if it will help to keep the heat in. She looks at them as she edges toward an answer that gets lost somewhere off in the distances of her stare.

From behind her a dark-haired man in an immaculate white shirt and black pants passes on his way to the cash register. He bends over almost beside us and then holds out a wallet.

"Excuse me. This was on the floor," he says with an easy smile and a trace of an accent. "I think you may have dropped it."

Elena glances at it for only an instant. Then she looks up at him. "It's not mine," she says.

The man looks to me, holding out the wallet, one of those expensive-looking French fabric creations that seems strange in a hand such as his. "Thanks. But it's not mine either," I say.

"Strange when you can't even give wallets away." He smiles. With one of those Latino accents that are more common at the lower elevations. "I'll leave it at the cash register," he says turning away. "My apologies for interrupting."

I struggle to find the thread again. "Where were we?"

She stares out the big window.

"What's wrong?"

She continues to look away as if something far off had caught her attention and the chatter around us was drifting into the distance. And then she gets up and leaves.

We are back at the Colonel's house, on the deck that overlooks the edge of America. "I wasn't sure how to tell you," she says. "After what just happened."

"What just happened?"

"Back at that restaurant—Mother's? The man with the wallet…" She stops, waiting for me to complete it *one of those expensive-looking fabric creations* in my thoughts.

"How do you say it? *La cicatriz?*" She's pointing to the back of her hand. "Right here."

I see images of the wallet thrust back at me, repeating again and again—*that somehow looks strange in a hand such as his.*

"A scar?" I say, remembering now, remembering the welt like a—

"A scar. Yes."

"What about it?"

"Antonio had a…"

"*Cicatriz.*"

"That was Antonio."

"Other people have scars on their hands."

"No. Not *that* scar. I know it almost like I know my own hand. Dr. Reyes had photos of it hanging in that house they kept me in. Big photos. Because Antonio wanted Dr. Reyes to make the *cicatriz* go away."

For a moment I struggle to bring the man's face, and that easy smile, back into focus. But something isn't emerging from whatever it is that Dr. Herrera would chart as the dendritic pool of memory.

"What was he doing?"

"It is his game. He loves games. He plays with people before he kills. I have seen it."

We hear the sounds of Doc and the others returning to the compound. A metal gate scrapes across asphalt. She stares out across the folds of the mountains and hills descending toward the border.

"Now other people are going to die in order to protect me," she says. "This was not part of the agreement."

"I wasn't aware there was any agreement."

"With the man who was killed in the Bosque," she says. "You remember? My agreement. The one I made when he was shot."

In this instant it is only her face I see now and nothing else matters because I know I have let my guard down. I am vulnerable. Over all these years—since Lightning, since Tommy—I have succeeded beyond measure in never suffering. Loss has not been in my lexicon. Because there was no one to lose.

Until now.

So for a moment I close my eyes to make sure I can still see those large dark eyes when she is not there—the curtains of gleaming black hair shifting around the smile that flickers like a distant beacon at the commencement of some long night of my own.

When I open my eyes she is not there. There is only the fading light softening the folds of the mountains on the edge of America.

Oh no no Mikey—

On my way to the dome I again stop at Mother's.

The waitress is in the kitchen when I find her. A wallet? She thinks and then asks the cook. Yes, one was turned in an hour ago. From under the cash register she extracts a small cardboard box marked in crayon *Lost/Found.* In it is the same expensive-looking French fabric creation dripping with the designer's initials. I open it and stare into the photo on the driver's license.

"It's a friend of mine," I say. "I'll give it to him."

In the car I wait until turning onto the South Road before I open the wallet again and look into the tiers of credit cards.

All of them bearing the name of Dr. Francisco Reyes.

And his Mexican driver's license with the image on it slashed as if by a razor.

Oh Be A Fine Girl Kiss Me.

After all these years I still remember the categories of stars from the mnemonic.

OBAFGKM.

And tonight we're in an improvised search for some of the Os and Bs, the young blue giant stars blazing away at 50,000 degrees Kelvin (our own puny sun is a mere 5,500 degrees). Twilight is already settling over us as I open the dome to the gathering darkness.

Yannic's run is finished. Tonight I am with a surly little Scotsman who is as intense as he is humorless. Carl is assisting as a favor, along for the infrared part of the ride, but tonight it is the Scotsman who calls the cosmic shots. He has showed up with his faithful dog, some anorexic breed with haunted, guilty eyes that he installs on the swivel chair. It's not the dog's fault, but watching the Scotsman coo and fawn over it, I just want to stand up and announce, "Dewpoint depression!" then shut the dome and go home.

I make excuses to go outside onto the catwalk encircling the dome, even though I know the wind, the air temperature and all the rest are, as we say, highly photometric.

But I am somewhere else. I am in Havana. I am in Tijuana. Penetang. I am out there—some place untold parsecs out in our internal cosmos where time curves back and starts again.

Oh Be A Fine…

Elena.

She is safe at the Colonel's. Again I can look out to the mountain and pick out the sentry positions established by the Colonel's men. But still my mind is playing tricks on me, running out of control.

The second law of thermodynamics has taken hold of my thoughts. I am hurtling into entropy: everything is going from order to disorder.

I cannot concentrate.

Back in the data room the Scotsman is squinting into a blur on the computer screen. "You see the continuum here from the quasar?" he says. And then to the dog: "You see it too, don't you, Bootsy?" The dog only looks guiltier, its ears pinned back. Or maybe it's just from listening to the Scotsman's dirge-type music on the data-room speakers, which after twenty minutes is making my hair hurt.

The Scotsman's real quest is ULIRGS—ultra-luminous infrared galaxies, which basically are cosmic head-on collisions. Not just one galaxy ramming into another—no, this is a Demolition Derby pile-up on the curve with three, four, five galaxies smashing into one another all at once.

When I sit in the warmth of the data room zooming in on these cataclysms befalling entire worlds out there in space, I usually never think of the Copernican principle: The earth is not special.

But tonight Copernicus rules. I see dread in everything. Everything is special. Dangerous.

The Scotsman is throwing out Right Ascensions and Declinations from his logbook and I obediently slew the telescope. But then Carl calls out from the computer. An urgent e-mail has just come through from an observatory in Chile. Something worth investigating is going on in the Orion constellation, which the massive star Rigel dominates.

Orion is lower in the sky than I would like, about three air masses. Within moments we're off in pursuit of Rigel, chasing it before it vanishes beneath the horizon. We are the hunters again, stalking lightpoints of prey as they flee into the cover of their own corners of eternity.

Once again I'm almost holding my breath as I start lowering all those tons of steel, glass and mirrors into the west. From the other side of the data-room wall, the Druids' telescope is groaning under the limits of its tolerance.

Rigel is one of the monster B-class stars that spend their vast cosmic inheritances so recklessly, so spectacularly, that they plunge into an early death. They are the stars' stars, burning through their fuel and dying young, blowing themselves to bits. But before they go, they sear the cosmos with a blue light far hotter than our sun, which only hits a mere orange on the spectrum.

Rigel is 44,000 times brighter than our sun. To which I ask: How does anything get to be 44,000 times brighter than our sun? What is that all about?

That's the problem with all this stuff. The numbers outrun your imagination in a flash. You're left with dust where images should be in your brain.

But there's nothing about Rigel's optical beauty that we'll capture tonight, not when we're working in infrared, which cannot pick up its eerie blue light reflected off the witch's head nebulae, all those trillions of miles out there. In astronomical terms Rigel's not that far away, only about 850 light-years, practically right in the next block, a mere five thousand trillion miles from us.

Or 260 parsecs if you're into all that.

But I always wonder if what we're seeing is even still there. Because what we're looking at is the light from Rigel that has taken 850 years to reach us.

So what if He got bored a few hundred years ago and decided to blow up a nearby swollen monster star the size of Rigel just for the hell of it? Back when Napoleon was marching on Moscow? And for the whole time ever since, we haven't had a clue what's barreling toward us?

Like what happened out there where Scorpius met the Centaurus constellation about two millions years ago? When whatever it was that blew itself to bits ripped the ozone layer right off our planet and hurled us right through the Pliocene Age and into the Pleistocene Age?

Doesn't this kind of thing completely screw up the concept of progress? That's what I want to ask. What's the point in all these human advancements that we've been struggling with for centuries?

We've just been busily cleaning up our act in our nice little part of the cosmos, trying to refine truth and justice and beauty and decency and all that—not knowing that this supernova death ray of gas and electromagnetic energy could be blasting toward us somewhere around the speed of light?

And He's sitting up there waiting for the action to start when it vaporizes our ozone layer off just for starters? Like some big dopey kid ripping the wings off a fly?

And then afterwards we get to start all over again, trying to raise ourselves up out of the muck for another few million years?

What is *that* all about?

Or maybe I'm really just preoccupied with those *sicarios* out there somewhere. But it is more than that.

It is a skill you will acquire soon.

Dr. Herrera.

Less than an hour later Rick, the other night assistant, has taken over from me. Family emergency, I tell him.

I am heading into the shadows of the forest. First up to the intersection at Mother's Kitchen and then down the mountain road, sweeping through the curves, through the dread seeping up from this *Malava,* as the Indians called it. And in the headlights everything takes on its own kind of mysticism, its own meaning. Every oncoming car is filled with *sicarios*, every glint from the forest is a weapon, and every curve the place for a roadblock.

The mountain has its ways.

I stop briefly at the Colonel's house, where Doc and Harry and the others have set up perimeter outposts—that's the term they use—across the mountain's folds and undulations. In the darkness, the men from the mountain are ready, some hidden, others scattered throughout the woods in knots of camouflage, metal and whispered wisecracks. Computers and GPS devices and cell phones throw sleek, faint glows across the sniper scopes and modified semiautomatic rifles.

Elena is safer here than anywhere else I can think of.

Charger hurries over to me. "I don't like this," he says, leaving the deep conversational spaces as he always does. "Doc has got us ready to shoot this guy with a new face. This Antonio. But tell me something."

"What?"

"How do I know who to shoot?"

"Where's Elena?"

"She's safe. Inside. Talking to someone who came up to see her." He looks away the way he always does when he doesn't want to talk any more.

"Who came up here to see her?"

"Father Nunzio," he says, his gaze searching the darkness for something to latch on to.

Tijuana

Highway 15 splits the towering hills, a crevasse of beaded lights plunging south, winding through the darkness toward San Diego. This darkness yields to the terraced illumination of houses on the lowering hills and then to the compressed rush of San Diego itself. It is just over an hour since I was looking into the mysteries of Rigel.

But there is one other mystery. Closer and more personal. And ultimately more terrifying to me. It revolves around the remembered fragments of Dr. Herrera's words. Not only his words.

You mean like this Elena who you're—

I keep playing what has been—is being—said through the filters of what I want to remember. But I cannot. Not now.

I am doing over a hundred miles an hour when I look at the speedometer.

Not far off another highway in the Hillcrest area of San Diego is the address he gave me. His office is in a three-story neo-Mediterranean building that is in darkness when I arrive.

He is standing in the faint glow of a solitary reading lamp on a desk swept clean of any documents. It takes a moment for me to register the cardboard boxes piled high in the unlit recesses of the office. The painted walls are bare but the unfaded rectangles are like echoes of photos, diplomas, that had hung there when the place had life. Now it is embalmed. It is an office at an end. Packed up. Something is over. There is no forwarding address on any of the boxes. No name. No Magic Marker scrawls of *Office* or *Patients* or *Records.* Just boxes overflowing with papers as if someone had just dumped them all into some kind of trash.

"Are you moving?"

It's as if he didn't hear the question. "I'm in a hurry," he says.

"Are you moving?" I ask again.

"In a manner of speaking," he says.

"Where are you going?"

It's as if he hasn't heard. "One of my patients is in crisis tonight."

"You seem to have a lot of them."

"I do."

"I need some answers."

"A lifelong craving for which there is no permanent cure," he says, settling into his chair. "You are here because you remembered something?"

"What violence am I going to be explaining away?"

"Ah. That."

"Yeah. That skill I will acquire soon."

"What else?"

"The tape recording you made with her."

"Ah."

"What was your answer?"

He sits staring off into the darkness. "My answer?" he says finally.

"When the tape ran out. After she asked you why you would give her sodium amytal the first time you ever met her." His eyebrows raise imperceptibly, acknowledging the challenge. "What was your hurry?"

"I was concerned—"

"Since when does any doctor jam sodium amytal into someone they've only just met?"

"Ah. You have experience in this, I take it," he says, the irritation weaving through the fatigue of his expression.

"Did you answer her?"

"No."

"Why?"

"I thought my answer might be"—he searches for the word—"destructive."

He finds the tape after rummaging through the chaos of several boxes and plays it as I ask him to. It begins as it had before:

You know that I am taping this?

...Ah.

Is that a yes?

Yes.

"Go to the end," I say. "Or almost the end."

He obliges. And then:

No. But I thought that in your case there was some urgency.

Why? Doctor, what was the urgency? Elena's voice is languid, almost dreamy.

The tape clicks off.

"You shut it off when she asked you that question."

"Yes. Yes, I did."

"What was the urgency?" I ask. "What is it you needed to know?"

He is looking up at the darkness of the ceiling, sitting in a large chair that swivels slowly back and forth.

"I needed to know if she—Elena—was the one who had done it."

"Done what?"

He sits, thinking. Staring into darkness. "All right," he says. "All right."

Only a few minutes later we are approaching the Mexican border.

"This business of saints hearing voices," he's saying. As if we'd talked about nothing else. "They were at the very least bipolar. But then most of the bank robbers whose cases I've been called in on were bipolar too. Stalin started as a bank robber, you know."

"Why are we going into Mexico?"

"You wanted answers."

"And Mexico is the only place to give them?"

"There are either answers or just more questions. Mexico has both."

The traffic bunches up in front of the Mexican border inspectors. Dr. Herrera's big black Lincoln is waved through. "Just wait," he says. "It's the plainclothes guys. They always cause problems. They take one look at me driving a car like this and—" A man with a plastic ID holder on his belt steps out in front of the car and snaps us to a stop. Dr. Herrera is ordered out of the car, the trunk is opened and something is said.

And then we are driving into Tijuana.

My thoughts are running away with me. Why exactly am I with a man who has more or less been on the payroll of the Cabrera family? "Tell me something," I say. "I've just had my home destroyed by Antonio's people and you're taking me to the place they come from?"

"The ones who destroyed your home were from San Diego, not Tijuana. Antonio has more men there than he does here. For them there is no border, not any more. Besides, they're not really sure what you look like. They're still arguing over different descriptions of you."

"How do you know so much about this?"

"I know," he says, dismissing the possibility of any further inquiry.

He has driven around the traffic circle and is heading into the neon blur of tourist bars on Avenida de la Revolución, and then is diving into the urban chaos of Tijuana, small streets strewn with repair shops, garbage and dusty cars, and then cutting across to a wide boulevard. At the tallest building for miles around, he pulls in. It is a hotel, oppressive in its massed and towering sterility outside and in.

The lobby is cavernous, dim and filled with stark, garish furniture surrounded by nicotine-colored marble. A mariachi band woefully serenades one of the empty corners. "If anyone asks just say you're one of my associates," he says, his eyes always in motion, scanning the width of the lobby. "But no one will," he adds. Yet his eyes never leave the people milling around behind me as we sit with our glasses of rum and Coke.

"They own this hotel," he says.

"They?"

"The Cabreras. Ramon. Antonio."

"Is this common knowledge?"

"No," he says, cuffing aside whatever challenge was implied.

"Is it the money," I ask, "that keeps you faithful to them?"

"Faithful?" He almost laughs. Without a trace of humor. "Is that what you think it is?"

"Then what? Why?"

"Why?" The jangled finale of the mariachi band drowns out whatever was to follow. The music is replaced by a cavernous rustle.

"Do you remember that priest I was telling you about? The one with the pigs?"

"What has this got to do with why I am here?"

"Everything," he says. There is a moment when neither of us talk. "You don't understand, do you?"

"Am I supposed to?"

"If you want to, you will," he says.

"When I had been there in that jungle town for about a year, the Indians began trusting me. The Indian women would come to see me asking if I could help them not to have any more babies. Most of them got pregnant once a year and ended with at least a dozen children. So I started implanting these birth control devices, IUDs, into these women. But the only nurses I could get at my clinic were the nuns, who were under the control of the priest. They were appalled at the idea of birth control—and assisting in it would be the sin of sins.

"When the priest found out he went on a rampage and I got myself denounced all over again. An instrument of the devil. But I kept implanting IUDs. The Indian women were coming from all over.

"And I said to the nuns: 'Do you want to help me? Or do you want to see some of these Indian women die?'

"The nuns agonized over this for a few days and then one morning showed up to help me implant IUDs. They thought they were doing the devil's work. But still they worked beside me in the operating room. Even when the priest threatened to have them all excommunicated.

"But the priest got his revenge.

"Sonia and I were not married back then. And living together was causing problems in the town. You have to remember that these little jungle towns feared the big-city ways of living. One day the mayor put on his white linen suit and came to see us. He was a bulky, rumpled man, only at ease when he'd had a few drinks and was making a speech in front of other peasants. To him, a doctor was someone who was far above his own station.

"With great awkwardness he said that an unmarried man and woman living together was an offense to the community. He kept apologizing as he said it.

"Sonia ran the entire clinic and she knew before I did that if we wanted to continue our work there we had no choice but to get married. Which we'd planned to do anyway. So we announced to the town that we were getting married.

"Sonia was amazing, the way she handled it all. It was all arranged—except for one detail. Which even she could not control.

"The only person who could marry us was the priest. And to our surprise he said he would be overjoyed to bless us in holy matrimony.

"Which is where his revenge came in. Because three days before the wedding he sent word that of course he could never marry anyone who had not been to confession. The entire town was watching us. I knew it was a trick of some kind. I was going to refuse to go to confession, but Sonia would not hear of it. She was afraid the priest would not marry us. So she went immediately to confess to the priest. When she came back she would not talk about it.

"All she said was, 'It's your turn.'

"And Sonia is a woman you ignore at your peril. She is as passionate as she is soulful. Do you know what a combination that is, my friend? If you are lucky you will. All I had ever wanted to do was marry her. It was my reality, my hallucination. I was in love. Am in love. It is the greatest gift you can ever have bestowed on you.

"So of course I went. It was a summer morning, when the sun was high up in the sky and the heat was already coming off the earth in waves that sucked the breath right out of you. All the Indians came and stood by the side of the dirt road watching me go to the church. The priest had told them I was going to confess. To them it was as if the priest had won.

"Inside the little church with its whitewashed walls it was already like an inferno and I should have known then because when it was this hot the priest never heard confession until later in the evening. In the confession box I started off the way you're supposed to: 'Forgive me, Father, for I have sinned.'

"Then after a long pause where he expected me to keep going he said 'So? How have you sinned?'

"I said, 'I have lost my faith.'

"Then he waited and said, 'That is worse than a sin. And what else?'

"I told him that was all. I could feel his fury coming through from the other side.

"He didn't want to say it but finally he did. 'And what about these evil devices you have put into the Indian women?'

"I said, 'That is not a sin.'

"'Then we will sit here until you admit it is a sin,' he said.

"So I said, 'All right then, we will sit.'

"And we did. All through the brutal heat of the morning and into the afternoon. And it was far worse in the confession box that had been built with a ceiling on it so all the heat stayed inside with no air. After about an hour I was starting to have trouble breathing. He was too.

"He was not a young man and I could hear him rasping. 'Are you ready to confess?'

"'No,' I said.

"'As you wish,' he said, and we sat there. My mind started buckling under the heat. I removed my shirt. Then my pants, sitting there in my underwear, sweating so much I was dripping. I heard a clunking sound and I realized he had hit his head on the other side of the confession box, probably passing out.

"'Father?' I said. 'Are you all right?'

"After a while he said, 'Fine,' but it sounded like his tongue wasn't moving when he talked.

"And the strangest thing began happening. I was coming to feel almost a love for him. I was overwhelmed by a kind of admiration.

"I felt humbled by the depth of his belief. And a terrible understanding descended upon me.

"I realized I could no longer hate this priest as I had.

"I wish it had not come to me. It was all so much easier before. Through all those years as my own gods crumbled I had been borne aloft by my scorn for people like the priest and his kind. And this was the great and terrible change that came over me at that moment.

"I lost my scorn.

"Do you have any idea what happens to a revolutionary who loses his scorn? It is a kind of emasculation. Because scorn makes everything possible, all the terrible things you do or say.

"I was told later that night that the Indian women found both of us unconscious on the floor on the opposite sides of the confession box.

"And two days later in the same church the priest married Sonia and me. And blessed us.

"The church was filled with Indian women. All of them implanted with IUDs. They came from all over the area, from far upriver, just to sit in the church when Sonia and I were married. And when the priest turned and saw all these Indian women he said, 'It is a great day for God.'

"Even a week earlier I would have reacted with scorn. But now all I said was, 'It is.'"

"Why are you telling me this?"

"Because I want to remember the day I was married." The neon from the bar reflects off his features in some impassive spectrum, yielding nothing but distance.

"Sonia died. Three days ago."

And then only the jangled buzz of the hotel lobby. As if he is in a trance.

"It was a long illness."

"Why didn't you—?"

He waves my words aside. "For almost two weeks Sonia was in and out of consciousness. And I told myself nothing—*nothing*—would prevent me from being there with her for the rest of her life." *The rest of her life.* It catches inside him as he says it as if struggling not to be said, and his accent flattens, with certain words punching through an anguish I have never seen in him. "Which really only meant weeks, maybe even only days.

"But then this... this business of the woman, Elena, happened. And I believed that if she was indeed the one they were hunting, then there was a second death about to happen—but one that I could prevent. If there was nothing I could do to stop death from overtaking Sonia, at least..." The words unwind, uncompleted.

"But hanging over everything was Antonio's wrath. Anything I told you, Antonio might have found out within hours. Word could spread. It always does here. And I would end up fleeing. Or a charred corpse like Dr. Navarro. Either way I could not be there with Sonia when she most needed me. But nothing—*nothing*—was going to stop me from being with her. I was at the hospital hour after hour, leaving only when I knew she was sleeping or when the sedation had overwhelmed her. I *vowed* Sonia would not be alone on that day..." His voice trails off for a moment.

"But she *was* alone. Three nights ago." Everything about him is clenched, with sharp angles overtaking his expression as he avoids looking at me. "I was there earlier that night. I had seen her myself. She was *sleeping*. I had talked to the nurses at the hospital. She was fine. *Fine!* They said that. Their exact word. It was at that same time that the reports of Antonio's killings, the massacres, started coming in. I phoned the only numbers I had on the mountain and no one answered. So I told myself I had to go up the mountain. To warn the woman. And you. For only a few hours, I thought.

"But death is quicker than any of us. It is the invisible beast always waiting to pounce.

"And when it did, *I was not there!* She died *alone*—as I told myself she would not. How many couples do you know who remain... in love? Over all those years? Do you know how rare that is? In my practice I have seen it once, maybe twice in all those decades.

"God, I wish I'd been the one to go."

We wait.

He stares into some nothingness only he can see as the noise from the bar rises unheard around him.

A woman approaches. She is an Indian, short, dark-skinned, and young but with an older woman's face, wide and worried, overlaid on younger features in that way that belies age. Her shiny black hair is tied behind her in braids.

She nods to Dr. Herrera and says something in Spanish or some dialect that has Spanish mixed in. He nods.

"I have learned to place more trust in the Indian women," he says, getting up. "It is a kind of superstition of mine. I believe educated people discard too much of their superstitions. Which are often more accurate than their intellect."

In the acrid night air the hotel valet drives up in the Lincoln and the Indian woman gets into the back. Dr. Herrera talks to her in that language and the woman falls into a nervous silence.

"I explained how you are an associate visiting with me for a few weeks," he says and makes a quick, subtle hand motion indicating that I should not respond.

We circle back, going north and then turning off the wide boulevard, plunging into the darkened side streets and emerging at a big, brightly colored restaurant with a stone courtyard filled with Cadillacs, Mercedes and dark-colored SUVs with tinted windows. A combination of salsa and rock blares over outdoor speakers as young men with tinted glasses and tattoos not quite covered by silk shirts cluster in groups that coalesce and then burst open like pods. Dead eyes and vacant smiles are all over.

"Juniors," says Dr. Herrera. "But we're fine."

"I'm sure."

"This is, or was, one of Ramon's restaurants."

The little Indian woman is our guide, slashing through the thicket of dark glasses where some forms of light never reach, pushing straight through the clusters of gold neck chains with pendants in the shape of AK-47s or daggers.

"This is the only place you will get the answers you want. Or the answers you *claim* to want," Dr. Herrera says as we reach the entrance.

Inside the restaurant the little Indian woman marches over to the *maitre d'*, a pulpy older man with a thin mustache on a wide face.

His normal balance of disdain and obsequiousness is instantly shifted toward the latter by the presence of this tiny peasant woman. She unnerves him in some way that does not fit with the bureaucrat's power he has honed to a blunt edge of superiority.

He stoops to hear her, his hands twist together as if he is washing them in air.

Then she vanishes.

We are escorted to a table in the bar under imitation Diego Rivera murals. At the table next to ours an expensively dressed young woman is flashing perfectly manicured signals to the waiters. The man she is with—young, dark-haired and getting drunk—has an expression held together by the leer of too much liquor. She signals the waiters and flashes American money at them. The man is suddenly surrounded by a phalanx of grimly jovial waiters.

What is obviously a house specialty is played out, an intricately choreographed ritual where one of the waiters blows a whistle, another grabs the man's head, a third pours a shotglass of rum into his mouth and then the other wipes his face with a towel. All accompanied by triumphal yells and a feverish mariachi overture. Then the waiters and the mariachis decamp with the precision of a marching band, leaving the young woman to rake the man's hair with her manicured fingers and smile at him seductively from close range.

She wears a thin, pale beige sweater like a second skin over enormous breasts that rub up against her man's hands. He clings to the table as if he's on a ship in a storm. He is well dressed, in his late twenties, with short dark hair and a crooked grin. He could possibly be described as handsome, but under the weight of the latest infusion of liquor his features sag out of any definition like stretched rubber. She kisses him on the mouth and then signals to the waiters for the ritual to begin again.

"He is one of their best killers," says Dr. Herrera, "and she is determined to marry him. I have seen her here before doing the same with another man. One from San Diego who was killed before she could marry him. Caught in the crossfire by a stray police bullet. He bled to death not far from here. He and some other Juniors were trying to assassinate a journalist. Just last year."

The waiters arrive again with smiles fastened tightly across their faces as they stand at the ready under the fake Rivera murals as the mariachi band does its best to provide a soundtrack.

"Ah, Freud...," says Dr. Herrera over the music. "In the unconscious it is impossible to separate powerful fantasies from actual experience. In her fantasy this woman has already married this dangerous man many times over."

The man falls drunkenly into the welcoming breasts of the woman, who flicks dollars at the waiters.

"But then illusions, like delusions, are derived from the deepest longings within us," he says. "It might even be why you're here right now. I suspect there's more to your relationship with the Cuban woman than you can admit to."

The neon beer signs play colored lights off his cheekbones, giving his face the sculptured look of a patrician with his steel-gray hair flowing back as a Medici might have looked, a look of fearsomeness or compassion depending on how the beholder perceived it.

"Some of the strongest people I know need illusions more than others. Forgive me, Freud is an old habit. But neuroscience has rushed in to save us. Now we'd say you are being held captive by the limbic part of your brain."

At the next table, as the perfectly manicured hands are guiding the clumsy pawing at her breasts, the woman smiles into the liquored grin before her.

"Like her. She will never understand the choice she is making—almost certain disaster with a terrible partner. The neurons firing connections to her limbic brain are taking the most well-worn path in her circuitry. Filled with neocortical memories, or chemical reactions within her, that match the code of someone, something, she once cherished.

"She doesn't know how much this tiny part of her brain craves the misery ahead of her.

"As is possibly the case with you."

Some sign that only he sees summons us to a corridor at the back of the restaurant.

The little Indian woman flashes her dark eyes, motioning us to wait in there, the light fading as the noise and the music become echoes. She vanishes into the gloom and then through a door at the end of the corridor.

"Now then, there are things you need to know before …" He stops and looks around as if someone might be listening.

"Before what?"

"Before. Just before. A year ago, maybe more, when the Mexican election was being held, Ramon and Antonio decided to kill some political leader as he came into the airport. But something went incredibly wrong.

"Bishop Montini was passing nearby on his way to catch a plane and several of the bullets struck him. Ramon and Antonio's men had accidentally murdered the bishop. The whole family went into fits of contrition. And their mother especially has never been the same since.

"Their mother is a simple, devout woman who fifteen years ago was just the wife of a garage mechanic living in a shack with one cold-water faucet. Her sons changed her life and she had always refused to believe they could be involved in anything bad. But this—gunning down a bishop! This was beyond even her superhuman powers of denial.

"Since the murder of the bishop, Ramon and Antonio's mother has been coming to see me as a patient four times a week. Usually at my office. Occasionally at her luxury condominium on Coronado Island in San Diego. And in the case of extreme emergencies—such as tonight—I am summoned to Tijuana to see her."

"Summoned?"

"Yes," he says sharply. "Summoned."

A shaft of light opens. The little Indian woman appears in a doorway, a silhouette motioning to us. She leads us down another corridor, the light fading as the noise and the music become echoes. We enter a darkened, silent room with a large round table made from rough-hewn wood. High-backed chairs made from the same wood and slung with leather are arranged symmetrically around it. A light hangs over the table, burning away the gloom in a receding circle of brightness.

We sit in silence, the little Indian woman standing behind us until, at some invisible signal, she goes to a door and opens it. An older woman enters, barely taller than the Indian, with piercing, almost frightening dark eyes set deep within the fleshy roundness of a tiny face.

I recognize her. From the television. Ramon's funeral. The mother wailing over the leathery death mask that once was her son's face as it stared upward in mummified fierceness.

But now she sits in the chair pulled out from the table for her by the Indian woman, her sclerotic stare giving off the aura of an indignant lapdog. Her left wrist is a cascade of thin gold bracelets. The rest of what she wears is cheap and synthetic. Her eyes are on me as she speaks sharply in Spanish.

Dr. Herrera answers. After several minutes of conversation he turns to me and speaks in a formal, almost stilted cadence. "She understands that you are an associate of mine. She agrees that this is not an appointment but a conversation. I have requested, however, that I not be the one to do the translation. I would rather you hear her words from someone else."

And with that he nods to the little Indian woman, who speaks for the first time. "Señora Cabrera wants to be sure that what she talks of here will never be spoken of anywhere else," she says in flawless English.

I nod slowly. "Of course."

Ramon and Antonio's mother sits across from us, her mouth working itself tighter in barely perceptible little twitches, and then she leans farther under the overhead light that bleaches her forehead as she talks.

"She says she wants a different medicine," translates the Indian. "She's already been through Prozac and Celexa and she tried Zoloft on her own. She says she cannot get rid of the nightmares."

"And this," says Dr. Herrera to me in a low voice, "is why she continues to see me but not the priest."

In Spanish Dr. Herrera asks her to describe the nightmares. She talks slowly at first in awkward, emphatic bursts of words. "She says she has nightmares about Ramon. She had some of these nightmares after the bishop was killed. And she saw Ramon in hell with fires burning all around him."

The translation from the little Indian woman with the face of an Aztec mask flows serenely, almost beautifully in strangely perfect English, nearly upper-class British in its intonation. As her employer is expelling anguished gasps of contrition and anger. Twisting and pulling at her fingers as if that will release the words.

"She has had this dream before," says the Indian woman, "but this time it was different. This time she saw him in hell with that terrible new face they stitched onto him. She says she knows why. She is afraid for Ramon's soul. Because of what Antonio is going to do to the woman who murdered his brother."

"Murdered?" I say almost by reflex.

"The Cuban woman," comes the reply, and I feel something vital slipping away, something beneath me that gives me sanctuary.

"The one who murdered her son."

Sometime after, maybe five, maybe two minutes later, I resume listening.

The gold bracelets are still making their own fearful music, tinkling as her little manicured hands jab back and forth into the light. "She says that she has not seen her son Antonio in weeks because he too has a new face, a beautiful face he tells her when he phones. She talks to him on a cell phone, a new one she is given every two or three days so the Americans will never be able to trace the calls. Antonio is in America now with his new face.

"And he does not want anyone to know what he looks like until he has avenged Ramon. And killed the Cuban woman."

I do not want to look at Dr. Herrera but I cannot avoid his gaze, his silence that comes at me in waves.

"And how will Antonio take his revenge?" I ask.

"Fire," she says.

There is another chiming of the bracelets. "Ever since the… the accident with the bishop, Antonio had become—how do you say it?—more aware of the Church. And in the same way that the Church once burnt sinners at the stake, in the Inquisition, Antonio has come to believe that fire is purity."

"Fire is purity?" I ask before I can stop myself.

Hey hey, now we're getting somewhere—

"*Si.* And he intends to purify this Cuban woman for the sake of Ramon."

As Dr. Reyes was purified? And Dr. Navarro? Purified at the tip of an oxy-acetylene fire?

"But she says the fire she saw in her latest dream was different, it was the fire of hell. This is what has upset her so much today. And she needed to see you because none of the pills have helped. So she wants something different, some other pill that is stronger, to make it go away."

"I don't know if I have pills for the fires of hell," says Dr. Herrera.

"She says you must. She says they have pills for everything now."

There is more talk but I hear nothing now, not when their voices have drifted off and I am staring across the table at Tommy, who is laughing the way he always laughed.

"Toldya," Tommy says with that big grin of his. "But you wouldn't listen would you?" No, I wouldn't. I couldn't. It scared me so much. "*Fire is a thing of sheer beauty. See? Even they know it—that fire is life! It makes everything possible. I mean c'mon, burning down all those old forests so new stuff can grow. It's fire Mikey, fire! Wiping out the old crap and releasing all that good stuff, the minerals and all that locked in those old charred trees and—*

—fire is life, I remember you saying that. And watching your fascination with the flame you made. But I did not want to know Tommy *It's like people Mikey. We all need the fire to release—*

They are all looking at me.

"Excuse me?" I say.

"She wants to know what is your assessment of her condition," the Indian woman repeats. "You are Dr. Herrera's associate, yes?"

I grope through a thicket of thoughts, feeling Dr. Herrera's tension.

"Tell her," I say, "that someone very close to me always used to say, 'Fire is life. Not death.'"

When the translation is completed those dark little eyes glitter for the first time. "*O gracias!*" she says, jumping to her feet, beaming and holding her arms apart as the bracelets chime.

He does not start his car immediately. He stares straight ahead, through the windshield into the ceaselessly changing configurations of young men with concealed weapons clustering outside the restaurant.

"What you heard tonight I was told almost a full day before you found the Cuban woman on the mountain.

"Ramon's wife, his widow now, is more, shall we say, objective than the mother. It's one advantage of loathing the man you're married to. Hours after Ramon died, she came to see me, telling me he had been murdered on the operating table." Another pause. "His wife, by the way, did not exhibit the same grief symptoms as his mother."

"How do they know it was murder?"

"They knew. And that if it was indeed the Cuban woman you had found, they would slaughter you, her, everyone they could find there. I simply wanted to get her away from there."

I am recycling moments. Precious, terrible moments. "What part of the brain is it again? The one that holds you captive?"

We have reached the traffic funnel to the border, a circling ramp leading to America, clogged with barely moving vehicles and street vendors, who weave in and out of the cars as they crawl toward the checkpoints.

He says, "I never gave her sodium amytal."

"What are you talking about?"

"I needed her to talk. In order to be sure that she was the one whose life was in danger. But the whole sodium amytal thing never happened."

"You injected her. Charger saw you."

"No. He saw me inject her. He *thought* it was sodium amytal. So did she."

"But I heard her talking on the tape. After you injected her. That's what made her talk."

"It was just a saline solution I injected her with. A placebo, if you like. I didn't have any sodium amytal when I first saw her. I had left in such a hurry. And because of the urgency of it all, I had no choice but to let her think I was injecting her with something that would work its medical power on her.

"She made herself talk. She only thought she couldn't talk."

"You told us she had some trauma-induced—"

"Out of either fear or calculation her mind just needed some excuse to shut down. While it rearranged the events of her recent past. It wasn't a real conversion reaction she was suffering from."

For what seems like a slow mile I am silent. "I've spent most of my life trying to rearrange the past."

"We all are," he says. "More than we want to know."

The lines of cars funneling toward the checkpoints are longer and slower than the usual weeknight. His Lincoln jostles into position behind an old pickup truck with Arizona license plates.

"9/11" says Dr. Herrera. "It added fifteen minutes at the border."

I'm still way behind him. "The past," I say.

He waits, expecting me to complete the thought. "Ah, the past," he says finally. "Even it is under attack now. They're saying the past may not exist—except back when it was the present.

"Sitting at that table with Ramon's mother an hour ago exists now only in the cerebral cortex of the four of us in that room. Except for a chemical reaction in four brains, it simply does not exist."

From somewhere in the lost terrain of my thoughts I see the cosmos and the inner workings of the human brain in some bizarre alignment. Einstein's theory of relativity, which drives almost everything in the universe, works both backwards and forwards in terms of time. As do Newton's laws. There is no past or future, just an unending string of beads of time, each one being the present. Strung together with all the other presents.

"There's something else you need to consider," he says. "It's almost certain—she murdered Ramon. There is no other way to put it."

I say nothing.

"You are acquiring the skill I told you you would. You are learning to rationalize acts of violence. But is it evil? Probably not. But who knows? Besides, you have no choice now. You're in love.

"I see it all the time" he says.

"*Toldya,*" says Tommy, laughing from somewhere off in the darkness. You did Tommy, you did.

And I have learned nothing over all these years—until the moments when I could afford to.

I know it now, that I am here because of you.

These nights on the mountain are as much destiny as my life has ever possessed—nights of routinely peering into violence that consumes entire worlds. Terrible fires that spew flames through galaxies, far worse than anything you ever did. Fire is what joins us, the buried link between you and me.

Attaboy Mikey. See? It's pretty isn't it, all those flames. But have you figured them out yet? Have you really understood them? Not just all the crap that sounds like a bunch of fire insurance actuaries writing a textbook about the horror—the horror—of it all. Listen to me Mikey, I'm talking about beauty here. Know why?

Through the telescope we look back in time. To what once was and is no more.

Somewhere far back in a different kind of time I am trying to see you, Tommy. As I never could back then.

Aw c'mon Mikey, it wasn't like I ever hid anything from you.

There are different kinds of conversion reactions. Not just the kind where people lose sight or speech after having been overpowered by the trauma rampaging within their own minds. There is mine: I see what is in front of me and turn away from whatever does not fit.

A different kind of blindness. Muteness.

It is the legacy Lightning bequeathed us. In the name of hope, the truth must be turned away from. Until it fits. Even in the wisest of us. There are some things we are simply unable to know. Our brains reject. Expel.

The woman? Aw no, c'mon, you're losing—I'm tellin' you, just like Lightning didn't want to know. And just like we didn't want to know about him. It's not just that this woman of yours wipes out some guy and— What is there to understand? I am at my own event horizon, hand in hand with a woman I met only days ago. *Oh get a grip for godsakes.* I have never believed in this kind of love, this gale force that gloriously batters loose everything that has been fixed and known, sweeping you far out into some riptide of need and longing.

But right now I can no longer see the shore. Nor do I want to.

Because a man in a uniform and a U.S. government badge is looking down from his station at the border checkpoint and asking, "Where do you live?"

For a moment I am not sure.

There are no real good-byes with Dr. Herrera. He is too full of patrician defenses for that. Instead he sends elliptical messages of farewell arcing out like tracers from some darkened part of his life. He talks of Che and of how he has always regretted not staying in the jungle, even if Che never got there. This life, the one with the cars and the houses and the wealth, somehow it is suddenly a withered appendage, a limb trailing uselessly behind him.

"Sonia's funeral was this morning. It is over. All over," he says in a voice so soft I can barely hear the words.

He is driving into the airport that juts out into the sea from the middle of San Diego and he stops at the terminal, oblivious to the incessant recorded voices warning of parking in the white zone. "Antonio will know by now that I was there tonight," he says. "He will soon know I have been trying to help Elena.

"Sonia would have approved. She was the one who always wanted to help others. But she loathed the Cabreras, all of them. She refused every gift I gave her once I started treating their wives and mistresses."

A blast of blue-and-red light from an airport police car ricochets across the surfaces of the car. "Sonia wanted to go back to the life we once had. But I kept finding reasons not to. And now?" he loses the words for a moment, "I have no reason to stay. I really didn't expect it to be like this. Not this difficult. Once she died."

He gets out and opens the trunk. "My mind has never dealt well with irony." He takes a single small suitcase from the trunk.

"One favor I would ask," he says, handing me the keys to the car. "It's leased. Just park it in the garage under my office. Earlier tonight I mailed an envelope to the leasing company telling them the keys would be under the floor mat." Then he nods. A kind of finality indicating that all that has to be said has been said.

"Where are you going?"

"Looking for Che," he says. And then turns and walks into the nearly deserted terminal, where the last flights of the night are being readied for takeoff.

Palomar

I have never felt silence like the one in which I am suspended on the drive back up to the mountain. It is a silence that blasts from somewhere within me and obliterates anything else as I replay every moment I have spent with Dr. Herrera. But like that old saying about the problem with life being that it has to be led forwards but can only be understood backwards, I start from the last glimpse of him walking into the airport. And replay the moments with him, all the way back to that night in my cabin when he first hurried up to the mountain.

And only then, by retracing, can I understand all the stern hesitation and formality, all the etched contours of fierceness he projected that now seem like nothing more than threads of grief pulled tightly together.

And the need, as some kind of tribute to the life most precious to him, a life that was ebbing away, to save another life.

That, I understand.

We are circles, all of us, intersecting from different planes.

In the hours before dawn a full ripe moon hangs over the valley below the dome. A funnel of smoke stretches all the way back toward Bailey Meadow, leaving stagnant air in its wake. The air is acrid as if it too has been charred.

It is the Colonel who meets me there first. The volunteers are still hosing down the charred cedars around the smoldering rubble where his garages had been. "They opened fire. Sprayed everything with automatic weapons again. Must have hit the propane tank."

Inside the Colonel's house there is silence except for the crackle of the radios and walkie-talkies drifting through the darkness. I call out for Elena and there is no answer. In the bedroom the covers on the bed are rolled back and her clothes are draped over the chair.

From somewhere in this hollowness I hear her calling my name. When I find her outside on the deck, a long T-shirt pulled down around her legs that extend out to the railing in front of her, she does not look at me. She keeps staring into the sky.

"I phoned everyone, trying to find you," she says.

After a while I say, "I was with the psychiatrist."

"Where?"

"His office."

"That's all?"

"We went to Tijuana."

She takes a breath that can be heard. Then she looks out into the darkness. "Show me something," she says. "From what you do."

"From what I do?"

"The stars."

I search through the needlepoints of light. "That's Scorpius," I say, trying to show it to her by tracing the winding constellation with my finger, but it's like drawing an intricate design in the sand. "That star up there, the brightest one." She squints and points. "Yeah, that one. It's Antares. It's in the process of dying."

"But it's brighter than the others."

"They do that. Before they die."

She keeps looking at the sky. Only the crickets can be heard now.

"Xylocaine comes in two dosages," she says.

It seems like minutes before she speaks again. "1,000 milligrams. And 100 milligrams. Hospitals are always afraid of mixing them up. Usually it is the circulating nurse who is in charge of making sure the dosage is correct. But since we had no circulating nurse I knew it would be up to me."

Again silence.

"And this is what killed him?"

Her answer unfolds quietly, without the urgency I somehow

expect. "When I was being held captive in that house of theirs listening to the screams coming from the basement I made a decision that my life was no longer mine to preserve. If I lived or was murdered and thrown to the dogs it was not something I could think about. Instead I had been handed a duty. To kill Ramon. He was a monster, a murderer, a dangerous and crazy person. But I knew that if I didn't kill him, sooner or later someone else would have to do it. You don't understand, do you?"

Baymer.

"Everything he was doing was, how do you say, laughing at? mocking? what I had promised the man who had been shot by the soldiers in the Bosque de la Habana when I was a girl. I hated what I was a part of now—using what was meant for good to help spread evil. I was a part of the devil's medical team. I had betrayed my promise to that man who died in the Bosque.

"And the only way I knew to stop it—stop Dr. Reyes—was to quietly change the dosage to 1,000 milligrams of Xylocaine. Enough to kill Ramon. And so end forever what Dr. Reyes was doing. And Dr. Navarro too. If Ramon was taken away from this earth, they would be too. Antonio would make it happen.

"So I watched the Xylocaine drip into Ramon and it was like all my—my *ansiedad?* was over. I was calm now.

"They could kill me and somehow I did not care. Truly. I did not.

"Because I told myself it was necessary. That there was a need to do it for the good. The good was more... how would you say? greater? than the bad."

All I see before me is that fierce little woman with her lapdog face, jumping to her feet and exclaiming *O gracias!* as the bracelets chime.

And keep chiming.

My hand cascading from her hair to her shoulders. And still farther down her back around to the curvature where we are born and reborn. With arias of wild gentleness and laughter filling the silence of some moment in a universe racing along beside us, we tumble back into the soft folds of the bed. And from somewhere beyond where we exist now, I learn for the first time about a kind of absolute submission. A kind of love that hurls aside all the traces and hurtles blindly into the purest darkness.

And as I lose myself within her I know. I know for the first time in all these years. I know why Lightning stayed.

I can almost reach out and touch him.

In the last moments of night, the darkness clinging to the edges of the world before it is pried loose by a first faint light: She is talking to me. In low, gentle tones.

I drift in and out of her words, cresting the silken waves of her voice, parsing the fragments of what she says, hearing but not hearing. Yet understanding all in some fractured jumble of meaning. She is telling me about that first morning when I fell asleep, exhausted, and awoke to find her standing over me with a knife.

About how I cried out in my sleep. Words. Names. She was not sure which. But in some way sensing that we shared something. *Sharing? oh no no no, for godsakes Mikey get real. I mean okay so you blew someone away too—check that, you just took out the nose, but she! She got the whole megillah, corpse and all. Okay so the stiff was stitched up a tad around the gills and pumped full of medical rat poison, a neat job, ring one up for the little lady but don't go thinking Bonnie and Clyde et al. here because you and I have got some living to do—*

Even before I awake in the light of dawn I know she is no longer here. Some instinct is at work even in the depths of sleep, before I reach over to the other side of the bed and feel its coolness, its emptiness. The Colonel's house is as still as a tomb.

The phone rings again and again.

It is Father Nunzio.

The Colonel is outside near the road, haggard and talking hurriedly to the men driving his water trucks.

"She left," he says. Like a betrayal had occurred.

In a gentle way it had. She had given him back a few fleeting moments of his youth. And now he looks older, as if something vital has been cut out of him.

"She left me a note," he says almost defensively, looking at me like he can't figure out what I'm doing here. And then he turns back to his drivers before striding off toward the white Jeep. He's back to being the way I remember him, sulfurous and unapproachable. His pale blue eyes burning off any trace of the last few days.

As I'm leaving he turns and holds out his hand like he's some kind of traffic cop. "Don't spread it around that she's not here any more, okay?" he whispers. He taps the side of the car like an exclamation mark and walks away.

"Why not?"

He turns with a look like he can't believe what he's just heard.

"If those Mexican drug bastards know she's gone," he says as if he's talking to a slightly slow student, "they won't attack again, will they?"

"Probably not."

"This is where clarity sets in. We've waited a long time for this."

In the parking lot outside Mother's Kitchen the sheriff's cruiser and Doc's pickup truck are the only two vehicles parked out in front.

"Hear your lady friend had to leave," the deputy says, warming his hands around the coffee, his hair the color of tarnished silver in the oblique light forcing its way through the trees.

"You know more than I do." Which is pretty much an obvious assessment because the deputies know everything that happens on the mountain.

"Too bad. She seemed nice." He's stalling until he can find an opening. "Real nice."

"She was. Is."

He looks around. "I was real surprised to see the Colonel having company."

"So was he."

"This morning when he found out she'd left, it really choked him up," Doc says. "Although he'd never admit it."

"Lemme tell you something, Doc, and I'll deny it if you ever tell him," says the deputy, "but your old man is a long-ball hitter when it comes to women. He and I grew up here together. Served in the same damn marine base in I Corps up a piece from Da Nang. Never saw a man so damned fool sentimental when it comes to women. Fell in love about as often as a rabbit breeds. No offense to your mother."

"My mother's still good friends with him."

"Hell, he's on better 'n lawyerly terms with all of his exes. All but one," says the deputy.

"The one in the photograph?" I ask.

"If the photo is a dark-haired woman like one of them old-time movie stars, you broke the code, son. He still rubs up against a tree every time he thinks of her. But see, she wouldn't stand for it all."

"Stand for what?"

"All his craziness. Man's tore up more bars, rolled more cars and sponsored more recreational mayhem than any human I ever met. Why do you think he's so damn tight-assed rigid? Needs a steel fence full of rules around his mind to keep the springs from flying loose. But then I seen this with a lot of wild men when they get old."

Father Nunzio has been waiting for me, sitting in a booth by the window. At this early hour he is the only customer. And still cranky from having been kept waiting while I was outside talking to the deputy and Doc.

Behind him a lone waitress is setting tables with cutlery and cups.

"I've been here since before it opened," he says, trying to fix me with an accusatory stare.

But the thick glasses only magnify those rheumy old eyes, making him look like a slightly scarier Mr. Magoo. Not like the old days where every time he looked at you, you felt like you were getting jabbed by a needle.

"You helped her leave," I say, furies struggling to reach the surface. Once again he is in my life. "All this was planned."

"Only since last night. When she knew she was going to tell you what she did to Ramon."

"How many Hail Marys did that get?"

"She wanted to protect you."

"I'm not sure I'm the one who needs protecting."

"You do," he says. "Antonio will be like the abbot of Citeaux—eight hundred years ago when he was waging the Albigensian crusade and couldn't be bothered going to the trouble of finding out who was a heretic and who was a believer. So he came up with a solution. 'Kill them all,' he said. 'God will know His own.'

"Antonio will be like the abbot. To get to Elena he would not care who was slaughtered. Whether they were protecting her or not. She is saving you by leaving. She knew that if she stayed she would not be the only one to die."

"Father, go back to your church and let other—"

"I put her in my car and sent two of the best Indians with her to drive." He looks at his watch. "She'll be in Los Angeles by now."

He's in control again. That's the key to it all with him. *I put her.* Information is power and he knows her secrets now and I know nothing. I am the supplicant who must reach up and grapple for whatever news of her he deigns to dispense.

"Los Angeles?" There must be something about the look on my face that completes the thought.

"You should have paid more attention," he says, grappling to keep his reservoir of righteous indignation from leaking away. *Oh yeah right Mikey, is that ever rich, this big glorified turd hiding out behind his—*

"What do you know about paying attention to another human being?"

His face cinches up like a change purse pulled tight on strings. "She *asked* me," he snaps, "not to tell you before now. She was afraid of telling you. Afraid you'd try to talk her out of leaving."

"Yeah? Well she'd be wrong," I say.

He absorbs this, making chewing motions. Finally he looks directly at me. "We have a sanctuary in the heart of Hollywood. Originally started years ago when the death squads were roaming through El Salvador and Nicaragua. We smuggled refugees in from those countries. But the network has stayed intact and once in a while we use it to shield people who need it. Like her."

"Where is it?"

"I can't tell you."

He thrusts a letter at me. His way of choreographing it all for maximum drama. Right after the Albigensian stuff, bring in the letter.

"It's from her," he says.

Michael it says on the outside in wildly flowing handwriting. It is as if the envelope can barely contain the word. I take it but do not open it.

"Now then, I'm late," he says. "Some Mexicans came across the border to the Centro de Guadaluparno last night. I am needed there. So drive me there, please."

Thanks to god for you being with me... I am thinking of you as I am going away ... I will keep going for a long time... I already miss you... I already reach out and want to know why your arm is not there to touch... but I still see the man in the Bosque and I have to do what he deserves from me... and I do not want more hurt than I cause already.

Te quiero

Elena

Do you understand?... For a while. Okay?

Okay.

It's as if the mountain is having a seizure. Everything gives way at once.

The two-way radios and the cell phones suddenly explode with voices, all calling in with reports of simultaneous attacks. The Colonel gets back from Temecula, his rear window shattered by bullets, and exhilaration pumping through those steel-blue eyes. "History is dealing hands," he says to those of us behind the water tanker that blocks his driveway. "Time to place the bets."

But I barely hear him. It is Charger I am listening to. From whatever the outpost is, somewhere down near the edge of Mendenhall Valley far below us where Doc is fixing binoculars.

"I seriously don't think you should come down here, Michael." Charger's voice comes through the phone talking faster than I have ever heard him.

"Charger, what's happening?"

"Sort of like they're running a reverse on me, Michael." And then his voice turns to static as the cell phone scrambles whatever it is he says next.

There is a large cloud of smoke way off in the distance. A few seconds later the sound reaches us in a booming thud.

"Charger?" I yell into the cell phone, dialing again and again. *You have dialed a number that is no longer in service. Please hang up and...* On redial the phone just rings and rings.

From the two-way radio his voice comes in again, panicked and angry all at once. I yell for Doc, who has already loaded up one of those dirt-bike motorcycles that clutter up the Colonel's garage and now hurtles off down a hill, followed by two others.

By the time I get onto the horse they are far in front of me, plunging toward the flames that shoot in scrofulous geysers of dirty colored fire, blasting into the low gray clouds that press down on this endless sea of green.

Charger is somewhere in those flames.

One of the motorcycles is shot out from under the man riding it. Doc is hurt or wounded in the underbrush near the footpath on the side of the hill. I dismount below them while the horse I am riding sidesteps and spins in panic so that even getting out of the saddle is difficult. I run toward the hillside firing the automatic rifle and yelling for Charger.

I am all reflex and impulse, not really having any plan except one—

to save Charger from whoever, whatever, is attacking him. The sheer desperation carries me ahead, stumbling and yelling for Doc and the others as I fire blindly with a weapon I barely know how to hold.

And then something makes a terrible noise, hideous and whistling before it blows up in the middle of the flames and all hinges of perception are ripped loose. I am pinwheeled through the air and find myself inexplicably on the ground listening to screams in two different languages that seem to come from everywhere.

In the gathering darkness, any one of those faces whipping through the forest behind the automatic rifles could be Antonio.

Maybe it's the light but they all look the same.

The Colonel is waiting, standing on the mountaintop overlooking the valley when we return. He looks right over us, out into the valley like someone impatient with the preliminaries and waiting for the main event to begin.

"Finally!" he says quietly. And then he glances down at us with what might be a smile.

I make a run for the dome, shaking off the warnings about traveling the roads. Even an hour later from the catwalk of the dome I can hear gunfire and watch the flames spread up the side of the mountain into Mendenhall Valley. But it is a different direction I turn to, north with the wind, north into the lights of Los Angeles that are still visible in the distance beneath the tumbling grayness of the skies. Then the rains come from behind, putting out the fires to the south.

And silently smothering with mist the lights to the north.

Three days later, in the place where the lights came from, I stand in a small cemetery not far from where the 405 Freeway meets Wilshire Boulevard. Marilyn's grave vault is over in a corner just as Charger had described it, with office buildings rising in a palisade of steel and glass behind it. I lay the flowers beneath the simple inscription *Marilyn Monroe,* making sure the card saying *With Love—Charger* is discreetly placed the way he would want it to be.

Charger always felt uncomfortable with open displays of affection.

And then I take out the little glass jar filled with ashes I got from the place where Charger died. I have no way of knowing if they're his exactly. But they came from as close as I could get to where I last saw him, the place at the edge of the valley where the trees are now just charred spires. I scatter the ashes beside Marilyn's grave and watch as they settle into the dampness at the base of the vault. I figure he won't mind. Of course he'd be embarrassed and shy about imposing on Marilyn this way, being with her like this. "She won't mind. You guys are going to like each other," I say, whispering in case anyone else is around.

The Catholic churches on the list of Hollywood-area sanctuaries take two days to visit, all of them rustling inside with whispered Spanish amid the teeming silence.

Elena Garcia Molina?

Shrugs. Whispered consultations over lists of names.

And who is it who wants to know?

More whispered consultations.

We have to protect—

There is no Elena Garcia Molina known to any of the priests or the workers. Or so I am told. But at one of the churches not far from Hollywood Boulevard, where tourists are roving in search of glamour, there is a compound fenced in from the streets with a large house behind the church. It is a kind of dormitory, and in the little office next to the front door the impassive dark-skinned woman is politely insistent. Information cannot really be given. This is a place of protection, she says. As all the others have said.

But she flickers a trace of recognition at the mention of Father Nunzio. Yes, there may have been someone by that name here for a day or two.

But she has gone. And no one knows where.

Palomar.

The sum total, expressed in material terms, of these years here on the mountain is my one small suitcase. It sits amid the flattened wreckage of my cabin like a peg.

For one last time I walk back toward the stream, the shaded grove of trees where dappled light comes through in beams. My Bosque. Where images dance, fueled by memory. The past. It does exist.

It lives in something other than light-years or megaparsecs. Or neocortical phantoms that dance alone in a solitary mind.

Hey hey now we're talking Mikey

Tommy…

Listen listen, I got an idea for my new guaranteed bestseller You're Looking Good and Other Horrible Lies. *See Mikey I figured out that no one under—*

Tommy, I can't do it any more.

—under the age of thirty is ever told they're looking good. They don't have to be told. They naturally look good—they're young! It's just the crones and geezers who—

It's over, it's time. I have to leave.

—look like shit who have to tell each other how great they look. Lying through their teeth—

Tommy, good-bye.

What!? Mikey no. No. Don't mess with me like—

I have to.

Have to? Well please, thanks and fuck you too Mikey. You gonna burn my letters too? Huh?

Why would I burn your letters?

Snuff out all traces of my existence? Huh?

I've been your brother—

Well what do you think you've been you moron? My fairy fucking godmother? Mikey—it's that's tomato can, ain't it? That Chiquita banana you've been boinking. I shoulda known—shack up for a night and whammo, an instantaneous case of shit for brains. Goddammit I—

I love you.

Fuck your love you homo you incestuous deviant dipshit drooler. There's wackers like you in the nuthouse with wires tied to their wieners Mikey, which is what's gonna happen—

Tommy.

...Ohforchristsakes Mikey c'mon... You're kiddin' me. Right?... Right?... Hey hey. No! Okay? Enough of this crap...

...

Are you listening to me Mikey?

...

I know you are, you moron.

...

Okay, okay, okay... two can play this game you know

...

Fine. Just fine.

...

See ya.

...

Oh by the way Mikey—you're looking good.

Penetang

At twilight in the warm summer months the bays and inlets are scattered with little fishing boats searching for pike or bass. It is in shallows like these that she seems happiest, the places where there is the nestling shelter of land around us but the vastness of Georgian Bay stretches out into the fading light of the sun.

Marlee is my sister. Until the day last summer when I returned from America I had not seen her since she was an infant. I had stopped uncertainly at the end of the lane in front of the little house on a hill between Penetang and the open water. She was standing silhouetted against the sky. "There's a stranger here," she called out. Mother appeared and from behind the veil of the screen door, the uncomprehending confusion surged until she let out a cry and rushed down the lane to throw her arms around me.

For a moment I hardly recognized her, not just because of the gray hair or the etchings in that once porcelain face. Instead it is because of the image of her, the one that froze in my mind two decades ago, and that now in one jarring instant is instantly erased by the older woman I see before me.

Marlee is almost twenty now, suspended by her autism in some world of her own where connections to others are tenuous and so often framed in narrow fields of repetition. It was her bedroom, when Mother showed it to me, that gave off the ghostly family imperatives tracing their way back through the genetic entanglements of whatever made us what we are.

What we were.

A man, a woman, two sons. And now Marlee. In the bedroom Tommy and I once shared. And all I could think of looking at this room in the little house on the quiet bay, the repository of what was once *us*, was the old saying: Be kind, for everyone you meet is fighting a terrible battle.

There is a sense that our terrible battles are over. For now.

Baymer, Oinky, Oinky's mother, Myner, the three aunts, Father Nunzio, Grandmother: Gone. Moved. Or vanished. With Tommy and Lightning.

All of them winnowed, scattered. And with them whatever battles or anguish that cloaked them: gone.

And Dr. Baymer, the Crown attorney who was going to prosecute me, and any witnesses who could testify against me are either dead or lost to the farthest reaches of the elderly hospice system.

My crime, such as it was, has been expunged.

Penetang, the specter that has roiled in some world I remembered and never understood, is in a kind of remission.

And yet sometimes for a moment or two it all comes rushing back, but in ways that are emptied of all the spent furies. In a pile of old papers in the garage I find the *Gone With the Wind* poster and I am struck by how much Mother really did look like Scarlett O'Hara. I could never have seen the resemblance years ago. Back in the days when she was Mother.

Now the memories send me back into brittle photo albums and the uncertain smile on a beautiful young woman preserved in fading images. Later, I hang the poster in its old place in the hallway and twice she walks past it without noticing. The third time, she stops, backs up and looks at it, imperceptibly shaking her head.

She looks from the poster to me. "Fiddle-dee-dee," she says and then laughs, almost embarrassed. Then she takes the poster down. I never see it again.

That evening, she sits on the porch facing the bay. For a while her eyes are closed, the last burnished moments of the day casting soft shadows across the threaded contours of her face.

"Your father would have made a wonderful Rhett Butler," she says. "Much better than Clark Gable."

And then she closes her eyes again. Serene in the final warmth of the sun.

On the wall of Marlee's room were pencil drawings she had made at the age of four. They were drawings of boats—wooden boats like the kind Lightning had wanted to make. Perfectly rendered mahogany-planked boats, meticulous in their perspective and detail, drawn over and over again by a little girl, renditions of ads she found in a scrapbook Mother kept of our life with Lightning.

But then the other drawings came in a torrent, dozens of them so sophisticated that an illustrator could barely have matched them. Sleek wooden boats, meticulous in a lap strake construction that Lightning would have been proud of.

A day later, I dig up Lightning's old tools, the wooden-handled planes and saws and vises. Opening the metal case that has been buried amid all the glass up behind our old house. Feeling for the first time something actually passing from his hands into mine. A continuation of what was begun and then stopped shines out of the metal case like some mystical light of revelation.

Removed from their shrouds of oilcloth and grease, the tools give off some dull glint of purpose that cannot be ignored. At first I merely return them to their positions in the old garage, arranging them as I remembered Lightning might have done.

Then one morning one of Marlee's drawings shows up in the garage, a drawing of a sleek mahogany boat, the kind of small cruiser the Italians made half a century or more ago.

Not a word is said. It all progresses on unspoken understanding, as Marlee sits silently watching. One of her vaguely related great-uncles, an old man from the French-Canadian side of the family, shows up to instruct me in the use of the tools.

Then, each day more drawings appear in the garage. Until the dust-covered wooden beams and walls are almost obscured by them.

What Marlee cannot know is that mahogany is back. The wooden boats made from these designs are now symbols of understated elegance plying the lakes and gracing the covers of boating magazines. Just as Lightning had insisted they would be. Years too late. And too early.

From what I am told on the phone it remains pretty much the same back there on the mountain.

Even though the *sicarios* are seldom seen on the mountain now. Their occasional forays are almost taunting in the way that they deny the Colonel the great battle that forever exists just beyond his reach.

Accounts of the Colonel's restlessness are told with differing degrees of intensity. As everything about him always has been. Some are tales of him stalking the edges of the mountain, standing guard on the fault lines of the civilizations. Waiting for it all to begin.

While others tell of it all being over. Even as he still prowls the night.

Stories of sporadic assaults occasionally cascade down from the TV news satellites and come already equipped with their own legend, their own mythology.

And every stranger on the mountain is suspected of being Antonio. Or so they say.

I tell myself I don't miss it.

But I do. I think of Palomar often, especially on the nights when I am alone out in the boat staring up at the silence of the sky. Filled with wonderment. Knowing that almost everything about the sky that was held to be fixed and true a hundred years ago is now known to be wrong. Even at the beginning of the twentieth century and right up past World War I, the High Priests were decreeing that our Milky Way was the entire universe. Which is pretty much like looking at a grain of sand and insisting you're seeing the whole beach.

And what of everything we now hold to be fixed? What chance does that have of being true in a hundred or a dozen years.

But what has become fixed for me ever since those days on the mountain are the questions that won't go away. The ones that come from watching entire worlds blow up like kernels of popcorn.

And so still I wonder sometimes. Why?

And yet I do not want to give into the accompanying thoughts.

So right now I have chosen to believe in different truths. And today my quest is to make Marlee laugh.

It is what gives me meaning now.

Savant is the term Mother says the local doctor uses to describe Marlee. An autistic savant with the mental age of a child and the windblown blonde hair and pretty tanned face of a mystery I cannot unlock, only accept.

I have come to love Marlee and the subtle games she sneaks into our life. It is my aim to get through all the seriousness that envelops her and make her laugh. I sense that she wants to and sometimes I probably imagine that she is on the verge of breaking out of this strange shroud that settles around her spirits.

On one of our twilight journeys out into the bay in the old mahogany boat I am restoring with Lightning's tools, I am close to making her laugh. I am telling her about Father Nunzio, doing an imitation of him yelling at his students. I'm sure I can see a smile forming in her eyes, the tiniest beginning of a laugh.

And then it fades.

She sits in the back of the boat looking around with that solemnity that settles around her in the silence of the lake at night.

As if pulled by some genealogical force, Marlee has taken as her own private domain the little plateau up behind our house. It is her sanctuary to which she retreats, lying on the lushness of the grass that she tends with meticulous, obsessive care. When I first see her lying there, staring up into the twilight sky, I call out, telling her to be careful.

"Why?" she calls back, puzzled.

"The glass."

When I get up there, she is leaning back on her elbows staring at me with that look of hers, simultaneously blank and profound. "What glass?"

Standing there for the first time in years, I wait for just a moment, expecting voices I do not hear.

I run my hand through the smooth carpet of grass. Waiting to feel the sharpness of jagged edges, menacing, glinting in what is left of the light. But they too are not there any more.

The earth has done its work.

"What are you looking for?" Marlee asks.

"Something that used to be here."

"Know what I'm looking for?"

"What?"

"Bootes?" At first I think she's looking for her shoes. But she leans back and looks up at the sky and I realize she is talking about a constellation even most astronomers couldn't identify without consulting their sky charts.

"Ah," she says triumphantly. "Right there, under Arcturus."

She pulls out the pad of sketching paper she always carries and says, "Shine the light." I turn on the flashlight, its beam catching a pad of paper, on which she starts drawing the entire sky—Canis Minor, Cancer, Hydra, Ursa Major, Draco and on and on, working toward the Northern Cross, all of it dashed out in dots and lines and letters by the flashing pencil. Not once does she look up.

And then with those serious eyes she finally looks up and hands it to me. "It's for you," she says.

"Thank you," I say. I cannot believe what I am looking at—a complete sky chart that no other human I know of could reproduce like this. "How did you do it?"

"I looked at your star book," she says in that casual voice of hers.

Two nights later, under a barrage of starlight as we're pushing the boat away from the dock: "I like Elena too."

"What?" I've never mentioned her name since I've been back.

"You got mail from her."

"Yes."

"E-mails?"

"Yes."

"From Havana," she says. "Is she coming here?"

"Soon."

"Cubana Airlines Flight CU088, Saturday. It arrives at 12:20 p.m. from Havana via Veradero, Saturday," Marlee says. "An Airbus. I checked for you."

"Thank you." Said in a mixture of amusement and amazement.

"I'm glad for you."

The winter just ended was cold in so many ways until the February afternoon when a large envelope arrived. It bore the postmark of Escondido, California. Inside was a scrawled letter. It was from Father Nunzio... *I think of you and of her... I pray for both...* Garrulous and taciturn at the same time. *I have often reflected on the possibility that a different kind of divine intervention was at work for you both.* Attached to his letter was yet another envelope, this one addressed to him at the mission. It bore a return address of a M. Nadeau at a television production company in Montreal. It too had been opened.

Cher Padre,

I am writing to you at the request of a young woman my wife and I met recently while on vacation in Havana, Cuba. It told of making an emergency visit to a clinic where his wife was treated for an ear infection. Treated by a young doctor. A woman. Who asked M. Nadeau if he would take a letter back to Canada, the mail from Cuba being too unpredictable, held up in Havana for weeks, months, sometimes forever, and mail it to a priest in California who might have the address of someone she once knew.

Dear Michael:

I am saying prayers that this gets to you because I do not know where you are. I am hoping it is all good for you. I forget that I lose some of my English but I have enough to tell you that I have never stopped, for one little moment, of thinking about—

As I have not. For one little moment.

My grandfather, he died after I came here just for him. Coming back was not such a big problem because he was still one of the old men who had power. I came because it was not finished. Nothing was finished. Not with him. Or with me too. I had to finish. I hope you can see why I had to—

I can.

—and now it is done. Even in the Bosque. It is done.

Almost.

It is as close as Marlee comes to excitement. Wanting to know how Elena's getting out of Cuba, not being satisfied with the answers I give her about why she is being allowed to leave the country.

And whether we are getting married.

"*What?*"

"That Father Nunzio asked you," she says. "In his letter."

"He doesn't know anything."

"Maybe you don't know anything."

"You weren't supposed to read that."

"You probably wanted me to."

"Absolutely not."

"Well? Will you?"

"Hey. She's just coming here for a visit, okay?"

"Yeah." And then silence. "Yeah, yeah, yeah."

We are drifting past the foreboding Victorian building on the south shore, the Mental Health Centre, as it is called by everyone now, surrounded by angular new buildings that only enhance the sense of ugliness and menace I feel emanating through a filtering curtain of trees as its lights flash glinting reflections onto the water around us.

"Tommy was in there, wasn't he?"

"Yes."

"I read all Tommy's letters. Every letter he ever wrote to you," Marlee says, pointing to the looming old building on the shore, "from in there.

Whatever it is emanating from those buildings intensifies. I feel a chill.

"I like Tommy," she says instantly. "Tommy's good."

"He is."

"One looney got out of here last week. Word is he's going back to politics," says whatever voice it is that comes out of Marlee. I know it, I'm sure of it—it *is* her voice. But somehow I hear her differently.

"I WILL get out of here, you know."

"Marlee?"

Her expression widens like the first light of some dawn never seen before. She almost smiles. A kind of sly grin that speaks of mischief and secrets and hidden little joys wriggling their way to the surface.

And from somewhere far away, I'm sure I can hear another voice.

Then in her own way, she laughs.

And there in the darkness of the water and the sky, broken only by the reflections of lights from differing origins, something is completed.

Acknowledgments

My gratitude for the courtesies extended in the writing of this book began one freezing January afternoon when Bob Thicksten invited me to join him far above the ground on the uppermost icy surfaces of the masssive Palomar dome. My introduction to the lore of the 200-inch telescope began on those vertiginous heights, watching Bob clamor over the dome, kicking sheets of ice off it. Coming only a few minutes after we'd introduced ourselves, the invitation was the first in a long series of remarkable Palomar experiences and friendships for which I am truly grateful. As the man who has nurtured the telescope for years, Bob, more than anyone, has honored the original reverence for this awesome instrument that is part science and part spiritual. He and his wife, Debbie, were also wonderful guides into the communal labyrinths of mountain society.

To the Caltech astronomers, particular thanks to Keith Matthews, whose wry insights into the meeting places of science and absurdity were treasured. And also to Ben Oppenheimer, who ably represented the next generation.

I am indebted to Dr. Jorge Barrera for introducing me to the world of psychiatry on the Mexican-American border, a task he carried out with great wit and grace. Thanks also to Dr. Saul Levine and Dr. Bill Johnston, both Toronto psychiatrists. To Saul for helping me while establishing his new Southern California practice, and to Bill for facilitating my research into the Penetang Mental Health Center.

Gracias to Sol Benarroch, my friend and guide through the Spanish language, not only in this book but in so many colorful ventures in Cuba. And also to Señor Reyes in Havana, who provided so many memorable translations.

Finally, thanks to the ladies in my literary life: Phoebe Larmore, my agents, for being the muse of Casa del Mar in Santa Monica; and Elaine Markson in New York for her soothing mixture of reality and optimism; and to Iris Tupholme, my editor in Toronto, who made the marathon worthwhile.